**Praise for *New York Times* bestselling author
Heather Graham**

"Graham's tight plotting, her keen sense of when to
reveal and when to tease...will keep fans turning the
pages."

—*Publishers Weekly* on *Picture Me Dead*

"Graham weaves history, ghosts and danger into a
gripping story like no other."

—*Fresh Fiction* on *The Summoning*

"An incredible storyteller."

—*Los Angeles Daily News*

**Praise for *USA TODAY* bestselling author
Delores Fossen**

"An entertaining and satisfying read...that I can
highly recommend."

—*Books & Spoons* on *Wild Nights in Texas*

"Clear off space on your keeper shelf, Fossen has
arrived."

—*New York Times* bestselling author Lori Wilde

New York Times and *USA TODAY* bestselling author **Heather Graham** has written more than two hundred novels. She is pleased to have been published in over twenty-five languages, with sixty million books in print. Heather is a proud recipient of the Silver Bullet from Thriller Writers and was awarded the prestigious Thriller Master Award in 2016. She is also a recipient of Lifetime Achievement Awards from RWA and *The Strand*, and is the founder of The Slush Pile Players, an author band and theatrical group. An avid scuba diver, ballroom dancer and mother of five, she still enjoys her South Florida home, but also loves to travel. Heather is grateful every day for a career she loves so very much. For more information, check out her website, theoriginalheathergraham.com, or find Heather on Facebook.

Delores Fossen, a *USA TODAY* bestselling author, has sold over seventy-five novels, with millions of copies of her books in print worldwide. She's received a Booksellers' Best Award and an RT Reviewers' Choice Best Book Award. She was also a finalist for a prestigious RITA® Award. You can contact the author through her website at www.deloresfossen.com.

New York Times **Bestselling Author**

HEATHER GRAHAM

OUT OF THE DARKNESS

**HARLEQUIN
BESTSELLING
AUTHOR
COLLECTION**

**HARLEQUIN®
BESTSELLING
AUTHOR
COLLECTION**

Recycling programs
for this product may
not exist in your area.

ISBN-13: 978-1-335-40630-9

Out of the Darkness
First published in 2018. This edition published in 2022.
Copyright © 2018 by Heather Graham Pozzessere

Marching Orders
First published in 2003. This edition published in 2022.
Copyright © 2003 by Delores Fossen

For questions and comments about the quality of this book,
please contact us at CustomerService@Harlequin.com.

Harlequin Enterprises ULC
22 Adelaide St. West, 41st Floor
Toronto, Ontario M5H 4E3, Canada
www.Harlequin.com

Printed in U.S.A.

CONTENTS

Also by Heather Graham

Harlequin Intrigue

Undercover Connection
Out of the Darkness
Shadows in the Night
Law and Disorder
Tangled Threat

MIRA

Krewe of Hunters

Dreaming Death
Deadly Touch
Seeing Darkness
The Stalking
The Seekers
The Summoning
Echoes of Evil
Pale as Death
Fade to Black
Wicked Deeds

New York Confidential

The Final Deception
A Lethal Legacy
A Dangerous Game
A Perfect Obsession
Flawless

Visit her Author Profile page at Harlequin.com,
or theoriginalheathergraham.com, for more titles!

OUT OF THE DARKNESS

Heather Graham

For Saxon and Joe, two of the nicest and most talented young men I know. May their move to New York be filled with dreams—and, of course, all kinds of visits from West Coast friends!

Prologue

What Davey Knew

The Bronx
New York City, New York
Ten Years Ago

The eyes fell upon Sarah Hampton with a golden glow; the woman's mouth, covered with blood, split into a diabolical smile as she cackled with glee, raising her carving knife and slamming it down on the writhing man tied to the butcher block in the kitchen. Blood seemed to spurt everywhere. Screams rose.

And Sarah, laughing at herself for her own scream, grabbed Davey's hand and followed Tyler Grant out of the haunted house.

"Fun!" Tyler said, laughing, catching his breath.

It was fun. Though Sarah had to admit she was glad she was here as part of a party of six. Fun? Yes, sure…

And creepy! The weapons had looked real. The "scare actors" could have passed for the real thing quite easily as far as she was concerned.

"Ah, come on, the guy on the butcher block—his screams were nowhere as good as they should have been," Hannah Levine said. "He must be getting tired of screaming—long season, long night. But I guess it is Halloween."

"Yeah, I imagine that the poor kid has been at it awhile," Sean Avery agreed. He looked at Sarah's cousin, Davey. "Then again, this place opens for only four weekends, with Halloween weekend, the last, being the boss. Coolest thing ever, Davey!"

Davey gave him a weird little half smile.

Suzie Cornwall—Sarah's best friend—frowned. "What's the matter, Davey? Was the haunted house too scary for you? We were all with you, you know."

"That one was okay," Davey said.

"But now...drumroll! We're moving on—to the major attraction!" Sean said.

"No, no, no!" Davey shook his head violently. "I'm scared!" He clearly didn't want to go into Cemetery Mansion, another of the haunted houses; he seemed terrified.

Sarah looked at her cousin with dismay.

She loved Davey. She really loved him. She had never met anyone who was as kind, as oblivious to what others thought, as willing to help others.

But Davey had Down syndrome. And while most of Sarah's friends were great, every once in a while they acted as if they didn't want to be with her, not if she was bringing Davey along.

And tonight...

Well, it was almost Halloween. And she and her friends had scored tickets to Haunted Hysteria in a radio contest. It was the prime event of the season, but one they couldn't actually afford. Well, to be honest—and they all had to agree—it was Davey who'd won the tickets. They'd asked him to dial the radio station number over and over again, and Davey hadn't minded.

The place itself was fabulous. Decorated to a T. Bats, ghouls, ghosts, vampires, witches and more—young actors and actresses, of course, but they walked around doing a brilliant job. The foam tombstones looked real and aged; the makeshift mortuary chapel was darkened as if older than time itself. Lights cast green and purple beams, and fog machines set in strategic places made for an absolutely immersive experience.

And now they were all here—she, Davey, Tyler, Sean, Suzie and Hannah. Suzie, tall and well-built, perfectly proportioned to be dressed up as Jessica Rabbit for the night, was her best friend. Tyler was the love of her life. And most of the time, both of them were truly wonderful friends. Tyler had even told her once that he knew right off the bat if he'd like people or not—all depending on the way they treated Davey.

Hannah was a stunner, olive skinned and dark haired—and as an evil fairy, she was even more exotically beautiful than usual. Sarah was pretty sure she'd caused one of the "scare actors" to pause—too startled by her beauty to scare her!

Sean… Sean was charming, the old class clown. Apropos, he was dressed up as the Joker. Every once in a while, his wit could be cruel. Mostly, though, he was a great guy, and the five of them had been friends forever, even though Sarah and Tyler were the only duo in their group.

She had come in steampunk apparel; Tyler had matched her with an amazing vest and frock coat. Davey had come as his all-time favorite personality—Elvis Presley.

They were all nearly eighteen now. Come October of next year, they'd be off at their different colleges, except she'd be at NYU with Tyler, as they'd planned. But for tonight…

It was fricking Halloween. Aunt Renee had asked her to take Davey with her. Yes, of course, Sarah was very aware the tickets really *belonged to Davey.*

Sarah always tried to be helpful. It was easy to help care for her cousin.

Aunt Renee wasn't in any kind of financial trouble—she had a great job as a buyer for a major chain store—and she had household help and could afford to send Davey to a special school.

But Aunt Renee wanted Davey to have friends and spend time with people his own age—Sarah's age. Aunt Renee wanted a wider world for Davey; she did not want his mom to be his only companion.

Sarah's friends were usually happy to have Davey with them.

But now Sarah could feel that Davey was holding them all back—and they were kids, with a right to be kids. The others were looking at her. Sure, they loved Davey. They were good people. But she could see them thinking *screw it!* They'd come to Haunted Hysteria; they were going in the haunted houses, and Sarah was welcome to sit outside with Davey.

Tyler, of course, had the grace to look guilty. He

wasn't eighteen until January, but he was already over six foot three, heavily muscled in the shoulders and extremely fine in the face. Hot, yes. Tyler was hot. And he loved her. He really did. Then, she hoped she wasn't exactly dog chow herself. She was, she admitted, the typical cheerleader to his football hero. Yes, she was blonde and blue-eyed, the fault of her genetics. She was a good student and coordinated enough to be a great cheerleader. She liked to believe she'd been taught by her family to be a lot more, too—as in decent and compassionate and bright enough to see and understand others.

She thought Tyler was like that, too. No matter how cool he was.

They were just right for each other—and their group of friends was nice, too! Something she considered extremely important. Tonight, they wanted to be seniors—they wanted to be a little bit wicked and have a great time.

But being Davey's cousin had long ago taught Sarah about the importance of kindness in the world. Patience, sharing, caring…all that.

All that…

Seemed to go out the window right now.

"Davey, I know you were scared in the first house, but we're all with you," she said.

"Hey, buddy," Tyler told him. "I'm bigger than the damned ghosts!"

"You can go between Sarah and Tyler," Suzie said. "They'll protect you."

"No! No—the things in this house—they were okay. They weren't real. But that house…that one, there. There are things in it that are real. That are bad. They're evil!" Davey said.

"Oh, you're being silly," Hannah said.

"It's true," Davey said.

"How do you know?" Sean asked him.

"My father told me!" Davey said. "He helps me see."

Sarah bit her lip. Davey's dad had died over a year ago. Aunt Renee was alone with Davey now. Davey's dad had been a marine, and he had been killed serving his country. Her uncle had been a wonderful man—good to all the kids. She'd loved him, too, and she'd known he loved her.

"Davey, your father isn't here," she said. "You know... you know your dad is dead."

Davey looked at her stubbornly. "My father told me!" he insisted.

"Davey," Sarah said softly, calmly, "of course, the point is for it all to be very scary. Vampires, ghosts—but they're not real. It's a spooky fun place for Halloween. There are all kinds of made-up characters here."

"No. Real bad things."

They all let his words sit for a minute.

"The actors in there—they're not evil, Davey," Suzie said. "Come on, you've seen creatures like that before—and the ones who walk around, they're high school kids like us or college kids, and now and then, an adult actor without a show at the moment! You know all about actors, buddy. There are pretend vampires—and werewolves, mummies, ghosts—you name it."

"No. Not werewolves. Not vampires," Davey insisted. "Bad people. Like my dad said!"

"You love actors and movies," Sean said. Sean knew Davey had a skill for remembering everything about all the movies and, because of that, he always made sure Davey was on his team for trivia games. When they weren't playing trivia, however, Sean had a tendency to ignore Davey.

Sean seemed to be trying with the rest of their group to engage Davey, but he kept looking at his watch. He wanted to move on.

"You shouldn't go in! You shouldn't go in. It's bad. Very bad," Davey said.

"It's just a haunted house!" Tyler said.

"I love you, Tyler," Davey said. "Don't go. My father… he was next to me. Yes. He was next to me. All the things he taught me. He's dead, I know! But he's with me. He said not to go in. He said there would be bad men and you have to look out. He was smart. My dad was a marine!" he added proudly.

"That's kind of sick!" Hannah whispered to Sarah. "Does he honestly think…"

"Davey," Sarah said softly. "Your dad loved you— you loved your dad. But he's gone."

"I'm not going!" Davey said stubbornly.

"He should come," Tyler told Sarah. "If you give in to him all the time…it's not good. Don't make him into a baby. He's several years older than we are." He turned to Davey. "You know I love you, buddy, right?"

Davey nodded. "We don't have a weapon. I'm not going."

"Davey, I'm begging you…please?" Sarah asked.

Davey shook his head, looking at her. There were tears in his eyes; he was obviously afraid she was going to make him go into the haunted house.

"Just go," Sarah told the others. "Davey and I will get a soda or…hey, there are a bunch of movie toys over there. We'll go look at the toys."

Tyler sighed. "I'll stay with you."

The others had already fled like rats.

Not even Suzie—some best friend—stayed behind. Just Tyler. Staring at her.

"Go," she told him, suddenly feeling put-upon.

"Sarah—"

"Go!"

He stiffened, squared his shoulder, shook his head— and walked on quickly to join the others.

"I'm still so confused. What scared you so badly?" Sarah asked Davey, leading him to a bench. At least she could sit. Her steampunk adventurer boots were starting to hurt like hell. "You were fine when we first got here. The haunted house we went in was made up to look like that one from the movie—you know, when the kids get lost in the woods and they find the house, but every- one in it is crazy! The father likes to hang people, the brother plays with a Civil War sword, the sister sprays poison and the mother chops up strangers for dinner. It was creepy cool—and they were all actors."

"Yes, they were actors," Davey said.

"Then why are you afraid of that one?" She pointed to the house where her friends were now in line, Cem- etery Mansion. It was a good, creepy representation from a horror film where people had built over a grave- yard and the dead came back to kill the living for dis- turbing them.

"It's evil," Davey said. He shoved his hands into his pockets and shivered. "I saw them. Dad told me to watch—I watched. That house is evil."

"How is it evil? It's honestly much the same. The themes are different. There are a lot of fabricated creatures—some cool motion-activated stuff, like robots—and then more actors. People just pretending. We went through the one house—it was fine."

He nodded very seriously and then pointed at the Cemetery Mansion.

"That one," he said. "It's wrong. I'm telling you, Sarah—it is wrong. And I like Tyler. And Suzie," he added. He didn't say anything about Sean or Hannah.

"You mean—you've heard they got the characters wrong somehow? We haven't been in it to see what the house is like, Davey."

"No, we can't go in," he said insistently, wetting his lips as he did when he got nervous. "No. It's wrong. You can feel it. It isn't scary—it's bad. Evil."

She looked at the house. It *was* spooky—the theme park had done a good job. Images were hazily visible in the windows: creatures that had just crawled from the grave, bony, warped, black-and-white, like zombies or ghosts, horrible to behold.

"You should stop your friends from going in there. Make Tyler come back. He wanted to stay with you. But you were all stubborn and mean."

Sarah heard the words and spun around to stare at Davey. But he didn't even seem to realize he had spoken to her.

He was looking at the stand where there were all kinds of toys.

Sarah suddenly smiled. His eyes were wide; he was happy to look at the toys. Davey loved the movies and he loved toys—that made movie-inspired props and toys extra special.

"Let's go see what they have," she told him.

* * *

"This is wrong," Tyler said as he got into the line for the haunted house with Suzie, Hannah and Sean. What was one more haunted house? he asked himself, irritated that he had let Sarah push him away. No matter if it was their idea or not, Davey had gotten them the tickets. He'd been patient enough to dial his phone over and over and over again.

And Tyler knew that Sarah was feeling alone—as if Davey was her responsibility, and she wasn't about to burden anyone else.

Tyler loved her. He knew they were both lucky, both blessed. People referred to them as the "Barbie and Ken" of their school. He liked to think it wasn't just that he played football and she was an amazing cheerleader—for any team the school put forth. He tried to be friendly, kind, sympathetic—and he worked hard in class.

Naturally, he and Sarah had been intimate—though not in a way that would give others a chance to tease them. They were discreet and very private; Sarah would never do anything to disappoint her parents. But in their minds, marriage was a given. Sometimes, in the middle of a class, Tyler would smile, imagine being with her in such an intimate way again, when they both laughed, when they grew breathless, when the world seemed to explode. She was an amazing lover and he hoped he reciprocated. Sex was fireworks, but life was loving everything about her—her great compassion for others, her integrity. He liked to think that he was similar in his behavior.

Leaving her on her own tonight hadn't been considerate in any way.

"I'm going to go back and wait with Davey and Sarah," he said flatly.

"Go back where?" Hannah asked him. "They're already gone. And besides, Miss Stubborn Pride isn't going to let you stay with her. I'm sure you already tried to and she sent you after us. She doesn't want you to have a lousy time just because she has to."

Tyler gritted his teeth and looked away. "She isn't having a lousy time—and neither am I, Hannah. I love Davey. No one out there has a better heart."

It was true, though, that Sarah and Davey had walked off somewhere.

He should have firmly ignored Sarah when she'd pushed him away. She was usually bright enough to be angry if someone didn't understand that hanging out with Davey was like hanging out with any friend…

And Tyler was suddenly angry himself; they wouldn't be here at all without Davey. Davey had won the tickets.

"Oh, come on, Tyler!" Hannah said. "It's okay! The retard is *her* cousin, not yours."

He wanted to slap Hannah—and he was stunned by the intensity of the feeling. In his whole life, he'd never hit a girl. And Hannah was a friend. She was usually…fine.

"Hannah, you know calling him that is not okay. Not cool. He's just like you or me," Tyler said.

"Maybe like you!" Sean said, laughing. "Not me. Hey, come on—this is supposed to be the coolest thing here, ghosts coming up out of the ground from all over. They say the creatures—animatronic or whatever—are the most amazing, and they put their best 'scare' actors in this one. Tyler, come on, we take Davey with us all the time. But this is our night. It's our last Halloween together. If he doesn't want to come in, screw it!"

"Not to mention that, as I already pointed out, we don't even know where they are anymore," Hannah said.

"Yep, well, I do have a cell phone," Tyler said.

"Tyler, leave it," Suzie said. She looked guilty, too, he thought. But maybe she was right. "We have VIP tickets—we get to move into the express lane up there. We'll be out soon and then we'll explore the food booths—Davey will like checking those out! And we'll hug him and tell him that he was right—we should have stayed out. It was really scary, so now we're all hungry!"

An actor in some kind of a zombie outfit came toward them, using a deep and hollow voice to ask for their tickets. They showed their passes and were moved up quickly in the line.

They entered the mudroom of the Cemetery Mansion. Bloody handprints were everywhere. They were met by a girl in a French maid outfit—with vampire teeth and blood dripping down her chin.

"Enter if you dare!" she said dramatically.

A terrified scream sounded from within. And then another. And another.

The place had to be amazingly good.

"Ah!" said the maid. "I say again, enter if you dare! Those who have come before you seem to be just... dying to get back out!"

She opened the door from the mudroom to the foyer and stepped back.

Tyler thought she looked concerned. As if...

As if people actually were dying to get out.

* * *

"Can we go look at the booth over there?" Davey asked Sarah.

He gave her a smile that made her ashamed. She had been secretly bitter; she'd wanted to go with her friends. It wasn't terrible that she should want to; she knew her feelings were natural. But she felt guilty, anyway. Davey wasn't being mean, she knew. He wasn't hurting her on purpose. He had his irrational fear set in his mind.

"Come on!" She caught his hand and led him to the toy stand. This one was stocked with prop weapons.

There were all kinds of great things: realistic plastic ray guns, gold-gleaming light-up lasers and much more. There were fantastic swords, like from some 1950s sci-fi movie, she thought. They were really cool—silver and gold, and emitting light through plastic blades that shimmered in a dozen colors.

They were cheap, too. Not like the licensed merchandise. It was called a Martian Gamma Sword.

Sarah smiled, watching Davey's fascination.

She worked three days a week after school at the local theater and could easily afford the toy sci-fi sword. She paid while Davey was still playing with it.

"Okay, good to go," she told him.

He looked at her, surprised.

"I bought it, Davey. It's yours."

His eyes widened. He gave her his beautiful smile again. Then he frowned, appearing very thoughtful.

"Now we can go," he said.

"Pardon?"

"We have to go," he insisted. "I can save them now—Tyler and Suzie. I can save them."

Sarah couldn't have been more stunned. She smiled. Maybe they could catch up—and if not, well, she'd still be able to say she'd experienced the most terrifying haunted house in the city—the state, maybe even the country!

"Come on!" she said. "Sure, I mean, it will be great if we can save them. So great."

"I have to go first. I have the Martian Gamma Sword."

"Okay, I'm right behind you!" Sarah promised. She hurried after him.

"They don't like this kind of light, you know."

"Who doesn't like it?"

"Those who are evil!" he said seriously.

He had his sword ready and held in front of him—he was prepared, he was on guard!

Sarah smiled, keeping behind him. She hoped he didn't bat an actor over the head with the damned thing.

Tyler didn't know when it changed.

The haunted house was incredible, of course. He knew the decorations and fabrications, motion-activated creatures and the costumes for the live actors had been created by some of the finest designers in the movie world.

The foyer had the necessary spiderwebs dangling from the chandelier and hanging about. As they were ushered in—the door shut behind them by the French maid—a butler appeared. He was skinny, tiny and a hunchback. Igor? He spoke with a deep voice that was absolutely chilling.

Tyler had to remind himself he was six-three and two hundred and twenty pounds of muscle. But just the guy's voice was creepy as hell.

"Cemetery Mansion!" the butler boomed out. "The living are always ever so careless of the dead! Housing is needed…and cemeteries are ignored. And so it was when the Stuart family came to Crow Corners. They saw the gravestones…they even knew the chapel housed the dead and that a crypt led far beneath the ground. And still! They tossed aside the gravestones, and they built their mansion. Little did they know they would pay for their total disregard. Oh, Lord, they would pay! They would be allowed to stay—forever! Forever and ever…with those who resided here already!"

Suddenly, from thin air, haunts and ghouls seemed to arise and sweep through the room. Suzie let out a squeal. Even Hannah shrieked.

Good old Sean let out a startled scream and then began to laugh at himself.

It was done with projectors, Tyler realized.

"To your left, ladies and gentlemen, to your left! The music room, and then the dining room!"

They were urged to move on. The music room hosted a piano and rich Victorian furniture. There was also a child sitting on the sofa, holding a teddy bear. She turned to look at them with soulless eyes—and then she disappeared. A figure was hunched over the piano. Suzie tried to walk by it; the piano player suddenly stood, reaching out for her.

She screamed. The thing was a motion-activated figure, one who would have done any haunted mansion proud. It was a tall butler—blond and grim-looking, with a striking face made up so that the cheeks were entirely hollow. It spoke with a mechanical voice. "Come closer, come closer… I can love you into eternity!"

It was nothing but a prop, an automaton. But it was real as all hell.

Suzie ran on into the next room.

The dining room…

At the head of the table was a very tall man—an actor portraying the long-dead head of the household; a man in a Victorian-era suit, wearing tons of makeup that had been applied very effectively. He was sharpening a knife.

There were dummies or mannequins or maybe animatronics slumped around the table. At least their bodies were slumped there. Their heads were *on* it. Blood streamed from their necks and down their costumes.

"One of them is going to hop up, I know," Hannah murmured.

She bravely stepped closer to the table. No one moved.

Tyler noticed there was a girl about their age at the end of the table. She was wearing one of this year's passes to Haunted Hysteria around the stump of her neck.

Good touch, he thought.

The bodies around the table did not move. The master of the house watched them with bloodshot eyes. He sharpened his knife.

A girl suddenly burst into the dining room from the music room. "Run! Get out—get to the exit! He's in the house somewhere!" she screamed.

"Yes, he is. He's right here," the master of the house said. He reached for her and dragged her to him. She screamed again, trying to wrench herself free. He smiled.

He took one of the knives he had been sharpening.

And he slit her throat.

* * *

Sarah didn't know what had gotten into Davey; he was usually the most polite person in the world. He'd been taught the importance of *please* and *thank you*.

But he was almost pushing.

And he knew their radio station tickets gave them VIP status.

Light sword held before him, he made his way to one of the actors herding the line. "VIP, please!" he told her.

"Uh, sure. Watch out for that thing!" She started to lead them up the line, toward the house. As she did so, there was a scream, and one of the actors came bursting out the front door.

She was dressed as a French maid—a vampire or zombie French maid, Sarah thought.

She stumbled out of the entry and onto the porch, grabbing for one of the columns. Blood was dripping down her arms and over her shirt—she appeared to have a number of stab wounds.

"Don't!" she shouted. "Don't… He's a killer!"

Applause broke out in the line. But then someone else burst out of the house—a ghoul dressed in an Edwardian jacket.

He crashed down, a pool of blood forming right on the porch.

More applause broke out.

"No, no, that's not supposed to happen," the zombie leading Sarah up the line murmured.

Davey burst by her; he was headed to the house, his light saber before him.

"Davey!" Sarah shrieked. Something was wrong; something was truly wrong. They needed to stay out, needed to find out if this was an excellent piece of play-acting or...

Or what?

Imaginary creatures came to life and started killing people? Actors went crazy en masse and started knifing the populace? Whatever was going on, it seemed insane!

The sensation that crawled over Sarah then was nothing short of absolute terror—but Davey was ahead of her.

With his Martian Gamma Sword.

He was charging toward the house.

Davey! She had to follow him, stop him and get him away—no matter what!

Tyler could hear nothing but diabolical laughter.

And screaming—terrified shrieks!

Suzie hopped on a chair and grabbed a serving platter for defense.

The master of the house turned toward them, dropping the body of the girl whose throat he had slit. It fell with a flat thud.

Sean squeaked out a sound that was nearly a scream.

Hannah grabbed Sean, thrusting him between her and the big man with the massive knife.

"Back up, back up, back up!" Tyler said.

Hannah did so. Sean turned to flee.

The master of the house went for Sean. He picked him up by the neck.

"No! Stop, stop it!" Tyler shouted.

This couldn't be happening.

"This isn't funny. It isn't right!"

The character didn't seem to hear Tyler. And Tyler had no choice. He leaped forward, shoving Hannah away, and tried to wrest Sean from the killer. He grabbed Sean's arm and pulled.

"No!" Suzie shrieked.

Tyler looked up.

The master of the house was approaching her with the massive knife, dragging Sean along with him. Then he turned. He came swinging toward Tyler, still dragging Sean. Tyler held on to his friend and jerked hard; Sean came free and they staggered back—Hannah, Sean and himself—until they crashed into the table.

Hannah began shrieking in earnest. As she did so, Tyler became aware of the tinny scent of blood.

Real blood.

And he looked around the table and he knew.

They were people. Real people. And they were dead.

Really dead.

"No!" Suzie shrieked.

She slammed her serving platter at the master of the house.

He just laughed.

And raised his carving knife.

Davey raced across the porch, pushing aside the bleeding maid and hopping over the body of the man in the Edwardian dress.

Sarah had no choice but to follow.

He burst through into a mudroom. There were bloody handprints all over it.

Some were fake—stage blood.

Some were real—human blood.

She could tell by the smell that some of the blood was real.

Davey rushed through to the foyer, his Martian

Gamma Sword leading the way. But there was no one there. He threw open another door.

"Davey, stop! Please, Davey, something is going wrong. Something is..."

They were in a music room; it was empty—other than for a bloody body stretched across a floral sofa.

"Davey!" Sarah shrieked. "No, no, please..."

She started to whirl around. There were holograms everywhere. A child in black with a headless doll appeared. And then a hanged man, the noose still around his neck. All kinds of ghouls and creatures and evil beings began to appear in the room and then disappear.

"Davey, please, we've got to get out. Davey!"

She gripped his arm as the terrifying images swirled around them.

"Not real," Davey said. "Sarah, they're not real."

He was moving on—and she heard screams again. Terrified screams...

He went through a black hazy curtain and they were in the dining room.

And there were Tyler, Hannah... Sean and Suzie... It appeared that they were all being attacked by...a creature, by someone or something. They had fallen back and were struggling to rise from the dining table, where there were...

Oh, God, corpses, real corpses. Dead people, all around the table. Suzie and Hannah were yelling and screaming, and Tyler was reaching out, but the carving knife was coming down and it was going to sink into Tyler's chest at any minute!

She heard a terrible scream—high-pitched and full of fear and horror. And she realized it was coming from her...

And she had drawn the attention of the...

Man. It was a real man.

An actor gone insane? What the hell?

No, no, no, no. It was impossible. It was Halloween. It had to be a prank, an elaborate show...

The man was real.

Absolutely real.

He was tall and big and had long scraggly white hair and he might have played a maniacal killer in a slasher movie.

Except this wasn't a movie.

And he was coming at her.

He opened his mouth and smiled, and she saw his fangs. Long fangs that seemed to drip with something red...stage blood...

Real blood.

She screamed again.

It sounded as if it was coming from someone else, but it was not. It was coming from her.

Tyler struggled up from the table. He slipped.

He was slipping in blood.

"No, no, no!" Sarah screamed.

And then Davey stepped up. He thrust her back with his arm and stepped before her, his cheap little plastic sword at the ready.

"Leave her!" Davey shouted, his voice filled with command.

The man laughed...

And Davey struck him. Struck him hard, with all his strength.

The man went flying back. He slammed into the wall, and the impact sent him flying forward once again.

He tripped on a dead girl's leg...

And crashed down on the table.

Right on top of Tyler and Sean and Hannah, who had already been slammed down there. It was too much weight. The table broke with an awful groaning and splintering sound.

Shards and pieces flew everywhere as what remained of the table totally upended.

Tyler let out a cry of fear and fury and gripped the man's shoulders, shoving him off with all the force of a high school quarterback.

To Sarah's astonishment, the man, balanced for a matter of seconds, staring furiously at Davey—and then he fell hard. And didn't move again. She saw that he'd fallen on a broken and jagged leg of the table.

The splintered shaft was sticking straight through his chest.

Tyler got up and hunkered down by the man carefully, using one of the plates off the table as a shield.

"Dead," he said incredulously. He looked up at the others. "He's dead… He fell on the broken table leg there and…oh, God, it's bad."

"Out of here! It's evil!" Davey commanded. "It's still evil."

They were all shaking so badly no one seemed able to move. Davey reached for Hannah's arm and pulled her up. "Out!" he commanded.

And she ran. Suzie followed her, and then Sean, and then Tyler met Sarah's eyes and took her hand, and they raced out, as well, followed by Davey—who was still carefully wielding his plastic sword.

They heard sirens; police and security and EMTs were spilling onto the grounds.

The medics were struggling, trying to find the injured *people* among the props and corpses and demons and clowns.

When the group of friends reached a grassy spot, Sarah fell to the ground, shaking. She looked up at Davey, still not beginning to comprehend how he had known...

Or even *what* it was he had known.

"I told you—that house is evil," he said. "I told you— my dad. He taught me to watch. He stays with me and tells me to watch."

It had been the unthinkable—or easily thinkable, really, in the midst of all that went on at a horror-themed attraction at Halloween.

Archibald Lemming and another inmate had escaped from state prison two weeks earlier. They had gotten out through the infirmary—even though he had been in maximum security. News of the breakout had been harried and spotty, and most people assumed the embarrassment suffered by those who had let them escape had mandated that the information about it be kept secret.

Archibald Lemming had been incarcerated at the Clinton Correction Facility for killing four people— with a carving knife. The man had been incredibly sick. He'd somehow managed to consume some of the blood in their bodies—*as if he'd been a damned vampire.* He'd escaped with a fellow inmate, another killer who was adept with a knife and liked to play in blood— Perry Knowlton. Apparently, however, Lemming had turned on the man. Knowlton's body had been found burned to little more than cinders in the crematorium at an abandoned veterinary hospital just outside the massive walls of the prison.

Sarah knew all that, of course, because it was on the news. And because, after the attack at Cemetery Mansion, the cops came to talk to her and Davey several times. One of them was a very old detective named Mark Holiday. He was gentle. His partner, Bob Green, was younger and persistent, but when his questions threatened to upset Davey, Sarah learned she could be very fierce herself. The police photographer, Alex Morrison— a nice guy, with the forensic unit—came with the detectives. He showed them pictures that caused them to relive the event—and remember it bit by bit. The photographer was young, like Bob Green. He tried to make things easier, too, by explaining all that he could.

"Archibald Lemming! They found his stash in prison. Idiot kept 'history' books. Right—they were on the Countess Bathory, the Hungarian broad who killed young women to bathe in their blood. The man was beyond depraved," one of the cops had said that night when he'd met with the kids. He'd been shaking, just as they had been.

People were stunned and angry—furious. If there had been better information on the escape, lives might have been saved. Before the confrontation with Davey and his friends, the man had killed ten people and seriously injured many more. He'd managed to escape at a time when it was perfect to practice his horror upon others—Halloween. He had dressed up and slipped into the park as one of the actors.

But many survived who might have died that night. They had lived because of Davey.

It did something to them all. Maybe they were in shock. Maybe denial. Guilt over being the ones who made it out. And confusion over what it meant, now that the normal lives ahead of them seemed all the more precious.

Sarah was with her cousin and her aunt when Tyler came to say goodbye.

He was leaving the school, going into a military academy and joining the navy as soon as he could.

Sarah was stunned. But in an odd way, she understood. She knew she had closed in on herself. Maybe they all had, and needed to do so in order to process that they were alive—and it was all right for them to go on.

She, Tyler and their friends had survived. And it was too hard to be together. Too hard to be reminded what the haunted house had looked like with all the dead bodies and the blood and things so horrible they almost couldn't be believed.

So she merely nodded when he told her he was leaving. She barely even kissed him goodbye, although there was a long moment when they looked at each other, and even *this*—losing one another—was something they both accepted, and shared, and understood.

Sarah gave up cheerleading and transferred to a private school herself, somewhere that hadn't lost any students in the Cemetery Mansion massacre.

When college rolled around, she decided on Columbia and majored in creative writing, veering away from anything that had to do with mystery or horror. She chose a pseudonym and started out in romance.

However, romance eluded her. She was haunted by the past.

And by memories of Tyler.

She turned to science fiction.

Giant bugs on the moon didn't scare her.

Except…

Every once in a while, she would pause, stare out the window and remember she was alive because of Davey and his Martian Gamma Sword.

Still, by the time she was twenty-seven, she was doing well. She had her own apartment on Reed Street. For holidays she headed out to LA—her parents had moved there as soon as her dad had retired from his job as an investment banker. Of course, they always tried to get her to join them with a permanent move, but she was a New Yorker and she loved the city. Sometimes she guest-lectured at Columbia or NYU. Upon occasion, she dated. Nothing seemed to work very well. But she was okay. She had college friends, and since she'd worked her way through school waitressing at an Irish pub, she still went in to help out at Finnegan's on Broadway now and then. The Finnegan family were great friends—especially Kieran, who happened to be a psychologist who frequently worked with criminals. He always seemed to know when Sarah wanted to talk a little about what she'd been through—and when she didn't.

It wasn't the happiness she had envisioned for herself before the night at the Halloween attraction.

But it was okay.

She hadn't seen Tyler—or any of her old friends—for over a decade.

Sarah had been living in the present.

And then she heard about the murder of Hannah Levine.

Like it or not, the past came crashing down on her.

And with it, Tyler Grant reentered her life.

Chapter 1

"Tyler!"

Davey Cray greeted Tyler with a smile like no other. He stepped forward instantly, no hesitance after ten years—just a greeting fueled by pure love.

It was as if he had expected him. Maybe he had.

Tyler hugged Davey in return, a wealth of emotions flooding through him.

"I knew you'd come. I knew you'd come!" Davey said. "My mom said you were busy, you didn't live here anymore. You work in Boston. But I knew you would come." His smile faded. "You came for Hannah." Davey looked perplexed. "Hannah wasn't always very nice. And I watched the news. She wasn't doing good things. But…poor Hannah. Poor Hannah."

Yes, poor Hannah. She'd disappeared after leaving a bar near Times Square.

Her torso and limbs had turned up on a bank of the Hudson River.

Her head had come up just downriver about a half mile. She had been savagely cut to ribbons, much like the victims ten years past.

According to the news, Hannah had become a bartender, and then a stripper—and then a cocaine addict. Had that already been in the cards for her? Or had her life been twisted on that horrible night?

"Poor Hannah, yes. Nobody deserves to have their life stolen," Tyler assured Davey. "Nobody," he repeated firmly. "Had you—seen her?"

Davey shook his head gravely. "My mom doesn't let me go to strip clubs!" he said, almost in a whisper. Then he smiled again. "Tyler, I have a girlfriend. She has Down syndrome like me."

"Well, wow! That's cool. Got a picture?"

Davey did. He pulled out his wallet. He showed Tyler a picture of a lovely young girl with a smile as magnificent as his, short brown hair and big brown eyes.

"She's a looker!" Tyler said.

"Megan. Her name is Megan." Davey grinned happily.

"That's wonderful."

"Sarah set me up on the right kind of page on the internet. It really is cool."

"I'll bet it is! Leave it to Sarah."

"She loves me. And, you know, she loves you, too."

"Of course. We all love each other."

By that time, Renee Cray had made it to the door. She was a tall, thin, blonde woman in her late forties, with big brown eyes just like Davey's. "Tyler!" she exclaimed.

And then she, too, threw her arms around him, as

if he was the lost black sheep of the family being welcomed back into the fold.

Maybe he was.

"Tyler! How wonderful to see you! We knew, of course, that you'd joined the navy. And I know Sarah had heard you're living in Boston, working there as some kind of a consultant. Police consultant? PI? Something like that?"

"Exactly like that," he told her.

Renee continued to stare at him. "You're here...because of Hannah Levine, right? But...what can you do? What can anyone do? Is it horrible to say I'm glad her parents died in a car accident years ago? But what..." Her voice trailed off, and then she straightened. "Where are my manners? Come in, come in—you know the way, of course!"

He entered the parlor; Renee and Davey lived in a charming little two-story house in Brooklyn that offered a real yard and a porch with several rocking chairs. Renee was a buyer for a major retail chain and was able to keep up a very nice home on her own salary. Since the death of her husband, she had never done much more than work—and care for Davey. Tyler doubted she had changed. She was, in his opinion, a wonderful mother, never making Davey too dependent and never becoming codependent herself.

"Sit, sit," Renee told him. "Davey, get Tyler some tea, will you, please? You still like iced tea, right?"

"Still love it," Tyler assured her.

When her son was gone, Renee leaned forward. "Oh, Tyler! It's been so hard to listen to the news. I mean, bad things happen all the time. It's just that...you all escaped such a terrible thing, and now Hannah. Of course, her lifestyle...but then again, no one asks to be murdered... They haven't given out many details. We don't know if she was raped and murdered, but she was…decapitated. Beheaded. Just like—"

She broke off again, shaking her head. "It's like it's the same killer—as if he came back. Oh, I'll never forget that night! Hearing what had happened, trying to find Davey, trying to find you children… Oh, Tyler! Hannah now…it's just too sad!"

"It's not the same killer," Tyler said quietly. "I saw Archibald Lemming die. I saw him with a wooden table leg sticking straight through him. He did not miraculously get up and come back to kill again. Hannah had demons she dealt with, but they were in the way she looked at life. It's tragic, because no one should ever die like that. And," he reflected softly, "she was our friend. We were all friends back then. We haven't seen each other in a while, but…we were friends. We knew her."

Renee nodded, still visibly shaken.

Maybe they hadn't seen Hannah in a long time, but she had still been one of them.

"Tyler, I guess it's been in the media everywhere, but…you weren't that close with Hannah, were you? Had you talked to her? How did you come to be here?"

He smiled grimly.

Sarah. Sarah was why he had come. He thought back, hardly twelve hours earlier, when he had heard from her. He had received the text message from an unknown number.

Hi Tyler. It's Sarah. Have you seen the news?

Yes, of course he'd seen the news.

And he'd been saddened and shocked. He'd been there the night of one of the most gruesome spree killings in American history, and then he'd gone on to war. Not much compared to the atrocities one could see in battle. Between the two, he was a fairly hardened man.

But…their old friend Hannah had been brutally murdered. And even if her life had taken a turn for the worse lately—which the media was playing up—neither she, nor any victim, should ever have to suffer such horrors.

While Tyler hadn't seen Sarah in a decade, the second he received the missive from her, it felt as if lightning bolts tore straight through his middle and out through every extremity.

They said time healed all wounds. He wasn't so sure. He never really understood why he'd done what he'd done himself, except that, in the midst of the trauma and turmoil that had swept around them that night in a long-gone October, Sarah had still seemed to push him away. She always said she was fine, absolutely fine. That she needed to worry about Davey.

She had rejected Tyler's help—just as she had refused to understand he'd been willing to make Davey his responsibility, just as much as Davey was Sarah's responsibility.

They'd all had to deal with what had happened, with what they had witnessed.

Tyler had always wanted her to know he loved Davey, and he never minded responsibility, and he didn't give a damn about anyone else's thoughts or opinions on the matter. They had to allow Davey a certain freedom. When they were with him, they both needed to be responsible. That was sharing life, and it was certainly no burden to Tyler.

But Sarah had shut down; she had found excuses not to see him.

And he'd had to leave.

Maybe, after that, pride had taken hold. She had never tried to reach him.

And so he had never tried to get in touch with her.

But now...

Now Sarah had reached out to him.

He'd kept up with information about her, of course. Easy enough; she kept a professional platform going.

He liked to think she had followed him, as well. Not that he was as forthcoming about where he was and what he was doing. He had become a licensed investigator and consultant. Most of his work had been with the Boston Police Department; some had been with the FBI.

He knew she hadn't gone far. Her parents had rented out their Brooklyn home and moved to California. Sarah was living in Manhattan. She'd found a successful career writing fiction—he'd bought her books, naturally. Her early romances reminded him of the two of them; they'd been so young when they'd been together, so idealistic. They'd believed in humanity and the world and that all good things were possible.

Her sci-fi novels were fun—filled with cool creatures, "aliens" who seemed to parallel real life, and bits of sound science.

Part of why he'd never tried to contact her again had been pride, yes. Part of his efforts had actually been almost noble—her life looked good; he didn't want to ruin it.

But now...

Yes, he'd seen the news. Hannah Levine had been murdered. The reporters had not dealt gently with the victim because of her lifestyle. They hadn't known her. Hadn't known how poor she'd grown up, and that she had lost both parents tragically to an accident on the FDR. They did mention, briefly, that she'd survived the night of horror long ago.

As if reading his mind, Renee said, "They're almost acting as if she deserved it, Tyler! Deserved it, because of the way she lived. I'm wishing I had tried harder. Oh, look! If she hadn't been an 'escort,' this wouldn't have happened to her. I feel terrible. I mean, who ever really understands what makes us tick? Not even shrinks! Because…well, poor child, poor child! She never had much—that father of hers was a blowhard, but he was her dad. Both dead, no help…and she was a beautiful little thing. She was probably a very good stripper."

That almost made Tyler smile. "Probably," he agreed. "And yes, she was beautiful. Have the police let anything else out yet?"

"We know what you know. Her body was found… and then a few hours later, her head was found. First, we heard about the body in the river. Then we heard that it was Hannah."

The front door opened and closed. Tyler felt that same streak of electricity tear through him; he knew Sarah was there.

Renee frowned. "Sarah must be here."

"I'm sorry. I should have said right off the bat that she was meeting me here," Tyler said. "That's why… why I came. She didn't tell you?"

"No, but…that's great. You've been talking to Sarah!" Renee clapped her hands together, appearing ecstatic.

"We've exchanged two sentences, Renee," he said

quietly. "Sorry, four sentences, really. 'Did you hear the news?' 'Yes.' 'Will you come and meet me at Aunt Renee's?' And then, 'Yes, I'll come right away.'"

Renee just nodded. Davey was coming back in the room, bearing glasses of iced tea. "Sarah is here," Renee said.

Davey nodded gravely. "Of course she is."

Tyler watched as she walked into the parlor. Sarah. Whom he hadn't seen in a decade. She hadn't changed at all. She had changed incredibly. There was nothing of the child left in her. Her facial lines had sharpened into exquisite detail. She had matured naturally and beautifully, all the soft edges of extreme youth falling away to leave an elegantly cast blue-eyed beauty there, as if a picture had come into sharp focus. She was wearing her hair at shoulder length; it had darkened a little, into a deep sun-touched honey color.

He stood. She was staring at him in turn.

Seeing what kind of a difference a decade made.

"Hey," he said softly.

"Hey!" she replied.

They were both awkward, to say the least. She started to move forward quickly—the natural inclination to hug someone you held dear and hadn't seen in a long time.

He did the same.

She stopped.

He stopped.

Then they both smiled, and laughed, and she stepped forward into his arms.

It was impossible, of course. Impossible that they had really known what the depths of love could be when they hadn't even been eighteen. Then he'd felt as if he'd known, right from the first time he'd seen her at school, that he loved her. Would always love her.

That no one could compare.

And now, holding her again, he knew why nothing had ever worked for him. He'd met so many women—lots of them bright, beautiful and wonderful—and yet nothing had ever become more than brief moments of enjoyment, of gentle caring, and never this...connection.

Sarah had called on him because a friend had been murdered, and he was the only one who could really understand just what it was like. This didn't change anything; whether he loved her or not, she would still be determined to push him away when it came to relying on him, sharing with him...

Back then, she hadn't even wanted him near.

They drew apart. It felt as if the clean scent of her shampoo and the delicate, haunting allure of her fragrance lingered, a sweet and poignant memory all around him.

"You are here," she said. "Thanks. I know this is crazy, but... Hannah. To have survived what happened that October, and then...have this happen. I understand you're in some kind of law enforcement."

"No. Private investigator. That's why I'm not so sure how I can really be of help here."

"Private investigators get to—investigate, right?" Sarah asked.

"Why don't you two sit down?" Renee suggested.

"Sit, sit. Have tea!" Davey said happily.

Once again, Tyler sat. For a moment, the room was still, and everyone in it seemed to feel very awkward.

"I'm glad you came," Sarah said. "Not that I really

know anything. I belong to a great writers' group that brings us down to the FBI offices once a year for research, but… I really don't know anything. I don't think the FBI is involved. New York police, high-crimes or whatever they call it division… I just— The killing… sounds way too familiar!"

Tyler nodded. "Yeah. Though psychopaths have beheaded and sliced up victims many times, I'm sorry to say. And, of course," he said, pausing then to take a breath, "well, we were there. We saw the killer die back then." He looked over at Davey and smiled tightly, still curious about how Davey had sensed so much of what had gone on. "We were all there. We saw him die. Davey was a hero."

"My dad. My dad was with me," Davey said.

"In all he taught you, and all you learned so well!" Renee said, looking at her son, her soft tone filled with pain for the husband she'd lost.

"The police may already have something," Tyler said. "When a murder like this occurs, they hold back details from the press. You wouldn't believe the number of crazy people who will call in and confess to something they didn't do, wanting what they see as the credit for such a heinous crime. I have friends in Boston who have friends in New York. Maybe I can help—all depends on whether they want to let me in or not."

"Sarah has friends, too!" Davey said.

Sarah looked at him. "I do?"

"Kieran!"

"I haven't talked to her in a while," Sarah murmured.

"Who is Kieran?" Tyler asked.

"A friend, yes," Sarah said, looking at him. "She and her brothers inherited a very old Irish pub on Broadway—downtown, near Trinity and St. Paul's. The old-est brother manages, Kieran works there sometimes."

"You worked there!" Davey said.

"I did—I worked there through college," Sarah said. "Anyway, Kieran is a psychologist who works with two psychiatrists, Drs. Fuller and Miro. They often work with the police—they're geniuses when it comes to the criminal psyche. And her boyfriend is a special agent with the FBI. So, yes, if I asked for help…"

"That's excellent," Tyler told her. "And it could re-ally help, as far as finding out whatever information there is forthcoming. Other than that… I'm not law enforcement."

"But people hire PIs all the time," Renee said.

"When someone is missing, the family might hire someone. In murder investigations that go cold…"

"We can hire you!" Davey said happily.

"We're not her family," Sarah said.

"That doesn't matter. We were her friends," Davey said. He was quiet a minute and made one of his little frowns. "She was mean to me sometimes, but she was my friend, too. Mostly she was nice to me."

They all fell silent.

"I'll figure something out, and I'll keep you posted. I do have a legal standing as a private investigator, but it's a lot nicer if the police want me involved."

Sarah nodded. Again, they were all quiet.

"So, what's happening in your life, Tyler?" Renee asked. "It's so very long since we saw you. Davey has missed you."

"I know what Tyler has been doing! I follow his page," Davey said. "He dated a model! Pretty girl,

Tyler. I think, though, Sarah is prettier. But I saw the pictures of you."

"She's very nice," Tyler said. "She's—in Romania now. Shooting a catalog, or something like that."

"You must miss her," Davey said.

"We were casual friends."

"BFFs. That's friends with benefits," Davey told his mother, certain she wouldn't know.

"Davey!" Renee said. "Please, Tyler came as a favor. Let his private life be private."

Davey had lowered his head. He was chewing on a thumbnail, something he did, if Tyler recalled rightly, when he was nervous—or hiding something.

"You've got to be able to help somehow," Sarah said, as if she hadn't heard any of their exchange. "I'm so frustrated. I feel so worthless. And I feel terrible that I didn't keep up with her. I mean…we were friends once. I don't know what that night did to her. We all dealt with it differently. But…" She paused, inhaling a deep breath. "Sean suggested there was something—"

She broke off again. He knew what she was going to say. In the confusion with police and parents—and the horror that seemed almost worse when it was over and the garish lights were on—both Sean and Hannah had suggested there was something weird about Davey.

That it was downright scary, the way he had known something was really wrong.

"We talked. Davey told me. I think the police understood, but others didn't. My uncle taught Davey to watch people—to have excellent situational awareness, like an operative or a cop. Because people can be so cruel and mean. My uncle wanted Davey to be able to protect himself from that. Davey knew when kids wanted to—to make fun of him. He was good at avoiding such people. He was amazing at looking out for bullies. He saw that man… Archibald Lemming. He'd noticed him earlier. And he'd seen him go into that particular haunted house, and that was how he knew. But…"

"I told them," Davey said, nodding grimly. He brightened. "But they lived!"

"You were a hero," Sarah assured him.

Davey's smile faded and he looked grim. "But now Hannah is dead. And I'm afraid."

"You don't need to be afraid, Davey," Sarah assured him quickly. "You'll never be without one of us."

"Or my girlfriend!" he said brightly. "Megan," he reminded Tyler.

"Trust me, young man. Megan's mom and I will make sure you two aren't in any danger. Someone will be with you," Renee said.

"Can we still kiss and all?" Davey asked.

"We'll look away," Renee promised. She shook her head. "We're trying to keep it real—they have ten-year-old minds in grown-up bodies."

Davey giggled. Then again he looked grim. "It's scary. Sarah has to be with somebody, too."

Sarah smiled and reached over and patted his hand. "Davey, I won't be out late at night. I won't be anywhere without friends."

"You live alone."

"You could come stay here," Renee said.

"Aunt Renee," Sarah said, "I need to be near the universities. And here's the thing. We know Archibald Lemming is dead. What happened to Hannah is tragic, and one of those horrible events in life that happen to mirror another. I'll be careful. But I'm always careful.

I grew up as a New Yorker, remember? I've been savvy and wary a long, long time. Besides..." She paused and looked over at Tyler. "This must be...random. The act of some horrible, twisted thing that parades as a human being. Tyler... Tyler went to war. He knows very bad things happen."

"We followed you when you were deeped," Davey said.

"Deployed," Aunt Renee said.

"We were afraid you wouldn't come back," Davey said.

"Well, I am here, and I will find out what I can to help see that this man who killed Hannah meets a justice of his own, I promise," Tyler said.

He rose. He did need to get checked into his hotel room. And he needed to find out if the people he knew had been able to pull any strings for him.

"You have my number?" Sarah asked him.

He smiled at her curiously. Of course he did. They had been texting.

"Same number, right?"

She shook her head. "Well, it's the same as about five years ago?"

Tyler frowned. "But...you have my number?"

"Has it changed?"

"Never. It's the same one I've been texting you on."

"I—I didn't get a text. Davey told me you were coming."

Davey was up on his feet and running out of the room.

"Get back here!" Sarah commanded.

Davey hadn't quite made the door. He stopped and turned around.

He looked at Sarah.

"He needed to come. Tyler needed to come. I..."

"You pretended to be me," Sarah said. "Davey! You must never do things like that!" she added with dismay.

"Davey, I should cut your texting time with Megan!" Renee said firmly.

Davey sat down, crossing his arms over his chest, his lips set stubbornly. "Tyler is here. He needed to be here." Then he threw his arms out dramatically. "Do what you will!"

"Just don't do it again! Ever!" Sarah said, horrified.

She looked at Tyler. "I'm so sorry. I never would have twisted your arm, made you come here. I mean, it was on national news, you'd hear about it, but..."

"I need to be here," Tyler said softly. "Davey is right. I've got some things to do. I'll be back with you later. We may need help from your friend."

"Kieran," she said. "Kieran Finnegan. And she's living with a man named Craig Frasier. He's—he's great. I don't know if the FBI will be investigating this, but..."

"We'll talk to him."

He wanted to hold her. To pull her to him. But she was already trying to back away. She hadn't done it—hadn't contacted him. Davey had. And Tyler needed to remember that.

"I'll be in touch later tonight," he said.

He didn't hug her goodbye. But as he went to the door, Davey raced to him. "I'm sorry, Tyler. I'm so sorry."

"It's okay, buddy, it's okay. You're right. I need to be here. The police might already have a lead on this madman, okay? But I'll be here."

He nodded to Renee and Sarah, then headed out of

the house. He imagined Sarah might follow him, tell him that the years had been wasted for her, too, that she knew, just seeing him again, that...

Didn't happen.

He drove into the city and checked himself—and his car, which was as expensive to park as booking another room!—into his hotel. He had barely reached his suite before his phone rang.

And this time, it was actually Sarah.

"Tyler," she said excitedly. "We're in!"

"What?"

"This makes me feel worse than ever, but... I just got a call from a lawyer. Tyler, Hannah left a will. She has me listed as next of kin. She didn't have much money—barely enough for her funeral," Sarah said softly. "But that means that I can hire you, that it can all be legitimate, right?"

"I can work the case—even work it as if you've hired me. That's not the point. I have to form some relationships, step carefully, keep in with the police. We need everyone working together."

"But I am next of kin. You will stay, you will—"

"I will stay," he promised her softly.

And a moment later, he heard her whisper, "Thank you. Thank you!"

And then...

"Tyler?"

"Yes?"

"I am so sorry. I don't know why... I lost everyone. I should have been her friend. I really should have been her friend."

He didn't know what to say.

"Time doesn't change things like that. You were her friend. And...you're still my friend, Sarah. I still love you. I will see this through, I promise."

And he hung up before she could say anything else.

Chapter 2

"Survivor's guilt," Kieran Finnegan said softly.

Kieran was a good friend. While the hectic pace of her life—she worked as a psychologist for a pair of psychiatrists who worked frequently with the police, FBI and other law enforcement agencies, *and* helped out at the family pub—often kept her in a whirlwind where she didn't see much of her friends, she was the kind of person who was always there when she was needed.

Sarah had called her that morning.

It was Sunday noon. Hannah's body had been discovered the morning before; last night, Tyler had come to Aunt Renee's house.

And while Finnegan's on Broadway was doing a sound weekend business—they had a traditional roast entrée every Sunday that was very popular—Kieran was sitting down with Sarah. Of course, Finnegan's was in good shape that day as far as staff went, and since Sarah had once worked there, she could probably hop back in to help at any time herself, just as Kieran would do if the need arose.

Kieran had assured Sarah she would be there to spend some time with her, talk to her. As a very good friend would do.

That made Sarah feel all the worse about the lousy friend she had been herself.

"Survivor's guilt?" she repeated, shaking her head. "Honestly, I don't think so. I mean, what happened years ago...all of us survived. We survived because of Davey, though, honestly...some of the guff he had to take afterward! People wanted to know what kind of a medium or seer he was. 'Down Syndrome Boy Sees Evil.'" She was quiet for a minute. "Well, I have to admit, I was young and easily irritated, and Hannah..." She bit her lip and shrugged. "I was annoyed. She liked to have Davey around for the publicity, but then wanted me to leave him home if we were going out for the night or clubbing. She would use him when it seemed he was drawing a lot of attention, and then be irritated if we were spending any real time with him. But now..."

"From what I've gleaned through the media, her murder was brutal," Kieran murmured. "And far too similar to the method of the massacre at the theme park. Here's the thing. You're experiencing terrible guilt because Hannah is dead, and she was your friend—even it was a while ago. You both survived something horribly traumatic. But now she is dead. And you are alive. And all that happened before is rushing back. But, Sarah, you're not guilty of anything. Hannah survived that night— along with your other friends—because of Davey. You felt protective of Davey. That was only right. So quit feeling guilty. Hannah did choose to live a dangerous lifestyle. That doesn't mean what was done to her isn't every bit as horrid and criminal. But she may have put herself in danger. You have done nothing wrong. Of course, you could learn to be a bit more open to the possibility there are good people out there, and good things just might happen—and most of your friends truly love Davey."

Sarah leaned back and picked up her coffee cup, grinning. "Do I have a really big chip on my shoulder? I'm not sure whether I should enter therapy or say ten Hail Marys!"

"Do both!" Kieran suggested with a shrug. She let out a sigh. "Sarah, if you weren't really upset, you wouldn't be human, and I'd have to worry about you. Or rather, you would be a sociopath and I would have to worry about you." She shook her head. "Craig was saying that it was uncanny—the remarkable resemblance to what happened before." She hesitated. "In the actual killing, that is. Archibald Lemming found himself an amazing venue in which to carry out his bloodlust— what better than a haunted house? But it isn't him."

"It could be someone who studied him or knew him."

"Possibly."

"And someone like that doesn't stop, right?" Sarah asked.

"No," Kieran admitted unhappily. "When such a killer isn't caught and the killing stops, it's usually because he's moved on, been incarcerated for another crime or he died. This kind of thing…"

"It's not just someone who wanted Hannah dead?"

"I doubt it. What was done was overkill. Now, overkill can mean just the opposite. You see it with victims who are stabbed or bludgeoned over and over again—their killer was furious with them. Or sometimes, with someone else—and the victim they choose is the substitute for the one they want to kill. But again, remember I'm going from what was in the news. The way that this was done..."

"You think there will be more victims."

Kieran was thoughtful. "Yes—if we're talking a copycat killer who had a fan obsession with Archibald Lemming. I am afraid there will be more victims. Then again, people are clever. Maybe someone had it out for Hannah and wanted her dead specifically. Make it appear there is a psychopath or sociopath on the loose. There have been cases where several people were murdered in order to throw off suspicion when just one was the real target."

"Archibald Lemming was a psychopath, right?"

"Yes, the term applies to someone who is incapable of feeling empathy for another human being. They can be exceptionally charming and fool everyone around them—Ted Bundy, for instance. There are, however, psychopaths who turn their inclinations in a different direction—they become highly successful CEOs or hard-core business executives. They will never feel guilt. A sociopath, on the other hand, reaches his or her state of being through social factors—neglectful parents, bullying, abuse. Some function. They can be very violent, can show extreme bitterness or hatred along with that violence, but they're also capable of feeling guilt and even forming deep attachments to others."

Sarah nodded, listening to Kieran. It was good, she

figured, to have a concept of what they might be dealing with.

But dead was dead. Hannah was gone. And it didn't matter if she'd been viciously murdered by one kind of killer or another. It had been brutal.

Kieran smiled at her grimly. "I know what you're thinking. But when hunting a killer, it's helpful to have a concept of what you're looking for in his or her behavior."

"Of course! And thank you!" Sarah said quickly.

"So… Tyler Grant has come back to help?" Kieran asked. "And you were listed as Hannah's next of kin. That's good. It will allow him a lot of leeway."

"The FBI hasn't been asked in yet, right?"

"No, but Craig has a lot of friends with the police."

Kieran was referring to Special Agent Craig Frasier, FBI. They were living together—sometimes at Craig's and sometimes at Kieran's. He had the better space in NYC, so Kieran would eventually give up her apartment, most probably, and move in with him. They were a definite duo; Sarah was sure marriage was somewhere in the future for them, especially since Kieran's brothers—Declan, Kevin and Danny—seemed to accept him already as part of the family.

"Do you think…" Sarah began.

"Yes, I think!" Kieran said, smiling. She inclined her head toward the door. Tyler must have arrived. Sarah found herself inhaling sharply, her muscles tightening and her heart beating erratically.

Why? She wanted him here; she wanted…a solution. Hannah's killer caught and put away for life. She wanted…forgiveness.

Maybe it just seemed that their lives—so easy a de-

cade ago—had come to an abrupt break. It had become
a breach, and she wasn't sure things could ever be really right for her if she didn't come to terms with that.

*Once upon a time, she had been so in love with him.
High school! They'd been so wide-eyed and innocent,
and the world had stretched before them, a field of gold.*

Kieran stood, waving to him.

"You've met Tyler?" Sarah was surprised. She hadn't
known Kieran in high school.

"No," her friend said, shaking her head. "He called
about meeting up with Craig. I looked him up after—
found some pictures online. Rock solid, so it seems."

Rock solid.

Yes, that had always been Tyler.

"But how…?"

Kieran laughed. "How do you think?"

"Davey!" Sarah said. She wasn't sure whether to
be exasperated or proud of her cousin. Devious! No,
being devious wasn't really in his nature. Pretty darned
clever, though!

Tyler reached the table. Sarah stood, as Kieran had.
It was still awkward to see him. He'd grown into a truly
striking man with his quarterback's shoulders and lean,
hard-muscled physique. There were fleeting seconds
when they were near one another that she felt they were
complete strangers. Then there were moments when
she remembered laughing with him, lying with him,
dreaming with him, and she longed to just reach out and
touch him, as if she could touch all that had been lost.

He was obviously feeling awkward, too. "Sarah," he
said huskily, taking a second to lightly grip her elbow
and bend to kiss her cheek—as any friend might do.

That touch…so faraway and yet so familiar!

"Hey, I hear Davey has been at it again," Sarah said. "This is Kieran, of course."

"Of course," Tyler said, shaking her hand.

"Craig should be here any minute. He had to drop by the office," Kieran told him.

"Thanks," Tyler said.

"Coffee? Tea? Something to eat?" Kieran asked. "We are a pub. Our roast is under way."

"I'm sure it's wonderful," Tyler told her, smiling. "I've heard great things about this place—you're listed in all kinds of guidebooks."

"Nice to know."

"I would love coffee."

"I'll see to it. Black?"

"Yep. It's the easiest," he told her.

Kieran smiled pleasantly and went to get a cup of coffee for him.

Tyler looked at Sarah.

"Craig is great. You're going to like him a lot," Sarah said. "I can't believe Davey is making all these connections."

"The kind we should have made ourselves."

Kieran was already heading back with coffee. And she was indicating the old glass-inset, wood-paneled doors to the pub.

Craig had arrived.

He hurried to the high-top table where they'd been sitting. "Hey, kid," he said to Sarah, giving her a quick kiss on the cheek. He looked at Tyler. "Tyler, right? Grant?"

"Tyler Grant. And thank you, Special Agent Frasier."

"Just Craig, please. And sorry," he added, watching Kieran arrive with coffee, "you're going to have to slurp that down. We need to get going. The man on this particular case is a Detective Bob Green. He's a twelve-year homicide vet—he worked the Archibald Lemming case years ago. You might know him when you see him, though he wasn't the one doing the interviews back then, his partner was. He's senior man on his team now. Good guy. We can join him for the autopsy."

"That's great! Thank you," Tyler told him. "I know you have other cases."

"This caught up with me in the midst of a pile of paperwork," Craig told him. "My partner is handling it for me, and my director knows where I am, so it's all good."

"What about the site where Hannah was left?"

"I can take you there." Craig turned to Kieran, slipping an arm around her. "Save us supper, huh?"

"You bet."

The affection between them wasn't anything overt or in-your-face. It was just that even the way they looked at one another seemed to be intimate.

"Okay, we're on it," Craig said. He turned and headed toward the door. Tyler looked back and nodded a thanks to Kieran. He glanced at Sarah and gave her something of an encouraging smile.

She remembered his words from last night. He would stay on this.

He loved her still.

Friends...

Yes, sometimes friends loved each other forever. Even if they couldn't be together.

Autopsy rooms could be strange places. It was where doctors and scientists studied the dead and did their best to learn from them. The NYC morgue downtown was huge; the body count was almost always high. It wasn't that so many people were murdered; New York had had less than a hundred homicides in the past year— a large number, yes, but considering that it was home to eight million-plus people, and double that number came through almost on a daily basis, it wasn't such a massive amount.

But the homeless who died so sadly in the street came to the morgue, as did anyone who died at home or in hotel rooms, or anywhere else about the city other than with a doctor or in a hospital or directly under a doctor's care and with a known mortal disease.

Autopsy was no small neat room with refrigerated cubicles. Those existed, but for the most part, the place was a zoo comprised of the living and the dead—doctors, techs, photographers, cops, receptionists, computer crews and so on.

The living went about living—joking, taking lunch breaks, grabbing time to make appointments for themselves, call the cable company or check on the kids.

Detective Bob Green was a man in his late forties or early fifties with a thatch of neatly cut blond hair that was beginning to veer toward white, a slender face and dark almond eyes that contrasted with his pale skin and light hair. "Special Agent Frasier!" he said, greeting Craig.

Then he turned to Tyler.

He had a grave smile and a sturdy handshake. "I remember you," he told him. "I remember you all from the night at the horror park. Do you remember me?"

"Yes, I do. You were with an older detective, Mark Holiday. And a police photographer—I think his name was... Morrison. You were great with us back then, so thank you. It was hard. At first, I remembered little from that night except for the carnage and worrying about my friends," Tyler told him.

"Alex Morrison… He's still with us. So—you headed into the military and became a PI," Green said.

"I did."

"Thought you might become a cop. You were good that night. Composed. You're good in a crisis."

"Glad to hear it," Tyler told him. "Thank you."

"To be honest with you two, the autopsy already took place. But Lance—sorry, Dr. Layton—is waiting with the corpse." He paused, eyeing Tyler again. "You were there when Archibald Lemming killed all those people. We didn't know if…well, this does beat all. Of course, at this time we just have one dead woman— your friend," he added softly. "And it would be great to keep it that way. But… I was there, you were there… See what you think."

He led them into a room where a number of bodies lay on gurneys, covered properly with sheets.

A tall, thin man who reminded Tyler of Doc from *Back to the Future* stood by one of the gurneys. The ME, Dr. Lance Layton.

The man was waiting patiently for them. He greeted Craig with a smile and a polite nod. And Tyler realized he was curious about him, watching to see how he was handling being in a room with corpses. The doctor didn't extend a hand; he wore gloves, Tyler saw.

"You've seen your share of the dead, I take it?" Layton said.

"Four deployments in the Middle East, sir. Yes, I've seen my share."

Layton nodded and pulled back the sheet.

And what he saw was Hannah. What remained. She'd been such a pretty girl, olive-complexioned and with a bit of a slant to her dark eyes. She'd grown up to be an attractive woman—or she would have been, in life. If she had been alive, her eyes might have narrowed and hardened; she might have looked at the world differently. She hadn't always been the kindest or most sympathetic human being, but she'd never deliberately caused pain. She loved partying; she loved a good time. Beaches and margaritas. She'd gone toward the "dark" side—though she might have been nothing but light, had life not touched her so cruelly.

But not as cruelly as death had.

Her head sat apart from her torso and limbs. They were in different stages of decomposition.

"How was it done?" Tyler asked, and his voice was, to his own ears, thick.

"A knife. I believe she was lucky. Her killer hit the artery first. She would have bled out quickly while he continued—sawing at her."

Beheading a human being—with a knife—wasn't an easy thing to do. Strong executioners with a honed blade still had to use formidable strength; English axmen had been famous for botching the job. With a knife...

And this was Hannah.

Tyler remembered the last time he had seen her, not long after the night at the horror attraction. They hadn't talked about it the way they might have. The pictures of the dead in the "dining room" had been all too fresh in their heads. She had been quiet and grim, as they all had been, with the police. Each had been asked to give an account of what had happened. They'd been kids, ushered in and out, with protective parents or stepparents with them. A silver lining, one of the detectives had said, was that Archibald Lemming was dead. There wouldn't be a trial; they wouldn't have to stand witness.

And God help them all—they didn't need another Archibald Lemming on the streets.

Now, here, looking at the body of a young woman who had been an old friend, he found his memories were vivid and they were rushing back.

Archibald Lemming had decapitated four young people; the bodies had been seated around the table.

The heads had been upon it.

Tyler looked up at the ME and asked, "Drugs, alcohol? Anything on her, anything that would help explain how she was taken?"

Layton glanced at Detective Green. Tyler figured that Layton's loyalty was to the cop first; he'd obviously worked with Craig Frasier before. Layton wasn't telling him anything until he knew Green approved his sharing of details.

"Alcohol. And, yes, cocaine. At the rate she was imbibing... I'm not sure she'd have been long for this world as it was. She had been partying, I take it. She was last seen at a bar in Times Square," the ME told him. He glanced at Green again, and Tyler realized he must have learned that through the detective.

"It doesn't look like she put up much of a fight, but then again, the state of the body... Being in the water can wash away a host of evidence," Layton continued. "Thankfully, she wasn't in long. Her, uh, body pieces were found at several locations along the river, but we believe they were disposed of at the same site. The current washed her up...the parts...just a bit differently.

Since they were separate locations, they were discovered by different people."

"The body was cut up," Tyler noted.

"Yes, but most of the cuts are postmortem. If there is any salvation in this, I think she bled out quickly. The torture inflicted on her after… I don't think she felt. I wish I could say all this with certainty. That's just my educated opinion."

Once again, Tyler remembered the bodies around the table. They had been posed. This could be the same handiwork, as far as the beheadings went. But Hannah hadn't been posed; she'd been thrown in the river.

"It might be a copycat, it might not be," Craig murmured, obviously thinking along the same lines.

"We'll release the body toward the end of the week," Dr. Layton said. "We're holding on just in case…"

Just in case another body or body parts wash up on the riverbank again.

Detective Green, Craig and Tyler thanked him and they left the morgue.

When they were out on the street, Green looked at Tyler curiously again. "Where are you going from here?"

"Site inspections," Craig said.

"We're going to the bar where she was last seen, called Time and Time Again," Tyler said. "Then we're going along the Hudson—where the parts washed up."

"I don't think the discovery sites will help you," Green said. "Not even the killer could have known just where she'd pop up—or if she'd be taken in by a fisherman or a pleasure cruiser or what. Maybe you'll get something I didn't get at the bar. Good luck with that."

"If we find anything, we'll call immediately," Craig assured him.

Green nodded. "I know you will. Good day, my friends."

He headed off in one direction. Craig and Tyler turned in the other.

"Time and Time Again?" Craig asked.

Tyler nodded.

Time and Time Again. How tragically apropos.

Kieran didn't want Sarah going home. "You shouldn't be alone right now," she told her. "I mean, not with what has happened."

Her words surprised Sarah. She hadn't thought about being in danger herself. "I'm not being judgmental—trust me, not in any way!—but I've never led a lifestyle like Hannah was living. I mean…she was trolling for tricks. She was stripping—and not in a fine gentlemen's club. Not that a fine gentleman can't be a psychopath, right?"

"Charming, well-dressed and handsome to boot," Kieran assured her. "But the murder was so horrible… people are scared. And not just hookers. And if you're not scared, I think you should be. Anyway, wait until the guys get back, at the least. I've talked to Chef. He's saving us all a nice dinner. Until then…"

"I need to be doing something," Sarah said. "I can't just—sit here."

"What do you want to do?"

Sarah hesitated. "Look up what I can find on the past. Find out more about Archibald Lemming. Find out about the prison break. About him and his friend."

"The pub office here is all yours. We have a very

nice and well-behaved computer on the desk. No one is making any entries on a Sunday. We'll be busy. Make yourself comfortable."

"Kieran, that's Declan's computer," she said uncomfortably. She knew the Finnegans, and she knew the pub. She had been grateful for such a great place to work when she had been in school.

Declan was the oldest of the Finnegan clan. He had taken on the responsibility of the pub. The others all pitched in, but Kieran's brother Danny was a tour guide and her other brother, Kevin, was an actor. The workload fell to Declan.

Kieran grabbed her hand. Declan, a handsome hunk of a man with broad shoulders, a quick smile and dark red hair, assured her that she was more than welcome to the computer, to his office and the run of the pub if need be.

Sarah found herself led down the hall to the office; Kieran signed on to the computer there.

"Knock yourself out," she told her cheerfully once Sarah was set. "I'll be wherever for the moment. When Craig and Tyler get back, you can tie up, we'll have roast and we'll see you locked in for the night."

Sarah frowned; she didn't want to be afraid. She was a New Yorker! She had never feared the subway, though she did carry pepper spray. If she'd been afraid of every perceived threat, she'd never have made it in the city.

But Kieran was gone. And Sarah didn't know where to begin—other than to key in the name "Archibald Lemming."

His crimes—even his initial crimes—had been horrendous. He'd received the death sentence, but under pressure by right-to-life groups after his sentencing, the death penalty had been altered to "life and ninety-five years." To make sure that he never got out.

But of course, he had gotten out.

Lemming's first known victim had been a kindergarten teacher. She'd been found in her home, her head almost severed from her body. He'd managed to get his second victim's head off. It had been left on a buffet table in the dining room while she'd been seated in her favorite chair. He hadn't discriminated by sex—his third victim had been a man, a plumber, who'd been found with his fingers wrapped around a beer, his torso in a recliner in the living room, his head atop the TV.

Lemming had been interviewed by the police, since he had hired the plumber to do some work in his home. It was also discovered that he'd had a flirtation going with the first victim, who had lived in his building. He'd been let go—there had been no evidence against him. Then the body and head of his landlord had been found—set up much the same as the others. And despite his "charming" protests, he'd been connected to the crimes via DNA—he'd cut himself during the last murder, and his own blood had given him away. He'd been incarcerated, where, according to prison officials, he'd been a model prisoner. Until, with Perry Knowlton—another murderer who used a knife—he'd escaped via the infirmary.

And gone on to kill and kill again in a frenzy in the "haunted" house.

Sarah sat back and breathed for a minute.

This was crazy.

She had seen the man die. He had no children—none known, at any rate. And if he'd had any offspring, it was unlikely that they knew he was their father. He'd been a loner: no wife, no girlfriend. He'd gone to work every day on Wall Street—and he'd killed by night.

She scanned the information on the page again. He was, by pure definition, the perfect psychopath. No emotion whatsoever. No regret. He was cold and brutal. He'd even murdered the man with whom he'd escaped.

Sarah frowned and started reading again.

Yes, she'd seen Archibald Lemming die.

But...

She sat back, still staring at the screen. And to her own amazement, she thought she had a theory.

Chapter 3

Being escorted back to the office by Danny Finnegan, Tyler found himself grateful that Sarah had found such a supportive group of friends.

Just going through the pub, he'd heard people call out to Danny and to one another.

"Regulars?" he asked. "They all know each other?"

Danny, a leaner, slightly younger version of his brother Declan, shrugged and grinned. "Our folks—and theirs before them—wanted it to be a real Irish pub. Well, back in the day, men had a room, and women and families had a separate one, if they were allowed in at all. But hey, progress is a good thing, right? Yeah, we like to be an Irish American *Cheers*, and we want everyone to feel welcome."

"I do," Tyler assured him.

Danny pushed open a door in the long hallway. "Tyler and Craig are back, Sarah!"

She had been very seriously staring at the computer screen and looked up quickly, a question in her eyes.

Tyler wished he could tell her that yes, simply going to the morgue had solved the whole thing.

He prayed that eventually, and sooner rather than later, they would have answers.

It wasn't going to be easy; they had nothing to go on.

"Kieran will have roast out for you all in a few minutes. We've got you at a back booth," Danny said, and left.

Tyler dropped into a chair in front of the desk.

Sarah stared at him. "It was...horrible, wasn't it?" she whispered.

He nodded. "I can't help but remember—we all had such promise."

"But did you learn anything?"

"I'm heading to the bar where she was last seen, Time and Time Again, around eight or so. If they get some of the same clientele nightly, someone might know or remember something." He hesitated a moment. "She wasn't working at the strip club anymore—she hadn't been for about two weeks. From what I understand, it was a pretty decent place. I've heard it's easy for strippers to become involved in drugs—helps them through. But there are a number of clubs run fairly well, professionally—no touching for real, and no drugs. Anyway, Hannah was fired about a week ago. Craig and I dropped by the club after we visited the sites where she was found."

"So...wow. I feel worse and worse."

"Don't. Something happened that night ten years ago. We were incredibly lucky. Thanks to Davey, we weren't killed. But we all changed. We became introverted. And when we got over it, time had passed. This was in no way your fault—you have to know that. You couldn't have stopped what happened in Cemetery Mansion, any more than you could have saved Hannah now. You have to accept that."

"I know."

"The thing is… I do think this is random. The first suspects in a murder are always those closest to the victim. Except in a case like this. There's no one really to look at—her last boyfriend was in Chicago when it happened."

"Random…" Sarah paused and took a breath. "I know this may seem far-fetched, but I have an idea who we're looking for."

Tyler couldn't have been more surprised. "Who?"

"Perry Knowlton!"

He was still for a minute. "Perry Knowlton is dead. Archibald Lemming killed him, too. Police found the ashes in a veterinary clinic before they even caught up with Lemming."

She shook her head firmly. "They never proved it!"

"What do you mean?"

"I've been reading up on Archibald Lemming and Perry Knowlton all day. I've studied every newspaper article, every piece of video. They found a body so badly burned there were no DNA samples—maybe there might have been today, but not back then. They found his prison uniform. They found trinkets he carried. But they never proved without doubt that the bone fragments and ash they discovered were the remains of Perry Knowlton."

Tyler had read up on the killers, too.

And she was right.

Before, Knowlton hadn't been someone to consider. He hadn't made any appearances over the years and had been assumed dead. He was a killer, too. A serial killer. Like his prison buddy, Archibald Lemming, he had loved to kill with knives. He hadn't been known for decapitating his victims, but for slashing them, the kill strokes being at the jugular vein.

"Maybe," Tyler said.

"But how, and where has he been? Those are the things I've been wondering. I mean, he'd be in the system. If he'd been arrested for any crime in the past ten years, his prints would be on record. They'd have known it was him. What? Did he find a distant farm somewhere and hide out for ten years? Kieran said serial killers don't stop, unless they are dead or incarcerated somewhere." She flushed, her beautiful blue eyes wide. "I know I just write science fiction novels, but I am good at research."

"Sarah, your theory is just as sound as anything else we have at the moment, that's for sure," Tyler told her. "I—I don't know. We can look."

There was a tap at the door and Kieran stuck her head in. "Roast!" she said. "You need to keep your strength up if you're going to continue working on this thing. That means actually having a meal. Craig says you're going to the bar later. Nothing to do until then except fuel up!"

"Sounds good to me," Tyler said. He rose. Sarah still had a bit of a shell-shocked look about her. He walked around the desk and reached for her hand. "Let's eat," he said.

"Dinner," she agreed.

She stood. Her palm rested in his. He couldn't believe ten years had passed and it was still incredibly good just to hold her hand.

And then she smiled at him.

And he knew. He'd waited forever to be back with her. He sure as hell hadn't wanted it to be like this... But he had never managed to fall out of love with her. And that was why nothing else in his life had ever been more than a fleeting moment in time, sex between consenting adults, panacea to ease a pain he'd refused to admit existed.

Maybe it was true that there was one person in the world who was simply everything, one person you were meant to love for a lifetime. Still, neither of them had fallen apart; they had created good lives. Responsible lives.

So why had he left?

Because she had pushed him away. And that would never lead to a lifetime of happiness. And, of course, he was still afraid she would push him away again. But at least not in the middle of a murder investigation. Not this one.

"Thank you," she said quietly.

There was something soft in her eyes. Something that made him think of years gone by.

It hurt.

And it was good, too. Oddly good.

"You're welcome," he murmured.

They made their way back down the charmingly

paneled old hallway and out to the restaurant section of the pub. As promised, Kieran had a back booth for them, out of the way of the now very busy crowd. Sunday roast was apparently extremely popular.

Although Craig was careful about what he said, Tyler learned the FBI agent had been working on an organized crime case that included bodies found as the result of a rather old-fashioned but very efficient form of retribution murder—they had their feet stuck in concrete and had been dropped in the East River. "My partner, Mike, has been doing some cleanup paperwork for me, but we still have a few arrests to make. I'll be as much help as I can."

"You've opened doors for me. I'm grateful," Tyler said. "And Sarah might have a very good idea for us to pursue."

She hiked her brows in surprise and flushed again. "I hope you're not going to think I have an overactive imagination," she said.

"We definitely think you have an overactive imagination," Kieran told her. "But that's a good thing. It pays. On this, however, what do you think?"

"Tell them," Tyler urged.

And so she did.

Neither Kieran nor her boyfriend looked at her as if she were crazy.

"That's true?" Craig asked. "I remember the case—when Archibald Lemming died here on that table leg. Of course, the entire country talked about it. But I never studied anything on Perry Knowlton. As far as the public was concerned—as far as everyone was concerned, really—the man was dead, a victim of the man he had befriended. Now that is something I can look into for you."

"That would be great."

"Excuse me," Kieran said. "Drinks, anyone?"

They opted for iced tea all around and she disappeared to get it. Another smiling waitress arrived with their plates.

The food was really good.

The conversation became lighter. They learned that Kieran and Craig had met during a diamond heist. Because of Kieran's employers, Dr. Fuller and Dr. Miro, she was able to help Craig with a number of cases—recently one that had involved the deconsecrated old church right behind the pub. "My brother was affected by that one... He'd been in love with a victim," Kieran said softly. "That's Kevin. You haven't met him yet, Tyler. But I'm sure you will!"

Tyler told them he was living on Beacon Hill. He described his daily work. "I take on a lot of missing-children cases," he said. "When I'm lucky, I find them—most often, they're runaways. When they're not... I have a great relationship with the Boston PD, which is very important. I won't work possible-cheating-spouse cases—too sordid. I have worked murder cases—a number of cold cases. It wasn't always that way, of course, but working the cheating spouse thing just seems nasty—and finding justice for someone feels really good."

"Have you ever considered coming back to New York, Tyler?" Kieran asked.

"It's home. One never knows," he said.

"Boston, New York...so many great cities!" she said. And then she looked at her watch. "Whoa. Well, dinner with you two was great. I wish we were heading to a play or a movie now, but I know you want to stay focused. It's eight o'clock."

"Time to go," Tyler said, rising.

"Are you going with him?" Kieran asked Craig.

"I have to head to the office for at least an hour or so," he replied. "Hey, this man is a good investigator. He'll do fine."

Sarah had risen, as well. "I'm going with you," she said.

"Sarah," Tyler protested. "That's not a great idea."

"I can help."

"How?"

"I can make you look human and sweet—better than looking like a linebacker out to tackle someone!"

Time and Time Again was off Forty-Second Street and the Times Square area, but far enough away from the theater district on Ninth Avenue to just miss most of the theater-going crowd.

It would best be described, Sarah thought, as a *nice* dive bar.

She definitely wanted all her facilities about her, but deeply disappointed the bartender by ordering a soda with lime.

"Don't you want a Ninth Avenue Special, a Dive-Bar Exotic or a Yes, It's Time Again?" he asked her.

He was a young man of maybe twenty-five. Cheerful and flirty.

Sarah was sitting at the bar; Tyler was meeting with the night manager in his office.

"No, thanks. Just the soda water."

"Your friend a cop?" he asked her.

She shook her head, smiling though, and looked around. The place was decorated with old posters that depicted the city during different eras. They helped cover the fact that the bar really needed to be painted.

"No, Tyler isn't a cop."

"But he's in there asking about that girl," the bartender said. He had a neatly trimmed beard and mustache combo, and she wondered if he was a student at one of the city's colleges.

"Yes, he's asking about Hannah Levine," she told him softly.

"I'm Luke," he said, looking down the bar to see if he was needed. He wasn't. He leaned on it. "The cops have already been all over us. She was carrying one of our promo matchboxes—that's how they knew she'd been here." He grimaced. "They have raised lettering—really swank matches for this place, but we get a mixed clientele. We cater to the local music scene."

"Nice," she replied. He was friendly, and she decided she might be able to help the investigation. She could ask questions, too, and maybe in a different way. "Are you from New York?"

"Nope. Akron, Ohio. Loving being here. Don't be deceived by appearances. This is actually a great place. Yes, we have a few lowlifes hanging around. But it's honest work for me and helps pay the bills."

"Hannah was my friend," she said softly.

"Oh?" He seemed surprised. He leaned closer to her. "You don't look like a junkie."

"Hannah wasn't on heroin," she said defensively.

"No, just everything else. She came in here frequently.

The owner had barred her for a while, but...people liked her. She just—well, she looked for tricks here, you know."

Sarah winced.

"Hey, I'm so sorry. I guess you hadn't seen her in a while."

"No, I hadn't. But..."

"I can see you care." He straightened and said, "Excuse me," and hurried down the length of the bar, speaking to customers seated on stools along the way. He refilled a few drinks, whispered to someone and then headed back to speak with Sarah.

"I don't know what it was with her!" Luke said. He lowered his voice. "We dated a few times, but then... I found out she was hooking. I...well, that didn't work for me. I want to have a wife I'll grow old with, kids. Hannah said she'd never settle down. But we didn't part badly. We were friends. I tried to help out, give her food—pay her bar tab when she walked out. She was her own worst enemy. Sometimes I thought she was committing slow suicide. Even when she had people trying to help her, she'd laugh them off. She said she loved the danger of hooking, you know?"

Sarah did know. Hannah had wanted to be on the edge—she'd wanted to skydive, ride the fastest coaster, speed on the FDR.

"I don't care what she was doing. What happened shouldn't have happened to her or to anyone!" Sarah said passionately.

"No! Of course not! I didn't mean that. Just that... I don't know who she might have met, who could have done such a terrible thing..."

His voice trailed off as he realized he obviously didn't need to remind Sarah what had happened.

"Were you working when she was here?" Sarah asked him.

"I was coming for the late shift. But I was just outside. Coming in."

"And you talked to her?"

He nodded. Sarah thought she saw the glint of tears in his eyes and his voice was husky when he said, "She gave me a big hug and a kiss on the cheek and told me she 'was about to go roll in some dough.' I assumed that meant she had met up with a rich guy willing to pay a nice price. She was so pretty. Even...even with the drugs and alcohol. And nice. No matter what, she had something about her. A core that had some real warmth, you know?"

"I do know," Sarah assured him. She cleared her throat. "Did you tell the police what she said?"

"I wasn't interviewed. I wasn't actually in the bar when she was here, so the manager never called me to talk to the police."

"And you didn't volunteer to help?" Sarah asked.

"Hey. They were trying to paint a picture of her I don't agree with—that she was a druggie whore who got what was coming to her."

"That can't be true. Any sensible, decent person knows that, whatever someone's lifestyle, they don't deserve such a horror 'coming to them.' That can't be—"

She was suddenly interrupted by Tyler's deep voice right behind her. "Whatever made you think the world was filled with sensible and decent people?"

She fell silent. The bartender was looking at Tyler.

Sarah quickly introduced the two. They shook hands as Tyler crawled up on the stool next to Sarah's.

"You're not a cop?" Luke asked him warily.

Tyler shook his head. "I'm a PI, in from Boston. Mainly here because, as I'm sure Sarah told you, Hannah was a friend."

"Pity you guys weren't around when she was still living," he murmured.

"Yes, we're well aware of that," Sarah said.

"Hey," Tyler said. The word wasn't spoken angrily, nor was it shouted. But it was filled with the fact that Sarah could not be blamed—nor could any of them.

"A sick killer is responsible, no one else. When she was a kid, no one could tell Hannah what to do. I sincerely doubt she'd have listened now. But we were her friends," Tyler went on. "And we will see that justice is done for her."

"Okay, okay!" Luke said, hands in the air. "Look, I'm sorry I didn't go bursting into the office and say hey, yeah, I knew Hannah. I don't know who killed her..."

His voice faltered suddenly.

"What is it?" Sarah asked.

"A man."

"A man?" Tyler asked.

Luke nodded. "He was in here several times a couple of weeks ago. I thought that he was watching Hannah. No way out of it, with those cat eyes of hers... bedroom eyes, you know what I mean? Anyway, he was watching her."

"Was he...old, young? Can you describe him?" Tyler asked.

"Well, he was average. He wore a low-brimmed hat

all the time—I sure don't know his eye color or anything like that. Narrow face. Wore a coat, too. But then, you know, when it's cold, people don't always take their coats off in bars. Especially this one—the heating system isn't so great."

"Anyone else unusual?" Tyler asked him.

"I'll think…honestly, I'll think about it. But as far as this place goes… I mean, describe unusual. We get all kinds. Some hardworking, partying-on-Friday-nights kind of people. Drug dealers now and then. But Willie—you met Willie, the night manager, right?" he asked, looking at Tyler. "You were just in talking with him, right?"

Tyler nodded.

"He doesn't like drug dealers or junkies. He can usually ferret them out and he's as tall and muscle-bound as you are, dude," he said, glancing quickly at Tyler and then grimacing at Sarah as if they shared a great joke. "I think they hired him because they don't need a bouncer when he's on. Also, he's the owner's cousin. Owner is in Utah, so… But you see, Hannah left here— after that, we don't know."

"I know," Tyler said. "And, listen, the cops on this really are good guys. If I can get them to send a sketch artist down here, do you think you could help us get some kind of an image of the guy in the hat and the coat?"

"I'll go you one better," Luke promised. "Bring your guy down. We'll also post that we need any help—no matter how minute—anyone can give. How's that?" He pointed across the room to a large bulletin board. "Trust me. People will want to help. Kind of like back in the days of Jack the Ripper, you know? People may like to think this guy only went after a prostitute and he won't target them. But this kind of thing…" A shudder shook his whole body. "This is terrifying!"

"Hey, is there actually a bartender in here?" someone shouted from the end of the bar.

"Hang on, there, Hardy! Give your liver a breather! I'm on the way!" Luke said. He nodded to the two of them.

"Did you pay yet?" Tyler asked Sarah.

"No." She scrambled in her tote bag for her wallet, but Tyler had already set a bill on the bar.

"I think I'm supposed to be paying you," she said. "For your services."

He stared at her and smiled slowly. "I was that good, huh?"

She realized just how her words might be taken, and yet of course he was teasing.

Still…

Ten years between them.

She felt the blood rise to her cheeks. She had not blushed this much since…well, since forever.

"I meant I'm next of kin, or so Hannah said. I'm hiring you to find her killer."

He shook his head. "I'm going to find this killer for Hannah. And for all of us," he said.

Tyler had barely gotten into his hotel room after dropping Sarah off at her place when his phone rang.

"Tyler?"

He was curious the caller had voiced the question, as he always answered his phone with one word, his surname, "Grant."

But despite time and distance, he knew the caller.

"Sean," he said.

"Yeah, it's Sean. Hey, how are you? I know this is out of the blue, but…"

There was fear in Sean's slightly garbled and wandering words.

"I'm here. In New York."

"Because of Hannah?"

"Yes."

"Thank God!" Sean said. "I mean, you were in the military, right? You, uh, know your way around a gun and all that."

"I know my way around a gun and all that," he agreed.

"I'm afraid they're after us," Sean said.

Tyler hesitated. Then asked, "Sean, who are *they*? Everyone thinks what happened to Hannah is horrendous, but why would any 'they' be after all of us?"

"You don't know the latest. Oh, well, it just broke. Maybe you haven't heard."

As Sean spoke, Tyler realized he had another call coming in—from Craig Frasier.

"Excuse me. I'll be right back with you," he told Sean. "Craig?"

"There's been another murder. Body and head left in a park by the FDR. There was ID. Her name was Suzie Cornwall."

Suzie?

Sarah's best friend? God, no.

"Bob Green called me. You can join us at the park. I'll text the address."

He switched the call back over. "Sean, my God, I'm so sorry—"

"Oh, Suzie—our Suzie—is here with me."

"What? Listen, Sean—"

"No, no, I heard on the news. Suzette Cornwall was murdered. But it's not our Suzie. Our Suzie is here, with me. We're married now, you probably know, so she's Suzie Avery. The cops found me—I guess as a Suzie Cornwall's husband, in whatever database. She was Suzie Cornwall, too. But…oh, Lord! Our Suzie is here. She's fine. But that's just it, don't you see? He—or they!—got Hannah. They're looking for us, Tyler. They're looking for us—the group at Cemetery Mansion that year."

That was crazy. Just crazy. The only person who might want some kind of revenge was Archibald Lemming. And Lemming was dead. Tyler had seen the table leg protrude right through his body.

He'd seen the blood. The ripped and torn flesh, down to the organs and bone. Lemming was not alive. And Tyler had lived with the fact that he was at least partially responsible for that man's death…no matter if he was a murderer the world was better off without.

Perry Knowlton? Was he really out there? Had Archibald Lemming helped him pretend to die—so that he could live?

"Tyler? Help!" Sean said softly.

"All right, listen, Sean. You and Suzie stay close and keep your doors locked. Don't go out tonight. Stay in until I know what's going on. You hear me?"

"I hear you. Loud and clear. Door is locked. But please, don't you see? He killed Hannah Levine. Now he's killed a Suzette Cornwall. We're all supposed to die, Tyler. I don't know why, except that we were there. We were there."

"I'll be in touch. Just stay put. Where are you living now?"

"Brooklyn. Got a little house."

It was too bad Sean wasn't living in a tiny apartment with no windows and one door.

"Windows—check all the windows. Make sure you're secure."

"Got it. You'll call me?"

"As soon as possible. I'm meeting the cops at the site."

He hung up; he didn't have time to waste on the phone. He put a call through to Sarah. Her phone rang a few times, and in those split seconds he felt debilitating panic setting in.

Then she answered.

"Sarah, listen to me. I'm asking Detective Green to get a man out to your aunt's house. Now I do think we're all in danger."

"What? What are you talking about?"

"Have you seen the news?"

"No."

"Okay, it's not the Suzie who was our friend, but a Suzie Cornwall was murdered. I just talked to Sean. They're fine. But I'm going to stop by for you. I need to get you somewhere safe. You can stay at Kieran's with her for now. Craig has been living there, mostly, I guess, so I am assuming it's pretty darned safe. You have to lock yourself in…"

"A woman named Suzie Cornwall was murdered?" she asked.

"Not our Suzie."

"Poor woman. Oh, my God, poor woman!"

"Sarah, listen to me. Don't open your door until you hear my voice!"

"Right, right. I won't," she promised.

"And call Davey and Renee. Tell them to stay put until we figure something out."

Tyler hung up, and then, with his wits more thoroughly about him, he dialed Craig back. Craig let him know that yes, of course Kieran would be happy to have Sarah come stay with her. He should have said something; he had thought it was a given.

Tyler thanked him and headed out. His hotel wasn't far from Sarah's place on Reed Street. It seemed as if the distance had somehow become greater since the last time he drove it.

He left his car in the street, not caring what kind of a fine he might get, and took the steps to her apartment two at a time.

But Sarah was ready to go. She had a little bag with her. She looked at him with wide eyes, shaking her head. "That's too much to be a coincidence, right?"

"It's too close," he agreed.

"My theory… I think it has to be right!" she whispered.

"It may be right. Listen, I'm taking you to—"

"Kieran's. I figured. Where else could you drop me at midnight—or is it 1:00 a.m. yet?"

He just nodded.

Then he told her, "I'll find out more when I see the crime site."

They hurried out to the car and he got her in safely before he jumped back in the driver's seat. When they got to Kieran's place in SoHo, he parked the car in the street again.

"Go on—I'll run in!" Sarah told him.

"Not in this lifetime," he answered, leaving the car and taking her arm.

Kieran lived above a karaoke bar. Someone was warbling out Alice Cooper's "The Man Behind the Mask" as they made their way up.

The singer wasn't so bad. His choice of song seemed grating.

Of course, Sarah knew which unit was Kieran's door. She stopped in front of it.

Tyler reached out to knock.

And then it touched him that they were on the run from an unidentified threat, and he was on his way to go see the corpse of a woman—an innocent victim—who, just earlier today, had surely believed she had years left before her.

Life was fleeting.

He turned, pulled Sarah into his arms and kissed her. It was a hard kiss, hurried and passionate, hotly wet and very sloppy. She was surprised at first, but then she returned his kiss, and when he released her, she looked at him breathlessly, with confusion.

"Tyler—"

"I love you. I've always loved you. And so help me God, we will survive this!"

Kieran's door opened; she'd heard something. She

had expected them. Tyler saw one of her brothers was there, as well.

"Danny is going to hang with us," she said.

"Great," Tyler said. "Okay—"

"Don't even say 'lock up.' I'm a New Yorker, and I live with Craig!"

He actually smiled at that. Then he turned and left. No cops had ticketed his car and no tow company had taken it away.

He drove quickly and competently.

He needed to reach the crime scene.

To see everything in situ.

He had to get there.

And, dear lord, how he dreaded getting there, as well.

Chapter 4

Danny Finnegan was really a great guy.

Once upon a time, Sarah and he had almost dated. She'd somehow known that it couldn't be a forever kind of thing between them, so they'd stayed friends.

Danny, she thought, had realized the same thing. They were never going to be friends with benefits, either—it would be just too awkward for them and the entire family. And having the Finnegan family as friends was something special; they'd tacitly known that anything between them—other than great friendship—could destroy it all.

And still she loved him as a friend, as she did Kieran.

If it weren't for the fact that two people had been murdered in a fashion reminiscent of a decade-old massacre, it might have been just a late evening with friends.

Kieran made hot chocolate and set out cookies; Danny diverted Sarah with weird stories about the city. "Believe it or not, this lady kept her son's corpse in the house for years—up in Brooklyn. She didn't kill him— poor guy died young of disease. But she kept him—and the only reason the body was discovered was that she was hospitalized herself. A relative went to get some things for her and...well, the son was down to skeletal remains. I've heard stories about other people keeping corpses, but I know this one is true! The papers all covered it. We're a great state—and so weird. Oh, not in the city, but up in Elmira, John Brown's widow—she being the widow of the John Brown's raid John Brown!—received a head. A skull, really. Another man named John Brown died down in Harpers Ferry, a skull was found and everyone said that it was John Brown's—so they sent it to her."

"Ugh. What did she do?"

"Sent it back, of course!" Danny said.

Sarah smiled, knowing he knew she'd grown up in the city and would be aware of the history of the state, but maybe not all the most bizarre bits and pieces of fact and lore.

"Hey, Cooper Union had the first elevator shaft— not elevator, actually. Otis hadn't come along yet, but when building, Cooper had the basic idea, using a round shaft!"

Sarah laughed. "I think I did hear something about that years ago—NYU students often hung out with Cooper Union people."

Her phone rang. She glanced at the number and was surprised to see that despite a few hardware upgrades over the years, Suzie Cornwall's number was still in her contacts.

She answered quickly. "Suzie?"

"Hey. You okay? I'm sorry. I shouldn't have called. I mean, it was okay—not okay, Lord! I'm sorry, it was not okay, it was terrible, horrible, when Hannah was killed. But…it didn't really terrify me. It saddened me, but it didn't terrify me. Sarah, now he's killed a *Suzie Cornwall*. Oh, my God. That poor woman. She was killed for having my name! I'm so scared, Sarah. So scared. Do you think that… Davey could help?"

Stunned, Sarah stared at the phone. "Suzie, hey, hey, yes, of course I know you're scared. But… Davey is a young man with Down syndrome. He isn't a medium, he isn't magical. That night…he saw Archibald Lemming slinking around. He saw him go into the house. My uncle taught him to be wary. How to really notice things, to watch out for people because, sad as it may be, the world is full of bullies who want to hurt those who are at a disadvantage instead of helping them. He didn't want Davey to fall victim to someone who meant him ill."

"But…he *knew* that night!" Suzie whispered. "Oh, I'm sorry. Sean said this wouldn't make any sense."

"Congratulations, by the way. I 'liked' it when I saw that you two had married, but I figured a zillion other people did, too. You looked beautiful."

"Yes, yes. Thank you. I think I actually saw your 'like.' I should have called or written then, or…you know. Oh, but I've bought all your books!"

"Thanks. I didn't think you were a sci-fi fan."

"I'm not."

"Well, then, thank you very much."

"Oh, but they were good. Oh, Sarah! I'm so scared."

"You're home, right? Tyler told you to go home and stay there and lock in, right?"

"But what do we do in the morning? Sean and I both have jobs. He works down on Wall Street. I'm up by the park at the new department store there—I'm a makeup artist. Sean is a stock broker."

"Maybe, just tomorrow, you shouldn't go in. Maybe they can arrange police protection."

"For the rest of our lives? Sarah, they have to find this maniac."

Both Kieran and Danny could hear Suzie through the phone, she was talking so loudly. Sarah looked at them both, shaking her head.

"No," she said firmly, gazing at Danny and Kieran. "Until they find the killer."

"It's Lemming. It's Archibald Lemming. He's back. He's come back, and he knows we were there. He's going to kill us all."

"It's not Archibald Lemming. We saw him die."

"He's come back—somehow."

"No. It's someone just as sick, using what happened."

"But…how? How is this person finding us?"

"He made a mistake—he didn't find you. Unless this is sheer happenstance and he killed a woman who happened to have the same name, or your maiden name."

"Lemming must be whispering from the grave. He'll keep killing, it wasn't happenstance. He's after me."

"He'll be stopped."

"But what if—"

"Tyler is back in New York," Sarah said simply. "And I know he won't stop."

* * *

The body of the woman was seated on a park bench, hands rested easily in her lap. If she just had a head, it would have appeared she had simply decided to relax a minute and enjoy the beauty of the park.

She'd been wearing a red sweater and jeans. All around the neck area, the sweater was darkened; blood had dried into it.

As Tyler arrived, Craig came forward, telling the officer who was keeping the crowd back that Tyler was with him.

"We're on it now," Craig told him, referring to the FBI. "This morning, with this second kill and the name of the victim, the police chief decided to bring us in, along with every law enforcement agency in the near vicinity. He's a good guy. No jurisdictional bull with him. He wants murders solved."

He'd spoken as they came to the body. Police photographer Alex Morrison was there, snapping pictures quickly. Detective Bob Green was present, too, leaning close to the victim, but not too close. Dr. Lance Layton had been called out; he had already arrived, as well.

Thankfully, none of them looked at Tyler as if he didn't belong, or as if he were an interloper.

"No defensive wounds," Layton said. "But the bastard did saw through her neck with a blade—a serrated blade, so it appears. Might have drugged her first. Pray that he did, the poor thing! Had to have—no one could feel that kind of pain and not react."

"The head?" Craig asked quietly.

"It was left in a kid's swing," Green said. "Doc had it moved—it's in the back of the wagon."

He was referring to Dr. Layton's vehicle. The back

door to the van was open, an officer in uniform standing guard before it.

"We'll take a look," Craig said grimly.

They did; the officer knew Craig and gave way.

The head was in a sterile container.

Her hair had a brown base, but had been multicolored in blues and greens and pinks, just as many women were coloring their hair. Though it was difficult to tell from a severed head—all life and vitality gone—it appeared she had been a bit older than their Suzie. Judging from the headless body, she had probably been about the same height and weight.

"How did he get her here?" Tyler wondered aloud. The FDR was just above them. The park was surrounded by apartment buildings, all of which had storefronts at the bottom. It was a typical New York City neighborhood—the park offering some trees and fake grass, but all around it, the congestion of giant buildings and all the trappings needed to house millions of people on an island.

"She was found after dark by some folks who jumped the fence—a babysitter who'd lost her phone here. I don't think the killer thought she'd be found until morning," Craig told Tyler. "The media got hold of it just about the same time as the police, so God knows what pictures are out there. They had her name first—she lived in that building just over there. No ID on her, but our teenage babysitter knew her because they live in the same building. Her name is on the buzzer in the foyer. No night guard or desk clerk in the place. No cameras. The cops are doing a door-to-door now, but...so far, no one saw anything."

"He killed her elsewhere and got her in here fast."

Tyler looked out at the crowd watching the scene. The killer could be there—with the others, watching them all, enjoying the fruit of his labors.

"Crime scene techs are going over the place with a fine-tooth comb," Craig said. "We're hoping to hell the officers or the techs will find something—anything. And," he added grimly, "we're hoping Lance will tell us she was drugged and unconscious before this happened. Press conference first thing, autopsy right after. Until then..."

"I need to be with Sarah," Tyler said. But he paused, looking around the scene. The park, with the shaded benches for moms and dads and babysitters. The colorful playground created for children, with crawl bars, slides and multileveled platforms.

The park was fenced, but the fence was wood and easily scaled.

"Facts we have will be coming through email," Bob Green said, walking over to them. He always seemed to be studying Tyler. Tyler just stared back at him. He supposed he was a curiosity to the detective. He had been there when Archibald Lemming had attacked a group of teenagers in a haunted house. When there had been so much fake blood it had been hard to figure out where the real blood began. "We'll share all information on this immediately, to facilitate working together. This has to be stopped. The mayor called me personally. I have a meeting with my guys and the FBI at the crack of dawn, and we have to be ready for the press conference. We'll have the park roped off for the next week, at least." He lowered his head, letting out a sigh of disgust. "Kids.

Little kids come here. The babysitter...she's a student at NYU. All of about twenty. Can you imagine a little one walking in on a sight like that?"

"No one should ever have to walk in on a sight like that," Tyler said.

"Is there...anything you can think of, anything about Lemming, anything at all that might help?" Green asked him.

"Lemming died that night. We don't believe, however, that the man with whom he escaped is dead."

Green frowned. "Ashes and bone fragments and his prison uniform were found. Lemming used Perry Knowlton to escape, then he killed him."

"He's the only man who would really know exactly how Archibald Lemming worked," Tyler said. "And there was no DNA. There sure as hell were no fingerprints. There's no proof the man is dead."

"At my office we're going to work on the concept that he might be alive," Craig said.

Green nodded slowly. "And he's out for...revenge?"

"Possibly."

"Then you're all in danger. You, Sarah, Sean Avery and the other Suzie Cornwall. And Davey Cray," he added softly.

"And Davey," Tyler agreed. "Can you give them protection?"

"I can. And you might be right. Then again, the killer could be anyone. There are sick people out there who fall even more sickly in love with criminals and killers. Especially serial killers. Some of the fan mail those guys get in prison...it's enough to make your hair stand on end. But we need something to work with. Anything."

He was still looking at Tyler, apparently wanting an answer.

"As you said, our lives are in danger. If I had any kind of an idea, I guarantee you, I'd share it."

"There's nothing, nothing from that night...?"

"I remember Archibald Lemming coming at me with a blade. I was in shock. I was terrified for myself and the others. Sick from what I saw. And then Sarah and Davey were there—and I pushed Lemming off us, and we saw Lemming die. We can't look to the past. It isn't him doing these things. But I believe it is someone who knew him."

"Let's get out of here—it's nearly three in the morning," Craig said. "We can think it all out for hours, talk it all out...but there's nothing more we can do here."

There wasn't. The dead woman's torso was being loaded for removal to the morgue; they would, at that point, just get in the way of the officers and techs working. She obviously had been killed elsewhere; she'd been displayed. Not thrown in a river. Displayed.

"Interesting," Tyler said.

"Yep."

"Yep?"

"You're wondering how, if the park was locked, one man got the body over the fence. It's damned unlikely he just waltzed in with the corpse and a head."

"And yet, could two people working together be quite so sick?"

"I guess we need sleep," Craig said. "Clear heads are better."

They had separate cars; they headed to them, both aware they were going back to Kieran's in the Village over the karaoke sushi bar.

Walking down the street, Tyler was aware of the way his Smith and Wesson sat in the holster at the back of his waistband.

Because he couldn't help but wonder if someone was watching.

This was Kieran's neighborhood, not Sarah's. Sarah lived far down south on the island, on Reed Street.

And the killer didn't know everything; after all, he'd murdered the wrong Suzie Cornwall.

Tyler wondered how many other people might have the same names in New York City. None of the group had an unusual name.

Craig had parked ahead of him. He caught up and they walked together. "You think he's had enough for one night?" he asked Tyler.

"Hannah hasn't been dead more than a week—and from what the ME said, she's probably only been dead about five days. Water hides a lot of truths. And now... I don't know. Hard to tell if he's just getting started—if he's been locked up for years, or murdering kittens and puppy dogs for practice."

"I think this person has killed in this manner before," Craig said. "He knows just how hard it is to decapitate someone with a knife. He enjoys the struggle to manage it all, and he's proud of himself for doing it."

"There's got to be something on this guy some-where."

"Somewhere. Thing is, how do you suddenly do things so horrible? Where has this guy been? How do we have a repeat of Archibald Lemming now—out of the blue?"

"There is something, somewhere," Tyler said with determination. "We just have to find it."

They had reached the stairs to Kieran's apartment.

The karaoke club had gone quiet; it would be dawn in another few hours.

Kieran answered the door as soon as she heard Craig's voice. "Anything?" she asked anxiously. Danny and Sarah had come to stand behind her. They all looked at Craig and Tyler expectantly.

"A corpse, as grisly as you would expect," Tyler said.

"And her name was… Suzie Cornwall?" Sarah said. "For sure?"

"From everything we understand," Craig said. "Cops are canvassing the neighborhood and the forensic team is busy," he added.

"This one was more like…before, right?" Sarah asked.

Tyler hesitated to share the gory details. "She wasn't tossed. In two pieces. She was in two pieces, but set up for shock value. No haunted house, but an audience of children and young mothers, if she hadn't been found until morning."

"We'll know more then. Kieran, I think we should talk to your fine doctors, Fuller and Miro, tomorrow," Craig said. "There will be a press conference and then we'll go to the autopsy, but after that…"

"Of course," Kieran said.

"Not that you're not brilliant and haven't learned just about everything from them," Craig told her.

"Sure, sure…no charming sweet talk, huh? I was

about to pull out our blow-up beds. We all have to get some sleep, even if it's only a few hours. Danny is going to hang in and we've actually got it all covered. I figured I'd take Sarah and we'd pull a girl thing and claim the bedroom, and then one of you on the sofa and two on the floor—"

"I have a hotel room, and it's under the business name. I don't need to make it more crowded here," Tyler said.

"Oh, but it's so late," Kieran protested. "Or early."

"It's okay. There's no traffic," he insisted.

"I'll go with you," Sarah said.

"What?" He said the word sharply, though he didn't mean to be so abrupt.

It didn't matter. She ignored the tone. "I'll go with you."

"We should have gone to Craig's place—much bigger and nicer," Kieran admitted.

"It's all right, the hotel is great. I'm on the twentieth floor. There's security on at night. And I was in the service. I wake up at just about anything," Tyler said.

Sarah already had her bag. She was coming with him.

"All right. Let us know you get there okay, huh?" Kieran asked.

"Hey, this guy has hit only vulnerable women so far. I'm not vulnerable," Tyler assured her. "But yes, we'll text as soon as we're there."

He'd never agreed Sarah should come. Out in the hall, once Kieran had closed and locked the door, he turned to her. "This isn't a good idea."

"Probably not," she agreed.

"You can just stay with your friend—"

"Too crowded."

"You'd have the bedroom—"

"Look, you'll be leaving again, after all this, I know that. I don't really know what I'm doing, either. But this has happened. We're together now. And I... I know you. Whatever this is, for however long... I'd rather be with you right now. Kieran is great. Craig is great. Neither of them was at Cemetery Mansion."

"We need to be careful, over everything else."

"Yes, I know. But right now I want to be with you. Yes, you left me before. I expect you'll leave again. And that's all right. That's—that's the way it has to be."

He hesitated, ready to open the door to the street. He looked at her and said softly, "No, don't even try to tell me you believe it happened in that order. You left me long before I ever decided I had to go."

He didn't give her a chance to protest. He opened the door and hurried her out to the car.

He wondered if he should think it was wrong, crazy. He knew where this was going.

And he could only be grateful for the moment.

"So, welcome to my temporary castle," Tyler said, opening the door to his room.

It was a slightly nicer hotel room at a middling upscale chain hotel. There was a small sitting area with a sofa Sarah assumed opened up to an extra bed, a large bath and a very inviting, big bed with some kind of an extra-squishy mattress that promised a great night's sleep.

It was barely night anymore and she wasn't really intending to sleep. Not right away.

Tyler locked the door and slid the bolt. Sarah had wandered in and set down the small bag she had packed to head over to Kieran's.

"My favorite chain. I have one of those 'frequent stayer' cards with them."

"You're in hotels often?" Sarah asked.

"I travel around some. Business."

"But not often in New York."

"I avoid New York," he said.

"But you're here now," she said.

He turned, studying her, his hands on his hips. "And you—you're here right now."

She nodded, not sure about her next actions. She had forgotten just how she loved everything about Tyler. Even the way he stood now, curious and confident. Not aggressive—just confident. They'd both had it so easy when they'd been younger. She had known she'd gotten lucky—not just because of his easy laughter, kindness and natural charm. She was lucky because they had found each other. They'd never been the brightest, best or most beautiful; they had just fallen in together when they'd been fifteen and sixteen, when she'd dropped some papers, when they'd both reached down to gather them up and had crashed heads. And then laughed. They were new then—new kids at a new school.

She shrugged off the memory and took a hard look at the man standing before her.

"You said you still loved me."

"I do." He didn't hesitate. "And I believe you love me."

"And that sometimes, love just isn't enough."

"Right. Sometimes love just isn't enough."

"But for tonight…"

"Or today," he said drily, glancing over at the clock on the mantel.

"For now…"

She thought he was going to say something like "Come over here!" Or that he would take the few steps to reach her.

But he didn't. "For now… I really need a shower. I was…there. Anyway, a shower."

He turned away, pulling a small holster from the rear waistband of his jeans and setting it on the little table by the bed. He shed his jacket and shoes. She was still just standing there, and he shrugged and headed on into the bathroom.

He didn't close the door. She wasn't sure whether that meant she was being given an invitation or not.

Sarah quickly slid out of her sweater and jeans, glad he had gone into the shower. She wasn't sure she could have disrobed with anything like sensuality anymore— it had been too long.

Awkward! That was her theme emotion with him now. Once, everything had been so easy. And now…

Naked, she tiptoed toward the bathroom door. The shower was very large. Tyler was standing under the spray, just letting the water rush over him. She knew, of course, what he was feeling. He felt that he smelled of death and decay, and the water would never be cleansing enough. She had felt that way after the night at the Cemetery Mansion. And for a long time afterward.

She opened the shower door and slipped in behind

him, encircling his waist with her arms and laying her head against his back.

He turned, pulling her to him, gently lifting her chin and her face. His mouth moved down upon hers, soft and wet and steaming. He touched gently at first, so that she barely knew if the steam and heat was him or a whisper of the water beating all around them. Then the pressure of his kiss became hard, his mouth parted hers and she felt his tongue, and with it, wings of fire crept through her memory and more.

The water sluiced over and around them, deliciously hot and sensual. His hands held her tight against him first, and when it seemed her breasts were all but welded to his chest, she felt his palms slide seductively down her back, his fingers teasing along her spine. He pressed his lips to her shoulder, and her collarbone, and then his eyes rose to hers. The way he looked at her...the past and present rolled into one. They had been so young once.

His eyes were no longer young. And yet she loved everything she saw within them, even if that wisdom meant he would leave her again, and this, this thing between them that was so unique, would be nothing but a memory.

He reached behind him to turn off the water. And he grinned suddenly. "I was thinking of some great, cinematic moments of romance. I should sweep you up, press you against the tile, make mad love to you here and now..."

"Except one of us would slip on the soap and we'd end with broken limbs?" she asked, smiling in turn, a little breathless, surprised she'd been able to speak.

"Something like that," he said. "And we have a dreamy mattress…and, hmm, neither of us has to do the laundry. Let me try this!"

He thrust the shower door open and stepped out, and then surprised her so much she gasped before laughing as he swept her up in his arms. "There's no staircase for me to carry you up dramatically, but…"

"We're soaking!"

"The heat is on—no pun intended—and we'll dry."

And still she smiled. He walked the few steps needed and let her fall into the softness of the bed, and then he came down in turn. He was immediately by her side, half atop her, finding her lips again with his own, his hands skimming over her, touching her with caresses that made her forget everything but a longing for more. They seemed to meld into a kiss again, rolled with the pile of soft covering, and then his lips found hers, left them, moved down the length of her body, hovering here and there over her breasts, then snaking downward. He caressed her thighs with kisses and erotic finger play, and she writhed, twisting to come back around to him, to touch him, press her lips against his skin, taste the cleanliness of his naked flesh, the warmth of him, the fire, the essence…

She saw his eyes again as he came over her and thrust into her. She met his gaze squarely with her own, reaching for him, pulling him ever closer to her. The bed cradled them as they began to rock and twist and writhe together.

She remembered the way they had been…

And it was nothing compared to now. Memory hadn't served so well. He could tease so sensually with the lightest brush and then move hard, and the sensation would be almost unbearable. She was achingly and acutely aware of his body...muscle, bone, every movement. He was leaner and harder than ever; his shoulders had grown broader, his abdomen tighter...he moved with a fluid fury and grace that swept her into moments of sweet oblivion, lifted her, eased her down, lifted her again...and then to a climax that seemed to shatter everything, straight down to her soul.

They lay in silence, just breathing. For a few moments, the sound was loud. It began to ease. She felt the slowing of her heartbeat; she thought that she heard his, too.

She tried to think of something to say. Something... that explained her current emotion. Something deep or profound.

She didn't speak first.

He did.

"Hmm," he said lightly. "I guess I have missed you!"

"Well," she murmured, "I'm ever so glad."

He rolled up then, looking down into her eyes. "You really are beautiful, Sarah. Inside and out, you know."

She shook her head, confused. "Just decent, I hope, like I want to believe most people in the world are."

He rolled over again, plumping up a pillow. "Oh, Sarah. So far above decent! I'd definitely rate you an eleven this evening!"

"On a scale of one to ten?"

"One to twenty."

She hit him with a pillow.

And he laughed and moved over her again, smiling.

"On a scale of one to five...an eleven. Maybe a twenty or a hundred..."

He kissed her.

It had been a very, very long time.

They made love again. She thought it was dawn when they finally slept. And it was too bad. They really had so very much to do...

A killer to catch.

More murders to stop...

Including their own.

Chapter 5

Tyler was amazed that he hadn't had to drag himself out, almost crying from exhaustion. But he wasn't tired; he felt that he was wide-awake and sharp—as if some kind of new adrenaline was running through his system, something that changed the world.

Sex.

With Sarah. Different as could be…and sweet and explosive as any memory that he could begin to recall.

Biology, like breathing. Should have been. It just wasn't. Something made people come to other people and, whatever it was, it was strong. Sometimes, it became more. Sometimes it lasted forever. Sometimes it didn't.

He stood in the situation room at the precinct while the facts of the murders were laid out for the dozens of officers, agents and marshals crammed into it. All they really had were the facts that had to do with the murders—they had nothing on suspects, clues or anything at all. Dr. Layton was there, and he explained the cutting off of the heads; even some men Tyler knew to be long-timers looked a little pasty and green as they listened. Lance would be starting the second autopsy today and would soon know more. Bob Green asked Tyler to talk about their theory that Perry Knowlton might still be alive, as they knew for a fact that Archibald Lemming was dead.

Someone asked how the man could have been hiding for years and suddenly come out to commit such heinous acts. At this point, Craig asked Kieran to come forward and offer what insight she could. Tyler saw that Kieran must speak to various groups of law enforcement often; she was prepared and calm.

"As you all know, serial killers only stop when they're forced to stop. A trigger of some kind—death of a loved one, work failure, financial loss, or other traumatic losses usually start a killer off. Sometimes it's just an escalation, and it's sad but true, children who torture animals often grow up to be the next generation's serial killers. Perry Knowlton had been incarcerated for the murders of eight women in upstate New York. He and Archibald Lemming met in prison. For all intents and purposes, it appeared that Archibald killed Perry—it wouldn't have been against his nature, and he killed men and women alike. But the two might have had some kind of honor among killers—Perry Knowlton started the fight that got both men into the medical complex from which they managed to escape."

"But that doesn't answer where he's been all these years," an officer said.

"Possibly locked up."

"Fingerprints!" another agent reminded her.

"He might have been in a hospital or mental facility, or had a physical issue causing him to lie low. Or he might have been killing other places."

"Did you forget the killings at that haunted house years ago?" another officer asked, his tone derisive.

Tyler started to move forward again. He was surprised to see that Sarah had moved up to the front of the crowd, and she looked to Kieran and said, "May I?"

On Kieran's nod, Sarah took a deep breath and spoke. "I'll never forget that. I was there. With my friends. And we survived because my cousin had been taught to watch people—because people, in general, can be cruel. My uncle taught my cousin to carefully observe his surroundings and the individuals nearby. That night, he saw Archibald Lemming at the theme park before he went into the Cemetery Mansion. Lemming was alone when Davey saw him then—of course, that scenario fits if Knowlton is alive or dead.

"After Hannah Levine was murdered, I started researching everything that happened surrounding the escape. Nothing proves beyond a doubt that Perry Knowlton is dead. Also…there are over two hundred thousand unsolved homicides on the books right now in the US alone. Hannah was found in the water, so he might have been disposing of his victims in a way in which they weren't found."

There was silence around the room. Tyler was pretty sure everyone there was thinking about the one who had gotten away—their one case they couldn't crack. And it wasn't something that made them feel good.

"Thank you!" Detective Green said, moving in.

"Now, get out there, officers. This killer is not going to become an 'unknown' statistic!"

"One of the police spokesmen has been briefed on what we do and don't want out for public knowledge," Craig said quietly to Tyler. "He'll handle the press conference. We can get on to the autopsy—and then over to Suzie Cornwall's building. She wasn't working. She was a patient in a clinical trial, quite seriously ill, or so her landlord told the police. The odd thing is…"

"What?" Tyler asked.

"We have a picture of her—when she was living. She really did resemble the photos we've seen of Suzie Cornwall Avery—at first glance, they might have been the same person."

Tyler was quiet for a minute. He hadn't seen Suzie in a very long time, but human nature didn't change. Suzie had always been a good, sweet soul, with a high sense of social responsibility. It wasn't going to make her feel any better, knowing that while a woman had been killed because she happened to have been given the same name at birth, that poor woman had been ill.

The stakes were high; Sarah was right. The killer was out to find those who had been there that fateful night a decade ago at the Cemetery Mansion. The night Archibald Lemming had been killed.

Revenge?

Just a sick mind?

Whichever didn't really matter. They were in danger.

"Sarah…do we bring her?"

"No, I figured she'd be comfortable with Kieran, and I have an agent staying with them at Finnegan's. They'll be fine. Trust me—if this bastard is after Sarah, he'll know by now she's with Kieran. But in my line, if there's a threat, we shoot to kill."

"I'm getting more and more worried about the others. Especially Davey."

Craig looked at him while Sarah and Kieran walked across the room to join them.

"What about this," Craig suggested. "I can have Davey and Renee brought into the city. We have an amazing safe house—easy to guard. It also has escape routes in the event the officers on duty should be killed, automatic alarms in case of a perceived danger... And my boss, Director Egan, is huge on preventing bad things. He'll want them there."

"Really?" Sarah whispered. "That leaves only Sean and Suzie, and Suzie is so terrified by what happened that she's about ready to be institutionalized!"

"They can be brought there, too. It's big. I think there are actually three separate bedrooms."

"How long can we keep them there—or keep guards on them?" Tyler asked.

"This isn't going to take long," Sarah said softly. "You will catch him soon, or..." She paused and looked at them unhappily. "Or we'll all be dead. All of us who were in the Cemetery Mansion."

In Tyler's mind, Dr. Lance Layton looked more like a mad scientist than ever. His white hair was going everywhere, half of it standing straight up on his head. He was thoughtful and energetic. "I have all kinds of tests going on. Here's the thing—poor lady was not long for the world. Poor thing! She was undergoing a new kind of cancer treatment—meant she didn't lose her hair to chemo. She had liver cancer that had spread just about through her body. Death might have been a mercy, if it hadn't been so..."

He stopped speaking. "Well, small mercy. She wouldn't have been terrified or in pain long, but would have bled out within a matter of seconds. That's something that we can truthfully tell her loved ones."

The woman had been going to die, anyway, a slow, painful death. He hoped that would help Suzie live with herself.

The police photographer, Alex Morrison, was standing by quietly. Layton looked over at him. "You're—you're getting enough?"

"I am. But the head, yes, we need a few more angles on the head."

"Right," Layton said. "Thankfully, the powers that be are concerned enough on this case to keep everyone on it working together—it's harder when you have different techs and photographers and detectives. Well, I mean, not really for me. Other than that I have to repeat my findings, though some just prefer written reports, anyway, and a written report..."

"I'm not in your way?" Morrison asked.

"No, not at all," Craig assured him.

Morrison nodded to them both and began his work.

"Thank you, Morrison. All right, down to it."

He began to drone on. Tyler listened, mentally discarding the findings that meant nothing to their investigation.

But then Dr. Layton got to the stomach contents. "Here's what's interesting. Now our first victim, Hannah Levine, had eaten hours before her death. Miss Cornwall had eaten far more recently. Both had enjoyed some prime steaks. I don't know how much that helps you, but they may have dined at the same restaurant. I know that the city is laden with steak houses."

"Interesting—a possible lead," Tyler said. "And then again, maybe they just both enjoyed steak."

Morrison, working over by the stainless steel tray that held Suzie Cornwall's head, cleared his throat. "I think I have everything we might possibly need," he said.

He looked a little flushed. Tyler certainly understood. The head no longer really resembled anything human. It hadn't been on display long, but the sun, the elements and bugs—and the violence of being chopped off—had done their share of damage. The flesh was white, red, bruised and swollen.

"Thank you, Morrison," Layton said.

"I'm sure you've been thorough," Craig said, nodding to the photographer. "I know they want to have a decent sketch out by tomorrow. The photos we found of her on social media just aren't very good. If we use them along with the images you have, an artist can come up with something that will work well in the newspapers."

"Right," Morrison said grimly. "They're going to put an image out, correct? Ask for help?"

"That's been the decision, yes," Craig told him.

The photographer nodded at them all and left quickly.

Layton continued his analysis.

They listened awhile longer, looking at the body the whole time. To his credit, even Layton, long accustomed to being the voice of the dead, seemed deeply disturbed by the remains of the murdered woman.

Then it was time to try to find out how, when and where this Suzie had met her killer.

* * *

"Oh, lord!" Sarah said.

Kieran, who had been busy with her computer, looked up.

Sarah was at her own laptop, working in Kieran's office at the psychiatric offices of Fuller and Miro. She'd intended to be busy with her current novel, *Revenge of the Martian Waspmen*, but just hadn't been able to concentrate on her distant world.

"What is it?" Kieran asked.

"I finally keyed in the right words that led me to the right sites that led me to more sites. I've found so many unsolved and bizarre murders..."

"Show me!"

Kieran walked around her desk to stand behind Sarah.

Sarah pointed and spoke softly. "This one—up in Sleepy Hollow, and chalked up to it being Sleepy Hollow. 'Headless corpse found in ravine.' Then, here. 'Hudson Valley—help needed in the murder of local bank teller,' and, when you read further, you discover that she was found in two pieces—head on a tree branch, torso in the river. Then here's another in southern Connecticut—'Skull discovered off I-95, no sign of the body.'"

"There are probably more. I'm sure Craig has his tech guy working on it," Kieran mused. She sat again. "The guy's got to be living here somewhere. Somehow. But how? He'd need a credit check to rent an apartment. He'd need to make money somehow. And he'd have to pull all this off—and manage to look like one of the crowd."

"Is that so hard in New York City?" Sarah asked. "I

mean, think about it. In New York, whatever you do, don't make eye contact. We walk by dozens of down-and-outers on the streets and in the subway. A few years back, a newspaper writer did an experiment and gave one dollar to each person with a cup or a hat just on the streets. Within a mile radius, she'd given away two hundred dollars. He could have begged on the street. He could have done a dozen things. He could have robbed people—without actually killing them. No lost wallets are ever found. We're a city of tremendous wealth and the American dream, but when that fails..."

"It's a good theory," Kieran said. "We'll talk to Craig. Give me a minute!"

She disappeared and then returned to her office with Drs. Fuller and Miro in tow.

Fuller was maybe fifty, tall and extremely good-looking.

Miro was tiny, older and still attractive, with dark curly hair, a pert little gamine's face and an incredible energy that seemed to emit from her.

"Show them what you just showed me," Kieran said.

And so Sarah did. And when she was done, Fuller said, "I think you've found something. Sad to say, but in history, many people have gotten away with crimes for years. And if these killings are associated, he was careful to commit his murders in different places."

"But all close to the central point—New York City," Miro put in.

"I believe my esteemed partner and I are in agreement on this," Fuller said. "This could all be the work of one man. And," he said, pointing at Sarah's computer screen, "this is old. Dates back almost ten years. This could have been Perry Knowlton's first kill after the massacre in Cemetery Mansion."

Sarah felt a sense of panic welling in her; she wasn't afraid for herself—well, she was, of course—but she was terrified for Davey.

She looked at Kieran. "Can you make sure that my aunt and Davey are safe?"

"Absolutely," Kieran promised. "And I'll tell Craig that my good doctors have weighed in. We need to follow up on your theory. I'm not sure how, but we need to move in that direction."

Everyone was safe, and Sarah was extremely grateful.

"We had a cop at the house, or just outside the house, and of course I brought out coffee," Aunt Renee told Sarah. "I have to admit, I've been trying not to panic. This is…this isn't coincidence. This is terrible. If Hannah was a target, and then…seems they killed the wrong Suzie, but she was a target, and if I was to lose you and Davey, oh, my God, I'd just want to be dead myself. I can't believe this. It isn't fair. Of course, I do know," she added drily, "that life isn't fair, but still, you all survived such terror…"

Sarah gave her a big hug. Then Suzie and Sean hugged Renee, and then Davey, as their FBI guards stood back silently, letting the reunion go on.

A young woman with the leanest body Sarah had ever seen—she wondered if she even had 1 percent body fat!—came forward then. "Pizza is on its way," she said cheerfully. "We don't have any delivery here. An agent always acquires food. The Bureau has control of the entire building, with sham businesses and residences—used as office space, we're careful with tax-payer dollars!—but we want you to be relaxed enough to…well, to exist as normally as possible under the circumstances. I'm Special Agent Lawrence."

She indicated a tall man nearer the door. "That's Special Agent Parton. We're your inside crew for the moment and we work twelve-hour shifts. Our apartments are in this building—we're always on call. Tonight, however, you'll have fresh agents—nice and wide-awake, that is. The doorman and the registrar downstairs are agents, and there are two agents in the hall at all times. If you will all get together and draw up a grocery list, we'll see to getting what you need. The kitchen is there—" she pointed to the left of the front door "—and the central bath is there." She pointed to the right. "One of us will always be at that table by the door, while the other might be with you. In the very unlikely event that every agent between the entry and you is brought down, there is a dumbwaiter in the back that is really an elevator. Naturally, our engineers have worked with it—nothing manual, no pulleys or cranks. You hit a button, the door closes and it takes you down. It can't be opened on the ground level from the outside—it can only be opened from the inside once you're down there. Same button, huge and red. You can't miss it."

"This is wonderful. Thank you!" Sarah said softly.

"Catching the bad guys is our job—along with keeping the good guys alive!" Special Agent Lawrence said. "Let me show you to your rooms," she added.

The living room or parlor boasted a dual area—a TV and chair grouping to the right and a little conclave of chairs to the left. They were led down a hallway.

The bedrooms were sparse, offering just beds and dressers and small closets.

"The best place I've ever seen!" Aunt Renee said.

"This one? Can I have this one?" Davey asked, looking into one of the rooms.

They were really all the same. There had to be something slightly different for Davey to want it.

There were no windows. No way for a sniper to have a chance; no way for an outsider to see who was inside.

"Davey, whatever room you want!" Suzie said.

Davey grinned.

"What's special about it?" Sarah asked him.

"The closet is painted blue. 'Haint' blue, like they told us when my dad took me on a ghost tour in Key West. Haint blue keeps bad things away."

"Excellent," Sarah told him.

"I'll go next to Davey," Aunt Renee said.

"And we'll be across the hall," Sean agreed. "And Sarah—"

"I won't be staying. I'm going with Tyler."

Renee protested, "Oh, Sarah! The two of you should both be here—"

"Try telling a military man he needs extra protection!" Sarah said lightly. "I swear, we'll be fine."

"You're staying with Tyler?" Sean asked her. "Have you been seeing each other again? Last I heard, he was out of the military and living in Boston."

"He came because of Hannah. We'll see this through," she said.

She heard Tyler's voice; he had arrived at the safe house. It had, she realized, gotten late. She knew he and Craig had been going to the autopsy and then to interview the building owner and whatever friends—or even acquaintances—they could find of Suzie Cornwall's, to try to trace her steps before she was taken by her killer.

"Excuse me," Sarah murmured and hurried out. He and Craig had arrived together.

She gazed at him anxiously. She didn't ask any questions; they were all in her eyes.

Tyler nodded, looking over her head, and she realized that Special Agent Lawrence, Renee, Davey, Suzie and Sean had all followed her out.

"Suzie," he said softly, "this can't make it better, I know, but the Suzie who was killed was already dying a horrible death."

"What?" she asked.

"Cancer—it had riddled her body."

"Anything else?" Sarah asked.

"We went to her building and to the hospital. No one could tell us anything. She was likable, she kept to herself. She was polite and courteous, and I'm sure we would have all liked her very much. But even her doctor said that the experimental drugs weren't having the desired effect. She was going to die a slow and horrible death."

"Poor woman, to suffer all that, and then…"

"Dr. Layton, the medical examiner, said she died quickly," Tyler said.

They were all silent. It was impossible not to wonder which would be worse—a slow and horrible death as her body decayed around her, or the horror of having her throat slit, her head sawed from her body.

"It's my fault," Suzie whispered.

"No. It's the fault of a sick and wretched killer, and don't think anything else," Tyler said firmly. Again there was silence. Not even the agents in the room seemed to breathe.

"So," Tyler said. "We think that Perry Knowlton might still be alive. We're going to try to relive that night—together, all of us except for Hannah, of course. Try to remember what we saw in that haunted house— and if any of us might have seen Perry Knowlton."

"Might have seen him?" Sean said, confusion in his voice. "We didn't know what he looked like. Not then. I mean, later, there were pictures of him in the papers and on TV and all, but… I sure as hell didn't see him in Cemetery Mansion."

"Let's go through it. We came through at different times. Let's see what we all remember."

"It will actually be good for you all—from everything I understand from my police shrink friends, including the shrinks Kieran works with," Craig said. "And where is she, by the way?"

"She's with your partner, Mike, at Finnegan's," Special Agent Lawrence said.

"She's not a target, and Mike would die before anyone touched a hair on her head," Craig said. "Shall we?" He indicated the sitting area.

Sean and Suzie, holding hands, chose the little settee. Renee sat on one of the wingback chairs, and Tyler and Craig sat across from them. One chair was left, though there was room on the settee. "Sarah, sit," Davey said. "Sit, please."

She smiled and sat. Davey settled by her side on the floor, curling his legs beneath him.

"Davey," Tyler said, "let's start with you. You knew there was something bad going on. And I'm sorry. I know you've been through this before."

"I saw him. The bad man. Archibald Lemming," Davey said. "But I didn't know his name. My dad warned me about men like him."

"But your dad wasn't with you, whispering in your ear or anything?" Craig asked.

Davey gave him a weary look. "My dad is dead."

"Of course," Craig said, "and I'm so sorry."

"He said he would always be with me in all the good things he taught me," Davey said. "So I watch for bad people. He was bad. I saw him go in Cemetery Mansion."

"And that's why you didn't want to go in," Tyler said. He smiled at Davey. "And you warned us, but we were foolish, and we didn't listen."

"I was okay once I had my Martian Gamma Sword!" Davey said, perking up. He leaned back and looked up at Sarah. "And it was good, right?"

"It was excellent. You were a hero."

"Which is why the bad guy wants to kill me now," Davey said pragmatically.

Sarah set her hand on his shoulder.

Tyler told him, "Don't worry. We will never let that happen. So, Davey and Sarah stayed out, while Suzie, Sean, Hannah and I went in. There were people ahead of us, but the theme park was letting only a few go in at a time, so while there were people ahead and people behind, we were still more or less on our own."

"There were motion-activated animatronic characters everywhere," Suzie said. "I remember that."

"I remember when we were going in, the 'hostess' character stationed there—a French maid, I think—was acting strangely." Tyler went on. "I don't think she knew anything then, but I'm sure she felt as if something was odd. Maybe she was bright enough to have a premonition of some kind—maybe someone was late or early or had gone in or hadn't gone in. She seemed strange. Which, of course, would have been normal, since it was a haunted house."

"I remember that, too," Sean said. "As a high school senior I couldn't admit it, but...yeah, I was scared. But you know, we were part of the football team back then. We couldn't be cowards."

Suzie was nodding. "Honestly? I think—even though we were assholes about Davey not wanting to go in—I think we were a little unnerved from the get-go. Then there was the massive character in the music room. Very tall, and blond. That automaton, or whatever. Scared the hell out of me."

"What?" Sarah asked. "An automaton?"

"You couldn't have missed it," Suzie said. "Seriously, it was tall. Over six feet. It was creepy. Really freaked me out."

Sarah frowned. "You know, we talked to the cops, we talked to each other...and still, sometimes, it's like I remember new things. Maybe even my nightmares, I'm not sure. Honestly, I know we were almost running from the start, but when Davey and I came through, there was no character. There were no figures in the music room. Who could have moved an automaton in that kind of time? Especially a big one?"

Tyler leaned forward. "I remember it clearly—I remember how it scared Suzie horribly. It was definitely there."

"And when Davey and I came through, there was definitely not a character there," Sarah said.

"He was sitting at the piano," Suzie insisted.

"Not when we came through," Sarah said.

"Maybe it…"

"What? Just disappeared?" Sean asked her.

"But—I was so sure it was an automaton! It—it talked to me!" Suzie said. "Oh, my God! He saw me that night. He saw my face clearly. And yet…he killed another woman." Suzie stared at Tyler and Craig hopefully. "Was it possibly accidental? Was she old, was she…different…was she…not like me?"

"I'm sorry, Suzie. She wasn't your twin, but…"

"But he saw me over a decade ago. People change," Suzie said harshly. She sighed. "Okay, fine, so much for that theory. He meant to kill me. To behead me. To saw my head off!"

She started to sob. Sean pulled her close.

"Don't cry, Suzie," Davey said. "He wants to kill all of us. And he's a terrible person. None of it is your fault."

"Poor Hannah…but could it be? Could it really be?" Suzie whispered.

"Him," Davey said somberly.

They all looked at him. He had propped his elbows on his knees, folded his hands and rested his chin upon his knuckles. He looked like an all-seeing wise man.

"Him, the other killer, the bad guy," Davey said. He shook his head. "Yes, I think he was the other bad guy. If you saw him. He was gone when Sarah and I came through. He was gone, because he knew. The one guy—Archibald Lemming. He was meant to die. But his friend, the one everyone thought was dead—he meant to live. He was there that night, but he got away. It would have been easy. Everyone was screaming and running. Yes. It is him, right? He killed Hannah. And he's still out there, right? He's the one who is trying to kill all of us."

There was silence.

Then Tyler told Davey, "But you knew, Davey. You saved us then. And you know now, and so you're going to help us all save ourselves now." He smiled. "Because your dad taught you to be smart. He taught you to know people, which is something we who don't have Down syndrome don't always do."

Davey smiled back at him.

"Mom is good, too. Dad taught her to be a little bit Down syndrome."

Renee smiled and nodded. "Yep. I'm a little bit Down syndrome, thanks to your dad. He was a very good man."

Davey straightened proudly.

Tyler turned and looked at Craig. "I think that must be it—the character who was there, and then wasn't. Archibald Lemming didn't kill Perry Knowlton. I think maybe Lemming had a death wish—but he wanted to go out with a bang. Lemming had some kind of insider info about escaping through the infirmary. They killed personnel to escape, but even then they had to have timing information and all. So, say that Knowlton was the brains behind the escape. And then they found Haunted Hysteria. What a heaven on earth for someone who wanted blood and terror!"

"And all these years," Suzie said, "he's been just watching? Waiting? Is that possible?"

Sarah said softly, "We think he has been busy. Yes, he's been in New York City. This is theory, of course. But we've done some research. We think he's still been murdering people. He just takes little jaunts out of the city to kill."

"Oh, my God!" Suzie said.

"But now," Tyler said, "he's killing here. Right in the city."

"Revenge," Sarah said.

"But...he lived!" Suzie protested.

"Yes, but he might have idolized Lemming. And while he's a killer, and he's been killing, this is different. He's been imitating Lemming, but not making a huge display out of his crimes. But now...who knows? Maybe he was careful, but then saw Hannah on the street or something. Maybe he was just biding his time. But the thing is, now..."

"Now?" Suzie breathed.

Sarah looked at Tyler. "And now we have to have our justice—before he gets his revenge!"

Chapter 6

The safe house wasn't far from Finnegan's, making it simple to leave and head to Broadway and the pub. Kieran had gone there to help out, which she often did when she was anxious and waiting for Craig.

But by the time Sarah and Tyler reached Finnegan's, it had grown quiet and Kieran was back in the office. Declan, Kevin and Danny, Sarah had learned, had become accustomed to having their office turned into a conference room for Craig and Kieran when something other than inventory and payroll needed to be attended to.

An undercover agent, someone who worked with Craig, was sitting at the bar, watching the crowd while sipping a Kaliber, Guinness's entry on the nonalcoholic side of beer.

He greeted them with a friendly nod when they arrived. Declan, behind the bar, cheerfully sent them to the office. Kieran was at the desk.

"Everyone is good—safe?" Kieran asked as they entered and took up chairs in front of the desk.

"Safe and sound," Sarah said. "I'm just so glad Davey is there now. I have a feeling that Perry Knowlton must know Davey was the key to ending everything that night."

"Maybe not," Tyler said. "He didn't try for Davey first."

"No, he went for Hannah, who, sad to say, was an easy target. She wouldn't have recognized him, but maybe he recognized her. And she would have been an easy first mark because…because she would see men. She was working as a hooker," Sarah said sadly.

"And that makes sense—go for the easiest victim first," Kieran said, nodding.

"And we think we have a lead, though where it can take us, I don't know," Tyler said.

Craig went on to explain what they'd discussed.

"And no one really saw him, right? What he really looked like?" asked Kieran.

"I never saw him at all, and neither did Davey. We think he was pretending to be an automaton in the music room. From what they said, he scared Suzie half to death when they went through. But there was no such person—or automaton—by the time Davey and I arrived. He could have run out already—or he could have gone through any one of half a dozen emergency exits."

"But his picture was in the papers, on the web and TV screens, right?" Kieran asked.

"Yes, of course," Tyler said. "I did see him. He was

very distinctive. Tall, at least my height. And lean. With a long face with sharp cheekbones and jaw."

"Well, at least not a medium height—someone who blends in with the crowd. But there are a lot of men over six feet in New York City," Craig said.

"Maybe you should be staying at the safe house," Kieran said thoughtfully.

"No," Sarah said.

"Well, Tyler, too—he's one of you," Kieran pointed out.

Tyler shook his head. "I think Sarah and I will be all right. If he comes for one of us, it's going to be when we're alone. He isn't going to come to a hotel room. He doesn't kill with a gun, but with a knife. I have a gun. And it's always best to bring a gun to a knife fight. As long as you're steady, the gun is going to win every time."

"And we should have something to work with soon enough," said Craig. He looked at Sarah and nodded an acknowledgment. "Sarah had it right, we think, from the beginning. We found no less than ten unsolved murders that had to do with total or near decapitation, ranging from Westchester County—Hudson Valley and the Sleepy Hollow area, as Sarah found—to Connecticut and New Jersey. Regional police are sending us everything they have on those killings. We'll be able to go over them tomorrow. But most importantly, our tech department has entered the last known picture of Perry Knowlton into the computer. Tomorrow, we'll be starting off the day with images of what Perry Knowlton might look like now, and we're putting out pictures of Hannah and Suzie. Hopefully, someone might come forward, having seen them somewhere. Our appeal to the public will contain a subtle warning, of course. No one is safe while this man is at work."

"We should call it a night," Kieran said. "And get started again in the morning. I have a court appearance at nine, so I'll be out part of the day. Sarah, you should hang at the safe house during that time."

Sarah knew she probably should. That fear did live within her somewhere.

But she was going to be with Tyler.

She smiled. "I'll be safe," she promised.

Everyone stood. Out in the bar and dining area, they said good-night to Declan, the only one of Kieran's siblings still working.

Tyler and Sarah were silent as they drove to the hotel. The valet took the car; the hotel lobby was quiet. There was no one in the elevator with them.

"You think we're really safe here?"

"I think I'll shoot first and ask questions later," Tyler said.

She smiled.

"You should think about going to the safe house," he told her quietly. "It's one thing for me to take chances with my life, but… I'm not so sure you should have that kind of faith in me."

"I have ultimate faith in you."

That night, she didn't have to join him in the shower. The door was barely closed, his gun and holster were barely laid by the bed before he had her in his arms, before they were both busy grasping at one another's clothing and dropping it to a pile on the floor. His kisses had become pure fire, heated, demanding, like a liquid blaze that seemed to engulf her limbs and everything in between. She returned his hunger ravenously, anxious to be flush with him, to feel his flesh with every inch of her own, feel the vital life beneath that skin, muscle, bone, heartbeat, breath...

He pressed her down to the bed and made love to her with those hot liquid kisses...all down the length of her body. The world faded away in a sea of pure sensation. She crawled atop him, kissing, touching, loving, as if she would never have enough.

And then they were together, he was in her, and the sensation was so keen she could barely keep from crying out, alerting the world to their whereabouts and exactly what they were doing.

She bit her lip, soaring on a wave of sheer ecstasy. All that lay between them seemed to burst with a show of light before her eyes, a field of stars and color. Then she drifted into the incredibly sweet sensation of climax as it swept over her and shook her with a flow of little shudders and spasms. And then they were still, with the incredible sense of warmth and comfort and ease, her just lying beside him.

She felt she should speak; she didn't want to. They'd been this close once before, when life had been all but Utopia.

But everything had changed. He'd said that she'd left him—but he had been the one to walk away. Move away. Start a completely new life.

He pulled her close to him.

She thought he might speak.

He did not. He just held her, his lips brushing her forehead as they lay there.

She stared into the darkness for a long time, not sleeping.

There was sound. The slightest sound in the hallway.

Tyler was out of bed, his Smith and Wesson in his hands, before she could really register the noise. He went to the door. And then he came back, returning the gun to the side of the bed. Sliding in beside her, he told her, "Two girls in 708 returning from a night at the bar. They're trying to be quiet—kind of surprising one of them hasn't knocked the other over yet!"

She smiled. This time, when he pulled her close, they made love again.

And then she did drift to sleep.

She thought she would dream of sandy beaches, a warm sun and a balmy breeze—and Tyler at her side.

Instead, she dreamed of a tall dark man lurking in the shadows, watching her. She was back in Cemetery Mansion, racing after Davey, trying to stop him. And she was in the music room, with no one else there, and it seemed no matter how fast she ran, she couldn't reach the dining room, couldn't find Davey, couldn't get out. And though she couldn't really see him, she knew that he was there. The tall dark man.

Watching her.

Calculating when it would be her turn.

Tyler had never needed much sleep, and he was glad of it. At just about six in the morning, he woke; at his side, Sarah was twisting and turning.

He whispered to her, pulling her closer to him, not wanting to wake her, but not wanting her to suffer through whatever was going on in her dreams—or nightmares. He wanted to ease whatever plagued her, even while he marveled at being with her once again. Her body was so smooth and sleek, curved upon the snow-white sheets. Her hair had always been a sunny shade of gold, and it fell around her like a mantle.

"Sarah," he said gently.

Her eyes opened. For a moment, they were wide and frightened—just for a moment. And then she saw his face, and she smiled and flushed.

"Nightmare," she murmured.

"So I gathered. About?"

"Cemetery Mansion," she said softly. "You know, sometimes it takes me a few minutes to remember what I had for lunch the day before—but I remember everything about that awful night."

"So do I."

"Do you ever...dream?"

"I've had some dreadful nightmares, yeah, for sure."

She sighed. "I'm glad to hear it. I mean—I'm not glad you have nightmares. I'm glad I'm not the only one. I guess that's not really very nice, either!"

"You're human."

She stared at him for a moment, blue eyes still very wide, but her expression grim. "Human. So is this killer. He's human—and he's done these things!"

Tyler was silent a minute. Then he told her, "There's something wrong with people like Archibald Lemming and Perry Knowlton. You know that—you've been around Kieran enough. When they get to such a point, it's a fine distinction between psychopaths or sociopaths—whatever wiring they have in their heads, it's not normal. In a sense, they've lost all their sense of humanity. The normal person is heartsick to hear about an earthquake that killed hundreds, but this killer would want the pictures. He would relish the death and destruction. He would wish that it had been his handi-work."

She shook her head. "I can't feel sorry for him. He's sick, but after what he's done to people...that kind of sickness doesn't draw any sympathy from me. I guess it should, but it doesn't."

"The thing is...even if he were to finish this bit of revenge—"

"You mean, kill all of us."

"Even if he were to finish, he wouldn't stop. It's impossible to know now if he did commit any or all of the unsolved crimes you and the FBI found. It's impossible to know if he was gearing up, practicing for this—or if, in his warped mind, he realized that he should take his desire to kill and turn it into revenge."

"He's got to be stopped!" she whispered.

"He's careful. Hannah was an easy target. He found Suzie Cornwall—the wrong Suzie Cornwall—and lured her off alone easily enough. But now we're onto him. And he'll figure that out. I don't think he intends to take any chances, so we have to keep the others at the safe house and be incredibly alert and aware ourselves."

He heard his phone buzzing—it was time to be up and moving.

He reached for his cell. He wasn't surprised the caller was Craig.

"The pictures are about to go out."

"That's good."

"Yes, but you have to know something."

"What is that?"

He heard a bit of commotion. The next thing he knew, Craig was gone and Kieran was on the phone.

"Tyler! He's been at Finnegan's. This man...this

man who appears to be Perry Knowlton...he's been at Finnegan's several times. I'm not there all the time so I don't really know, but... I've seen him! I've seen him at least three times!"

It was early and that meant there was no problem for Declan to open the pub just for friends and family. His siblings along with his fiancée, Mary Kathleen, and Craig, Tyler and Sarah sat around two tables that they'd pushed together, drinking coffee.

Sarah made sure Tyler was introduced to Kevin, Kieran's twin—the one brother he'd not met yet. Kevin couldn't stay long; he was shooting a "Why I Love New York" commercial for the tourist board at ten.

"We shouldn't have asked you to come in," Tyler said. "Nice to meet you—and I'm sorry."

"It's all right. Declan called me as soon as he received the message from Craig with the police computer rendering of Perry Knowlton. I never waited on him, but I know I've seen the bastard in here."

"It's frightening—and interesting. Because if you recognize him, hopefully others will, too," Tyler said.

Craig had printouts of the composite lying on the table. He told them, "Perry Knowlton is forty-three years old now. He started his killing binge at the age of twenty-nine, and was convicted of five murders and incarcerated by the time he was thirty-one."

Tyler picked up the account. "In prison, he met Archibald Lemming, and they probably compared their methods for finding their victims—and for killing them."

"And," Kieran continued, "they would remember their crimes. They were probably thrilled to have someone to tell, trying to one-up each other all the time. They liked to enjoy their memories over and over again—just as others would enjoy talking about their vacation to Italy, or a day at a beautiful beach."

Declan tapped the image of Perry Knowlton that lay on the table. "A few times before—and then less than two weeks ago—he was at the end of the bar. He ordered whiskey, neat. He was polite and even seemed to be charming those around him. Easy, level voice."

"You're sure it was him?" Tyler asked.

"I'd bet a hell of a lot on it," Declan said.

"And I'm damned sure, too," Kevin said.

"He was at a table, maybe a month ago," Mary Kathleen told them all. "And he was quite amicable, very nice, complimented the potato soup and the shepherd's pie."

"I served him when he was hanging around with a number of the regulars," Danny said. "He had them all laughing."

"The all-around guy-next-door," Kieran murmured. "Historically, there have been several truly charismatic serial killers, the poster boy being Ted Bundy. He worked for a suicide crisis center, for God's sake, with Anne Rule—long before he was infamous for his crimes and she was famous for her books. But he wasn't the only one. I don't know that everyone would have fallen for Charles Manson, but he knew how to collect the young and disenfranchised. Andrew Cunanan—Versace's killer—was supposedly intelligent and affable. Paul John Knowles was known as the 'Casanova Killer.' The list can go on, but..."

"A charming, bright, handsome psychopath," Sarah murmured. "Great."

"But he's been exposed now," Tyler reminded her. "Someone knows him. Someone has seen him and knows his habits."

"Oh, aye, and sure!" Mary Kathleen said. "He likes good shepherd's pie, tips well enough and has lovely laughing green eyes. Ah, but how they must look when—" She broke off, shivering. "Horrible. Don't just shoot him. Skin him alive, saw him to pieces!" she said passionately.

Sarah set her hand on Mary Kathleen's. "But that's what makes the difference between us…" she said. "We wouldn't do those things to another human being. Although I understand completely what you're saying. I was there. The idea that killers find a little torture themselves does have its appeal."

"Do any of you remember the first time you saw him—and the last time?" Tyler asked.

"The first time…" Declan mused.

"Last October!" Mary Kathleen said. "Oh, I do remember—because I had to leave early that day. Me niece was coming over from Dublin. He offered to pay his check quickly."

"That was nearly five months ago," Kieran murmured.

"Do you think he's been looking for Sarah all that time?" Kevin asked.

"How would he have known that she worked here at all?" Declan murmured.

"He might have found her by accident. He might have seen her one day and followed her… It's a huge city, but we all know that sometimes it can be a very small world. And it's easy to discover personal details on social media," Tyler said.

"My address was never out anywhere!" Sarah said firmly.

"Of course not," Declan said. "But you might have written something about the pub. And that brought him here."

"Maybe," she murmured.

"He must have figured out after the first month or so that she wasn't working here anymore," Declan commented flatly, "But..."

Craig's phone rang and he excused himself.

"He thought that she'd come back," Tyler said. "He knew you worked here at some time or another, Sarah. And when was the last time anyone saw him?"

"Like I said," Declan told him. "Ten days to two weeks ago. Sorry I can't be more definite."

"He knows some things, but obviously not enough," Kieran said, looking at Sarah. "He didn't know Suzie wasn't using Cornwall anymore—he didn't know she and Sean Avery were married. He tries to find what he's looking for, but he hasn't the resources he'd surely love to have. That means we've got an edge on him," she added softly.

"Director Egan called," Declan told them. He was, Sarah knew, Craig's direct boss. "He says he'll keep Josh McCormack in here, watching over us and the pub, during opening hours. We are licensed to have a gun, which is behind the bar. But only the family has access."

"Oh! If something were to happen to someone in the pub, or to Finnegan's... I'm so sorry I seem to have brought this on you!" Sarah said.

"You didn't," Declan said. "We're tough. We'll manage, as we always have."

"*Sláinte!*" Mary Kathleen said, raising her coffee cup.

Smiles went around; coffee mugs were lifted in cheers.

Craig returned to the table. "Tyler, there's been a break in the case. The bartender at Time and Time Again also recognized Perry Knowlton from the composite. I think we should talk to him again."

"Ready when you are," Tyler said, standing. He looked down at Sarah.

"Hell, no," she said. "I'm not staying anywhere. I'm coming with you."

When they reached the bar in the theater district, Detective Bob Green and his photographer, Alex Morrison, were already there.

Tyler almost ran into Morrison. "Hey, you all made it," the man said, watching him curiously. "There are no security cameras here, so they want pictures of the bar and the entry. Seems our fellow Knowlton liked to hang around here a lot. He flirted with Hannah—sorry, you can talk to the bartender yourselves. I'll get on with it."

He seemed to be taking pictures of all aspects of the bar.

The place was still closed; it was ten thirty and Tyler imagined it opened by eleven or eleven thirty. They needed the time alone with Luke, the bartender.

Luke was already talking to Detective Green, who was seated on one of the bar stools. He saw Sarah coming and smiled and waved—obviously a bit taken with her. That was good; she had said she could be helpful, and though Tyler really wanted her safely far away from the action, she was useful. So far, she'd actually garnered far more info than he had, just by being friendly and curious, and he was supposedly the investigator.

Luke greeted them all and offered them coffee.

For once, Tyler thought he'd been coffee'd out.

"I should have been able to meet you wherever," Luke said. "I don't usually work days, but...the other bartender quit. She saw the picture and she just quit. That guy's been in here lots. He was teasing and flirting with Hannah the night...the night she...the night she was murdered. But can it really be him? He seems really decent. Nice—he tips big, unlike a hell of a lot of people around here. Are you sure that it's him?"

"We're sure we need to find him," Tyler said.

"Have you seen him since Hannah was killed?" Sarah asked.

"Oh, yes."

"Yes?" Tyler asked.

"Hell, he was in here last night! And, I mean, until the news this morning, I had no clue. No clue at all. I was nice, he was nice. Oh, God, he's good-looking, you know. Flirtatious. He talked to so many girls. I just hope...oh, God! I hope none of them turn up dead!"

"We're hoping that, too," Craig said.

Detective Bob Green looked at Craig. "You guys are handling the safe house. We'll see to a watch on this place."

"He won't come back here now," Sarah said.

"Well, he's pretty cocky," Luke said.

Sarah shook his head. "He didn't think that we'd know it was him—but now he knows we're looking for him, thanks to the picture we released to the press. I think he'll lie low for a while. But hey, sure—keep an eye on the bar."

"We don't have a hell of a lot else," Green said.

"She's right, though."

Tyler swung around. It was the photographer, Alex, who had spoken, and he was now coming up to join them. He flushed and said, "Hey, I'm with the forensic unit—civilian. Not a cop. But I've taken a hell of a lot of photos, and...well, here. Here's some of what I got at the park the other day. The park where Suzie Cornwall was found. If you look..."

He held his camera forward, twisting it around so that they could gather close and see the images right-side up.

"We're looking at the body of Suzie Cornwall in situ," Green said.

"Yes, yes, but I just realized what else I have here—studying it all. Let me enlarge it for you... Look at the people," Alex said. He clicked a side button; the image honed in on the crowd, growing larger.

And there he was.

Perry Knowlton, aged just as the computer suggested he would age.

Tall, with a headful of blond hair. Lean face, rugged chin, broad, high brow. Lean, long physique. Tall, yes, standing next to a rabbi with a tall hat—and a guy who looked like a lumberjack. He almost blended in with the crowd.

"He does come back to the scene of the crime," Sarah murmured.

"He's been everywhere!" Alex murmured. "He's been here. God knows, the man might have been in the city since the Cemetery Mansion massacre."

"You remember the massacre?" Sarah asked him.

"Anyone who was in the city at the time remembers it," Detective Green said.

"Some more than others," Tyler said, studying Alex. "Were you at the theme park?"

"Yeah. Oh, yeah, I was already there—when I was called in to work for the local unit that night! I was still so raw—I'd made it into the academy, but one time when I was sitting around sketching to pass the time, a colleague told me they were short in the forensic department. My curiosity was tweaked, and I figured I could always come back and finish the academy. I never did, but...anyway. I wasn't making any kind of big bucks, if you know what I mean, so I was moonlighting, too. Working part-time for the amusement company. That night, I was working as a float—you know, I was sent wherever they were missing an employee or actor. That night I was a ticket taker, not far from where the Cemetery Mansion had been erected. I can't believe I was there—that I might have seen the creepy bastard go running by me—as he escaped. I just remember the blood and the screams and the people who were so terrified, running, running, running..." He stopped, shaking his head. "Hell, I'd give my eyeteeth to help in catching this bastard, so anything—anything at all I can do to help, I'm there. I'm going to go back over the pictures we took of the crime scene when we found Hannah Levine...you know, um, both places where they found her...head and torso."

"Interesting," Tyler said. "Maybe you can find some kind of a distinguishing something about him that will give us a clue as to where he's been living—he has to be in the city somewhere."

"He wears black in these pictures," Alex commented. "A black coat."

"He wears a black coat when he's in here, too," said

Luke. He cleared his throat. "Do you think he will come back here? I mean, I should be okay, right? He's going after women."

Alex Morrison was flicking through his digital pictures. Tyler reached for the camera.

He'd just recently been taking shots of the place. The large, etched mirror behind the bar; the old wooden stools; the rather shabby booths out on the floor; and the tables there. He had taken pictures of the tables inside and of the outside of the establishment.

A large canopy awning hung down over the front of the building, though it hadn't become a warm enough spring yet for patrons to want to sit outside. Or even have a window open.

But Alex Morrison had taken pictures outside, of the streets leading east and west of the bar. He had caught other buildings in his shots.

And he'd caught a number of pedestrians.

Tyler studied the pictures. He felt Sarah's hand on his shoulder; she was looking over at them, as well.

Mostly, it appeared to be Manhattan's daily business crowd—rushing here, there, trying to get to work on time.

People were in line at the coffee shop toward the corner.

A woman had paused to adjust her shoe.

Tyler glanced up at Alex Morrison. He was probably just in his early to midthirties now.

Tyler vaguely remembered him as the photographer back then, but they hadn't had any real contact at the time. But Morrison had been decent, straightforward, yet gentle due to their ages.

However, not as brave or passionate as he seemed to be now.

His photos were good. He had an eye for focus and detail.

"Touch here, and you can enlarge wherever you want," Alex told them.

"Thanks."

"Go back a few," Sarah said. "There's a really great long shot. It brings in the street, going toward the Times Square area."

Tyler flicked back.

And at first, he saw nothing unusual.

No details at all. And then he paused.

There was a woman in the road. The street wasn't closed to traffic, but she was jaywalking and in the middle of the road as cars went by her.

All around her, neon lights blazed—even in the morning.

The pictures hadn't been taken an hour ago. Some had just been taken as Alex had entered the bar.

Tyler touched the screen as Alex had shown him. The image enlarged.

She was wearing a white dress, white coat and low white pumps. She had a bobbed platinum haircut—like Marilyn Monroe.

He could see that, compared to other people walking in the vicinity, she was tall. Really tall.

"She…" Green murmured.

"Oh, Lord!" Sarah said.

"What is it?" Alex Morrison asked them, frowning as he turned the viewing screen back toward himself.

"She is a he," Tyler said quietly. "She is Perry Knowlton. When did you snap that?"

"That's...that's one of the last images I took—maybe ten minutes ago."

Tyler was up and heading out before the others could blink.

No.

She was a he, and the "he" was Perry Knowlton.

And he was out there, close.

Closer than they had ever imagined.

Chapter 7

Sarah sat tensely on her bar stool.

Tyler had raced out; Craig rose, but hesitated.

"Go on—one of us should go, too, and hell, you're younger than I am, if you're going to be running around!" Detective Green said. "I'll stick here. Alex is with me."

Then Craig was out the door.

"He won't be there anymore," Alex said dismally.

"It hasn't been much time. And he's a tall man in drag. They have a chance at finding him," Detective Green said.

Alex shrugged; it was apparent he sincerely doubted that.

"He's picked up new talents," Sarah said.

"What do you mean?" Alex asked.

"I've been reading a lot about him. Loner. Had an

alcoholic, abusive father, but I really wonder what that might have meant. He was very young when he was apparently discovered cutting up little creatures in the park. And then..."

"So, what new habit?" Alex asked.

She smiled. "I guess he learned at Cemetery Mansion about costumes. There was nothing in his earlier history about him dressing up to perform any of his atrocities—or even to go and view the fruit of his labor. Nothing about wearing women's clothes."

As she spoke, her phone rang. It was Tyler. Her heart leaped with a bit of hope that he'd called to tell her they'd taken Perry Knowlton down.

Really, too much to hope.

"He's not on the street, but we're not ready to give up," he said. "I'm going to ask Detective Green to get you to the safe house. You can spend a little time with Davey and everyone."

She bit her lip. She didn't really want to go; she liked working with him and Craig—questioning people, listening.

But she couldn't keep Detective Green sitting here all day on a bar stool.

And she knew it was unsafe for her to stay alone.

"Sarah, is that all right?"

"Of course," she said. She handed the phone to Bob Green.

She heard Tyler's voice speaking, and then Green told him, "I'm going to get some men on the street, as well, but...we know now Perry Knowlton is capable of being a changeling. He could be anything and anywhere by now."

Sarah could hear Tyler's answer. "But that's just it—we are aware now. That makes a difference."

"I'll see Sarah to the safe house. More officers will be out immediately—I'll join the manhunt when I've made sure Sarah is with the others."

He hung up and handed the phone back to her. "I'll get you there now, in my car."

"You're going to leave already?" Luke asked, looking unnerved. "Someone needs to be... Am I safe?"

"He's on the run. He won't come back here," Green replied.

Luke swallowed. He looked at Sarah and said, "Um, come visit some other time, huh? We're not usually such a bad place. I'm..."

The detective had already risen. Luke was actually looking a little ashen, and Green clamped a hand on his shoulder. "You're okay. I will have a patrolman on his way here. You're going to be okay."

Perry Knowlton was tall and blond and had ice-cold dark green eyes.

Which really meant nothing now. Eye color could easily be changed with contacts. Hair color was as mercurial as the tide.

He couldn't change his height.

They started where Alex Morrison's digital images had last shown him.

Craig took the right side of the street.

Tyler took the left.

He entered a popular chain dress store. A number of shoppers were about, but he quickly saw the cashier's booth toward the middle front of the store.

"I'm looking for a woman, very tall, platinum hair, in a white dress," he told the young clerk. "Have you seen her?"

"Oh, yes! Your friend came in just a few minutes ago. She's trying on maxi dresses. I helped her find a size."

Tyler smiled. "She's still here?"

"Dressing rooms are at the back."

"Thanks!"

Tyler hurried to the rear of the store. There was a row of fitting rooms, five in all. Only one was in use; he looked at the foot-long gap at the bottom of the doors.

Someone was standing in a pool of white.

The white dress?

He drew his gun and kicked open the door.

A middle-aged woman, quite tall, with a fine-featured face, stared at him in shock.

"I'm so sorry. Oh, Lord, I'm so sorry—I'm after a killer," he said. Hell. That sounded lame; he was just so damned desperate to catch Perry Knowlton.

He was so damned close.

Now he might well be close to a lawsuit.

"I'm so sorry, honestly."

She smiled at him. "Sure, honey. But hey, you're the best excitement I've had in some time. I guess that was a gun in your pocket! Hi—I'm Myrna!"

The FBI safe house was really pretty incredible. Entering was like going into one of the hundreds of skyscrapers in the city. They had to check in at the door; the girl at the desk appeared to be a clerk. She was, of course, an agent.

And Sarah was aware that the man reading the paper in the lobby was an agent, as well.

They were given permission to go up. Bob Green paused to have a conversation with the agents on duty at the door. There was complete local-federal trust on this case with those involved, but there was still a conversation.

Aunt Renee was in the kitchen; she'd invited their FBI guardians to her very special French toast brunch that morning, and she was busy cooking away when Sarah arrived. "All done soon! Suzie and Sean are going to join us." She smiled lamely. "It's not so bad here," she said softly. "I wish you were hiding out with us, but... I do understand. As long as you're careful. Davey... Davey is in his room. He's doing okay. He understands."

"Of course he understands," Sarah said. She smiled. "He usually does. He plays us when he chooses!"

"I guess so," Renee said softly. "Sometimes, I wonder if I'm overprotective. But the thing is, there are cruel people in this world. Well, as we know, there are heinous crazy killers, but... I mean in general. Grade school children can be especially unkind, making fun of anyone who is even a little bit different. And there are adults...they may not even be bad people, but... they don't know how to manage. Honestly, sometimes neighbors will walk on the other side of the street if they see me coming with Davey. I need to let some of the good in. Odd thing to realize when you're hiding from a killer, huh?"

Renee smiled ruefully at her. Sarah bit her lip lightly and nodded.

She was overprotective of Davey, too. And, yes, the

world could be cruel—besides sadistic killers. But it wasn't a bad thing to protect those you loved.

Maybe it was just bad to assume others didn't love them equally.

"I'll go see how he's doing," Sarah said.

"He loves you, you know."

"And I love him."

"He loves Tyler, too."

"And I know that Tyler loves him."

Renee nodded. "Tyler does love him. He really does."

"Breakfast smells divine," she said. "Is it still breakfast?"

"Brunch!" Renee said.

"Yes, brunch sounds great. There's enough?"

"You know me. There's enough to feed a small army!"

Sarah left her aunt and headed to the room Davey had chosen. She tapped on the door and he told her to come in.

He was sitting cross-legged on the bed, with his computer.

He looked up at her. "I miss my girlfriend!"

"Of course you do. She's a sweetie. But I'll bet she understands."

He nodded. Then he said, "No, not really." He shrugged. "Her mama doesn't even want me talking to her now. Maybe…"

"It will be all right. You called Tyler in, and my friends, Kieran and her boyfriend, FBI Special Agent Frasier—they're all working on it. It's going to be okay."

"It will be okay," Davey said with certainty. He

reached behind his back. "I still have my Martian Gamma Sword!"

"Of course. You made it okay once."

He nodded. "You just have to know."

"We didn't see him, Davey. The others saw him. Perry Knowlton, I mean."

"But he knows. I'm so sorry he hurt Hannah. And the other woman."

Sarah was sure no one had described the grisly murders to Davey. Of course, there were TVs just about everywhere.

And Davey loved his computer.

"No more haunted houses," Davey said.

"No. Definitely not."

"Bad people use whatever they can."

"That's true, Davey." Sarah kissed his cheek. "We can all learn from you!" she said softly. "You have that Martian Gamma Sword ready. You just never know."

"You just never know," he agreed.

"What are you doing on the computer? Have you been able to talk to Megan through My Special Friends or any other site?"

He nodded, a silly little smile teasing his face. "Yeah, I talk to Megan. I love Megan."

"I'm very happy for you."

"It's forever kind of love," he said sagely.

"That's nice."

"Like Tyler," he said.

"Oh, Davey. I know…what you did was very manipulative, and yet…"

He grinned. "I think that's better than devious!"

"Well, anyway, it's good that Tyler is here. For now. But please don't count on forever, okay?"

But Davey shook his head. "Forever," he said.

"I think I'm going to go and see if I can help your mom. I got here in time for brunch. Cool, huh? You like being here, right?"

"I'm okay," he said.

He was looking at his screen again. She didn't know if he was trying to communicate with his girlfriend or if he was studying movies—looking up actors and directors.

At the doorway she paused, glancing back at him. "Tell Megan I said hi, okay?"

"I will. I'm not talking to Megan right now."

"What are you doing?"

He looked up at her, a strange expression on his face.

It wasn't mean. Davey didn't have a mean bone in his body, and in a thousand years he would never purposely hurt anyone.

"Davey?"

He smiled then, his charming little smile. "Research!" he told her.

"On?"

"On…whatever I find!"

"Ah. Well, breakfast—I mean brunch!—soon."

She left him and headed out to help her aunt. She wondered, even then, if she shouldn't check out just what he was researching on his computer.

If he'd been going to burst in on someone other than the killer he was trying to catch, Tyler had at least chosen the right person.

Myrna was Myrna Simpson, and it just happened that she was the wife of retired police lieutenant August Simpson. While Tyler had awkwardly tried to explain himself, she waved a hand. "Please, don't. I'm fine. No big deal."

"Thank you!" he told her and turned to walk away.

"I believe I know who you're after!" she said. "Tall woman—actually an inch or so taller than me. Very blonde. A drag queen? Or…just someone in costume?"

"Someone in costume, we believe."

"Too bad. He'd make a great drag queen," Myrna said. "He bought some things. I saw a few of them, but the clerk can probably give you a real list."

"The clerk said he was still in the dressing room."

"Two clerks are working. Mindy and Fiona. Come on."

It turned out he'd spoken to Mindy. Fiona hadn't been at the desk. She was then, though, a woman older than Mindy and the manager on duty.

She was suspicious at first. Tyler gave her his ID, but she remained skeptical, even with Myrna Simpson trying to help out.

Luckily, Craig Frasier walked in. His FBI identification made Fiona much more agreeable.

She gave them a list of the purchases made by Perry Knowlton.

"Is she here often?" Tyler asked.

"Often enough, I guess. Every couple of weeks," Mindy said.

When they finished, Tyler thanked Myrna again. "You really had no reason to trust me, but you did."

She laughed. "I told you. I've been married to a

cop—now retired—for thirty-three years. I learned a lot about sizing up people with first impressions. Though, to be honest, I mistook your man, Perry Knowlton, for someone with a few issues—not a serial killer. If I see him anywhere, I'll be in touch."

In the kitchen of the safe house, Aunt Renee had just about finished her special French toast.

"Want to set the table?" she asked Sarah.

After she set places, Sarah headed over to Special Agents Lawrence and Parton, who were by the door, diligently on guard.

"Brunch!" she told them.

"I'll stay. You eat first," Parton told Lawrence.

"You sure?"

"Just make sure you leave me some!" He glanced at his watch, then looked up and grinned at Sarah. "Sorry. We've been on a long shift. Reinforcements are coming in an hour or so."

"You've been great—and you must have my aunt's special French toast. It's really the best!"

She went to get Davey, Suzie and Sean from their rooms.

Of everyone, Suzie was looking the worst for wear. Frazzled.

"I'm just hoping I have a job when we get out of all this," she said. Then she winced. "Of course, I'm hoping to have a life first, and then a job."

Sean was dealing with it better. "I'm seeing it as a very strange vacation. She's usually too tired for sex!" he whispered to Sarah.

"Sean!"

"I'm trying to get a lot of sex in!"

"Sean!" Suzie repeated in horror.

"Oh, come on...hey, I'll bet you Sarah is getting a little, too!"

"French toast, at the moment!" Sarah said. She turned to head out; Suzie and Sean followed her.

They gathered around the table. Special Agent Lawrence said they were free to address her by her first name—Winona. She was a ten-year vet with the force, they learned as they passed eggs, French toast and bacon around the table.

"Agent Parton—Cody—is a newbie, really. He's been with us about a year and a half. Thankfully, there's a constant stream of recruits. It's a busy world, you know."

So it seemed, Sarah thought.

"Tell me about your books," Winona Lawrence said, looking at her. "I admit to being a sci-fi geek!"

"She's working on alien bugs now!" Davey said excitedly.

He explained. Sarah was glad he was doing the talking when her phone rang. It was Tyler.

"You okay?"

"Everything is good here," she said. And she added, "The agents are great."

"Some are more personable than others, so Craig has told me. That makes them good at different things. Anyway, I'll be a while. I wanted to make sure you were okay. We've found out Perry Knowlton has most probably dressed as a woman often. We have a list of his most recent purchases."

"But you weren't able to find him?"

"No." He hesitated. "There's some kind of a new lead. We don't really know what. Craig's director just called and asked him to come in. We have the image of Knowlton's latest appearance out with a number of patrol officers. They're still looking. I'll call back in when I know more."

"Okay, great. I'm fine here," Sarah assured him.

She hung up. Conversation had stopped. Everyone was looking at her.

"We're getting close, I believe!"

There was silence.

Then Special Agent Lawrence said, "Well! I can't wait to read your latest novel, Sarah! You have a wonderful fan club here."

Sarah smiled. And wished she could remember what they'd been talking about before Tyler's call.

She couldn't.

It didn't matter. She realized it was going to be a very long afternoon.

"Director Egan didn't mention what arrived?" Tyler asked Craig.

"I just got a message from his assistant—come in as soon as possible," Craig said.

Tyler thought he could have stayed on the streets, searching, but he didn't think Knowlton was going to allow himself to be found that easily.

He was out there, though. And he was a chameleon. That made the situation even more frightening than before.

He'd made the decision to come with Craig. The FBI just might have something that could lead them to Perry Knowlton. The man had no known address. According to all official records, he didn't exist. He'd died a decade ago.

But he was breathing and in the flesh—and killing people—whether he was dead on record or not.

They reached the FBI offices and went through the security check required by everyone, agents included, and then headed up to the director's office. Egan's assistant sent them in.

Egan was on the phone, but he hung up, seeing that they'd arrived.

"We've had a message from the killer," he said. "It literally arrived ten minutes ago."

"We've received hundreds of messages from hundreds of 'killers,'" Craig said wearily. He looked at Tyler. "You'd be amazed by the number of people who want to say they're killers, or to confess to crimes they didn't commit."

"I think this one is real," Egan said. He glanced at Tyler. "It was actually addressed to you, as well as this office."

"And?" Tyler said.

"Apparently, Perry Knowlton wants to be a poet, too," Egan said. He tapped a paper that lay on his desk and slipped on his reading glasses. "Don't worry—this is a copy. The real deal is with forensics. Anyway, 'Six little children, perfect and dear, wanting the scare of their lives. One little boy, smarter than the rest, apparently felt like the hives. They went into the house, they cried there was a louse, and one fine man was gone. But now they pay the price today...six little children. One of them dead. Soon the rest will be covered in red.'"

"Six little children. Well, we weren't exactly little, but in a way, we were still children," Tyler said. "But he makes no mention of having killed the wrong Suzie Cornwall."

"He might not want to admit that he made a mistake," Craig said.

"Sounds like it might be legit," Egan said. "Naturally, we're testing everything, finding out about the paper and the typeface and all…and what came with it."

"What came with it?" Tyler asked.

"A C-1, I understand," Egan said. "According to doctors, there are seven cervical spine bones in a human being. The C-1 vertebra is closest to the skull. We received one—and we believe it might well have belonged to Hannah Levine. When a victim has been beheaded, the neck bones may well be crushed or… We're comparing DNA. But I do believe that we'll discover it belonged to Hannah."

"So now he's taunting the police. But we just put the images of Perry Knowlton out today—how did he know so quickly that we know who he is?" Craig wondered aloud.

"This arrived via bike messenger. I've emailed you the address for the service. I'll need you to look into it. You should get going," Egan said.

"Yes, sir. We need to inform Detective Green…" Craig said.

"Already done," Egan assured him.

They left the office.

The messenger service's office was just north of Trinity Church, on Cedar Street.

The clerk behind the desk was pale. He was young and uncertain, with a pockmarked face and shaggy brown hair. "I know… I talked to a man from the FBI. I… I have a log, of course. I—I, oh, God! He didn't really say anything—just that the FBI had to know about a package! Was it a bomb? Did we handle a bomb?"

"It wasn't a bomb," Craig said. "What we need to know is who gave you the package to deliver?"

"Um…" The clerk fumbled with a roster on the counter. "Jacob Marley. He paid cash. It was a man…an old man, hunched over, crackling voice. Told me he didn't believe in those newfangled credit card things. He believed in cold, hard cash."

The clerk looked up at them. "Um, we still take cash."

"You're the one who received the package here?" Tyler asked.

"Yes, sir. Er, I should really see your credentials."

Craig flipped out his badge. The clerk swallowed hard.

"It was a transaction like dozens of others. People do still use cash. I mean every day, people use cash!"

"Did you notice where the man went?" Craig asked. "Or where he came from?"

The clerk shook his head. "It was a busy morning. But…there's a subway station just down the street." He tried to smile. "Don't think he'd use a newfangled thing like a car, huh? Then again… I don't know. But he didn't look like the kind of guy who'd be driving a car around the city. How old is the subway?" he wondered.

"Built in 1904," Tyler said briefly, wondering how he remembered the exact year. He'd actually seen a documentary on it, he recalled, and then impatiently pushed the history lesson aside. "But he was here not long ago, right?"

"About an hour ago…yeah!" He suddenly seemed proud of himself. "I have it on the roster!"

Craig started to say more; Tyler touched him on the shoulder.

"The subway," Tyler murmured. "There's no other way. He was just up by the theater district, and while we were going crazy running around and checking out the clothing store, he was on the subway headed here, changing his appearance. He left the package. And then he—then, hell, he went back to wherever it is he comes from."

"He's been in New York City a long time," Craig mused. "He knows the system."

"I'll bet that he more than knows it. Craig, long shot here, but he's had plenty of time to study it. I was watching a program on the roots of the subway and the progression through the years. We know he can leap quickly and know where he's going." Tyler paused and took a deep breath. "Long shot, like I said. I can't help but think that he really knows the subway and the history of it—knows it like the back of his hand. There are so many abandoned stations. We know that the homeless often find them in winter. Do you think it's possible he's living underground somewhere?"

Craig listened and then nodded slowly. "Underground New York. We just had a case that involved the deconsecrated church right behind Finnegan's. Yeah, the subway."

"We know that people do make use of the empty

space—warm, and out of snow and sleet and all in winter. An abandoned station—that might even be lost to the history books?" Tyler suggested.

"Surely, in ten years, the man has needed to bathe. Needed running water. A way to eat and drink and sleep and—survive," Craig said.

Tyler shrugged. "I know I'm speculating, but it does work. Okay. My mom told me that once, when I was a kid and we were traveling on vacation, we wound up in Gettysburg and couldn't get a hotel room. So she and my dad parked the car in the lot of a big chain hotel—so we could slip in and use the bathrooms in the morning. Maybe our guy is doing the same thing. Not from a parking lot, but an abandoned station somewhere near several hotels...places he could slip in to use the facilities. Maybe hotels with gyms that have showers—he's evidently good at changing his image constantly. Wouldn't be hard for such a con to snatch a key and learn the identity of a paying guest."

"Possible," Craig said. "Hey, we went on theory. Theory has proved true. We'll head back to the office. In fact..." He pulled out his phone. "Mike should be in. I'll have him get started, pulling up all the spec sheets we'll need."

"Sounds good," Tyler said, and then he was quiet.

"What?" Craig asked, clicking off after speaking with his partner.

"That poem...it still bothers me."

"Because it was bad? Because it mentioned Davey and Sarah and the others?"

Tyler shook his head. "Because it didn't mention

the Suzie Cornwall who is dead. He said 'one.' Made it sound as if he just killed one."

"Maybe he doesn't consider a mistake to be one of his kills."

"Maybe. Still..." Tyler shrugged. "You know, I can't help but want this bastard dead. By the same token, I want him alive. I want him answering questions."

"Well, we have to find him if we're going to take him in," Craig said pragmatically, "dead or alive."

Sarah was restless and didn't want to stay at the safe house any longer.

She wanted to be doing something.

Of course, she knew she'd be stupid to head out.

She did the dishes and played a Guess the Hollywood Star game with Davey—knowing full well he'd beat her soundly, and fairly.

Then Tyler called to bring her up to date—it seemed Perry Knowlton had sent a message and a bone to the FBI offices, taunting them.

She was glad when Kieran arrived with her brother Kevin. Due to Kieran's connections, she and Kevin had been given special dispensation to visit.

They sat together in one of the little chair groupings in the living room area. Craig, of course, had informed Kieran what was going on, and she and Kevin had come to tell Sarah about one of the recent cases they had wound up working on—or rather, that Craig had worked on, and which had involved them. It had revolved around the deconsecrated church and a killer who'd left his victims "perfect" in death.

"The point is, he liked the underground." Kieran

paused and looked at her brother. "He killed a young actress Kevin had been seeing."

"I'm lucky I was never charged with the murder," he said grimly.

"I think they're right. I think it's the only solution. This guy has been hiding underground and taking advantage of his obsession with dressing up and—so it seems—his ability to borrow other identities," Kieran said.

"It makes sense." Sarah added, "Tyler said they were going to find a place near hotels—somewhere he could use facilities when he needed them. He's probably a very adept thief—the kind who steals small-time and therefore is never apprehended."

"Quite possibly. Anyway, we think they're on the right track," Kieran said.

Tyler called again then. Sarah hastily told Kieran and Kevin it was him.

"They're at an abandoned station not far from here," she said when she'd hung up. "But so far nothing."

"They'll keep looking," Kieran assured her. "People have the images and they know."

Next, Craig called Kieran. Sarah saw her wince.

"What?" she asked when Kieran clicked off.

"Well, they're getting calls and leads," she said.

"That's good, right?"

"Yes, except it's hard to winnow through them. Apparently, someone even called in about Craig and Tyler. They're phoning in about every man over six feet in the city of New York!"

"Oh!" Sarah said.

"Don't worry, they'll keep working."

Davey peeked his head out. "Want to play a game?" he asked.

"Davey," Sarah murmured uncomfortably. "They're probably busy..."

"We'd love to play a game!" Kieran said.

And so they all played.

For once, Sarah won.

Davey was her teammate.

The day was long and hard.

When eight o'clock came around, Tyler and Craig decided to wrap it up and start again in the morning.

They didn't want to be obvious about what they were doing; they didn't want Perry Knowlton to know they were actively searching underground for him.

They'd been provided with a really good map of the defunct stations—those that had existed years ago and were not in use now.

They needed more, Tyler thought. More to go on.

But shortly after eight, they returned to the safe house.

Sarah looked at Tyler anxiously. So did the others.

"We'll be starting up again in the morning," he assured them all. "We did take a step forward today. Another step tomorrow. We will catch the bastard."

He once again tried to get Sarah to stay at the safe house.

She absolutely refused.

He was, on the one hand, very glad.

Because there was nothing like getting back to the hotel room with her. There was nothing like apologizing, telling her he'd been underground, digging around in tunnels.

And then having her join him in the shower. Hot water sluicing over her breasts, her naked body next to his...

Touching, caressing.

Feeling her make love to him in return.

Falling hot and wet and breathless on the clean sheets in the cool air...

Being together, laughing, talking, not talking, being breathless...

Feeling the release of a tremendous climax.

And lying next to her as the little tremors of aftermath swept through him, allowing a sweet relief and tremendous satiation.

He loved her.

He always would.

And she loved him, too.

He just wondered if being so much in love could be enough.

Love was supposed to conquer all. But not if she pushed him away.

He'd think about that later.

The day had been long, but the night could be very sweet.

He allowed his fingers to play over the curve of her back, caress the soft, sleek flesh and then fall lower again, teasing...

She let out a soft, sweet sigh.

"What are you thinking?" he asked her quietly.

"I'm not thinking," she said.

He didn't press it. He just held her. And they lay silently together once again.

A bit later, she moved against him. She teased along his spine with her tongue. Her fingertips were like a breath over his flesh. Her arms wound around him, and he curled toward her and she continued to tease and play and seduce.

They made love again.

And then held one another.

He should have had nightmares. He did not. He slept deeply, sweetly.

And then his alarm went off.

It was morning again. Perry Knowlton was still out there.

And God alone might guess what he would do next.

Chapter 8

"I wish I could go with you," Sarah told Tyler.

He hesitated. They were showered and dressed, ready to leave.

"I can be helpful—hey, the bartender at Time and Time Again liked me better than you."

He had to smile at that. "Yeah, so…most guys out there are going to like you better than me. And, yes, you have proved helpful."

He wasn't lying. She had been very useful. That didn't change the fact that her being in danger could compromise his—or Craig's—ability to work.

"You're just better at the safe house!" he told her gently.

"Time goes so slowly," she said. She brightened. "But actually, there were a few minutes yesterday when I almost had fun. Kieran and Kevin were by—we played

one of Davey's games with him. It was great. Kevin
acted out half of his clues for Kieran. We were laughing. I was so surprised they were willing to play."

"Why?"

"Well, they're busy, of course. They don't really have
time to play Davey's games."

He was silent. There it was. Her insistence that only
she could really be happy to play a silly game with
Davey.

"What?" she murmured, sensing the change in him.

"You can be really full of yourself, you know."

She frowned, stepping away. "What?"

"Never mind. Let me get you to the safe house."

He stepped out; she followed, still frowning. "Tyler?"

"Let's go."

He got her out of the room and down to the car. Once
they were in traffic, however, she pressed the point.

"What are you talking about?"

"Never mind. Now isn't the time to worry about it."

"When should I worry about it? When we're either
dead or you're back in Boston?"

He stayed silent; traffic was heavy. She waited.
When they reached the area of the safe house, she
pushed again.

"Tyler, tell me what you're talking about."

"Davey," he said simply. "Who do you think you
are, really? Other people like Davey, love Davey, and
enjoy his company."

"I—I…" Sarah stuttered.

He saw one of the agents—Special Agent Lawrence—
in front of the building. She waved at him, hurrying
around to the driver's side of the car. "I'll take it for
you—you can see Sarah safely up. It will be there…"

She pointed to a garage entrance down the street. "Agent Frasier will be by for you in about ten minutes."

"Okay, thanks," Tyler said, getting out of the car. He walked around, but Sarah was already out and walking in ahead of him.

The agent at the desk nodded to them.

Sarah was moving fast; she got into the elevator first. He had to put his arm out to keep the door open.

He stepped in. She was staring straight ahead. He wasn't sure if she was furious or in shock.

"I told you it wasn't really the time."

She didn't reply. The elevator door opened on their floor. She hurried ahead. At the door she stopped and turned and looked at him. "You're not being fair! Davey is like love personified. He doesn't have a mean bone in his body. Of course people...most people...love him!"

"Then let him enjoy them without you feeling you need to be a buffer."

"I—I don't!"

"You do. You push everyone away."

The door opened. Special Agent Preston was there. "Hey. Did you see Winona? She went down to take the car."

"Yes, we met her."

"Craig is on his way."

"I'm going right down," Tyler said.

Sarah was still staring at him. Now she looked really confused. And worried. Maybe she hadn't realized how overprotective she was—and how much she had doubted other people. Him.

"Go in!" he told her.

He started back toward the elevator. Sarah gasped

suddenly, and he spun around—ready to draw on Special Agent Preston.

But the FBI agent just looked puzzled. And Sarah was suddenly running toward him. "Tyler!"

"Sarah, we can talk later," he said softly.

"No, no, no! Nothing to do with us...with Davey. The poem—the poem Perry Knowlton wrote. It was about Hannah, right—not Suzie Cornwall."

"It seemed to be about Hannah." He paused, frowning, wondering what she was thinking.

He'd memorized the poem, and spoke softly, repeating the words. "'Six little children, perfect and dear, wanting the scare of their lives. One little boy, smarter than the rest, apparently felt like the hives. They went into the house, they cried there was a louse, and one fine man was gone. But now they pay the price today... six little children. One of them dead. Soon the rest will be covered in red.'"

"Hannah. We know—from Luke, the bartender—that Perry Knowlton hung around the bar near Times Square. And he went to a dress shop there semiregularly... He seemed to watch Hannah easily enough. Maybe he ran into her by chance one time. He was able to become a woman quickly. And then get to the subway to gather and then deliver the package. Tyler, you need to be looking for something underground not far from the bar and the shop."

He smiled at her slowly. "That would make sense. You've got it, I think. Although..."

"What?"

"I didn't really see anything in that area. He was a regular at the bar, yes, so we looked, but... We'll have to look again."

"But you will look?" Sarah asked.

"Yes, of course."

He gave her a little salute. Then he continued on to the elevator.

"I wonder what we're costing the taxpayers," Suzie said dismally. She had just flicked the television off. They had seen the artist's sketch of Perry Knowlton one time too many.

Along with pictures of Suzie Cornwall.

The young woman had been ill, and the artist's rendering had allowed that to show.

But Suzie had turned white every time a picture of her came across the screen.

Sarah leaned forward. "Suzie, stop blaming yourself. He's killed before. If we don't get him now, he'll kill again."

Special Agent Lawrence heard them talking and came forward, just a bit hesitantly. "Please! I know you won't stop, but you have to try to. It's not your fault, Suzie. It's not your parents' fault for naming you, or your dad for having that surname. It's the fault of a sick and pathetic and deplorable criminal mind. You have to accept that. If you don't, you will make yourself crazy."

"If I live to go crazy," Suzie muttered.

"You will live," Winona said, solid determination in her voice. She smiled, and then shrugged, sighing. "Okay, maybe I look a little worn, because I am. I need some sleep. But don't worry. We have replacements coming. Hey, Parton, who is coming on next?" she called.

Cody Parton was at the desk by the door. "Guzman and Walsh, so I've been told," he called.

"Ah, Walsh is a new guy. Guzman has been around forever and knows the ropes. Trust me, you'll be safe!" she said.

She smiled and walked away.

"People can say anything. I can even know it's true. But I can't help it. If that young woman's name hadn't been Suzie Cornwall, she'd be alive now," Suzie told Sarah softly.

"Maybe something worse was in store for her," Sarah said.

Suzie shrugged. "I wish I could think of something productive to do. It hasn't been that long, but I feel as if we've been cooped up forever."

Sean poked his head out of their bedroom. "Hey, guys, wanna watch a movie?" He shrugged. "They have all the movies we could possibly want. Reciprocation... or the cable company sucking up to the Feds, not sure which!"

"I guess so," Suzie said. "A comedy! Sarah, you coming?"

Sarah smiled. "No, I think I'll sit here and...plot."

"Alien bugs, huh? You're going to sit there and go crazy thinking," Suzie said.

Sarah offered her a weak smile. "Am I overprotective of Davey?" she asked.

Suzie hesitated. "Oh, Sarah! Sad to say, I haven't been around you that much lately, so I don't know if you are or not."

"Did I...in high school, was I overprotective?"

"Yes. Sometimes you had the right to be. We weren't cruel kids, but we could be careless. But..."

"But?"

"You really didn't have to be with Tyler and me. And

others, of course. Davey has to make a few mistakes on his own, but he's smart. He can handle it. Your uncle did teach him to watch out for the bad guys."

Suzie grimaced and went on into the room with Sean. Sarah sighed, sitting there, torn between thinking about her own mistakes and the fact that they were hunting for a killer.

"You doing okay?" Winona walked back over to her.

She nodded. "Fine, thanks. It just seems...seems like this is taking a very long time."

"This? Long? I was with the Organized Crime Unit for a while—oh, my God! We gathered info for months and months and...um, but this is different."

Sarah smiled.

It wasn't all that different.

It could take time. A lot of time.

"I'm going off in a bit. Can you think of anything I can do for you?" Winona asked.

Sarah liked the woman, really liked her. She smiled and shook her head.

"When do we see you again?"

"Two days. I'll be back on for the next three after that, twelve hours a day!"

"No offense, but I hope we're not here that long. Though you've been very nice."

Winona smiled. "You guys have been easy. I think your aunt and Davey are watching a movie, too. I'll check on everyone before I leave. The new agents are due here soon. Fresh agents. You know what I mean! Replacements!"

Sarah nodded and let her go, leaning back. She closed her eyes, wishing she could sleep, wishing Tyler was there, wishing...

Just wishing that she wasn't so tense, and so alone, wondering if she had pushed people away...

If only she hadn't been so young, so afraid and so unsure. Unable to believe not only in Davey, but in herself.

They were below the giant high-rises, great pillars of concrete, stone and steel that rose into the sky.

Once upon a time, the subway stop had been called the South Playwright Station. Back then, there had been no movies, and the station had actually been part of the Interborough Rapid Transit Company—one of the predecessors of the modern system.

In those days, the theater district had reigned supreme—there had been no movies. There had not been giant IMAX screens, 3-D, tablets, notepads, computers or any other such devices.

People had flocked here as one of the theater stations. Then a part of the subway had collapsed, and it had been closed off.

One of the city's engineers accompanied Craig and Tyler down to the station. The access was tricky; they had to bend over and crawl half of it. Broken brick lay with beautiful old tile; the station name was still mostly visible, all in tile that was now covered with the dust of decades that had passed without the station being used. The walls were covered in colorful but menacing graffiti from intrepid urban explorers and vandals. Tracks were intermittent, here and there.

The three men used high-powered flashlights as they went, moving cautiously.

"I don't know," Tyler murmured. "This seems a likely location, but how the hell could a tall man come and go, in all manner and mode of dress?"

"There could be another access," the engineer told them. "One that isn't on the maps. I did some digging. I believe there were a few entries in some of the old buildings—in the foyers or on the corners."

"Maybe," Craig said. "I don't think there's anything here, though."

"Wait, let's not head up yet. I think…there's something ahead," Tyler said.

"A door off to the side?" Craig murmured.

There was a door ahead, they discovered. An old maintenance door.

The three of them quickened their pace.

The new crew was coming on.

Agent Winona Lawrence impulsively gave Sarah a hug. "We really should move like professional machinery, but…come on, I want you to meet the new guys. One of them I've never met—the guy we were expecting called in sick. Oh, and you're going to have another female agent coming in tomorrow. Her name is Lucinda Rivera. She's super. You'll like her, too. But for now…"

The new agents were at the door. Guzman was older—maybe fifty. He had graying hair and heavy jowls, but a good smile when he met Sarah.

The other agent was younger—forty or forty-five, tall, with close-cropped dark hair, a large nose and dark eyes. She wondered if she had met him before, maybe with Kieran and Craig.

"Walsh called in sick," he told them. "I'm Adler. Jimmy Adler. Nice to meet you, Sarah."

"All right, then. We're out of here. Sleep!" Lawrence said.

"A beer!" Parton admitted.

"Parton," Guzman said softly.

"Hey…"

Sarah laughed. "Enjoy your beer, Special Agent Parton."

He grinned. "Just say 'Goodbye, Cody!'"

"Goodbye, Cody!" she repeated.

Guzman took up a position by the door after locking it. "You can take the desk," he told Alder.

"Sure thing." The other agent complied.

They weren't going to be as friendly or as easygoing as Lawrence and Parton, Sarah decided. She went back to her chair in the little living room grouping. There were magazines on a table by the sofa. She picked up a *National Geographic* and started leafing through it. There was an article about a new discovery of underground tombs and mummies in the Sahara Desert. She tried to concentrate on the piece, loving the concept of extraterrestrials possibly creating some of the great works in Ancient Egypt. Aliens arriving on Earth thousands of years ago could lead to some great sci-fi ideas.

The agents were making occasional small talk with each other, but Sarah wasn't paying attention. She could block them out. Well, she could tell herself she was concentrating all she wanted.

All she could really do was sit tensely, wishing that Tyler would call.

She had been there awhile when she heard one of the doors click open slightly, and she looked up; Suzie was at her bedroom door, looking troubled.

Sean was right behind her. He beckoned to Sarah.

She went to the door and started to speak, but Sean caught her arm and whisked her in. "You have to talk Suzie down. She's having daydreams, nightmares."

"You weren't there!" she whispered to Sarah.

"I'm confused. I wasn't where?"

"You weren't with us when we first went into Cemetery Mansion. He talked to me…he talked. The thing in the room…the thing we think now might have been Perry Knowlton. He beckoned to me. He spoke… I told myself he was a robot, an automaton, whatever. I was so scared…"

"She's dreaming that she hears his voice," Sean said.

Sarah wasn't sure what, but something suddenly went off inside her.

Instinct?

Like an alarm bell louder than could be imagined.

"We've got to get out," she said. "Now. And fast. Move—move toward that dumbwaiter-slash-elevator they showed us on the first day. Move now. Fast, and silently. I'm getting Davey and my aunt Renee. Go. Go now."

They'd been expecting Agent Walsh.

Walsh had "called in sick."

Maybe she was crazy—maybe she and Suzie were both cabin-crazy, paranoid—justly so, but paranoid.

Maybe.

But maybe not.

They moved as quickly as they dared over the rubble and through the dust they raised, to the door at the side of the tunnel.

"Careful," the engineer warned. "You guys want to make it, to keep on searching, right?" he asked cheerfully. "Of course, we could do this for days!"

"Let's hope not," Craig said.

The engineer shrugged. "It's okay by me. I like you guys!"

"Thanks," Tyler said.

Maybe they *were* wrong.

And maybe they were right, but they weren't looking in the right place. Besides tunnels, as Kieran had pointed out to Sarah, streets had been built on top of streets in New York City. Not to mention—as the Finnegan family had all known from a previous case—there were underground tombs scattered about, as well.

But logically, Tyler didn't think Perry Knowlton had been living in a tomb. Unless there was such a thing with easy access to the city streets.

Yet even as they reached the door, he couldn't help but remember the poem Knowlton had written and sent to the police with a bit of neck bone.

Six little children, perfect and dear, wanting the scare of their lives. One little boy, smarter than the rest, apparently felt like the hives. They went into the house, they cried there was a louse, and one fine man was gone. But now they pay the price today...six little children. One of them dead. Soon the rest will be covered in red.

He hadn't realized he'd spoken aloud. Craig stopped walking; Tyler nearly plowed into him.

"Poem still bothering you?" Craig asked. The engineer walked ahead of them.

"I don't know—I just think he would want to gloat over having killed two women so viciously," Tyler said.

"He is in revenge mode."

"Yes. Still, wouldn't he taunt us by saying, hey, and look what I did while I was trying to get the right people?"

"We need to catch him. Then we'll know."

"Wow, this is weird!" the engineer called back to them.

"What's that?"

"Door opens easy as if it had been greased yesterday!" And then he added a horrified "Holy crap!"

Tyler ran forward, Craig right with him.

The door opened to a little room lit by an electric lantern—a very modern electric lantern. There were boxes everywhere, an ice chest, Sterno...a mattress, pillows, blankets.

And in the middle of the floor, a man.

Stripped down to his underwear.

Blood streaked across his temple from a gaping head wound.

Craig was instantly down by his side. "Walsh, just met him the other day. He's got a pulse, slight... I'm pretty sure he was left for dead... His suit is...gone."

"You, sir! Stay with this man," Craig said. He was already trying his cell—and swearing when there was no signal.

"We've got to get to the safe house, have to send a warning. We have to get there!" Tyler said.

He wasn't sure he'd ever felt such a cold and deadly fear.

He was ready to rush back and crawl through the opening, ready to run all the way down Broadway. He was desperate to reach Sarah.

"There!" the engineer cried. "There's your entrance!"

And there it was. Across the little room was another door. Tyler rushed to it and threw it open. Stairs led up, and he took them to another door, then a hallway that twisted and turned.

At the end of the next hallway was a door that led to the foyer of a 1930s building. He burst out of it, with Craig behind him. He heard Craig dialing 9-1-1 for the man in the tunnel.

Tyler tried Sarah's number.

There was no answer.

Davey was paying attention. He wasn't watching his movie; he was at the door, ready when Sarah slipped across the hall as quietly as possible to open it. He brought a finger to his lips.

"What is it?" Renee asked.

"Shh, shh, shh, Davey is right!" Sarah told her. "Come with me. We have to get out of here."

"Get out of here?" Renee said, puzzled. "But we have FBI guards—"

"I think they've been compromised. If I'm wrong… we'll come right back up. But we're going to take the emergency exit. We have to get to the elevator—the escape dumbwaiter we were shown."

"Sarah, what has happened?"

"Nothing—yet. But please believe me—"

"I have my Martian Gamma Sword!" Davey said. And he did. He produced it, showing them that he was ready to fight.

"Please, I could be wrong, but if not, hurrying may be essential. Please, Aunt Renee!"

Renee still didn't appear to be happy. She looked out the door, down the hall to the living area.

Guzman and Adler seemed to be doing their jobs.

"Please!" Sarah said.

"Mom. Come!" Davey said. He looked at Sarah and said, "You know my mom. Really, sometimes she's a little Down syndrome, too. She concentrates, and you have to shake her up. You know that."

"Now!" Sarah said firmly.

She took her aunt's hand and led the way out. Renee grabbed Davey's arm. They headed silently out of the room and down the hall toward the little enclave where the dumbwaiter/elevator waited.

Of course, they'd never tried it.

Aunt Renee whispered that concern. "What if it doesn't work? What if five of us don't fit? What if the agents are furious?"

She'd barely voiced the question before they heard a thump.

Sarah stared back toward the door to the apartment.

Adler was standing over Guzman.

He still held the muzzle of an FBI Glock in his hand; he'd used the handle to cream the agent on the head.

"Go!" Sarah screamed as the man turned to look at them.

They ran.

"Hurry!" Sean beckoned from inside the elevator.

Sarah was still looking back as she ran. The others plowed into the elevator.

She stared right at the man. The thing. The monster the others had seen that night long ago—but she and Davey had not.

Because he'd already been out of the haunted house. Maybe he'd known that his fellow murderer was on a suicidal spree.

Now he looked right at her.

And he smiled.

He aimed the gun at her.

"Sarah!" Davey shouted.

She jumped into the contraption; they were on top of one another, like rats.

Sean hit the giant red Close Door button.

A shot went off.

The door shut just in time.

They heard the bullet strike…

"His voice! Oh, God, I knew that voice!" Suzie sobbed.

Yes! Thank God she had!

The elevator sped toward the ground floor, and Sarah prayed they could get out and get free and find help…

He didn't have just a knife anymore. Maybe, recently, he'd had a gun along with him as well for his murders. Maybe that was how he'd forced his victims to their murder sites.

Maybe…

"Oh, God, he's coming for us all!" Suzie cried.

All the official cars and all the official power in the world couldn't really move New York City traffic.

Up and out of the tunnel, Tyler and Craig didn't even try it.

On the street level, Craig was able to reach Dispatch to request help; officers would be on the way.

But so would they—via the subway.

Miraculously, they were able to hit an express.

And off the subway, they ran.

Bursting into the foyer of the safe house, Tyler stopped at last.

The desk clerk was on his feet, hurrying toward them. "Agents are up there," he said. "Guzman was down. That man came in with Guzman…he had credentials. There was no reason to suspect… He walked right in. Right by me and the backup. I'm here, but everyone else is out there, on the street. We have people going through the rooms, but…"

"But what?" Tyler roared. He realized that Craig had spoken at the same time.

"They got out, the witnesses… We don't know exactly where now—they didn't come this way. They sensed something was wrong somehow, but…they're out on the street. We have men out there, but—"

Tyler didn't give a damn just how many men might be out on the street. He turned, followed by Craig.

"Hey!" the agent called to them. "Hey, this is important!"

Tyler barely paused.

"He's armed! He has a service Glock. He doesn't just have a knife—"

As the clerk spoke, they heard the explosive sound of a gun being fired.

Sarah had remembered the door would open only from their side—and only when she pushed the button.

She did so. They'd come out in an alley. If they didn't move quickly, they'd be trapped.

"Run! Go!" she commanded.

They tumbled out and began running. The good thing for them was the main door to the building was around the corner; Knowlton had to leave the building that way—his only choice. That gave them precious seconds to get out of the alley, get somewhere…hide!

She had Davey's hand. He was not the most agile person she knew; he wasn't necessarily fast when he ran. She was desperate to find a hiding place before they were seen.

"Davey!" Her aunt cried her son's name with anguish. Sarah knew that she hated being even one second away from him when there was danger.

She paused, but her aunt, panting, looked at her desperately. "Take him! Take him, keep him safe!"

Sarah nodded. She tightened her grip on his hand and ran on.

Luckily, the street was thronging with people. She kept screaming for help.

They moved out of the way.

Some pulled out cell phones—she hoped they were dialing 9-1-1.

Gasping for air, Sarah soon felt she was reaching her limit.

Trinity was ahead of her.

She had Davey; she had to pray Aunt Renee and Sean and Suzie would run faster than she could with Davey. They could truly get away, would find a shop, a restaurant, anything! Duck in…

She was on the street, ready to run into the Trinity graveyard, when she heard someone shouting at her. She turned.

It was a police officer in uniform.

She drew Davey behind her. "He's after us! The killer is after us—Knowlton, the man who beheaded the two women…he's after us!"

"Now, now, miss!" the officer said. "Miss, I'm not sure what your problem is, but you're just going to have to try to calm down."

"My problem is that a killer is after us!"

"Is this some kind of a crazy game?" the cop demanded.

"No, dammit! Sorry, sorry, Officer, please, I'm begging you—listen to me. There is a killer—"

She broke off. The man who had claimed to be Special Agent Adler—and was, beyond a doubt, Perry Knowlton—was now casually strolling toward them.

"Get over the fence. Hide in the graves!" she whispered to Davey.

"I won't leave you!" Davey said stubbornly.

"Do it!" she snapped.

To her relief, for once, he obeyed her.

And it was all right; Knowlton was just staring at her. Smiling still.

"Special Agent Adler, Officer, FBI," Knowlton said, ever so briefly flashing a badge. "And that woman is a dangerous psychopath!"

"He's going to shoot me," she told the police officer calmly.

"No, no, miss. He's FBI. Now, I don't know the truth here, but he'll talk to you and—"

Knowlton took aim and fired.

Sarah gasped as the officer went down before her. He was screaming in agony.

Not dead.

Knowlton might be good with a knife—he wasn't that great with a gun.

Sarah was dimly aware of the sound of dozens of screams; people were shouting, running, clearing the street.

And then Knowlton was looking right at her. He was a few feet away from her.

His stolen gun was aimed at her.

"You don't want to shoot me," she told him quietly.

He paused and smiled, clearly amused.

"I don't?"

"You don't like guns. You use them only to scare and bully people—when you have to. This may be the first time you're really using one."

"Sorry—I used guns we stole off the guards when Archie and I escaped."

"Still, you're not very good with a gun. You're much more adept with a knife. And I'm assuming you have one. You like to torture your victims, and that's much better accomplished with a knife."

"Don't worry—I'm carrying a knife. And," he added softly, "when I finish with you, I will find that cousin of yours. Oh, I read the papers, I saw the news! He was the hero, huh? Let's see if he dies like a hero. Oh, dear! Look around. A graveyard. How fitting!"

He smiled. Whether he liked a gun or not, he still had the Glock aimed at her.

"Drop it!" she heard someone say.

She smiled with relief. Sanity! Someone who realized that Knowlton wasn't the law—that he was a killer.

Someone...

Her turn to know a voice.

"Drop it!"

Knowlton stared at her. Smiled. Took careful aim—and then spun around to shoot at whoever was behind him.

A gun went off.

For a moment, it felt as if time had been suspended. As if the world had frozen—it was all a special effect in a movie, because, dear Lord, this couldn't be real. The killer, there, posed before her...

And then he fell.

She looked past him, her knees wobbling, something

inside her desperately fighting to keep her standing, to keep her from passing out.

There, past the prone body of Perry Knowlton, was Tyler.

She stared at him for a moment.

And then she ran, and he was ready to take her into his arms. She knew she wasn't shot; she wasn't sure about him.

"Tyler, Tyler…"

"I'm fine. I'm fine, I'm fine," he assured her, holding her, smoothing back her hair. "Are you…?"

"Fine. I'm fine. He aimed at you, Tyler, he aimed at you. He—"

"I'm okay. We're okay," he said firmly.

She was aware that Craig was with them then, briefly checking on the two of them, then hurrying forward to hunker down by the body of the fallen killer.

Others were moving in.

Davey had crawled back over the fence. He raced to them.

Tyler pulled him close, as well.

"Group hug!" Davey said.

Sarah drew back, looking anxiously at Tyler. "Aunt Renee, Suzie, Sean…?"

"They're all right. They went into a clothing store. They're good. We're all alive. All of us… Guzman and Walsh are being rushed to the hospital, and—"

Sirens suddenly screamed.

Chaos seemed to be erupting with a flow of agents and police, crime scene tape—a flurry of activity.

But none of it mattered.

She was being held in Tyler's arms. And anything

could happen around her. They had survived again. And this time...

She wouldn't just survive. She would live.

Chapter 9

Sarah and Kieran Finnegan helped serve the table.

The pub wasn't so terribly busy. It was Wednesday afternoon and the after-work crowd had yet to come in.

Sarah hadn't worked in the pub for years, but Kieran seemed to know that helping with the simple task of supplying wine, beers—regular and nonalcoholic— and a Shirley Temple for Davey was busywork, and sometimes it helped.

They should have all been more relaxed.

Knowlton had been dead now for several days. All the paperwork was done. There had been a dozen interviews with all manner of law enforcement, and then with major broadcasters and newspaper journalists. The Perry Knowlton story was still holding reign over the internet, TV, and papers and magazines everywhere.

That day, however, had not been about Perry Knowlton for Sarah and her friends.

That afternoon, they had gathered to bury Hannah Levine. There had been tears of sorrow and regret; friendship was a terrible thing to lose. And as they'd gathered at the grave after services, Sarah was pretty sure they were all looking back over the years and wondering how the killings at Cemetery Mansion had cost so many their lives—and left behind survivors who were emotionally crippled. There was no way out of wondering how they had let Hannah down. Each individual alive was responsible for his or her own life—they knew that. But they also knew human relationships were priceless and, for most, essential for living.

Sarah had been named as Hannah's next of kin. She arranged for a really beautiful nondenominational ceremony. Hannah's dad had been Jewish, her mom a Methodist, but Sarah wasn't sure Hannah had adhered to either religion. Or any.

But she had been left in charge. And Sarah wanted very much to believe in God and goodness and a higher power. She thought the service was not religious, but spiritual. She guessed Hannah would have liked it.

After the funeral and burial, they gathered at Finnegan's. And just as they had felt lost before, they were all trying to tie up the last little skeins of confusion in their own minds.

"I wonder… I mean, when you were trying to find Knowlton, find out if he could be alive…you found so many other victims. How will…how will you make all that go together?" Sean asked, sipping his beer.

"Agents in my office will do what they can to find out what happened where and when," Craig said. "Most forensic work does take time. We were incredibly lucky—beyond lucky, considering Knowlton's sudden surge toward suicide in his determination to kill you all—that we did make the right calculations in following his movements."

"And we're lucky Sarah got us out!" Suzie said, lifting her glass of white wine to Sarah.

"You knew his voice. After ten years, you recognized his voice," she answered.

"And Davey was ready to move quickly!" Sean said.

"To Davey—our hero!" Tyler said.

They all lifted their glasses to Davey. He smiled and lifted his Shirley Temple. "To best friends forever!" he said, and then grinned. "And to Megan. I get to see my girlfriend tomorrow!"

Everyone laughed. He passed a picture of Megan around. They all assured him she was a pretty girl, and she was.

There was a stretch of silence around the table, and then Tyler spoke.

"I really wish we could have taken him alive," he said. "There was a lot we could have learned from him. I still want to know how the hell he broke in to the playground to be able to display the poor woman he killed, thinking she was our Suzie."

"I do, too," Craig said. "But since he was aiming at your heart, you had no choice but to fire. You know, he would have shot you—and then Sarah. And then he'd have gone for Davey and killed anyone else in his way—until he was stopped. Our agents are still in the hospital. Guzman might be out in a day or two. Luckily, Knowlton didn't really know how to kill someone with a knock on the head. Walsh—the fellow we found in the subway tunnel—will be another week or so. But his prognosis is good. Then there's the cop he shot on the street—he'll be in the hospital for a few weeks. Needs several surgeries. So, Tyler, yeah, you shot and killed him. You saved your own life—and probably others."

Sarah made a mental note to visit the agents and the police officer in the hospital. She hadn't done so yet.

"How did he find us?" Suzie wondered.

"He wasn't just good at hiding," Tyler said. "He excelled at being a people watcher. He was excellent at observation, something he learned—according to earlier notes we recently dug back up from the horror park murders—from the man he admired and all but worshipped, Archibald Lemming. The guards had said that Lemming loved to hold court—and Knowlton loved to listen and learn. Patience, Lemming had taught him, was a virtue. So Knowlton discovered the safe house—by lurking around in any number of his disguises and maybe by following one of us. He watched, and he found an agent he could take by surprise. He was adept at so many things, and he was able to bide his time and wait."

"And," Craig said, "we found out that he stole his 'Adler' FBI identification three years ago. The man did know how to wait and bide his time. He took Special Agent Walsh down for his plain blue suit—and to keep him from showing up at work. He called in sick on Walsh's phone, left him to die in the tunnel—after stealing his gun. Once you all escaped him and he was out on the street, I think he decided he'd kill until he was killed himself—but of course, we were the focus of the rage he's had brewing for the last decade."

They talked awhile longer; they enjoyed shepherd's pie.

Then Suzie and Sean prepared to leave, hugging everyone.

"We need to keep in touch this time," Suzie said. "I think... I think we're relieved and grateful—and sad. But..."

"But we will keep in touch—I've missed you, Suzie. Yes, we will be haunted by what happened to Hannah. But we'll stay friends this time. And I think it will help," Sarah assured her, hugging her tightly in return.

Sean shook hands with Tyler, then the two embraced. "Hey, Boston isn't that far, my friend. We have to all keep in touch," he said.

Tyler nodded. "Yes. Of course."

Sarah noted he didn't refute the fact that Boston wasn't far.

Her heart sank a little. He was returning to his old life; she would be returning to hers.

She thought of the nights they'd been together since Knowlton had died. They had been intense.

They hadn't talked yet. Not really talked. They had made plans for Hannah's funeral. They had answered any last-minute questions they could for the police and the FBI.

It had been easier just to be together.

Davey got up from the table. He was anxious to leave; Renee was taking him for a haircut so he could look his best when he saw Megan.

"I got a girlfriend!" he reminded them all.

Soon after, Tyler smiled at Sarah and asked her softly if she was ready to go.

She nodded.

They weren't staying at the hotel any longer. They went to her apartment on Reed Street.

When the door was closed, he pulled her into his arms and very tenderly kissed her lips.

And suddenly, all the things she wanted to say came tumbling out of her mouth. "I'm so sorry. I don't know why. I think I was always afraid…maybe I didn't want to be hurt myself, and so I tried to make sure Davey wasn't hurt. It seemed to be a way to cope. There are bad people out there…or sometimes, just rude and unkind people. I haven't been… I've been… I just knew how some people felt some of the time, and I love my aunt and Davey and my family, and… I…there was really no excuse. I never meant to push you away. I just didn't want others to feel they had to take on my responsibility—"

His finger fell on her lips. "Some people want part of your responsibility."

"Oh, I know that! And I should have had faith in Davey being sweet and wonderful in his own right, I just…"

To her astonishment, Tyler slipped down to his knees. He looked up at her, eyes bright, and pulled a small box from his pocket. He flicked it open, offering it to her.

"Sarah, I've loved you forever. I've loved you when I was with you and when I wasn't with you. When I was away, you interfered with everything I would try to do, because I could never get you out of my memory…my heart, my soul. Sarah, we've wasted a decade of life, and life, as we all know, is precious. So…will you marry me?"

She was speechless, and then she fell to her knees in turn and began to kiss him. And they both started to shed their clothing, there on the hardwood at the entry to the apartment. When they were halfway stripped, he suddenly laughed, stood and pulled her up. "Let's not celebrate with bruises!" he said. She laughed, too, and she was in his arms again.

Making love had always been amazing. That afternoon...

Every touch, breath and intimacy seemed deeper, more sensual, more erotic. More climatic.

He stroked her back. Rolled and kissed her shoulder.

"Hmm. I think we celebrated. But you haven't actually said yes!"

"Yes! Yes...yes..."

She punctuated every yes with a kiss.

"I can go anywhere. I mean, we are New Yorkers, but Boston is a great city," she said breathlessly. "I can and will go anywhere in the world with you. We can have a big wedding, we can elope, we can do anything at all. None of it matters to me, except being with you, waking up with you, going to sleep with you..." She stopped, then straddled him with a grin. "My Lord! I could write romance again. Giant bugs—and romance!"

He laughed. He pulled her to him, and they talked and talked, and made love again.

No big wedding. They weren't going to wait that long. A small ceremony at Finnegan's, applauded by whomever might be there, with just Kieran and Craig and Suzie and Sean—and, of course, their families, including—very especially—Davey and Aunt Renee.

Sometime that night, very late that night, they finally slept.

Sarah felt that she was walking on air. She'd called Kieran, who was at work at the offices of Fuller and Miro, but she could meet for lunch.

Relief was an amazing thing. Or maybe it was happiness. So much time wasted, and yet maybe not wasted. She and Tyler had both grown through the years.

And now...

Now they were together. And she was going to marry him. It wasn't even that marriage mattered so much to her—that she would wake up every morning next to Tyler did. That wherever they went, whatever they did, she could go to sleep with him at night.

She'd loved him as long as she could remember.

And now...

The morning had been good. She had worked on her latest manuscript; an Egyptian connection, not through Mars, but through a distant planet much like Earth. The people had been advanced, kind and intelligent, and very much like human beings. A war with a nearby hostile planet had kept them away, and a shift in the galaxies had closed the wormhole they had used to reach Earth. But archeologist and mathematician Riley Maxwell had been with an expedition that had found a tablet, and the tablet had told them about the "newcomers," the "gods," who had come down from space and taught them building and water usage. Soon after her discovery, she was visited by a newcomer to their group, Hank McMillan, and he had been just as anxious to destroy all that she had discovered. And as they worked together and came under attack by a group with strange and devastating weapons, she'd begun to fall in love...all the while discovering Hank was an ancient alien, trying to close all the doors before the still hostile and warlike tribe arrived to devastate Earth...

Of course, they solved it all and lived happily ever after. Her outline was complete!

At eleven thirty, she left her apartment, smiling as she headed toward Broadway to walk down to Finnegan's.

Her steps were light.

She forgot all about the fact that New Yorkers supposedly didn't make eye contact.

She smiled and, yes, people smiled back.

It was a beautiful day, chilly, but with a bright sun high in the sky.

She was surprised when a police car pulled up by the corner ahead of her. She heard her name being called and, frowning, she hurried forward.

Happiness could be its own enemy. She was immediately afraid something had happened to Tyler. Or that something was wrong somewhere. Davey! Her aunt!

She rushed over to the car. Alex Morrison was at the wheel, and he was smiling.

"Hey, I'm glad I found you so easily!"

"You were looking for me? You could have called."

"Well, this just all came about. Hop in. I'll take you to Tyler."

"Oh. Is he all right?" she asked anxiously.

"He's fine, he's fine. We're working on putting some pieces together. With other events, you know?" he said somberly. "Anyway, come on, I'll get you to him and Craig."

"I have a lunch date with Kieran. I'll just give her a call."

"No need. We'll pick up Tyler and Craig and head to Finnegan's." He grimaced. "I can park anywhere with this car, you know."

"Sure. Okay." She walked around and slid into the passenger's seat and grinned at Alex. "You know, I've never ridden in a patrol car!" she said. "I'll give Tyler a call and then let Kieran know that we might be a few minutes late."

"Oh, that won't be necessary!" he said, reaching over. She thought he was going for the radio.

He wasn't.

He made a sudden movement and backhanded her so hard that her head spun, then crashed into the door frame. Stars went reeling before her eyes.

Shadows and darkness descended over her, but she fought it.

Not now. Even as she felt her consciousness slipping away, she struck out.

"Damn you, tough girl, huh!"

Before he could hit her again, she scratched him. Hard. And as the darkness claimed her from his second blow, she knew that, at the very least, she'd drawn blood.

Tyler was back in Craig's office at the FBI. The Bureau's analysts had pulled up a number of murders, facts and figures, and they were still going over them. Victims had families. And, Tyler had discovered, not knowing what had happened to a loved one was torture for most families. "Closure" was almost a cliché. And yet it was something very real and necessary.

He was frowning when Craig asked him, "What? What now? There's something you don't like."

"There's something niggling me about that damned poem. I wanted to take Knowlton alive."

"Yeah, well, better that *you're* alive," Craig reminded him. "But… I do see what you mean. Knowlton claimed Hannah. She was dumped in the river."

"And Suzie Cornwall was left in a park."

"He could have been working on his methods. What he did wasn't easy—getting himself and a body over the fence. Setting the body up. The head—in a swing."

"Have they found any kin for her?" Tyler asked.

"No, but she had friends. Only, her friends didn't really seem to have much of anything. No one has offered a burial. Instead of the potter's field on this one, I thought the four of us might want to chip in quietly and bury her."

"Works for me," Tyler said.

He was quiet again. Then he quoted, "'But now they pay the price today...six little children. One of them dead. Soon the rest will be covered in red.'"

"I admit it bothers me, too."

"But I shot and killed him. So we'll never know."

"Is it possible for us to look through the photographs again?"

"Of course."

Craig left the office. Reports lay on the desk. Tyler started going over them again.

DNA.

The little vertebra Knowlton had sent to the FBI with his poem had proved to belong to Hannah Levine, not Suzie Cornwall.

That bothered Tyler as much as the poem. If the bone had just belonged to Suzie Cornwall...

He started reading the autopsy reports again. So much was so similar. Except...

Hannah had alcohol and drugs in her system. Suzie...

She'd had her medication. Dr. Langley believed her throat had been slit, prior to her head being removed.

Hannah...

Hard to tell, with the way her head and torso had been found, washed up from the river.

He drummed his fingers on the table. No usable forensics had been found at the park. It was almost as if whoever had done the crime had studied books on how the police found killers, on what little bits of blood and biological trace could give them away.

Craig walked back into his office. "I got what I could. I called over to Detective Green, asking if Morrison could make sure we had everything, but Alex Morrison called in sick today. He's not there to help me get everything, but at this point, I do think I have it all."

Tyler looked at Craig, listening to the words. And suddenly, he was up and on his feet, not even sure why, thoughts jumbling in his mind.

Alex Morrison had been at the theme park the night Archibald Lemming had killed so many in Cemetery Mansion.

He'd started out in the academy and had gone into forensics.

He knew what was going on with the police—and the FBI.

"We need to find him," Tyler said. "We need to find Alex Morrison."

Sarah came to very slowly.

She wasn't at all sure of where she was. Somewhere deep and dank... It had a smell of mold and age and... earth.

She tried to move; she was tied up, she realized. Fixed to a chair. Her ankles were bound, her arms had been pulled behind her and her wrists secured.

Her head pounded. Her arms hurt. She ached all

over. The world was horribly askew. She had to blink and blink.

Reality overwhelmed her. She was a prisoner. And it was perfectly clear. Knowlton hadn't committed all the murders. They had known something wasn't right. Alex Morrison had been a living, breathing, functioning psychopath all the time. So helpful! So helpful as he used everything they had learned, so helpful as he ever so subtly turned them toward Perry Knowlton.

A functioning psychopath? Maybe Kieran could explain such a thing...

She tried to move.

She realized she could struggle, but the best she could ever do would be tip the chair over.

Panic seized her. There was barely any light. She heard a strange droning sound, like a piece of machinery moving...

She grew accustomed to the dim light. Blinking, she saw that, ten feet from her, Alex Morrison was busy at some kind of a machine. She realized, nearly passing out again, it was some kind of a knife sharpener. Battery operated, certainly, but...

Did it matter how the hell it was operated? He was sharpening his knife. To slit her throat, and then decapitate her.

This was where he had killed Suzie Cornwall. He'd made the mistake—not Knowlton. He'd killed her here, then he'd used a patrol car to dump her body. Easy enough. People seldom questioned a patrol car in a neighborhood, or an officer checking out a fence, or a park, or—

He turned.

"Ah, awake, I see! Oh, Sarah. I could have been nice

and seen to it that I dispatched you before…well, you know. Before. But then again, your kind deserves to feel some pain!"

"My kind?"

She wished Kieran was with her. Kieran might know how to talk to such a man. A functioning psychopath.

But Kieran wasn't here. Sarah had to think as her friend might—as any desperate person might think! Think to talk, think to survive—until help could come!

But how and why would help come? No one knew where she was. Everyone thought all the danger was over. No one knew…

There was no chance of help!

And still she had to hang on. While there was breath, she had once heard, there was hope.

And everything suddenly lay before her. Tyler, their future life together that they had managed to deny one another years ago…

"What is my kind, Alex?" she asked again.

He looked at her, leaning against the shoddy portable picnic table that held his knife sharpener.

"Cheerleader!" he said.

"What?"

"Cheerleader. You know your kind!"

"Oh, my God, Alex. I haven't been a cheerleader in over a decade."

"You were a cheerleader then."

"When?"

"Oh, come on, Sarah, give me a break! That night… at Cemetery Mansion. You were a cheerleader. Oh, yes. You had your football-playing hunk with you and your retard cousin."

"Don't you dare use that word around me!"

"Whatever."

"Oh, you idiot! That's why people suffer so much in this life—that's the reason Tyler and I haven't been together. How dare you! Davey is an incredible human being. But I didn't believe Tyler really saw that—*because of people like you, you asshole!*"

She was startled to realize her rage had apparently touched him.

"Okay, okay, well, maybe you're right about Davey. I mean…from what I understand, it was somehow him who managed to bring about the fall of Archibald Lemming. A brilliant man like Lemming."

"A brilliant psychopath and killer, you mean. Not so brilliant, was he? He's dead. And Perry Knowlton, well, what an idiot!"

"Ah, but you aren't seeing *my* genius. Knowlton got sloppy. He got sloppy—because he was afraid I would strike again before he could. He wanted so badly to kill you all himself! Not to mention it was useful to me for everyone to suspect him. I overheard that bit about their stomach contents—steak. Oh, I loved it! What a cool clue to lead nowhere—the women just both liked steak. I wished that Tyler had gone a little crazier on the hunt for a steak house, but still! So gratifying. I did such a good job. I followed Knowlton, and I learned from watching. I learned my lessons well. And I was a step ahead."

"You're an ass. You killed the wrong Suzie Cornwall."

His eyes narrowed. "Well, I won't kill the wrong Sarah Hampton, will I?" he asked her.

"How did you get your victim over the fence?" she demanded.

He laughed. "Databases! I found a way to get a key.

I opened the lock. I walked in with her leaned against me, like someone who needed assistance—maybe lost something like a cell phone, you know? I just looked like a city worker, a peon. It wasn't so hard. In fact, it was exciting. I had her body leaned against me, her head in a cooler, and I opened the lock and just walked on in. Then…fun. Setting her up. Locking the gates again. Exhilarating! It was great."

Sarah forced a smile. "They will know it's you. You've gotten away with a lot. Let me see…the night at Cemetery Mansion. You thought you wanted to be a cop— that would be a way to see murder and horrible things… and get paid for it! You were in forensics and you were called to the scene. And you saw exactly how gruesome all the blood and guts and gore could be."

"I admired Archibald Lemming to no end," he agreed. "Even as I took pictures of his cold, dead body."

"And you knew Perry Knowlton was still alive."

"I watched him leave the park."

"And you spent the next years trying to find him. Did you?"

"I did, about a month ago. But I never let on. I just watched. And after he killed Hannah…well, I thought I'd help him along. I have access to all kinds of information. I wanted to give him all the precious scoop I could get my hands on. Then maybe we could become partners. But hey…he ignored me. Ignored me! But now the police and your precious FBI friends are all patting themselves on the back. They think they're all in the clear. Well, I've got you—and before they find you, I'll have your darling Davey, too!"

"Davey is too smart for you," she said. "He was too

smart for Archibald Lemming, and for Perry Knowlton—and he'll be too smart for you!"

Alex Morrison smiled. "You try to protect him—well, you would have. Too bad I didn't have you around...before. Oh, but you wouldn't have helped me. The cheerleaders laughed at me. The football players... well, I spent some time stuffed in a locker. Oh, and I had my head stuck in a toilet. And you know what my folks did when it happened? My mother put my head in the toilet, yelling at me to stand up. And my old man—you know what he did? He beat me with a belt—told me a man would handle himself. Well, I'm handling myself now. I'm ridding the world of cheerleaders and football players and popular people who stuff others in lockers. I mean, come on, seriously—they all need to go, right?"

"Can it be this easy?" Craig asked.

Tyler wasn't thinking anything was easy. Sarah wouldn't answer her phone.

She was supposed to have met Kieran.

She hadn't.

Alex Morrison was nowhere to be found.

Craig hadn't tried to placate Tyler. He'd never suggested Sarah was all right somewhere, that she'd just forgotten her phone. That she was an adult and had just gotten busy.

There was no lie to believe in, and they hadn't tried to invent one. Time was everything; they didn't have much.

They had to find Sarah.

But Craig was right. They'd easily used the system to find the patrol car Morrison had been using.

And now they were using GPS on his phone.

Tyler was functioning. Get in the car, move, walk, use his mind...

Find Sarah, find Sarah...

But all the while, he was fighting terror again, that almost overwhelming terror he'd felt when they'd realized Perry Knowlton had taken down an FBI agent and was heading to the safe house.

Did Alex Morrison really believe he could get away with this? Would it matter, would anything matter, if he managed to kill Sarah?

"He's here, right on this spot," Craig said, frustrated. "We've got the old subway map, but I can't find anywhere that's an entry." He paused, looking around the street.

Tyler did the same; he stared at the map again. He scanned the buildings intently.

At the corner was an old stone apartment block. There was a grate, a vent from the massive subway system and underground city below.

It was New York. There were grates in sidewalks everywhere.

But the building appeared to have gone up in the early 1900s.

Right about the same time as the subway.

And the facade had never been changed.

He didn't speak; he rushed ahead of Craig and bent to pull on the grate. It seemed too tight. Craig reached past him, helping him twist the metal.

It gave.

There was a short leap down to an empty little room.

But as his eyes adjusted, Tyler saw an old wooden door.

And the door opened to a flight of ancient, worn stairs.

He and Craig looked at one another.

Tacitly silent, they started down.

At least Tyler prayed that he was silent. To him, his heart seemed to be beating loudly in an agonized staccato.

Alex Morrison came and hunkered down before Sarah, studying his well-honed knife and then looking at her with a satisfied smile.

"I guess I did want to torture you in a way. I mean, I spent days with my head in a toilet due to a cheerleader."

"I never did anything to anyone, Alex. I just liked cheerleading—I was good at gymnastics. And Tyler was never cruel to anyone in his life. He worked with a lot of the kids who weren't so good, on his own time. He got the coaches to have special days and special races... You're so wrong! Yes, people can be cruel. Kids can be cruel. We all know that, and to most of us, it's deplorable. I didn't have enough faith in people. But you... you're just a truly sad and pathetic case! Kill me. Do it. But it will never end what you feel. It won't help the hatred and rancor that fester constantly within you!"

As she finished speaking, she heard something.

She wasn't sure what.

Rats?

And then she saw. She didn't know how. It seemed impossible.

Tyler was there. Tyler and Craig. They had somehow known, had somehow found her...

Tyler made a motion to tell her to keep talking.

And she realized her position. Tyler was there, yes. And Craig. But Alex Morrison was in front of her. All but touching her. And he had his freshly honed, razor-sharp carving knife in his hands.

"You're wrong!" Alex was saying. "You're wrong. Every time I kill, I feel a little better. I feel I've sent one of you bitches or bastards on to a just reward!"

"You really should have gotten to spend a lot more time with Kieran Finnegan. She's a psychologist, not a psychiatrist—though her bosses are psychiatrists. She could explain to you that no, you were never going to feel better. I don't really get all of it—I majored in English and mass communication—but there are sociopaths and there are psychopaths. I believe, by the definitions I've heard, you might be the first. I'm not all that sure."

He moved the knife, waving it in an S through the air.

"She could help you."

"I don't want to be helped."

Sarah had never thought it was possible for such large men to move with such silent ease.

But Tyler and Craig had moved across the floor. Tyler was almost at her side. Craig was slightly behind Alex and to his left.

"Alex—"

"Hmm. Maybe I'm...oh, I don't know. But you know, Sarah, I think that if we'd been in high school together, you wouldn't have made fun of me. I think I will be merciful. I was merciful with Suzie. I wasn't so good to that bitchy runaway up in Sleepy Hollow. I sawed at her neck while she was alive. You—I'm going to see to it you bleed out quickly, quickly, quickly!"

"Hey, you!" Tyler called.

Stunned, Morrison swung around. He had his knife

out and slashing, but it never made contact. Tyler slammed his arm down on Morrison's so hard and fast the knife went flying and the man screamed in pain.

Craig dived for the chair, spinning Sarah around, then cutting the ropes.

Sarah saw Alex Morrison was on his knees, staring up at Tyler with pure hatred.

His arm dangled at his side.

"I didn't shoot him, Craig," Tyler said. "Maybe we can get something out of him."

"After he's locked up," Craig said.

Sarah could hear sirens again.

Broken arm or not, Craig Frasier was seeing to it that Alex Morrison was handcuffed.

And Sarah was back in Tyler's arms.

"It's over," he told her as she broke into sobs. "It's truly over."

And she knew it was.

Only the nightmares would remain, and if she could wake from them in Tyler's arms, eventually, they would be over, too.

It was a strange honeymoon, Tyler thought, but a great one.

The wedding, just as they had planned, took place at Finnegan's. They'd spent a few days alone in the Poconos, and now...

Sarah had needed to see Davey, and Tyler understood. Best of all was that Sarah believed he understood.

And so...

Buzzers were ringing. Bells were chiming. Neon lights were flashing.

There really was nowhere like Vegas.

And it was great; the actual "honeymoon" part of their extended honeymoon had been personal and intimate and amazing.

And now...

Sean and Suzie had joined them. They were seeing shows, going to music events, hanging out at the hotel's stunning pool. And at night...well, they were making love in their exquisite room.

Ever since the day Tyler had rescued Sarah from Morrison, they'd planned their lives, and were living them to the fullest.

He was coming back to New York. He was going to move his investigations office there.

He could consult with police, or the FBI, since now he had some useful and friendly connections.

And Sarah would keep writing.

She was really much better than ever, she assured him. He had given her that—a greater passion for her work!

It was their last night in Vegas. Tomorrow, they'd head back and get on with their regular lives. Somehow, to Tyler, those words held a touch of magic. Real magic. They'd weathered so much.

They would continue to weather what the future might bring.

They were playing slots at the moment, because Davey loved them so much and could spend hours at a machine with a twenty-dollar bill.

Tyler was pretty sure that Davey's greatest pleasure was hitting the call button for the waitress, smiling broadly when a pretty woman brought him a Shirley

Temple and then grinning toward Tyler or Sarah so that one of them would tip her.

Tyler was watching Davey when Sarah finished playing at a silly cow slot machine that said, "Moo!" every few minutes. He reached out a hand, pulling her over to sit on his lap at the stool where he'd found a place to perch.

She leaned against him. They didn't speak.

Life…

It was full of relationships. Cruel parenting had helped shape Alex Morrison. A brutal lack of empathy and lack of friendship had helped put the nails in the coffin of his psyche.

Tyler knew he'd been lucky.

He'd had a great family. And so had Sarah. And now, so close, they both had Aunt Renee and Davey.

Love was an amazing thing. There could never be too much love for many people in one's life.

And, of course, there was that one special love. Some people were lucky enough to know it when they had a chance to hold it, and hold it fast.

A forever kind of love.

Sarah was smiling at him.

He smiled back.

And it was evident, of course, but he whispered the words.

"I love you," he said.

"And I love you," she whispered back.

Davey had risen. He threw his arms around the both of them. "And I love you!" he said. "Come on, we gotta go up! Gotta get home tomorrow. I have a girlfriend, you know."

Laughing, they rose. It was time to go up to their rooms.

Tyler thought there was nothing wrong at all with a last night with Sarah in that exquisite bed!

* * * * *

MARCHING ORDERS

Delores Fossen

To my editor, Priscilla Berthiaume.
Thanks so much for your guidance and support.

Prologue

Monte de Leon, present

A bullet slammed into the crumbling chimney just inches from Captain Rafe McQuade's head. He mumbled some vicious profanity and flattened his body against the battered roof of the abandoned hacienda.

"I've got an admirer," he snarled into the thumbnail-size communicator on the collar of his camouflage uniform. "Do me a favor, Rico, and take him out, will you?"

"I'm trying" was the reply he got from Captain Cal Rico.

All hell was breaking loose on the ground twenty feet below him. Artillery shells. Frantic shouts. The smell of battle, smoke and gunfire.

None of which was supposed to be happening.

Talk about Murphy's Law. Anything that could go wrong, had. And now his Alpha Team members—and Anna—were neck-deep in cross fire between two warring rebel factions that had chosen this godforsaken place for a showdown.

Rafe inched forward, leaving the meager cover of the overhanging tree that he'd used to climb onto the building. His equipment belt and assault rifle scraped along the bleached roof tiles.

Come hell or high water, he would get Anna out. Failure was not an option.

"Infrared shows no one else inside the building. For now," Rico informed him through the receiver in Rafe's ear. "But Anna just moved into the cellar. You can access it through a door beneath the stairs."

"Atta girl," Rafe mumbled. With gunfire riddling the papery walls, the cellar was her best bet. Now, hopefully, she'd stay put until he got to her.

"I'm going in," he informed Rico.

Rafe scrambled to the lip of the roof, gripped onto the eaves and launched himself over the side. His feet crashed through the second-story window just below, and with his weapon ready to fire, he hit the floor running.

The hacienda had obviously been abandoned for months. Rafe fought his way through the litter of bashed furniture and debris to get to the stairs. He stopped at the landing and glanced down at the glass-strewn foyer. No sign of gunmen, but someone had shot out the windows and ripped off the double doors. The muggy breeze stirred what was left of a pair of ghostly white curtains. Just curtains.

Maybe.

Just outside the doorway, he saw a shadow of motion that had him holding his tongue.

Silently repositioning his weapon, Rafe waited. A second. Then two. Before he saw the man step into the foyer. A rebel fighter with an angry-looking machete and a semiautomatic. And he had his attention focused on the door that led to the cellar. Maybe the guy had actually seen Anna run in there. It didn't matter. There was no way Rafe would let him get to her.

No way.

The man looked up. A split-second glance as he tried to take aim. It was the last glance or aim he'd ever attempt. Rafe took him out with two shots to the head. The rebel fell into a heap on the floor.

"I just lost an admirer," Rafe reported to Rico.

Rafe barreled down the wide spiraling steps and made his way to the arch-shaped door beneath. "It's me—Rafe," he called out. "Open up, Anna!"

Almost immediately he heard her footsteps on the cellar stairs. With each one, his heart was right in his throat. There was a shuffle of movement before she opened the scarred door a fraction.

Rafe came face-to-face with a handgun.

Anna peered out at him, her gaze combing the foyer. Relief raced through him. And a whole host of other emotions that he didn't want to take the time to analyze.

"You came," she whispered, her voice shattering. She lowered her weapon. "I can't believe you came."

He pushed her back into the cellar and kicked the door shut, barricading it with the two-by-four and equipment bag already on the stairs. "Of course, I came. I'm an Air Force Combat Rescue Officer, darling. A highly trained CRO. Saving beautiful photographers is what I do best."

She made a soft sound of frightened laughter, slipped her firearm into her pocket and caught on to him.

Rafe was about to tell her how ticked off he was that she hadn't evacuated with the other journalists, but Anna stopped him. She latched her arms around him, and her mouth came to his. One kiss, and he forgot all about chewing her out.

Hell, he forgot how to breathe.

All Rafe knew was that he'd never, never wanted a kiss as much as he wanted that one.

Anna broke the mouth-to-mouth contact but held on tight. Rafe pushed the damp strands of honey-colored hair from her face and looked down at her. Her dark eyes shimmered with tears. Outside, the sounds of the fight began to fade, a clear indication that the Alpha Team was closing in.

"Anna's alive and well?" Rico asked into Rafe's earpiece.

Before he could answer, Rafe had to clear away the lump that'd settled in his throat. "Affirmative. Are we secure yet?"

"Only the area immediately surrounding the hacienda. Colonel Shaw's arranging transport for Anna, but you're looking at two hours, maybe three. I'll give you a rendezvous point and time when I have it. Hold your positions until further orders."

"Copy." Rafe clicked off the audio portion of his communicator. Two hours, maybe three. He could have waited weeks now that he knew Anna was all right.

"How did you find out I was here?" she asked, lifting her head from his shoulder.

"The Alpha Team's doing some jungle maneuvers so I've been keeping track of you since you arrived in Bogotá on assignment three days ago."

Anna gave him a considering look. "And with all the jungles in South America, you just happened to choose the remote village of Monte de Leon for those maneuvers?"

Rafe decided it was best to avoid answering that truthfully. "In a way."

A troubled sigh left her mouth, but she didn't ask for an explanation. Which was a good thing. He couldn't tell her about the classified mission that involved the Alpha Team, or the fact that he'd made sure he was close by in case something went wrong.

Rafe led her down the narrow steps and into the heart of the cellar. It was clammy, and the only light came from a bread-loaf size ventilation window at the back. He moved them as far away from that as he could, and with her snuggled in his arms, he sank onto a crumpled blanket in the corner.

"Soon we'll both be on our way back to Texas. Promise. Everything will be all right," he assured her.

Rafe leaned in and brushed his mouth over hers. It might have been just a brief kiss if she hadn't made a sound of relief, and pleasure. A throaty, feminine sound that sent a trickle of fire through his blood.

So, he kissed her, really kissed her, and deepened it when she responded.

Their bodies moved together, completing the intimate embrace. She wound her arms around him. Rafe did the same. Until they were plastered against each other.

Not good.

She latched on to his shoulders when he started to move away. "Is there any chance those rebels can get into this place?"

"Don't worry. We're safe."

Something he couldn't quite distinguish went through her eyes, and before he could figure out what, her mouth came to his again. Rafe felt the difference in her kiss. Not fear. Not this. This was all fire and need.

"Anna," he warned when she lay back onto the blanket. If he wanted to keep things in check, this probably shouldn't continue.

But it did.

Anna caught on to the front of his uniform and pulled him down with her. The logical part of his brain yelled that this would be hellish torture, but the rest of him didn't seem to care. While still holding on to his weapon, he buried his other hand in her hair and took her mouth as if it were his for the taking.

Rafe kissed her chin. Her neck. And the tender flesh that he found in the vee opening of her shirt. Anna arched against him, whispering his name.

When her leg brushed against the front of his pants, she stiffened slightly, obviously noticing that he was a dozen steps past basic foreplay. She didn't pull away, though. Not that he gave her much of a chance. Rafe knew this couldn't go where his body wanted it to go, but he wasn't ready to stop just yet.

While he kept up the assault on her neck, he opened the buttons on her shirt. One at a time. Slowly. As he bared her skin, he dropped kisses along the way until he reached her bra. It wasn't much of a barrier, a little swatch of pale-colored lace. He eased it down and took a moment to admire the view.

Thankfully, there was just enough light that he could see her. She was beautiful. And he didn't mean just her breasts and her body. Rafe stared down at her face and wondered what the hell he'd ever done to deserve her.

He lowered his head and brushed his tongue against one of her tightened nipples. She clamped on to her bottom lip, but not before she moaned with pleasure. He hadn't especially needed that kind of encouragement, but it sped up his plans a little. He drew her nipple into his mouth.

Anna's grip tightened around him. She arched her back and forced him closer. Rafe feasted. First one breast and then the other.

She stirred restlessly. Seeking. She pressed her lower body to his and had him seeing double when she moved against him in the most intimate kind of way that a woman could move against a man.

"I've been in this building for what seemed like an eternity," she whispered. "Thinking about you. About us. About how fragile life is. I want to be with you, Rafe, and I don't want to wait any longer."

He watched the words shape her lips. He'd already geared himself up to resist the need raging in his body. That's what he'd done for the past four and a half months since Anna had told him that she was a virgin and wouldn't give herself to a man she didn't love.

But those words changed everything.

He was about to remind her that it was the adrenaline talking, but Anna stopped him. She pressed her fingers to his mouth. "I love you, Rafe, and I don't want you to say anything. I just want you to do something about it."

His heart slammed against his chest. He had two simultaneous thoughts. *Thank goodness* and *oh, hell*.

Her timing couldn't have been worse. Ditto for the location. In fact, everything about the moment was wrong, wrong, wrong except for one major thing: somehow or another, it was right.

Totally, completely right.

Rafe let that sink in for a couple of moments. It sank in and went straight to his heart.

Maybe Anna didn't want the words now, but he sure as heck would say them to her later. Words to let her know that he didn't want to be just her first, or even her last, but her *only* lover.

He reached out, pulled her to him and took everything she offered.

Chapter 1

The moment Rafe slid his arm around her waist, Anna felt the jolt. Definitely not passion. Something else. Something she'd felt stirring just beneath the surface since his return three days earlier.

"No turning back now, darling," Rafe drawled, his voice low and intimate. The corner of his mouth hitched, causing a dimple to flash. "We've officially been joined at the hip."

"Yes," Anna managed to say.

She swallowed hard.

Rafe gently cupped her chin and leaned closer for the kiss that would seal the vows they had just taken. His hand trembled a little, and he closed the already narrow distance between them.

Their bodies came together. His crisp uniform whispered over the delicate layers of her silk-and-lace gown. Beneath her own trembling hand, Anna felt the strip of cool medals on his jacket and heard them jangle softly. All things considered, it was as perfect as it could be.

Except for that jolt.

Rafe kept the kiss brief, not much more than a touch. Breath met breath. His was warm and mint-scented. It mingled with the sweet fragrance of the pale peach roses in her bouquet.

"Don't worry," he murmured. The trace of Texas in his voice danced right off his words. "We'll make up for lost time. Promise."

It was the right thing to say. Ditto for the grin that curved his beautifully shaped mouth. But neither of those things made the jolt go away.

What in the name of heaven was wrong with her? She had it all. A mouth-watering husband that she loved. A life she wanted. This was her own personal version of a fairy tale come true. There was no reason for jolts or doubts.

None.

So, why didn't that make her feel better?

The chaplain placed a hand on each of their shoulders and turned them toward the guests. "I'd like to present Captain and Mrs. Rafael McQuade."

Applause rippled through the handful of people. Close friends and Rafe's co-workers, including his commanding officer, Colonel Ethan Shaw. The wedding had been so hastily thrown together that there hadn't been time to invite anyone from out of town. As unsteady as she felt, maybe that was a good thing.

When Rafe stepped away to speak to the guests,

Anna saw her best friend, Janine, make a beeline right for her. Janine didn't waste any time. She draped an arm around Anna's shoulders and pulled her aside. "Okay, is this the part where you tell me what the heck's going on with you?"

Anna didn't stand a chance of denying that jolt. Not with Janine. So, she went for what would hopefully be a believable slant on the truth. "I guess my nerves are still a little raw. I just keep thinking that those rebels could have killed Rafe."

"Uh-huh." Janine gave her a flat look. "That sounds, uh, good, and it might even fool a few people. Not me, of course. Because you see, I'm not buying this I'm-worried-about-Rafe stuff. I was with you during those two months he was held captive in South America. I've seen the look you get when you're worried about him, and this isn't it, Anna."

Maybe not. But this wasn't the place to try to discuss something that might simply be a figment of her overactive imagination.

"Everything will be fine," Anna quickly assured her. With any luck, that was true. "By the way, thanks again for helping put this wedding together. I couldn't have done it without you."

Another flat look. "Does that mean if I keep asking what's wrong, you'll continue to make small talk?"

Anna nodded and put some grit in her voice. "That's exactly what it means."

"Okay." Janine shrugged. "Then small talk it is. Mmm, let's see where we were."

"I was thanking you for your help with the wedding."

"Yes. And I was about to accept your thanks along with any future gifts of gratitude." Janine smiled, caught Anna's hand and lifted it so the light glimmered off the wedding band. "A one-carat, emerald-cut diamond, nearly flawless. Rafe did good by you, huh?"

Anna stared at the ornate band. Since Janine owned a jewelry store and had perhaps helped Rafe pick it out, she wouldn't dare say that it wasn't her style. But it wasn't. Nowhere close.

Funny that Rafe hadn't known that.

She kissed Janine's cheek and got her moving toward the door. "I'll meet you at the reception after the photographer's done."

"More small talk?" Janine questioned.

"Yep. Now, get going."

Janine looked more than a little skeptical but thankfully didn't press the issue. She followed the rest of the guests when they began to trickle out to go to the Officers' Club at the base.

Anna stepped around the photographer, who was making adjustments to his equipment. She knew him and offered a friendly smile. They often did freelance work for the same company.

Rafe sank onto the pew, folded his hands behind his head and stretched his legs out in front of him. There was nothing remotely odd about it. Anna had seen him do that a hundred times. Rafe didn't sit. He lounged. And it was that familiar pose that had her relaxing. It was *normal,* and if that was normal, then probably everything else was, too.

Probably.

As if he'd sensed that she was staring at him, Rafe looked up. "What? Having second thoughts already?" he asked, another grin shoving up the corner of his mouth.

She didn't have time to answer. There was a soft beep. Just one. It came from Colonel Shaw's pocket, and it was more than enough to get her complete attention.

The colonel pulled out the tiny phone and pressed it to his ear. "Alpha One," he said to the person on the other end of the line.

It seemed as if time ground to a screeching halt.

But only for a moment.

Something shattered. A loud deafening blast. Anna whirled toward the sound and saw the jagged multicolored pieces fly through the church. They'd come from the stained glass window behind the altar. Or rather, what was left of it. God, someone was shooting at them.

Just like that, Rafe sprang into action. He whipped out a sleek matte black gun from his shoulder harness and yelled for her to get down. Colonel Shaw did the same and hurried to turn off the lights.

The place was suddenly pitch-black, the darkness closing around her, and Anna found herself standing alone in the middle of a deadly silent room. She dropped to the floor, made her way to the organ and ducked behind it.

Lots of thoughts crossed her mind. None good. This was the culmination of all her nightmares. The rebels had come for Rafe, again, and this time he might not get so lucky.

She heard the footsteps. Barely. They were more movement of air than sound, but she didn't know what direction they were coming from. Not until the hand slid over her mouth.

"It's me," Rafe whispered. "Shhh."

He eased his hand from her mouth and moved her farther behind the organ. Without warning, he pushed her to the floor, a cloud of silk and lace fluffing up around her.

Anna held her breath and tried not to make a sound. Hard to stay quiet though when fear kept trying to grab her by the throat.

The moments crawled by. Slowly, her eyes adjusted to the darkness, and she peered out from behind the thick wooden base of the organ. Colonel Shaw was nowhere in sight. She prayed he hadn't gone outside, alone.

Of course, there weren't many alternatives.

Were there gunmen still out there? Maybe members of the rebel faction that had taken Rafe hostage? Or was this some other special ops mission? Maybe it didn't even matter. After all, a bullet could be deadly no matter what the motivation or cause behind it.

Only threads of moonlight filtered through the thick stained glass windows. It was too dark to see the photographer on the other side of the church, but she could hear him. His breath came out in short, fast spurts.

Unlike Rafe's.

Even though he loomed over her, only inches away, he was completely silent. If he had any reaction to the situation, he certainly didn't show it.

Something darted past one of the windows, casting a sinister shadow over the sanctuary. Rafe must have felt her body tense because he pressed his hand on her shoulder.

"Stay put," he warned in a rough whisper.

Anna latched on to his arm when he moved slightly. "You're not going out there, are you?"

"No. Colonel Shaw would want me to stay here with you. We have people all around the place. They can take care of the situation."

Anna hadn't known about the *people* who were outside guarding the church. But Rafe had. And so had his commanding officer. They obviously assumed something like this could happen, or they wouldn't have made such security arrangements.

What else did they know?

Another shadow slashed across the window, and a swish of sound followed. Maybe a gun rigged with a silencer and maybe just the wind rustling through the trees. But Anna didn't think it was the wind.

"At your six, Rafe," Colonel Shaw called out.

Rafe pivoted, took aim and fired twice. There was a spray of hot lead and glass. A sharp groan of pain.

And then the silence returned.

Anna counted off the seconds with each thud of her heartbeat. She wanted to ask Rafe if he was hurt, but she didn't dare risk it.

"The situation's contained," she heard a man announce. His voice hadn't come from inside the church, however, but out there somewhere on the other side of that shattered window.

The lights flared on, and in the same motion, Rafe sprang to his feet. Seemingly as an afterthought, he held out his hand and offered it to her so he could help her up from the floor.

"Are you okay?" he asked. Rafe reholstered his gun as calmly as he'd drawn it.

No. She wasn't. Along with the incident in Monte de Leon, these had been some of the most terrifying moments of her life. Anna gulped in a huge breath of air and glanced back at a gaping hole in the glass. She caught a glimpse of an Alpha Team member before he darted out of sight.

"What just happened?" she managed to ask.

"We'll know more when the colonel's had a chance to meet with the team." Rafe turned toward the photographer who was cowering near a pew. "Why don't you go ahead and pack up? We'll have pictures done some other time, okay?"

The man eagerly nodded and began to take down the equipment. Anna didn't intend to be placated quite so easily. "What's going on here, Rafe?"

He brushed a kiss on her cheek, took her by the hand and led her to a pew at the back of the church. "I'll go over everything with you after I've spoken to Colonel Shaw."

"In other words, there's something you don't want me to know." And by the time he did tell her, it most certainly wouldn't be *everything*. It would have been processed through layers and layers of debriefings until it was sanitized beyond recognition. "Who was out there?"

"Rafe?" Shaw again. "Come over here. I need a word with you."

Anna grabbed his arm. "I want to know what happened."

It seemed as if he was about to tell her, but then Shaw repeated the order he'd given just moments earlier. "It won't take long," the colonel added. This time, there was some impatience in his voice.

"We'll talk later," Rafe assured her. "And don't worry, everything will be fine."

"It'll be fine when you tell me—"

"Not now, Kate," he snapped. Rafe started to walk away but then came to a complete halt.

Kate.

He'd called her Kate, the name of Colonel Shaw's latest girlfriend.

Anna stared at him and felt her blood run cold.

Oh, my God. Who was this man she'd just married? Who?

One thing was for certain, it wasn't Rafe McQuade. Behind those familiar eyes and face, her husband was a stranger.

Chapter 2

*K*ate.

He'd called her Kate. Talk about a stupid mistake. It could jeopardize everything.

Rafe stared at her while he quickly tried to come up with an apology. Or at least a reasonable explanation. But she didn't look very receptive to whatever he had to say. There were a lot of questions in her eyes. And doubts. Doubts that he'd put there with that slip of the tongue.

How the devil could he have gotten her name wrong?

He lifted his hand to Colonel Shaw in a wait-a-minute gesture and went toward her. She stepped back. Not once. Twice. A clear signal that this wasn't a good time to try to pull her into his arms.

"Why?" she asked, shaking her head. That wasn't the only thing shaking. Her bottom lip was none too steady.

"Because I made a mistake." It was a good start, but he was a long way from undoing the damage. "Because I was scared. The thought of losing you has a way of doing that to me. Believe me, I know who you are."

"Do you?" she demanded.

It wasn't anger he heard in her voice but fear. He would have preferred the anger.

"I know," he assured her. "You're Anna, the woman I love. The woman I married." He eased closer. Baby steps. And kept eye contact with her. Until he could finally reach out and touch her. He ran his fingers along her arm and rubbed gently. "And I'm so sorry."

Her breath settled a little. It wasn't an acceptance by a long shot, but it would have to do for now. Behind him, he could hear Colonel Shaw's impatient murmurings.

"I really need to do this debriefing," Rafe continued. "But when we're done, we'll talk. And if necessary I'll do some groveling, okay?" He threw in a grin, but it did nothing to soothe the tension on her face.

Rafe waited a moment to see if she had anything to say. She didn't. Anna only stared at him.

All right. So, this wasn't a five-minute fix. Not that he'd thought it would be. It was yet another contingency, a bad one, in a day already filled to the brim with contingencies.

"I won't be long." He gave her arm a gentle squeeze, turned and went to his boss.

"Problem?" Shaw asked the moment Rafe joined him on the other side of the church.

Rafe hesitated, debating how much he should tell, but from his boss's demeanor, he already had enough to deal with. "I can handle it. What's the situation with the shooter?"

"The guy's alive but not talking. No ID on him, but they might be able to get something when they run his prints."

It was a long shot, and they both knew it. "Any idea what he was doing out there?"

"He tried to tamper with the communication equipment. The team scoured the area and didn't find anyone else. Seems he was working alone."

Rafe had already figured that part out for himself, but it was good to hear his commanding officer verify it. If there had been others, they wouldn't be having this conversation, and his bride wouldn't be in the pew staring craters in him. The three of them would still be in the dark waiting for the remainder of Alpha Team to contain the situation.

He almost wished they were still waiting it out. Then, he'd have a second chance to take back what he said to Anna.

"I've got someone checking over the equipment to make sure everything is fine," Shaw said, his explanation low enough that Anna wouldn't be able to hear. "And it looks as if we'll have an all clear for you two to leave in a couple of minutes. I'll stay here to wrap up things."

Rafe made a sound of agreement and issued an obligatory thanks and farewell to the photographer when he hurried out the door. The guy looked scared out of his mind, and probably was. A definite case of the wrong place at the wrong time, but at least everyone was alive. It could have been much worse.

Much worse.

Shaw tipped his head to Anna and kept his voice to a whisper. "Is she all right?"

Rafe wanted to say yes, but he couldn't. Besides, with that stunned expression on her face, it was obvious that she was far from all right. "I called her by the wrong name."

"Hell," Shaw mumbled. "How did you explain that?"

"Slip of the tongue. The pressure of the situation. Imperfection." But it wasn't the explanation or excuses that mattered. "Sir, I'm not sure she believes me."

The colonel added another four-letter profanity. "I'll do some damage control," Shaw assured him, his voice a low, rough bark. "Anna trusts me."

It was true, but Rafe almost wished she didn't. If Shaw had been just another officer assigned to Alpha Team and hadn't been close friends with Anna's late father, then maybe the colonel would have come up with a different plan.

One that didn't involve a wedding by direct order.

"She'll find out, eventually," Rafe said more to himself than to Colonel Shaw. From all accounts Anna was a bright woman, and he was bound to make other slipups. Sooner or later, she'd catch on.

If she hadn't already.

Shaw looked him straight in the eye. "But she won't find out until this is over, understand? I won't have you jeopardize the lives of those men—or her—because your conscience is bothering you."

"It isn't my conscience that's giving me a problem, *sir.* It's the notion that we could have gone about this in a different way. We shouldn't have involved her in this."

"She's involved whether you want her to be or not," Shaw declared. "Besides, Anna wanted this marriage."

He could have argued that. He could have reminded the colonel that Anna Caldwell actually wanted to marry Captain Rafe McQuade. When Anna learned that he wasn't that man, she wouldn't be pleased. Worse, there was nothing he could do to stop it. Things had already been set into motion.

Hell, legally he was married to her.

"Just stick with the plan," Shaw continued. He motioned for a team member, Special Agent Luke Buchanan, to join them when he entered the church. "We're too deep into this to back out now. Other than putting her under lock and key, this is the best way to keep her safe."

Rafe was afraid that's what the colonel would say. It didn't make it easier to swallow. "But what about the reception? We're expected there." In fact, it was more than expected. It was a vital part of the plan to generate some publicity.

Shaw blew out a long, frustrated breath. "We'll postpone it. I don't want you out in the open, not after what just happened. I'll come up with an excuse why neither of you can be there."

Rafe followed that through to its logical conclusion. If Anna and he didn't go to the reception, there would be no public appearance. No picture of the happy bride and groom in tomorrow's newspaper. No illusion to build a safety net for Anna and the others. And no diversion for him to make a much-needed exit.

Rafe repeated the four-letter word the colonel had just used.

Shaw checked his watch. "The limo will take you and Anna to the VIP quarters at the base. I'll be here for the next few hours if you need to get in touch with me."

VIP quarters. That wasn't the way things were supposed to work tonight. Shaw didn't give him a chance to remind him of that, but instead stepped away and headed toward Anna. Rafe watched as his boss took his bride's hand and urged her to her feet. Shaw leaned closer and whispered something that had her offering him a thin smile.

"It's apparently show time," Special Agent Buchanan mumbled when he walked closer to Rafe. "Again."

Yep. *Show time* was the right term for it. For the last three days, that was pretty much what all of them had done. It turned Rafe's stomach.

"By the way," Buchanan went on, "have I mentioned that I'll tear you limb from limb if you don't do everything in your power to stop Anna from getting hurt?"

"At least a hundred freaking times." But Rafe didn't hold the man's Neanderthal threat against him. Buchanan knew Anna and the other Alpha Team members. They weren't friends exactly, but this had to be taking a toll on him.

Too bad, though, that Rafe didn't see a way around this. He had to continue this charade, which would likely end with an innocent woman having her heart broken. It was the epitome of a rock and a hard place. And Anna was in the middle of it simply because she'd had the rotten luck to fall in love with the wrong guy.

He glanced over Buchanan's shoulder and saw the colonel and her making their way toward them. For a brief second, their gazes connected, but she quickly looked away. So, despite Shaw's confidence in his pseudo-fatherly relationship with Anna, he hadn't been able to smooth things over, after all.

"I was just telling Anna about that mud-for-brains idiot who thought it was a good idea to try to steal our equipment," Shaw announced. "Rafe winged the guy, but he'll be all right." The colonel passed the bouquet to her, and she gripped on to it as if it were a lifeline. "She's still a little shaken up. Heck, we all are. Right, Rafe?"

He mumbled a mandatory agreement and even tossed in one of his grins.

"How about it—are you sure you're okay?" Buchanan asked her.

Rafe didn't think it was his imagination that she gave Buchanan a suspicious glance, as well. With reason. Anna was probably trying to decide if she could trust any of them.

She finally nodded in response to Buchanan's question. "So, I guess you anticipated something like this might happen, or you wouldn't have had men outside the church?"

Rafe didn't even try to answer that. Thankfully, Colonel Shaw took the lead. "We didn't want to take any chances. Good thing, too, huh?"

"Yes. A good thing." But she didn't sound at all sure of the colonel's explanation.

Colonel Shaw put his arm around her shoulder. "Since you're probably not in a party mood, I thought it might be a good idea if we postpone the reception for a few days. Maybe you and Rafe could just go to the VIP quarters and leave for your honeymoon first thing in the morning? Don't worry. I'll let the guests know what's going on."

She eased out of his grip. "Was that man connected to the rebels who held Rafe hostage?"

"From all accounts, no, but we'll check him out. Don't worry. By tomorrow, we'll know everything about him, including his brand of toothpaste." Colonel Shaw looked at Buchanan and motioned toward the door. "Why don't you and I make sure the limo's ready?"

Rafe mentally cursed. This was a ploy to get him alone with Anna. It was Shaw's way of telling him to finish the damage control he started.

"So we're staying at the base?" Anna asked. Probably because the other two men walked away without answering her, she turned to him. "Is that where we're spending our honeymoon?"

Forcing himself to move, he hooked his arm around her neck. "Nope. That's a surprise, darling. We'll just stay the night there in case the local cops need to talk to me about the shooting."

At least that was probably how the plan would work. They would have to wait in quarters until he got further orders from Shaw.

"Look, I'm really sorry about what happened," he told her. "For the shooting and that stupid thing I said earlier. I'll do that groveling now if you like."

He said it lightheartedly, but there was nothing humorous about the look that Anna gave him. However, it didn't last long. By degrees, her expression softened. Or something. A frustrated sigh left her mouth, and she stepped into his arms as if she belonged there.

"I'm scared," she confessed. "And I'm tired of feeling this way. I just want things to be normal again."

Rafe automatically tightened his grip around her. "I know."

"It was just such a shock when you called me Kate. I mean, you've never done anything like that before. I always think of you as, well, unshakeable." She buried her face against his neck. "I guess the pressure got to you."

"Oh, yes. It definitely got to me. I'll try very hard not to let it happen again."

But now what? He could go two directions with this. He could blow it off and try to make her laugh. Or he could confess that he was scared, too. Damn scared. He didn't have time for either.

Anna came up on her toes, with plans to kiss him no doubt. It certainly wouldn't be the first kiss they'd shared, but from all the signals she was giving, it wouldn't be chaste like the one at the altar.

He was right.

She wound her arm around his neck, her eyelashes fluttered down, and she fit her mouth to his.

It sure wasn't innocent. Nowhere near it. It was the kind of kiss a woman gave her new husband.

Hot. Needy. Raw.

Still, he didn't stop it. Nor did he pull away from her or do what he'd done for the past three days—make some stupid joke to break the tension. He just stood there and enjoyed a great kiss that he had no business enjoying.

She gripped the front of his jacket and pressed herself against him. Her breasts against his chest. It didn't matter if he *shouldn't* react, he did. But then his body didn't seem to understand that this was a game he had to play. A sick game with lives at stake.

He cursed himself. He had no right to kiss her this way. None. And yet he had no way to stop it. If Shaw's plan was to work, then Anna had to believe he was the man she'd fallen in love with months earlier.

She broke the kiss but kept her mouth close to his. So close that he could still taste her. "I want to make sure that we're okay," she whispered.

He didn't have to fake a laugh, even though this one was filled with frustration. "Oh, we're okay."

Well, with one exception—he was aroused beyond belief.

Not exactly the military bearing he'd hoped to maintain.

"You guys need a few more minutes or what?" he heard Buchanan call out.

Rafe broke away from her as if he'd just been caught doing something wrong. Which, in a way, he had.

Buchanan flexed an eyebrow, but other than that, there was no change in his neutral expression. "Looks like you're ready to start the honeymoon. Come on. We'll get you to quarters as fast as we can."

It hit Rafe then. With all the chaos of the shooting and the name incident, he'd forgotten one important detail.

This was his wedding night.

With the change in plans, it was also a night he could be expected to make love to his bride. There was just one problem with that. He couldn't. Because Anna didn't know the truth. And the truth was something he couldn't tell her.

Because if he did, it could end up costing Anna her life.

Chapter 3

Had she imagined that something was wrong? Had she imagined that jolt?

Maybe.

Anna stared at herself in the bathroom mirror and ran her fingertips over her mouth, remembering the way Rafe had kissed her at the chapel. That certainly seemed, well, normal. And incredible.

Maybe Colonel Shaw was right, and this was just a case of nerves. Wedding jitters combined with that horrible shooting incident. With all that had happened recently, a case of frayed nerves certainly seemed a reasonable response.

She shook her head, embarrassed at the way she'd behaved. Not only had she given Rafe the cold shoulder, she'd actually thought maybe he had been brainwashed. Or worse. It'd even crossed her mind that he was some sort of spy sent to infiltrate the Special Ops Unit at the base.

Talk about jumping to crazy conclusions.

Bolstered by her pep talk, Anna swiped on some transparent lip gloss, ran a hand through her hair and stepped back to give herself one last look in the mirror.

Well. The image she saw wouldn't have a G-rating, that's for sure.

The fire-engine-red nightgown covered all three of the important *S*'s required for a hot honeymoon night. Skimpy. Short. Sexy. Definitely meant to seduce. And that was exactly what she wanted to do. Then, after making wild, passionate love with her husband, maybe they could sit down and just talk. She had so many things to tell him.

"This is what I want," she reminded herself. "I love Rafe. I really love him." And she reached for the door.

The sound of his voice stopped her. Anna peered into the room and saw him on the bed with the phone pressed to his ear. His shoes and jacket were off, and he was in his usual lounging repose with his back against the headboard. He had his shirt unbuttoned, revealing a toned, tightly muscled chest sprinkled with dark brown coils of hair.

It was provocative. No doubt about it. Just the sight of him caused the heat to roar through her skimpily clad body. Mercy, she was one lucky woman.

He took a sip of water, set the glass next to his holster on the nightstand and spoke in soft, murmuring tones. She only caught a word here and there. *Security. Colonel Shaw.*

She started to join him, but something in his tone stopped her. It wasn't the tone of a man who simply wanted to clarify information. He sounded a little angry. Rafe fired off his terse responses in clips, like gunshots. *Yes. No way. We've been through that.*

Anna stepped back into the bathroom and put her ear against the door so she could listen to the rest of the conversation.

"It wasn't supposed to happen this way, sir," she heard Rafe say.

She felt the wave of doubt creeping up again, but she refused to let herself jump to conclusions. This probably had something to do with the cancellation of the reception. That's all. Or maybe something had gone wrong with his plans for their honeymoon.

Rafe continued. "I can't do that to her."

Anna froze. Held her breath. And waited.

"This won't work," Rafe snapped. "She's not stupid. If I stay here, she'll know. I think we need to come up with another plan."

Oh, God. What plan? Anna squeezed her eyes shut and frantically tried to come up with a reasonable explanation to all of this.

She couldn't.

No, she wasn't stupid, and she couldn't dismiss the gut feeling that something was wrong. Terribly wrong. Her instincts were screaming for her to listen, and she would. Finally.

So, now what? She could get dressed and try to sneak out of the suite without him noticing. The chances of that were slim to none, and even if she managed it, then what would she do? She could go to Janine's house, but that would just involve her friend in something potentially dangerous. Besides, it might be Rafe who was in danger.

Anna leaned against the wall. If Rafe was in some kind of trouble, she wanted to know about it. She might even be able to help, but first she had to know the truth.

She tried to steady herself by taking several deep breaths. One way or another she would have to convince him to tell her everything. And maybe it'd be a truth she could handle.

Before she could change her mind, she pulled open the door and stepped into the room.

His gaze snared her right away. "I have to go," he said into the phone, and then hung up.

He stared at her a moment—the hesitation all over his face—as he got to his feet. Well, maybe it wasn't hesitation. Anna rethought that theory when Rafe's eyes skimmed over her. From head to toe. It was a long, smoldering, appreciative look that stole her breath.

Forcing herself to say something, anything, she clutched the sides of her gown. "Do you like it?"

He made a sound, a soft rumble as if clearing his throat, and nodded.

"I'll take that as a yes." Anna stepped toward him, all the while wondering if this was the biggest, and last, mistake she would ever make.

Well, hell.

Now, how the heck was he supposed to handle this? And why hadn't Buchanan called? He was supposed to come up with some bogus plan to occupy him half the night. It was obvious from the way Anna was dressed that she had an entirely different idea about how to occupy him. An idea that would involve clothing removal and hot, sweaty sex.

"It's a yes," he assured his bride after he found his

breath. "I definitely like the gown. Red, huh? It's a good color."

However, it was the woman inside it that he was really admiring. Rafe was glad he'd already loosened his collar, because just the sight of Anna would have required him to loosen something.

Damn. She was beautiful. Her dark-blond hair tumbled in a sexy heap onto her shoulders. Here was the sparkle he'd seen in the videos. Of course, he likely felt that way because of the barely there, devil-red nightgown that stopped at mid-thigh. High mid-thigh. If she bent just a little in any direction, he'd no doubt learn if her panties matched the color of the gown.

The blood rushed to his head. And other parts of him.

He couldn't let himself lose control. Nope. She might be his wife, but it was in name only. She certainly wasn't his for the taking.

Anna strolled toward him, her smile tentative. She was nervous. Rafe understood that feeling completely. He'd faced enemy fire and hadn't experienced the tangle of raw nerves that he felt right now.

He hitched a thumb toward a bottle of champagne. "It's from Colonel Shaw."

Rafe didn't intend to thank the man for it, either. Sometimes, he wondered if the colonel and he were on the same page. The last thing he needed tonight was to cloud his mind with alcohol.

Anna gave the champagne a passing glance. "That was nice of him."

Nibbling at her bottom lip, she stepped closer. And closer. Rafe just stood there while she lifted her hands and laced them around the back of his neck.

"I missed you so much when you were gone," she said softly. "I mean, when we left each other in Monte de Leon, we thought we'd only be apart a couple of days. It turned into two long months."

That comment ate away at him like nothing else could have. It was wrong to play with her emotions this way. Still, what choice did he have? He couldn't risk telling her everything. Not yet.

"I missed you, too," he answered.

Anna brushed her mouth over his. "But we're together now—just like you promised that day you put me on the transport to come back to the States. The day you asked me to marry you."

"I remember," Rafe lied.

She moved in for the kiss. He didn't quite manage to suppress a groan, but it didn't matter. Anna caught the sound with her mouth. She brought her sweet lips to his and gave him a kiss that nearly made him forget that this was supposed to be all for show.

She pulled back, slightly, and stared into his eyes. "I think we should start making up for lost time right now, don't you?"

But she didn't wait for him to answer that. She kissed him again.

Rafe braced himself for the assault. Or at least he tried to do that. It didn't work. Her taste slammed through his body. The energy. The intensity. And the distinctive feeling that he had lost his freaking mind. He had no business kissing her like this.

None.

Nada.

Zip.

He should be concentrating on a plausible lie to get

him the heck out of there before he stripped that gown off her and hauled her in the general direction of the bed. Still, he didn't move. He stood there and took everything. The kiss. The heat of her body. Her.

Anna slipped her hand into his hair. "You don't know how many times I wished that we hadn't agreed to wait until our wedding night to make love. Did you ever regret our decision to wait?" she asked, her voice as silky as the gown she slid against his body.

Rafe couldn't look at her. Not even a glimpse. If he did, she would know something was wrong. Instead, he stared at her earring. A small pearl dangled on a delicate thread of gold.

"You better believe there were times I regretted it," he managed to say. "In fact, the regrets went up a significant notch every time I laid eyes on you."

He didn't have time to pray that she wouldn't question him further about it. Or time to come up with a lie that would give him an exit. He felt every muscle in her body go stiff.

Anna jerked away from him, and in the same motion she reached for his shoulder holster that he'd left on the nightstand. He could have stopped her from pulling the gun, easily, but it would have been a huge risk. If something had gone wrong, she might have gotten hurt. So, he just stood there while she drew his own weapon on him.

"Answers," she said, her voice barely a whisper. "I want answers, and I want them now."

He tried to play it light, but inside it was a whole different story. She'd obviously figured out he wasn't the man she thought he was. Now, the question was—

what would she do about it? Would she really try to use that gun?

Maybe.

God knows what all of this would push her to do. If their positions were reversed, if he'd been kept in the dark about something like this, then he'd sure have that gun in his hand, and it'd be aimed at her.

"Answers?" he calmly repeated. He inched closer, but stopped when she lifted the gun and aimed it right at his heart. "What do you mean, darling?"

"The truth. There was no decision for us to wait," she clarified.

"Damn," he mumbled. Silently, he added some much harsher profanity.

He stared at her, cursing this stupid plan and cursing the fact that he hadn't stopped it. But there wasn't much he could do about that now.

Besides, he had a more urgent problem facing him. Literally. Somehow, he had to get the gun away from this woman without either of them getting hurt.

"Anna—"

But that's all he managed to say.

"Rafe and I were lovers," she whispered, a tear racing down her cheek.

There was no good comeback for that so he said the first thing that came to mind. "I'm sorry." He figured he'd be saying that plenty of times before the night was over.

"Sorry?" she snapped. Her eyes sliced at him with a scalpel-sharp glare. "It's a little late for that, don't you think? Two months too late. I'm pregnant."

Oh, man. That knocked the breath right out of him.

He couldn't speak. Couldn't move. All he could do was stand there and stare at her.

Pregnant!

Hell.

Anna was pregnant.

With her eyes brimming with tears, she levered the gun slightly higher. "And now I want to know what you've done with my baby's father."

Chapter 4

Anna's hands throbbed from the death grip she had on the gun. A dull ache drummed in her head, and her heart. What was left of her breath was lodged in her throat.

But those were the least of her worries.

Aches and throbs were nothing in the grand scheme of things. Not when her world had just spun completely out of control.

She tried to blink back the tears but failed. One slid down her cheek, and she feared others would follow.

"You're, uh..." He let out a ragged breath. "Pregnant?"

Anna nodded, not risking her voice. She hadn't meant to blurt it out like that. It'd been a secret, something wonderful and precious that she'd hoped to share with Rafe on their honeymoon. Instead, she'd shared it with this man.

This stranger.

He reached behind him, fumbled around until he located the bed, then sank down onto the mattress. He groaned and buried his face in his hand.

"Pregnant," he repeated. "Judas freaking priest! Why didn't somebody bother to tell me before now?"

His reaction confused her even more. He seemed far more concerned about her pregnancy than the fact she'd just discovered that he was an imposter.

"Who are you?" Anna asked.

He looked up at her and mumbled some words of frustration. "Why don't you put the gun down, and then we'll talk?"

"No." She had no intention of letting go of that gun. Not anytime soon. She already felt vulnerable enough standing there in the flimsy gown that she'd put on for what was supposed to be her wedding night.

Oh, God.

Her *wedding night*. And this man was supposed to be her husband. He wasn't. Anna was sure of that. But it suddenly didn't matter who he was. Because if he was there with her, then where was Rafe?

"Is Rafe dead?" She dreaded the question, but dreaded the answer even more.

He squeezed his eyes shut and groaned. "I knew this would happen. I just knew it."

That didn't do a thing to ease that ache. "Is he dead?" she repeated.

"No. Hell no."

She believed him. Or maybe she just wanted to believe him. It didn't matter. Anna latched on to that thread of hope. Rafe was alive, and as long as he was alive, somehow she would find him.

He opened his eyes, and his gaze snapped to hers. "I

have to call someone. I'd rather you not shoot me when I try to do that. Deal?"

The almost arrogant request didn't sit well with her. Of course, at this point nothing would sit well except maybe to see the real Rafe come walking through the door.

"I'm not in a deal-making kind of mood." Anna raised the gun so he'd remember that she was the one in charge here. "Where's Rafe?"

He tapped his forehead. "Right here, darling. And before we start a game of twenty questions, Colonel Shaw needs to know about this, understand?"

So, Colonel Shaw was in on this—whatever *this* was. It made the cut even deeper since she'd known him since she was a child. It didn't help, either, that she was holding a gun on a man who was a dead ringer for someone that she loved more than life itself.

Ignoring her and the weapon, he snatched up the phone and punched in some numbers. Anna didn't have time to threaten him again, and from his resolute expression, it wouldn't have mattered. If this man was some spy, or some enemy combat specialist, then he likely knew that she couldn't pull the trigger.

Not with that too-familiar face staring at her.

It would be like shooting Rafe.

"We've got a huge problem," he said into the phone, then hung up. "Colonel Shaw will be here in a few minutes," he relayed to her.

"I don't want to wait for him. I want answers now. Why are you doing this? Who are you, and what have you done with Rafe?"

He began to button his shirt. What he didn't do was even spare her a glance. "That's a real long story. Best to put away that gun before you do something we'd both regret."

"I won't regret shooting you if you've harmed Rafe," she informed him.

He laughed, a short burst of sound, but there was no enjoyment in it. "God, you do love him, don't you?" He didn't wait for her to confirm it. "Believe me, I'm sorry about that. Sorry about the pregnancy, about everything. If I could have done this a different way, I would have. You deserve better than this."

Anna pushed his apology aside. "Where is he?"

She'd meant to make that question sound more like a demand, but her voice crumbled. More tears welled up in her eyes. It was hard to stay resolute when her heart was breaking into a thousand pieces.

"Please," Anna begged. "I need to know what's happened to him."

He lifted his hands in a why-me gesture. "I didn't lie about that." He tapped his forehead again. "He's here. *I'm* here. Things are just a little messed up right now."

She shook her head, not understanding. A whirlwind of emotions went through her. Fear. Doubt. Dread. Mostly dread. If this was Rafe, then obviously something terrible had happened. "Did they brainwash you?"

"Not exactly." He motioned toward the gun. "Look, why don't you put that down—"

"Not until you answer me, damn it!"

"All right." He stood and crammed his hands deep into his pockets. He didn't avoid looking her in the eye this time. "You want the story? Well, here it is. My captors used a so-called truth serum. A nasty barbiturate cocktail that did a real number on me and some of my brain cells. It had an unexpected side effect—

retrograde memory loss—and the neurologist here at the base hasn't been able to reverse it."

She stared at him, afraid to feel relief that Rafe was alive, after all. "You have amnesia?"

He angled his head back and grimaced. "No. Well, not in the strictest sense of the word. Basically, I can remember everything except the last year of my life."

The last year. Twelve months. That didn't take long to sink in.

"We've known each other only a little more than a year," Anna mumbled.

He nodded.

And that brought her to the next logical conclusion. "You don't remember me?"

"No. Not really."

He didn't add anything to that for several long moments. Anna didn't dare try to speak. She just stood there, the gun gripped in her hand, and waited while her world fell apart.

"I remember meeting you right after I was stationed at Stennis Air Force Base," Rafe continued. "When I reported in to Colonel Shaw, you were in his office. You'd stopped by to tell him about a big assignment you'd just gotten."

Yes. She remembered. And that was several weeks prior to Rafe's and her first date.

Because she had no choice, Anna dropped down into the chair across from him. She fought hard to keep what little composure she had left. "Why didn't you tell me? Rafe, you married me, and you don't even know who I am."

He opened his mouth. Closed it. And shook his head.

What he didn't do was offer anything else. No explanations. No assurances. Nothing.

There was a sharp knock on the door. The sound rifled through the silence and sent her stomach to her knees.

"That'll be Colonel Shaw," Rafe said. He glanced at the door and then at the gun. "It's a good time to put that away."

He was right. The gun wouldn't solve any of this. Maybe nothing would. She was married to a man who didn't even know her.

Anna slowly released the grip she had on his pistol. Rafe eased it from her hand and placed it back in the holster on the nightstand.

There was another knock, but he ignored it. Standing over her, he reached out and brushed his knuckles over her cheek.

Anna flinched. "Don't," she insisted.

She had no idea what she should be feeling, but she knew for certain that she didn't want Rafe or anyone else to touch her. Too bad just looking at him caused her body to betray her. She had to battle the urge not to lean into his touch. To lean on him. Somehow, she had to convince her body that this wasn't the man her heart had fallen in love with.

He picked up his dark blue mess dress jacket from the foot of the bed and draped it around her shoulders. Only then did Anna remember that she had on just a nightgown. A nearly transparent one. She slipped her arms into the sleeves and hugged it to her so she was at least partly covered.

The jacket smelled like Rafe.

That too-familiar scent stirred an ache deep inside

her and spelled out the hard reality of her situation. The man she loved hadn't come home to her, after all.

Rafe answered the door, and she heard him whisper something to the colonel before Shaw entered. She didn't look at either of them. She couldn't. Anna kept her attention focused on the medals on the jacket.

"Pregnant?" Shaw whispered.

The barely audible conversation continued for several minutes, but Anna didn't even try to listen. She hated that the intimate details of her life were now part of some official discussion between two men she wasn't sure she could trust.

"I'm sorry, Anna," Shaw volunteered. "I didn't know about the baby. And I'd hoped things wouldn't have to come to this."

It wasn't the right thing to say. Her fear instantly turned to anger. "Did you think I was so stupid that I couldn't figure out something was wrong?"

"That's not what I meant." Shaw placed his hand on her shoulder. "We'd hoped that the blank spots in Rafe's memory would correct themselves by now."

"Blank spots," she repeated through slightly clenched teeth. The man was batting a thousand on the worst possible things to say. "I'm a blank spot, Colonel. And so is this baby I'm carrying. How the heck could you have let me go through with the wedding when you knew Rafe didn't remember me? I thought we were friends."

"We are." Shaw stepped around the chair where she was seated and stood in front of her. "Rafe was only following orders. *My* orders."

Anna looked at Rafe, but he didn't verify that. In fact, he kept his expression blank just as he'd done in the church during the attack.

"I can't explain everything that you probably want to know," the colonel continued. "But I can tell you that this is all part of a classified mission that involves other hostages—two CROs—who are being held by the same group of rebels who had Rafe."

Her fingers stilled on the Purple Heart medal that she was fondling. "What could our wedding possibly have to do with that?"

Rafe turned and faced her. "I have information the rebel leader, Len Quivira, wants to make a swap for those two hostages." He paused, glanced at the colonel, and Shaw nodded. "But there's a problem—I don't remember the information he wants. If he learns that, then he'll execute the men he's holding."

Anna hadn't thought things could get worse, but he proved her wrong. She clutched the jacket against her heart. It was as if she'd awakened in the middle of a nightmare. God. People's lives were at stake just as Rafe's had been only days earlier.

Shaw took up the explanation where Rafe left off. "The wedding had to go on as planned so we could make it seem as if everything was back to normal. The neurologist thinks Rafe's memory loss is temporary, that he should regain everything in the next couple of days."

"And if it's not temporary?" Anna asked.

Shaw never even hesitated. "We're working out a contingency plan. But we need some time."

Yes, and that's what her wedding had bought them. Time. Too bad it'd bought her much more than that. She was married to a man who didn't have a clue who she was. And she was pregnant with his child. A child he didn't even know he'd fathered. Heck, he hadn't re-membered even making love to her.

She tried to bolster her expression before she looked at Rafe. A nearly impossible task. Everything about him—his face, his voice, his hands—everything re-minded her that he was the man she loved. The man she wanted. And yet he wasn't that man at all.

"You could have told me all of this," she insisted. "I would have gone through with the pretense of the wed-ding to protect those men."

"We couldn't risk that," Shaw explained.

"But you could risk this?" She gestured toward the champagne and the bed. "Did you order Rafe to sleep with me as well?"

"No," the two men said in unison. It was Rafe who continued. "Buchanan was going to come over here with some bogus emergency. He'd have stayed until morning."

"Well, that would have taken care of ten hours or so. And then what, huh?"

Rafe shrugged. "And then there would have been another fake emergency, and then another, until either my memory returned or until we managed to free the hostages. I wouldn't have slept with you."

That confession didn't do a thing to ease the ache in her heart. "Well, we'll never know, will we?" she snapped.

Rafe met her gaze head on. "*I* know." He turned away from her and strolled toward the window. "I'm attracted to you. Maybe more than attracted, and I don't need a memory to tell me that. But I wouldn't have acted on that attraction without you knowing the truth."

She swallowed hard. Even with the memory loss,

he still felt the heat simmering between them. Heck, so did she. Anna cursed herself. Even now, she felt it. It was like a fire always smoldering inside her. That didn't mean, however, she would give in to it. After all, he'd lied to her about one of the most important things a person could lie about.

Colonel Shaw caught onto her hand. "We wouldn't have done things this way if there weren't so much at stake."

No, she didn't imagine he would. But she could guess where the rest of this conversation was leading. "What do you want me to do—pretend I'm Mrs. Rafe Mc-Quade?"

"For starters," the colonel said, "I need three days to put a plan into action. I can't negotiate with Quivira. That's against foreign policy. So, I'm stalling him, but he's suspicious because he knows what those truth drugs are capable of doing. Even if Rafe's memory returns, I probably can't trade that information for the hostages. In other words, I need a way to get my men out of there and put Quivira out of commission. All I'm asking is that you give me some time."

It was essentially an ultimatum. One she couldn't refuse. Either she continued this charade, or else she'd be responsible in part for those men's deaths.

Rafe was still at the window. He turned toward her and caught her gaze. The look that went through his eyes had her shivering. And aching.

Rather than speculate with a dozen different scenarios, none of which she'd probably like, Anna took the direct approach. "There's more?"

Rafe took a deep breath and strolled toward her. "We have an informant within the rebels' organization."

Anna shook her head. "Well, that doesn't sound like bad news—"

"The rebels plan to kidnap you," Rafe interrupted. "They want to use you for leverage to make sure I co-operate."

That nearly knocked the breath out of her. "Oh, God." Anna slid her hand protectively over her stomach. "When? How?"

"They won't get to you," Rafe assured her. "That's why we're here. I won't leave you unguarded until all of this is over."

It was too much for her to absorb. Anna blinked back the tears and cursed them. How had things gotten so twisted? A few hours ago, she was a happy bride. Now not only did her husband not remember her, they were all in danger. That included her baby.

"I know this is a shock, but here's what I need you to do," the colonel explained. "Tomorrow afternoon, Rafe and you will drive out to his aunt and uncle's cabin in the Hill Country near Canyon Lake. No one's using the place so you'll stay there until the situation with the hostages is contained."

She was already shaking her head before he finished. "What stops Quivira's men from finding out where we are and coming after us?"

"There'll be listening devices in the cabin. If anything goes wrong, all you have to do is yell, and we'll be there. We'll also have security specialists in the woods surrounding the cabin."

"That didn't do a lot of good at the church," she reminded him.

"Nothing like that will happen again."

Anna glanced at Rafe to see if he would second that.

He didn't. He was staring out the window. His pose seemed almost calm, but she noticed that his hands were clenched. Not exactly the endorsement she'd hoped he could give her.

"So, all I'd have to do is stay at the cabin with Rafe for a couple of days?" Anna clarified.

Shaw nodded. "Only six people know about Rafe's lack of memory. Luke Buchanan. Communications specialist Nicholas Sheldon. The neurologist. And us."

"Luke is in on this." Anna shook her head. "I'm surprised he didn't say something."

"He couldn't," Shaw reminded her. "It has to stay that way, Anna. Tell no one else, including Janine."

"Janine? She's my best friend. Why couldn't—"

"No one," Rafe insisted. "We can't risk it."

His tone didn't leave much room for argument. "All right." But that was easier said than done. Janine had a way of ferreting out the truth. Anna would have to be careful when they talked.

"We'll have to convince everyone that we're really married," Rafe continued. "That means even the other security specialists who might end up standing guard in the woods won't know the truth. We have to make everyone believe that things are as they appear to be. If Quivira's men hear anything to make them think I've lost critical pieces of my memory, then the plan falls like a house of cards. That can't happen."

Anna drew in her breath. Whatever he was implying, she didn't think she would like it. That was nothing new. She hadn't cared much for any of this. "So, what are you saying?"

"Colonel Shaw needs time to get those men out so

we can protect you. For that to happen, we'll have to pretend to be newlyweds."

She shook her head. "Yes, I got that. But how? In what way?"

Rafe turned and faced her. "*Every* way."

Anna pulled back her shoulders and waited for him to finish.

"The cabin has one bedroom. Just one," Rafe explained. "And we'll have to share it."

Chapter 5

With Anna right next to him, Rafe stood in the doorway and glanced around the living room of the rustic cabin.

"Man, talk about a blast from the past," he mumbled.

The place hadn't changed a bit. There was a massive bay window that provided a view of the lush Texas Hill Country. Battered hardwood floors dotted with colorful throw rugs. A well-worn leather sofa positioned right in front of a huge stone fireplace.

It was just as he remembered it.

Every strip of the golden pine paneling. Every picture on the wall. Every garage-sale knickknack on the mantel that Aunt Alice and Uncle Pete had placed there over the years. Rafe remembered it all.

Too bad he couldn't say the same for everything else in his life.

Especially his wife.

Not exactly the sort of thing a newly married man should have trouble recalling. But other than their first meeting in Shaw's office and the information he'd accumulated about Anna over the last four days, he knew practically nothing about the woman beside him. The woman he'd promised to love, honor and cherish for the rest of his life.

Ditto for that part about making a baby with her. That definitely was a piece of this freaking memory puzzle that he needed to recall in a hurry.

A baby!

How he could possibly not remember making a baby?

Anna stepped inside with him, her attention focused on the cabin where they would stay the next seventy-two hours. Together. Pretending they were newlyweds.

No pressure, right?

"We'll have the place to ourselves," he offered, forcing himself to say something. He put his duffel bag in the hall closet. "My aunt and uncle are in their RV headed off to the Grand Canyon."

And if his present situation hadn't been so uncertain, he would have called and asked them to come back for the wedding. In just about every way that counted, they were his parents. Rafe had never even met his own father, and he hadn't seen his mother since he was sixteen when she left their hometown of Crystal Creek, Texas, to *find herself.* Presumably, she was still looking since she'd been at it thirteen years and hadn't bothered to return.

"The kitchen's that way," Rafe said, giving her the nickel tour. He pointed to the pass-through on the other side of the room. "Colonel Shaw supposedly had the fridge stocked."

Anna made a sound of approval, but Rafe saw no such approval in her eyes. As she'd done since they left the base, she'd confined her answers to just a couple of words or those approving-disapproving sounds.

"It's all right for us to talk," he said. "Sheldon hasn't turned on the equipment yet. And if he has to switch off shifts with someone, he'll give us a heads-up so we won't say anything we shouldn't."

Another nod.

All right. He obviously wasn't making a lot of progress in the area of mending fences. Much more of this, and he'd have to start groveling.

"The bathroom and bedroom are down the hall," Rafe continued. "Just one bed. Sorry. I can sleep on the floor, but we have to stay in the same room in case something goes wrong and I have to get you out of here."

Anna gave him a look that could have frozen molten lava, then started to walk away.

He caught her arm to stop her, but Anna glanced at the grip he had on her arm and slowly lifted her eyes.

"Look, I'm not jumping for joy about these arrangements, either," Rafe informed her. "But there's not a lot we can do about it. Quivira and his men mean business. Trust me, you don't want them to get their hands on you."

The iciness in her eyes thawed a degree or two, but she still dropped back a step, putting some distance between them.

"I know what we have to do," she snapped. "Believe

me, I don't want to be kidnapped, but this is all just so…well, it's so…" Anna obviously gave up trying to get that particular point across and groaned. "Do you have any idea how hard it is for me to be here with you like this?"

Rafe nodded. "Yeah. I've given it some thought."

It had to be her own personal version of hell. By her own admission, she was in love with the man he used to be. But it damn sure wasn't a bed of roses for him, either. He was looking at a woman, a stranger, who happened to have his child inside her.

She made a helpless gesture with her hands. "It hurts to look at your face, to know that things might never be the way they used to be."

That touched him in a way that nothing else could have. Rafe reached for her, but she pushed him away.

"That won't help," she insisted.

He didn't press her, but Rafe wanted nothing more than to reassure her. Too bad that was the very thing he couldn't do. There were no reassurances. Until his memory returned or until those men were free, he was essentially in purgatory and Anna was doing penance right along with him.

"I need a couple of minutes to myself," she insisted. She pulled her phone from the purse she had hooked over her shoulder. "I'll call Janine and let her know that we arrived safely."

Rafe had to stop her again. "You can't use your phone. Sorry. It's not a secure line. You can use the one in the bedroom. It's cordless so you can take it anywhere in the cabin that you want."

"Can I give Janine the number, or is that not allowed?"

"It's allowed. The phone can't be traced to a specific location."

She mumbled a thanks, which had a get-away-from-me tone to it, and headed down the hall.

Rafe just stood there and stared at the empty space. Maybe it was time for that groveling. Either that, or the next three days would be even harder than he'd imagined, and he'd imagined a pretty tough time.

"A baby," he mumbled under his breath. He scrubbed his hands over his face. "A baby."

A child was the ultimate complication. And yet in some ways, it didn't feel so much like a complication at all. The baby was his. *His* baby. There was no doubt about that in his mind. Anna wasn't the sort to leave him and climb into bed with another man.

So, no matter what happened, the fact wouldn't change that she was pregnant. It created a bond between Anna and him, whether she wanted that bond or not.

Too bad that bond could also create a distraction that he didn't need right now.

For safety's sake, he had to put aside his impending fatherhood and press on with the plan.

Hopefully, he could do that.

Rafe started to check on Anna, but he heard Nicholas Sheldon's voice in the tiny earpiece that he was wearing. "Rafe, I connected a couple of minutes ago. I can hear you loud and clear."

Great. Just freaking great. That meant Sheldon had listened in on the very private conversation he'd just had with Anna. Sheldon wasn't supposed to turn on the equipment until Rafe gave him the go-ahead.

"I've got a good audio and visual of all rooms except the bathroom," Sheldon continued. "We opted to stay out of there for your bride's sake."

"I'm sure she'll appreciate that," Rafe grumbled.

"We aim to please, Cap'n," Sheldon countered. "I can pick up anything louder than a whisper. And just for the record—I don't plan to play Peeping Tom or Eavesdropping Eddie while I'm out here."

No, but Sheldon wouldn't have much of a choice. He had to monitor the place. If the rebels found out where they were staying, they'd likely try to come after Anna.

"I'm in a bunker in the bluff that's visible from the living room window," Sheldon went on. "It's a glorified hole, but I'll be monitoring the equipment from here. And I'm armed with some pretty nifty high-powered rebel stoppers in case something goes wrong. There's also a team at the bottom of the road to make sure no one gets through. That should give you a little peace of mind."

Rafe glanced out the window at the bluff where Sheldon had indicated. "You picked a good spot."

There were dozens of crevices in the side of that steep limestone bluff, and the bunker blended right in. But Sheldon was wrong about one thing. It didn't give him any peace of mind. Not much would at this point.

"Colonel Shaw asked me to pass on an update about that shadow you shot at the church. He didn't pull through."

"Damn," Rafe mumbled.

"Yep. That's what the colonel said, too, along with

some other creative profanity that blistered our ears. The guy was connected to Len Quivira and his rebels. No doubt about it. That means Quivira hasn't given up on his quest to kidnap Anna."

And he wouldn't give up. Rafe didn't have a lot of memories about his captivity, but he'd seen the look of absolute determination in the rebel leader's eyes right before the Alpha Team stormed the encampment and rescued him. Quivira managed to escape, but several of his men were killed that night.

No, Quivira wouldn't give up.

But then, neither would he.

"Just give a yell if you need me," Sheldon instructed. "I'll keep you and your bride as safe as I can. Until then—adios, Cap'n."

Rafe wished that assurance had come from his best friend, Cal Rico. But Rico was still undercover down in South America. Sheldon was the newest member of the team, and a civilian at that. A contracted communications specialist hired by the Department of Defense. Still, Sheldon seemed to have all the qualifications necessary to make this a successful mission. And if not, then Rafe didn't intend to stand around and let Quivira and his rebels take Anna.

Nope.

He ran his hand over the gun in his shoulder harness. This time he was on his own turf, not trapped in the jungle, and he was ready for them.

"Did I hear you talking to someone?" Anna asked.

Rafe looked up and saw her standing in the bedroom doorway. He didn't think it was his imagination that she looked pale.

He tapped his ear. "Nicholas Sheldon was just testing out the equipment. How's Janine?"

"Talkative. Don't worry—I didn't mention a word about your memory loss." She laid her purse on the dresser next to the door. "Am I allowed to ask how much privacy I'll have while I'm here?"

"Virtually none unless you whisper or go into the bathroom. Sheldon is monitoring everything. And those tiny black things on the ceilings?" Rafe pointed to the one just overhead. "Not spiders. Cameras."

She mumbled something under her breath. "You know, I wouldn't mind if I thought for sure it'd keep us safe."

"I'll do my best."

"Let's hope that's enough." She didn't even spare him a glance and walked right past him.

The hall was narrow, and when she moved, she brushed against him. Her hip against his. Not good. His body reacted not just to the brief contact but also to Anna. Cursing himself, Rafe pushed aside that reaction. He didn't have time for those kinds of reactions.

He followed her into the living room, dropped down onto the sofa and tried to get his mind on something else other than the too obvious heat that crackled between them. "If it'll help, you can go ahead and yell at me for not telling you the truth sooner."

Anna picked up a picture from the mantel, studied it and put it back down. "It wouldn't help."

"You sure about that? A good surge of adrenaline might get you past the I-think-you're-fungus stage."

If she had a reaction to his attempted humor, she didn't show it. "I've had all the adrenaline surges I need, thank you. My trip to Monte de Leon and that shooting incident at the church were enough to last me a lifetime."

"I know what you mean." He tucked his hands behind his head and sank deeper into the sofa. "And speaking of that incident, the guy didn't pull through."

She'd already started to reach for another picture, but her hand stopped. "Was he, uh, one of them?"

"Yeah. He belonged to Quivira's group."

She caught on to the mantel and closed her eyes.

Because she looked ready to faint, Rafe bolted from the sofa and hurried to her. "Are you all right?"

"Just a little light-headed. It might be routine for you, but I guess I'm just not accustomed to hearing about people dying."

"Believe me, it's not routine for me, either."

She stepped away from him when he reached for her. This time, Rafe didn't let her get away with that little evasive maneuver. He slipped his arm around her waist and held on. "When's the last time you had something to eat?"

"Uh, this morning at breakfast."

"Nearly six hours ago, and if I recall, all you had was toast and juice. No wonder you're light-headed. Come on, let's see what we can find in the kitchen."

He led her to the kitchen bar counter and eased her onto the stool. The silence suddenly seemed deafening. It was strange. They had so much to talk about, and yet even more that he wanted to avoid. For now, the baby had to be off-limits. It was too much like a walloping punch in the solar plexus to think about it. Still, it seemed with all that had happened, she would have something to say to him.

"Why are you looking at me like that?" she asked.

Only then did he realize he'd been staring at her.

"I was just thinking—about a lot of things. You never did tell me how you figured out that I didn't know who you were." It seemed a good time to turn away and do something that didn't involve staring. He rummaged through the fridge and came up with some sodas and turkey sandwiches. "What gave me away?"

She kept her attention focused on the food he put in front of her. "The kiss at the altar."

"Wow. The kiss?" He shook his head. "That stings a little. And here I thought there wasn't anything wrong with that." In fact, for him it'd been downright memorable. But then, he could say that about every kiss he'd had with Anna so far. "So, why did that make you suspicious?"

She pulled off a tiny piece of the bread and put it in her mouth. "Your hand trembled when you kissed me."

"A tremble gave me away? Jeez Louise." He darn sure hadn't noticed that. "Makes sense, though, I guess. Rico is always saying when it comes to tense situations, I'm as calm as a virgin taking a home-pregnancy test."

Anna sputtered out a cough.

The minute the words left his mouth, Rafe knew he'd made yet another mistake. For the next couple of days, he needed to strike the word *pregnancy* from his vocabulary.

"Say, are you all right?" Rafe asked.

She waved him off and downed a couple of sips of soda. "I'm fine. The bread just went down the wrong way." She paused. "Your friend's right—you're not the trembling kind."

Rafe stayed on his side of the counter, and while he took a bite of his sandwich, he gave that some thought. A tremble. Who would have thought something so simple would have blown the original plan? "Guess I was nervous standing there at the altar," he said almost idly.

"You're not the nervous kind, either," Anna informed him.

He nearly laughed. Man, she was *so* wrong. He had no idea how many nerves there were in the human body, but he felt every one of them. The woman certainly had an effect on him. Maybe it was a good idea to strike thoughts like *need* and *want* from his mental vocabulary, as well.

Rafe downed some of his soda. "I thought you figured me out because I hadn't remembered that we'd made love."

"That only confirmed it."

It was a subject he should leave well enough alone, but Rafe couldn't. It was something that had been niggling at him since she discovered the truth. "A couple of days ago, I read an old e-mail that you sent to me the morning you left on assignment to South America. You talked about...well, about us—"

"Making love." Anna moistened her lips. "Or rather *not* making love. I'd told you that I intended to wait... well, for whatever, but I changed my mind that afternoon in Monte de Leon."

Oh. So, they'd made love just that once. Well, maybe twice. He glanced at her. Yep. Definitely—at least twice.

Rafe tried hard to recall any little piece of that afternoon, but that particular pool of memories was blank. Too bad. He was sure it was an experience worth remembering. Plus, it seemed only right that he should remember the occasion where they'd created a baby.

"I might be twenty-five, but I have old-fashioned ideas about sex, I guess," Anna continued. She kept her voice at a whisper, probably so that Sheldon wouldn't hear her. "Catholic guilt coupled with crate-size personal baggage. My mother slept around a lot, and I saw how much that hurt my father." She cleared her throat. "It hurt me, too. The gossip. The endless stream of lovers that she brought to the house while he was at work."

He slid his hand over hers. "I'm sorry."

She grimaced. "I have no idea why I just told you that. It doesn't matter. It was a long time ago."

Rafe listened to the nuance of each word and didn't care much for his interpretation. "Did one of your mother's lovers try to touch you or something?" He whispered as well. Even though Sheldon had said he wouldn't eavesdrop, this was one part of the conversation Rafe intended to keep private.

Surprise sprinted through her eyes. "No. God, no. Nothing like that."

His stomach landed somewhere in the vicinity of his boots. "You were a virgin?"

Her silence, and the way her face bleached out said it all. Damn it. A virgin.

She pushed the sandwich aside, eased her hand from his and stood. "If you don't mind, I think I'll lie down for a while. I didn't sleep much last night, and I can hardly keep my eyes open."

He couldn't let her just leave again. Not without one more attempt to mend this vast bridge between them. "You do know I would have come up with a different plan if I could have?"

Anna didn't answer him right away. "I know. You might not remember me, but I don't think you'd do anything intentionally cruel. After all, buried beneath all those blank spots, you're still Rafe."

Yes, he was.

And that brought him back to something that had been on his mind since he'd stood at that altar—and trembled. This was a woman he'd already fallen in love with once. If things were different, if they hadn't been tossed into an impossible situation, it might even have happened again.

Might.

Unfortunately, he had a couple of strikes against him. He'd lied to her. Not a little lie, either. A bona fide whopper. Added to that was the fact he'd taken her virginity, gotten her pregnant and couldn't even remember doing it. And one more clincher—Anna no longer trusted him.

Not exactly a great recipe for building a loving relationship.

So, even if he fully recovered his memory, there was an ice cube's chance in a blazing furnace that she'd ever love him again the way she used to love him. He'd blown what was probably the best thing that ever happened to him.

"I should have said this before now," he whispered. "But thank you for everything. For the ceremony. For your cooperation. For this."

Anna just stood there, only inches away, her sweet feminine scent stirring around him. Rafe took in that scent. Cataloged it. Savored it. And forced away the ache that it awakened inside him. He prayed it'd give the blank spots in his memory a much-needed nudge.

It didn't. It only made that ache worse.

And it aroused him.

Before Rafe could do something stupid and act on that ache, Anna thankfully turned and walked to the bedroom. He waited several moments until he heard the springs groan on the old bed. Then he grabbed a beer from the fridge and went to the doorway to stand guard.

Since she was on her side with her back to him, Rafe looked at her. Like her scent, he cataloged and savored her curved body on the patchwork quilt. Her golden hair against the white pillow. Her creamy, pale skin.

She was an attractive woman. No doubt about it. But she was more than that. For lack of a better word, Anna was special. And to think, she'd given herself to him.

Only him.

Rafe twisted off the beer cap and brought the bottle to his mouth for a long, much-needed drink. His hand didn't tremble. Not this time. But deep inside him— well, that was a whole different story.

Anna and he hadn't just made love in that cellar in Monte de Leon. They'd made a baby as well.

His baby.

Rafe wondered just how long it would take him to absorb the enormity of that.

His baby!

Fury suddenly raged through him. Part of him wanted to take hold of every person who'd fired shots at Anna and beat them to a bloody pulp. How dare those SOBs risk Anna's life and the life of their unborn child.

However, another part of him wanted to surrender to the enormity of it all. It was humbling, and terrifying, like a mega jolt of reality. In seven months, give or take a few days, he'd become a father.

But first, he had to keep both Anna and the baby alive.

Chapter 6

"You didn't tell Rafe about the impending pitter-patter of little feet, did you?" Janine asked. Her skepticism came through even with Rafe's shower droning in the background.

As Anna had done with the rest of the telephone conversation, she chose her words carefully. Rafe had assured her that Colonel Shaw hadn't planted listening devices in the bathroom, but she didn't want to risk Sheldon or Rafe overhearing this particular part of her discussion. And she didn't dare move out into the hallway with the cordless phone because Rafe had insisted that he didn't want her out of his sight.

"I told him," she whispered to Janine.

"And? Don't make me beg here, Anna. How did he take the news?"

It was a good question, but Anna didn't know the answer. Rafe had said as little as possible about the baby. It was almost as if he'd been able to put something that monumental out of his mind.

Unlike her.

It was there. Always there. She worried both for her baby's safety and future.

"Rafe's very happy about it," Anna lied.

Janine's silence wasn't good. Anna could almost hear the wheels turning in her friend's head, so she went on the offensive. "We've been busy so we haven't had much of a chance to pick out names or anything. But there's plenty of time for that later."

Anna made sure she added enough inflection on the word *busy,* that it implied something of a sexual nature.

That wasn't a complete lie.

There was certainly a lot of intensity crackling between Rafe and her. Well, she felt the crackle and the intensity, anyway. That probably had something to do with the fact she was sitting on the bathroom floor only a couple of feet away from where he was showering.

The vinyl curtain didn't help, either. It was opaque and well worn in spots. The overhead light filtered right through the curtain so she could see in perfect detail the outline of Rafe's naked body.

Mercy, the man was built.

When he'd first informed her that he needed a shower, and that she'd be present for it, Anna figured out right away that it wouldn't be a comfortable arrangement. A huge understatement. Rafe had undressed behind the shower curtain. Thankfully. But Anna had been fully aware of each article of clothing that he discarded on the floor.

His white T-shirt.

Then, his snug jeans.

And finally, his steel-blue boxers.

By the time he was done, her pulse was hammering out of control.

"I won't be able to talk much longer," Anna continued. Best to say as little as possible to Janine to reduce her chances of slipping up. "Rafe's almost done with his shower. By the way, you haven't said exactly why you called."

"Well, it wasn't just to interrupt your honeymoon. I dropped by your apartment to water your plants and check your messages. Your obstetrician had called."

Anna went stiff. "What'd he want?"

"Nothing's wrong," Janine assured her. "He just said you needed to take some iron pills along with your prenatal vitamins. He called in a prescription and wants you to pick it up when you get back."

"You're sure that's all?"

"Absolutely." Janine paused. "I'm worried about you, though, you know. You just don't sound like a woman who's on her honeymoon."

"That's because I'm on the phone with you," Anna teased. "Would you feel better if I were breathing heavy and sounded exhausted?"

"Maybe."

Anna laughed. "You're my best friend, Janine, but don't expect me to share the details of my honeymoon with you." Her gaze drifted back to the man behind the curtain. "Let's just say that Rafe is everything I thought he'd be, and more."

"All right!" Janine laughed as well. "Now, that

sounds like a woman on the receiving end of a great honeymoon. So, why don't you give me a hint about where Rafe took you? I'm thirty-three and stand a better chance of being struck by lightning and eaten by a rabid shark than I do of going on a real honeymoon. The best I can hope for is a *few* steamy details so I can live vicariously."

"Live vicariously through someone else," Anna countered.

"Ah, come on. Just a few details. Are you out on a boat in the middle of a lake, sipping virgin daiquiris and rubbing each other down with coconut-scented suntan oil?"

It was a typical Janine-type question, but for some reason, it gave her another of those nasty jolts. Like the one at the altar. Anna wanted to push it aside but couldn't. Maybe jolts and uncomfortable feelings were now the status quo. And maybe blind trust was a thing of the past.

"Well?" Janine prompted. "Are you at the lake?"

"Not quite." They were in a tiny bathroom with the sticky steam and the scent of Rafe's deodorant soap in the air. "Suffice it to say we're alone."

"Aah. Sounds like heaven with a capital *H*. And since you don't need a friend for that, I'll just say goodbye. Enjoy every minute of it, Anna. Rafe and you deserve this."

"Bye." Anna listened to Janine's reminder about picking up the iron pills, clicked off the phone and got to her feet.

Sounds like heaven with a capital H.

Yes. It would have been if Rafe's memory were in

full working order. Then she wouldn't have been sitting on the floor gawking at him while he took a shower. She would have been in that steamy, hot water right along with him. They would no doubt be kissing.

Among other things.

Her hands would have been all over his hard, soap-slick body. And his hands—those magic hands—would have been all over her. Body against body. It certainly wouldn't have been doubts and regrets she would be feeling. No. It would have been heaven with a capital *H*.

Anna had to fan herself.

Great day. The fantasizing had to stop. If she didn't get her mind off Rafe's hot, soapy, hard body, she might self-combust.

Or something.

Talk about the ultimate irony. She'd waited all her life to be with a man like Rafe. Now, here she was married to him. Madly, hopelessly in love with him. And yet she couldn't have him.

Fate really did have a twisted sense of humor. Too bad it didn't cool the flames that her fantasizing had fanned. She ached to touch him. Ached to kiss him. And just plain ached for everything else that only Rafe could give her.

He turned off the shower, and one nicely muscled, tanned arm reached out from the curtain. He snagged the towel from the rack and stepped out, bringing some of the steam with him. It seemed to rise off his body.

Rafe knotted the towel at his waist. "A problem?" he asked.

Anna opened her mouth to tell him no, but nothing came out. No sound. Not even a syllable. Nothing.

Mercy.

If she thought the view behind the shower curtain was tantalizing, it was paltry compared to the view she had now. Rafe was only inches away. He was wet all over. Practically naked. With drops of water sliding down his face. Down his neck. Down his lean, muscled chest. Down his equally lean and muscled stomach.

And down the rest of him.

Only that fluffy white towel prevented her from getting the greatest of peep shows.

"That was Janine," Anna explained after she remembered how to speak. And breathe. Good grief, had the air been sucked out of the room? "She called. Good thing I brought the phone in here, or else I might not have heard it ring."

He stared at her a moment, studying her. Thank God he couldn't read minds.

Or hormone levels.

Anna firmly reminded herself that this wasn't really Rafe. Too bad, though, that all those blank spots were trapped inside the face and body of the man that she loved. A man she wanted. And it was also too bad that the want suddenly felt a lot like need.

"I'm sorry about the close quarters," he finally said. "I just didn't want to risk you being alone while I was in here." He combed his fingers through his hair. It fell into place as if he'd just come from the barber. "I needed a shower, and I didn't think you'd care to join me."

Her throat clamped shut. Not the best time for that to happen. Nope. Her silence must have alerted Rafe because his gaze landed on her.

He didn't move, but the narrow space between them

suddenly seemed to vanish. Anna couldn't take her eyes off him, and she stood no chance whatsoever of hiding the attraction she felt for him.

"You look…" Rafe shrugged. "Interested."

Oh. Maybe because she was. She was interested in the worst kind of way.

Anna decided she could lie and flat out deny it. Or she could take the ostrich approach and bury her head in the sand. But in the next couple of days, there would probably be other incidents just like this one. So maybe it was a good time to get a few things straight.

"I was *interested* the first time I saw you," she told him, trying to keep her tone clinical. "And I obviously stayed interested, or I wouldn't have said yes when you asked me to marry you. But it's not the same now. I mean, you're not the same. I'm not the same."

The clinical tone went south. God, she was babbling like an idiot and still hadn't gotten her point across. If there was a point.

Without taking his gaze from hers, Rafe came closer. "I'm willing to bet the attraction between us is the same as it's always been. I'm just at a different stage of the ball game than you are, that's all."

Anna took a step back, then another, but the closed door stopped her from going any farther. The look he gave her matched the heat of the steam lingering in the air. It also did an effective job of carving away at what little resolve she'd managed to hang on to. Her brain didn't quite grasp the notion that this was a man she couldn't have.

"You've got memories," he continued, his Texas

drawl kissing the words. "But I've got a good imagination to fill in all the blanks."

She laughed. A burst of nervous energy. "That's a dangerous combination."

"You bet it is."

Because he was so close, she could see the struggle going on in his eyes. There was raw attraction, definitely, but it was tempered by common sense.

It was a toss-up as to which would win.

With that water clinging to every inch of him, and his sensuous made-for-kissing mouth so close she could taste it, Anna was no longer sure which outcome to hope for. One thing was for certain—she definitely wanted Rafe.

And he knew it.

Still clutching the towel with one hand, he reached out and skimmed his thumb over her cheek. "I'd rather cut off my arm than hurt you again."

"I know," she managed to say.

Anna did know it, too. Even with everything that had happened, Rafe was an honorable, decent man. A man who just happened to send her body into overdrive.

"But this isn't about hurt," she explained. "It's about everything else."

And she still wasn't making any sense!

"I lied to you," Rafe admitted. "So, I don't expect you to just get over that because we've got the hots for each other."

The smile came before she could stop it. It was nerves. All nerves. She blew out a long breath of frustration. "This is hard for me."

He lifted an eyebrow. "Me, too, darling," he drawled.

That cocky grin returned in full force. She felt the impact of it, and of his dimples, all the way to her toes.

Anna clamped her teeth over her bottom lip to keep from smiling again. Part of her wanted to throttle him for making her remember why she'd fallen in love with him in the first place. Another part wanted to reach out, take hold of him and never let go.

Fighting back his own smile, he leaned in and brushed his mouth over hers. "Trust me, I know a little bit about torture. In the past four days, every time I kissed you, I knew it couldn't go any further than that." His lips touched hers again. "I wanted more. And I didn't have to rely on my memory to tell me that."

"Rafe—"

That was as far as she got. Anna didn't know whether to ask him to stop or beg for another kiss. Somewhere between the time he stepped out of that shower and now, she'd lost the battle with right and reason.

He slid his hand around the back of her neck. "Was that a no?" he asked.

But he knew the answer. Anna could see it in the depths of those cool green eyes. There was nothing about her body language or expression that was saying no.

"I've been trying to talk myself out of this," he whispered.

"Me, too."

"Yeah, and neither one of us is doing a very good job of it."

He was *so* right.

Rafe moved against her. Softly. Body against body. Until she was pressed between him and the door. Everything slowed. Like a lazy, hot breeze. It swirled around her until all she could see and feel was Rafe.

"My memories of you are somewhat limited, but you know what I remember about that first time I saw you in the colonel's office?" he asked.

Unable to speak, she shook her head.

"I remember your hair. It was shiny. And your face— the way it lit up the whole room. It was like you had eaten a whole constellation or something. Honey, you were sparkling." Her breasts brushed against his bare chest and sent her pulse out of control. "But what really got me was your smile."

"My smile?" she repeated. Sweet mercy, she sounded asthmatic. And she couldn't think. Her body was on the verge of begging him to take her where she stood.

"Yeah." He slid his hand to her chin, caressing her bottom lip with his thumb. "You looked up when I walked into that room. Our eyes met. And you smiled at me. Best damn smile I've ever seen, and I promise you, I've seen some smiles in my lifetime. I remember wondering if you tasted as good as you looked."

He held that long, lingering gaze a moment longer before his mouth came to hers.

Like everything else Rafe McQuade did in life, the kiss was potent and thorough. But surprisingly gentle. Anna felt herself melt against him. The heat of his mouth roared through her and ignited a raging hunger that only he could satisfy.

There was a good reason why Rafe was the only man she'd ever given herself to, and that kiss reminded her of it. He was truly the only man she'd ever truly wanted. Or loved.

Breathing hard, he pulled back and shook his head. "Know what? I was right. You do look as good as you taste."

That did it. The phone slipped from her hand and clattered onto the wet tile floor. Anna threw her arms around him and returned the kiss.

Their mouths came together, adjusted. Took. And claimed. Anna did the same with her body. She pressed herself against him, taking in his warmth and the feel of his corded muscles.

It was perfect. Like coming home.

She slid her leg along the outside of his. Rafe didn't let it stay merely a caress. He caught on to the back of her knee and positioned it so it cradled his hip. It also did an effective job of bringing the centers of their bodies into direct contact. *Very* direct contact. She felt him hard and hot as he pushed against her.

Anna sucked in her breath. Felt the heat surge within her. She fought to pull him closer, until they seemed one.

But that wasn't enough.

He took that fire bath of kisses to her ear and spoke against her skin. "I'm willing to bet my prize Harley that you're, uh, as uncomfortable as I am."

"Oh, yes." Her body screamed for more, but she forced herself to remember this shouldn't be happening. Even if she could forget the part about Rafe's memory loss, she couldn't forget all the danger lurking around. "But this probably isn't the best idea we've—"

He stopped her with a kiss and continued until Anna didn't think she had an ounce of breath, or willpower, left. Just when she was ready to strip off that towel, Rafe tore his mouth from hers.

"This is not easy for me to say, Anna, but you're right about this not being a good idea. I'd be lower than dirt if I made love to you while you still have so many doubts about me."

"Doubts?" Anna questioned. "What doubts?"

He smiled and groaned. "That's the fire in your blood talking, so I'll just grit my teeth and pretend you didn't say it. You have doubts, all right, and I don't want to take anything from you that you can't give willingly."

She cursed. He was right. It was the lust talking, and with everything so unresolved in their lives, making love should be the last thing on her mind.

"Tell you what, though, darling," Rafe whispered. "Here's Plan B. I keep on this towel but do something about your discomfort."

He slid his hand over her breasts, to her stomach. And lower. Each slippery caress stole her breath.

Rafe stopped, then added some well-placed pressure right on the zipper of her jeans. "So, what do you say? Want me to take the edge off for you?"

"I can't—"

"Trust me, I'd enjoy it as well. Not quite as much, mind you." He flashed those dimples. "But I'd love to find out if you look as good as you taste when I send you flying straight to the stars."

"Ooh." She groaned.

As offers went, it was the most tempting one by far she'd ever received. But while it might give her some temporary relief, it wouldn't solve anything, and it would complicate an already complicated situation.

With plenty of regrets and with some forced deep breaths, she stepped away from him.

Rafe ground his forehead against the door. "That's what I figured you'd say."

He pulled in several generous breaths of his own and reached for a pair of boxers he'd placed on the vanity. He slid them on beneath the towel. Anna tried not to notice that he was fully aroused, but it would have been impossible not to notice *that*.

"I have to know something," he commented. The towel slid from his waist and fell to the floor. "Did I make the experience as pleasurable as possible for you that afternoon I took your virginity?"

She'd already opened her mouth to answer, but he cursed and grabbed his holster off the vanity.

"Where? How?" he demanded.

It took her a moment to realize he was responding to something that someone had said into his earpiece. Sheldon, probably. And from the look on Rafe's face, it wasn't good news. Just like that, the passion evaporated, and in its place crawled the cold, hard fear.

Rafe flipped off the light, wrapped an arm around her and hauled her to the floor.

"How the devil did that happen?" he demanded.

Anna braced herself. But there was no way she could have braced herself for what she heard. It was the sound of a low-flying plane.

"I take it that's not one of ours?" she asked.

"No. And neither are the men who just parachuted out of it."

Oh, God.

While she sat stock-still in the dark room, the sound grew closer. And closer. Anna pulled in her breath and waited.

It didn't take long, mere seconds, before she heard the first shot.

Chapter 7

Gunfire pelted the cabin. Bullets tore though the thick logs and penetrated the interior near the ceiling. It was a barrage of ammunition, and Rafe had no doubt that it was coming from at least three automatic weapons.

Somehow, he managed to get the bathroom door open, and he shoved Anna into the pitch-black hallway, away from the windows. He followed on top of her, sheltering her from the flying debris.

"What should we do?" she yelled.

"Stay down until Sheldon and the others intervene."

It wasn't much of a plan, but at the moment it was the only one Rafe had. He had to trust that the team positioned at the end of the road would soon respond, and that the trained combat specialists along with Sheldon could put a stop to what was happening. If not, if the primary defense failed, he was armed and ready for a secondary assault.

Rafe resisted the instinct to join the fight then and there. He didn't dare leave Anna alone and unprotected. Instead, he forced himself to concentrate on the method of attack itself. Simple but effective. A light aircraft. Three armed men parachuting into the area at night. They were likely members of Quivira's group of rebels. God knows how they'd managed to avoid the detection equipment to get this close, but later he'd find out how they had accomplished it.

He listened to the sound of the striking bullets. And studied the pattern. There was no breaking glass. No concentration of gunfire in the bathroom, where the only light had been on only moments earlier. Just the nonstop blasts of lead through wood.

And that told Rafe loads about their situation.

The gunmen obviously weren't aiming to kill, so that didn't leave many possibilities. They either wanted him. Or Anna. Or both. But they wanted them alive. That meant they were using the gunfire as a distraction and were probably already closing in on the cabin.

"Where the devil are you, Sheldon?" Rafe called out. He levered himself up slightly in case he had to fire.

"Nearby," Sheldon barked into the earpiece. "Hold your horses. I'm trying to establish position here."

Easier said than done. It riled Rafe to the core that the rebels had put Anna's life in danger. Any one of those bullets could ricochet and hurt her or the baby. In hindsight he could see that bringing her here to the cabin had been a huge mistake. Too bad it'd taken hindsight for him to figure out that one.

"Rafe?" he heard someone say in the earpiece. Not

Sheldon this time but Luke Buchanan. "We're coming in. Stay down."

"No plans to do otherwise," Rafe assured him.

The gunfire assault continued. It was deafening, but Rafe tried to pick through it and figure out the positions of the rebels. North was his guess. They were clustered on the north side of the cabin. The side that faced the bathroom.

He heard the counterattack a moment later. Buchanan and Sheldon had obviously arrived. Still, the rebels didn't stop firing. Beneath him, he felt Anna's whole body tremble. God, he hated that they'd put her through this. She'd already been through too much already.

A spray of bullets slammed into the narrow window at the end of the hall. Glass burst through the air and landed on his back and legs.

"The angle of shots changed," Rafe mumbled.

Damn it. It was wrong. All wrong. And it blew his theory that the rebels were just trying to distract them. Unless...

Rafe put that thought on hold when a round of fire rocketed through the living room.

With his arm still looped around Anna, he dragged her forward to the hall storage closet. He opened the door, pushed Anna inside and positioned himself in front of her. Rafe braced himself to fire.

The shots continued. Only lower. No more bullets near the ceiling. Someone was aiming directly at the floor, and there wasn't a thing he could to stop it.

Anna mumbled something he couldn't understand. Something about the baby. She was scared out of her mind, no doubt about it. He was scared, too. Not for himself. But for her and his child. Somehow, he had to get them out of this alive.

More shots blasted through the bottom logs of the cabin. Several slammed into the old porcelain bathtub and toilet. Since the shots were coming from multiple directions at once, maybe that meant the team members hadn't been able to contain the rebels. The alternative wasn't something he wanted to consider yet, but he prayed to God it wasn't friendly fire that was coming so close to killing them.

The shots tapered off. Rafe kept count and timed the seconds in between until there was nothing but silence. He didn't dare move yet. He waited for a signal from Sheldon and Buchanan.

"Please tell me it's over," Anna whispered, her voice shaking.

God, he wished he could do that, but he couldn't. It was a worthless consolation, but Rafe reached behind him and touched her face. "I don't know yet."

The silence closed in around them. For Anna, it must have been smothering. Rafe had been trained to react to situations just like these, and he was damn good at his job. But there was just one little problem with that training. He'd never before had a scenario where he had to protect someone who happened to be carrying his child.

"I'm coming through the front door," Buchanan informed him. "Don't shoot."

"That better mean an all clear," Rafe countered.

"It does. For now."

Like the caress he'd just given Anna, that comment wasn't exactly reassuring. Maybe *for now* would last long enough so that he could get Anna out of there.

When the doorknob moved, Rafe got to his feet, but he kept his weapon aimed. He kept it aimed even after he saw Buchanan in the doorway.

Buchanan eyed the raised gun. "Trying to tell me something, Rafe?"

"No. I just want answers." And more than that, he wanted that nagging feeling in the back of his mind to go away. Something was wrong. But what? "What the heck just happened out there?"

"I'd like to know the same thing." Buchanan didn't holster his weapon, either, when he stepped inside. "Somebody jammed our equipment for a couple of minutes, just long enough for that crop duster to get past us."

"Us?"

"Me and Colonel Shaw. We were the team at the bottom of the hill."

That should have made Rafe feel a lot better.

It didn't.

"How's Anna?" Buchanan asked.

"I'm fine," she assured him. "But I'd very much like some answers."

Buchanan didn't have time to respond because Colonel Shaw stepped inside the cabin. Like Buchanan, he wore a dark battle-dress uniform—a BDU—and was armed to the hilt. They'd obviously been prepared for a fight.

Rafe gripped Anna's wrist and helped her to her feet. Because she didn't look too steady, he slid his arm around her waist and held on.

The colonel made a cursory glance of Rafe's attire. Only then did he remember he wore just his boxers. He was lucky to have those on. If the attack had happened moments earlier, he would have had on a towel.

"So, what happened?" Rafe asked.

Shaw shook his head. "Three men are dead. We had no choice but to take them out."

"Oh, God," Anna whispered. "Were they Quivira's men?"

"I wouldn't count on it," Nicholas Sheldon explained as he came through the door. He swatted the dust and bits of leaves off his camouflaged pants. "I managed to get some images just as the plane came into view. I'll check it out as soon as I can get back to the bunker, but I think we're dealing with the rival faction here."

Maybe. Rafe didn't intend to buy that scenario, hook, line and sinker. The angle of the shots told a powerful story. The first shooters had wanted them alive. The second hadn't.

"These guys didn't have kidnapping on their minds," Sheldon continued. "They were aiming to kill."

"So, you think this is *the* rival faction?" Rafe asked, keeping his other thoughts to himself.

Shaw relaxed some of the tension in his face and walked toward them. "We can get into all of that later, Rafe. Anna looks like she needs to sit down."

"No," she snapped. "Sitting down won't steady my nerves. I'd rather know the truth."

Rafe wanted to give her a round of applause. The woman sure had backbone. But he saw the steely look in the colonel's eyes. There was something that Shaw didn't want her to know. Maybe that just didn't apply to Anna, either. Maybe there were things Shaw was keeping from him.

Colonel Shaw reached out and took Anna's hand.

"Some of the things that went on out there are classified."

"Then give me the *official-use-only* version," she insisted. She pulled her hand from his and stepped back. "Because the way I see it, this just got official, and I have a need to know."

Despite everything, Rafe almost smiled. She definitely had backbone.

"All right." The colonel reholstered his weapon and nodded. "We have reason to believe that Victor O'Reilly has joined in on this fight."

"O'Reilly," Rafe repeated. And then he cursed. It wasn't news he wanted to hear, but it sure explained all those stray bullets. Quivira wanted him alive, to retrieve some information about God knows what. But O'Reilly, well, that was a whole different story.

In the simplest terms possible, O'Reilly was an expatriated American scumbag. He was just as powerful. Just as lethal. Just as mean. And he wouldn't hesitate to kill Anna or him if it meant keeping vital information from Quivira. That left Rafe with another question—why didn't O'Reilly want his old rival to get his hands on the information locked in those blank spots of his memory?

"Victor O'Reilly?" Anna questioned. "As in the man who's battling Quivira for control of the same territory in South America?"

"The very one." Rafe didn't have to give Anna biographical details about the man. After all, she'd been caught in cross fire in Monte de Leon between Quivira and O'Reilly's troops. "It could mean that whatever's trapped in my head, O'Reilly wants it to stay there, and he'll kill me to make sure it does. Or maybe he just wants me dead for another reason that I can't remember."

"Great," she mumbled, pressing her fingertips to her mouth. "Just great."

Yeah. And if he was in danger, so were Anna and their baby. If Quivira planned to kidnap and use her as leverage, then O'Reilly wouldn't hesitate to do the same. Or worse.

"There's more," Shaw continued, looking straight at Anna. "Sheldon listened in on your call from Janine Billings."

She shook her head. "Why?"

Hell. Rafe knew the answer, and he also knew that Anna wasn't going to like it.

"Janine knows Victor O'Reilly," Rafe explained, hoping it would sound better coming from him rather than Shaw. "They were, uh, friends years ago when he was in law school at the University of Texas."

"Friends?" she repeated. She sounded calm, but Rafe suspected there were at least a dozen questions going through her head. Ugly questions. And at least one of those questions would deal with why he hadn't mentioned this sooner.

"We've been monitoring her activity for weeks now," Shaw added.

Anna motioned toward the splinters, broken glass and other debris that littered the cabin. "And you think Janine had something to do with this?"

"She left her apartment immediately after she got off the phone with you. She walked two blocks to a café and is at this very moment having a double latte with a man who has close ties to O'Reilly."

"That proves nothing," Anna snarled.

But it didn't sound as if she completely believed that. Rafe groaned. He hadn't wanted her to learn about Janine this way. From all accounts, Anna and Janine hadn't known each other long but were as close as sisters.

"There's tracing equipment on her phone," Buchanan explained. "We don't know if she put it there or if someone else did. But at this point, we can't take any chances."

Anna turned to Rafe. "You knew about this?"

He nodded.

Her eyes darkened. "You listened to my phone conversation with her?"

"No. But Sheldon did."

She squeezed her eyes shut and made a shivering sound of anger. "Any other violations of my privacy that I should know about?" Anna demanded. She opened her eyes and stormed toward Sheldon. "How about it? Did you enjoy listening to a private conversation with my friend?"

"Just doing my job, Mrs. McQuade."

"Anna, the order came from me," Shaw assured her. "If you want to blame someone, then aim in my direction."

"All right, I will. Know what else? I'll blame you for the shooting, too. You shouldn't have had us come here. Those rebels nearly killed us."

"I know, and it's not going to happen again."

Rafe didn't add a vote of confidence to that, but he intended to be much more vigilant. Maybe he could even convince Anna of that.

"We're leaving here, right?" he asked Shaw.

"Yes. Get dressed." Shaw looked back at Buchanan

and Sheldon. "We go to the backup plan. Prepare the bravo location. We move immediately."

Rafe knew about the bravo location. It was another cabin at an undisclosed location. Suddenly the term "undisclosed location" made him very uncomfortable. If he was about to ask Anna to go anywhere with him, then he personally wanted to make sure it was safe.

He studied each man. Shaw, Sheldon, Buchanan. When it got right down to it, he didn't really know any of them. He'd known Shaw and Buchanan barely a year. A year he didn't even remember. He knew even less about Sheldon.

That made Rafe very uneasy.

Because despite all of Shaw's precautions, reassurances and backups, Quivira or O'Reilly had gotten through what was supposed to have been impenetrable security. And that left Rafe with one serious question.

How?

Chapter 8

Anna glanced around the tiny cabin. She could probably touch both sides at once if she merely stretched her arms out. If she'd been so inclined. She was too exhausted to test her theory.

There was a sitting area, such that it was. It consisted of a sofa and a lamp mounted on the wall above it. Across from that was a counter that could be loosely construed as a kitchen. There was also a bathroom, and sandwiched above it was a loft-type sleeping area.

"And here I thought the other cabin was small," Anna mumbled.

Still, she wasn't complaining. She hadn't wanted to spend another minute in that place. Every splinter, every shard of glass was a reminder of how close Rafe and she had come to being killed.

"Home sweet home," Rafe said from behind her.

From the sarcasm in his voice, he obviously wasn't impressed either with the accommodations of the bravo location.

Rafe eased her into the postage-stamp-size living area so that Luke Buchanan could join them. It was a good thing she wasn't claustrophobic because the three of them took up nearly every extra inch of available space.

Buchanan brought in with him the scent of gunfire and battle. She wasn't sure, but she thought there might be bloodstains on his shirt. Anna didn't want to know whose blood it was.

"I'll need to stay in here with you," Buchanan said. "Sorry, but I'm just following orders. Sheldon and the colonel left the car here in case we have to get out, but they're on foot at the end of the road."

"The road has two ends," Rafe informed him. "Let's hope they're watching both."

Again, she heard the sarcasm in Rafe's voice. Their eyes met for a moment, and in that brief encounter, Anna tried to convey her displeasure about their situation. She was especially displeased about him withholding information about Janine.

Now, if she could just figure out how she felt about that information, then she might be able to figure out what to do. And whom to trust.

God, was it possible that Janine was in on this?

She didn't want to believe it. Janine and she had grown close over the past couple of months. But Anna didn't intend to push anything aside. Not anymore. After all, Janine had never said a word about knowing any South American rebels, and that subject had come up numerous times after her return from Monte de Leon and during Rafe's captivity. It was definitely something Janine should have mentioned.

And then there was that coffee meeting with one of Victor O'Reilly's associates. No, Anna wasn't about to push that aside, even if she couldn't come up with a plausible reason as to why Janine would turn traitor and put people's lives—including hers—at stake.

"Anna and I'll try to get some rest," Rafe announced, not waiting to get Buchanan's opinion about it.

She almost resisted when Rafe took her arm and helped her up the ladder to the sleeping area. Almost. But there was something in his body language and firm grip that made her think he had more than just rest on his mind.

"Careful," he whispered. Rafe put his mouth close to her ear as they sank onto the narrow mattress. "The place is probably bugged."

Anna barely managed to suppress a groan. She'd had her fill of people listening in on her private conversations. Heaven knows if Sheldon had overheard her talking to Janine about the baby. It was bad enough that Shaw knew.

Rafe shut the curtain that separated their bed from the rest of the cabin. It prevented Buchanan from seeing them, but that didn't mean he still wasn't capable of hearing whatever they said. Of course, he might not have to resort to such primitive measures if the place was truly bugged.

"Don't know about you," Rafe whispered, "but I don't have a warm and fuzzy feeling about any of this."

"I agree, but what do we do about it?"

Rafe glanced out the tiny window at the head of their

bed. "I'm not sure." He partially shut that curtain, as well. "I guess that depends on how much you trust me."

There was still a thin light coming from the edges of the main curtain so she could see the expression on his face. It probably mirrored her own concern. At the moment, trust was a huge issue between them.

"I'm scared," she admitted, knowing it didn't answer his question. But the truth was she did trust him. A few blank spots in his memory couldn't erase the relationship she'd created with Rafe over the past months. With luck, he'd soon remember that relationship. And her.

"I know, and I'm sorry." Rafe shook his head. "I wish I could do something to make the fear go away."

He lay back, next to her. Side by side. And touching. The closeness stirred other memories within her. Ones that had chosen a bad time to be stirred.

She'd only slept next to Rafe once—in the cellar in Monte de Leon—and it'd been the most memorable event of her life. This one would be memorable, of course, but for all the wrong reasons. There was no surge of relief that Rafe was safe. No certainty that she'd indeed just been rescued from death itself. There was just the worry that it could happen all over again.

Rafe turned his head to the side so he could whisper in her ear. "How are you *really* doing?"

She heard the inflection and knew he wasn't just talking about her well-being. There was concern for her pregnancy and the child that they'd yet to discuss.

"I'm fine considering everything," Anna admitted. She paused, wondering just how far she should push this. After all, the place was probably bugged. But then, they might not have any quiet, perfect moments for a long time. This could possibly be as good at it would get. "You know, I was as surprised as you were when I found out I was pregnant."

"I can imagine," he mumbled.

There seemed to be a roadblock at the end of that comment, but Anna didn't let it stop her. "I'd planned on telling you on our honeymoon, but I blurted it out when I was holding that gun on you."

"I remember." He paused. "Look, I'm sorry it has to be this way. I mean, I'm sorry you're having to deal with all this uncertainty and the, uh, baby as well."

"You're having to deal with it, too," she reminded him.

"Yeah. I am." He groaned and scrubbed his hand over his face. "All of this would be a helluva lot easier if I just had my memory."

Yes, and then they could get on with their lives. Well, maybe. Maybe the rebels would still want them dead. And maybe their lives would never get back to normal.

"First chance I get, I'll try to get in touch with Cal Rico," Rafe said softly. "He's the one man I know I can trust."

"You really think Rico can find out who's behind this?"

"Maybe." He looked over at her. "All these what-ifs and maybes won't do us a bit of good right now. So, let's concentrate on the things we can do something about. How about let's play 'jog Rafe's memory'?" He picked up her hand and stared at her wedding ring. "Tell me about our first date."

It was probably a ploy to distract her, but Anna didn't care. Every time she closed her eyes, she kept seeing the bullets as they tore through the cabin. Any one of them could have killed Rafe, the baby and her. If she stood a chance of getting any rest, she had to stop thinking about that.

"You took me to a carnival in San Antonio," she whispered. "We rode the roller coaster until I nearly threw up."

He chuckled softly. "And I ate a couple of pounds of cotton candy."

"You did." Anna glanced at him. "Do you remember that?"

"No, I just remember I love the stuff. What else did we do?"

"Let's see." She closed her eyes and let the memories drift through her mind. "We played just about every arcade game there was to play. And you won second place in the mechanical-bull-riding contest."

"Second? I didn't win?"

Anna smiled. Rafe had had the same reaction that night. "There was stiff competition."

He stayed quiet for several moments, and Anna felt the light mood drain away. "I'm sorry I kept that information about Janine from you. Let me just say this— I'm not aware of any more secrets. But from here on out, I'll tell you the whole truth about everything, even if it's something that might upset you."

It was definitely the right thing to say. It made her feel marginally better about their situation. Too bad there were at least a dozen other issues to worry about, and one especially kept pestering her.

She kept her eyes closed, afraid of how he'd react to her question. "If you don't get your memory back—"

"It'll come back," Rafe interrupted.

"And if it doesn't, what then? It's something you have to consider."

"You're asking about us, aren't you? You want to know what'll happen to us if those blank spots aren't filled in?"

"Yes," Anna murmured. But she wasn't so sure she could manage the next part. She took a deep breath first and tried to prepare herself for where this conversation might end. "Will you get a divorce?"

Rafe never hesitated. "No way."

"But—"

He brushed a kiss on her cheek. "Darling, I've already consummated this marriage in my head at least a dozen times. That counts for something."

Maybe. But Anna couldn't rest her hopes on it. If Rafe got his memory back, or even if he didn't, his feelings for her might never be the same.

Never.

They certainly couldn't go back to where they had once been. There was a connection between them. And an enormous barrier.

Anna had no idea which one would win in the end.

"You're thinking too much again." Rafe pulled her into his arms. "Now, get some sleep. You'll need it if I can figure out a way to get us out of here."

Yes. She did need to sleep, but Anna didn't think it'd come tonight. Still, she eased herself deeper into Rafe's embrace and let the night and the safety of his arms take over.

Chapter 9

The nightmare raced through Rafe's head...

A brutal guerrilla-style ambush in the jungle. It was spliced with images from his own rescue two months later. Fragments of violence that followed a meeting gone bad. He'd been caught in a three-way cross fire between the CROs, O'Reilly's group of rebels and the men from Quivira's forces. A deadly triple ticket that could have easily left him dead.

And almost did.

Rafe had seen the bodies that littered the jungle. He'd studied the intel reports, had memorized them, so he could put identities with some of those dead faces. Quivira's own number-two man, Miguel Ramos. Across from him was Eve DeCalley, an agent from a private research facility, Sen-tron, who'd infiltrated Quivira's group a month earlier as part of Shaw's plan to draw out the rebel leader. The agent's death was a loss not only of life but of valuable information.

Just down the same bloody path lay Quivira's own son. Nineteen years old. Colonel Shaw had to shoot the kid or else be shot. In the end, the rebel leader's son had died along with the others. And in the end, before Rafe could make it out of that hellhole, he'd found himself facing the business end of an assault rifle held by one of Quivira's men.

Rafe still felt the sting of the ropes around his wrists. Even in sleep, he reacted as he'd been trained to react. His body prepared itself for the fight. He wouldn't die. He refused to die.

Evade and escape.

Those were his only options. Anna was safe. A few hours earlier, he'd put her on that transport himself, and somehow he had to make it home where she was waiting for him.

Pain from the brutal beating came back to him in broken, clipped images. The crack of his rib. The taste of his own blood in his mouth. The jab of the needle into his arm.

And there were questions. Always questions. His and theirs. About Shadow Warrior—a synthetic, weaponized strain of a deadly flu virus and its antidote. A virus and antidote that didn't exist outside the walls of the Sen-tron research agency. No one, especially the Alpha Team, had any plans for Quivira to get his hands on it, but Shaw had hoped Shadow Warrior would lure the rebel out.

Quivira definitely wanted the deadly virus to use against his enemies. But it wasn't the only thing. He wanted the information that Rafe had. It was Quivira's need for the information that'd caused him to fill the needle with the truth serum and shove it into Rafe's arm.

What had he wanted to know?

What?

It seemed there. Just within reach. Rafe felt as if he could almost touch it, but it faded before he could hold on to it.

"Rafe?"

His eyes jarred open. Rafe reached for his gun, but he felt her catch on to him. He almost broke her grip the hard way before he realized whose hands were on him.

"Anna," he whispered.

"You were dreaming." Her voice was a murmur. Soft. Warm. Reassuring. Like the hand she smoothed over his cheek.

"I don't know what he wants," Rafe mumbled. Remnants of the nightmare were still with him. Pieces of violence that wouldn't go away. The images still roared through his head, filling him with adrenaline. "Damn it, I just don't know what he wants from me."

"It's all right. It'll come to you."

Rafe latched on to every gently spoken word. God, did he need them. It didn't seem possible that a woman he hardly knew could make him feel as if everything would be okay. But that's exactly what she did. Maybe that's why he'd fallen in love with Anna in the first place.

She eased closer to him, her movements drowsy and slow. She slipped her hand around the back of his neck and into his hair. Her body brushed against him. And as if it were the most natural thing in the world, her mouth came to his.

Like the rest of the moment, the kiss she gave him was unhurried. The fingers that she trailed down his cheek, barely a caress. But that was all it took to erase the nightmare and make him want her more than his next breath.

Rafe fought through the sleepy haze in his head and tried to figure out if this should be happening. The answer he got was a no. And not just a plain *no,* either, but a resounding one. The timing sucked, no doubt about it.

Still, it felt damn good to hang on to what she was offering him.

He didn't hear anything suspicious. Just the drone of the air conditioner at the back of the cabin. Buchanan had turned off the lights in the main part of the cabin hours ago, just before Rafe allowed himself to doze off.

Rafe glanced out the tiny corner of the window—sunrise was still a half hour away. They were possibly in danger, and he needed to figure out how to get them out of there.

Still, he didn't pull away from her.

He cursed himself. It seemed wrong to take this intimacy from her when he couldn't remember the feelings that'd created the intimacy in the first place. But not all of those feelings were uncertain. He did care for Anna. A lot. That seemed, well, ingrained, as if destiny had paired them and wouldn't have things otherwise.

But just how deep did that caring and destiny go?

"You're thinking too much," Anna murmured against his mouth.

Mercy. The woman tossed his own words at him. He smiled in spite of the battle going on in his head. Too bad that battle didn't do a thing to cool his engines. That one little kiss from Anna quelled every argument he had for putting a stop to this. He wanted her gentle words.

Her touch.

Her mouth.

He wanted *her*.

Rafe gave up the fight that he knew he wouldn't win and hauled her to him.

"Restraint," he reminded himself. As if a mere reminder could stop this.

He couldn't keep the kiss lazy and gentle as she'd done. No way. He dove in headfirst. The energy from the nightmare and the leftover adrenaline fused with the need he had for her. Just her. Memories weren't necessary for him to know that he'd never needed or cared for a woman as much as Anna.

This was all need. All flames. It scared the devil out of him, and yet he wanted it to consume him.

They both fought to deepen the kiss. Her tongue mated with his. His grip on her tightened. They clung to each other. And the need just simply kept on building.

Rafe pushed some strands of hair away from her face and stared down at her. "Did we do this when I made love to you?" he whispered.

"Oh, yes. And more."

Good. So he hadn't just taken her in a flash of heat. How he'd managed not to do exactly that, he might never know. As it was, he had to fight not to take her right then, right there. He couldn't afford to lose himself inside her.

And that's exactly what would happen.

He'd lose himself and forget all about the danger that was still around them. She deserved a lot better than that. So, he had to play this safe even if it drove him out of his freaking mind.

Anna pulled him right back to her, her mouth hungry and hot, and she moved herself against him. He knew what she wanted, what she needed, and cursed the fact that his need matched hers. Too bad his would have to wait.

But he had other plans for her. Rafe undid her buttons and pushed open her shirt.

"Is it all right if we do this?" she mumbled.

"It's better than all right."

He would have liked to take a fire bath of kisses to her stomach and lower, but there was no way he could manage that in the tiny space without making a ton of noise. Logistically, the cabin wasn't a prime location for a long night of lovemaking. Still, where there was a will, there was a way. The will part was a given, and he'd already thought of a way.

He ran his hand over her stomach, and while he kissed her mouth, he opened the snap on her jeans. She reached for his zipper as well, but Rafe stopped her. One touch from her, and he wouldn't be able to think straight. For about a million reasons he needed to keep a clear head. Hopefully, that was possible. With the scent of her arousal all around him and the taste of her in his mouth, it would be a tough fight.

"Did I touch you like this when we made love?" he asked against her ear. He slipped his hand past the opening of her jeans and into her silky panties.

Her breath came out in short, hot bursts, and her grip tightened on his shoulders. "You did."

"How about this?" He went lower. And lower. Slowly. Until he slid his fingers into the wet heat of her body.

"Yes," she managed to say. She arched against his hand. "Definitely yes. I liked it then, and now."

The honest answer was nearly his undoing. It fueled his own heat, but because he had no other choice, he pushed that desire aside. Rafe ran his tongue over her earlobe and matched it with the strokes of his fingers. She gasped softly and frantically sought out his mouth.

He obliged. And kissed her.

She pulled him hard against her. The kiss didn't stop. Neither did the rhythm of his fingers inside her. She lifted her hips off the mattress, deepening the pressure of his touch.

"Did we do this?" he asked, fighting to keep the flames inside him in check.

"We did more. A lot more. It was magic. We were good together, Rafe."

He ached to join her in the most intimate way. To slide into that heat and move with her in an ancient cadence that would send them both over the edge.

But he couldn't do that and keep her safe.

Instead, he did the only thing he could do. He touched. And coaxed. He whispered words, and with each stroke of his fingers, he learned how to pleasure this woman he'd married.

She wrapped her arms around him and buried her face against his neck. "I shouldn't—"

"Wrong. You definitely should," he insisted. Rafe pulled back slightly so he could see her face. "Let me do this for you."

"I'd rather wait until both of us are ready to do this together."

He groaned. It wasn't the best time for that old philosophy to rear its head. "I'm ready," he assured her.

"Make that more than ready, but I just can't give you my undivided attention right now."

"I know, and that's why we should wait."

She slid her hand over his. Stopping him. Unfortunately, the back of her hand rubbed over the front of his jeans. The worst place possible. Other than nearly jumping out of his skin, he damn near embarrassed himself.

Alarmed, she shifted her position so she could look into his eyes. "Did I hurt you?"

"No." Rafe brushed a kiss on her mouth. "Why don't you let me finish what I started here?"

Anna shook her head and rebuttoned her top and jeans. "Believe me, I want that. Well, part of me does, anyway. But this isn't the right time or the right place."

"No. It's not," he confirmed.

She stared at him, apparently a little surprised that he'd agreed so readily. "And all this fire and, uh, whatever, apparently isn't going anywhere. It'll keep until we've...well, it'll keep."

Rafe had already geared up to agree to that as well. Reluctantly so, but he still would have agreed.

However, something stopped him.

Not a sound, exactly. And not even anything specific. It was just the feeling that something wasn't right. He lifted his head a fraction and listened.

She started to say something, but Rafe motioned for her to stay quiet. He eased back the curtain and looked out into the cabin. Buchanan was on the small sofa beneath them, but his eyes flew open the moment that Rafe's gaze met his.

"Problem?" Buchanan mouthed after a noisy yawn.

"Maybe."

He caught on to Anna's hand and helped her off the

mattress. Buchanan got to his feet and met them at the bottom of the ladder. Silently, both men checked out their surroundings. Without releasing his grip on Anna, Rafe went to the door and glanced out the tiny window next to it. Buchanan did the same on the other side of the cabin.

"Anything?" Rafe asked Buchanan.

"Negative."

That didn't do a thing to reassure Rafe. Something was wrong. Too bad he couldn't quite figure out what. There seemed to be a fog thickening in his head.

He put his hand on the doorknob and sifted through the sounds of the predawn. The air conditioner was still running. But what Rafe didn't hear was anything else. No sound of the woods. No sound of anything. And that made the hair stand up on the back of his neck.

Anna yawned and slumped against him. Rafe yawned as well and tried to shake off the dizziness. The dizziness he shouldn't have been feeling.

"I'm getting Anna out of here now," Rafe informed Buchanan.

"My orders are to keep you here."

As if that would stop him. Buchanan moved toward the door, but Rafe just muscled him aside. "Then, you'll have to disobey them because I'm not staying."

Rafe heard it then. The sound that his body had already braced itself to hear. Not the air conditioner as he'd originally thought. No. This was a car engine. And it was too damn close to the cabin.

"Get out!" Rafe yelled.

He threw open the door, pulled Anna out with him and began to run as fast as his feet would carry him.

Her steps were sluggish, and he finally lifted her off the ground.

Rafe looked back only to make sure that Buchanan had evacuated. He had. And Rafe saw something else. The car. With a hose running from the exhaust into the cabin.

Someone had just tried to kill them.

And that someone apparently wasn't finished.

Rafe skirted to the other side of an embankment just as the artillery shell blasted through the cabin. Fiery debris launched through the air in every direction. He didn't stop. Rafe kept a death grip on Anna and headed straight for the woods. It might be the only chance they had for survival.

A bullet ricocheted off the branches of a dead oak, sending a spray of splinters into the air. Anna ducked her head down, but somehow managed to get her feet on the ground so they could run even faster. She let Rafe lead the way.

She risked a glance behind her. The sun had just risen, but she didn't need the morning light to see the angry coils of black smoke and fire that rose from what was left of the cabin. It confirmed what she already knew—they'd barely made it out of there alive.

Buchanan and the others were nowhere in sight. Hopefully, they'd made it away from the attack, as well. Like them, they were probably running for cover. Anna didn't want to think beyond that.

They scrambled over a rocky outcropping. She saw a cactus, a mound of low-growing, flourishing spikes just as Rafe hurdled himself over it. She hurdled, too, but not before one of the needle-like teeth syringed its way through her jeans and into her leg. She clamped her teeth over her lip to keep from crying out in pain.

More bullets.

These sprayed into the ground around them, kicking up dirt and small pebbles. Rafe shoved her in front of him, keeping a tight hold on her shoulder. He was pushing her to save them both, but in doing so, he had also put himself in the direct path of the bullets.

She thought of the baby. The risk, not just from the bullets but also from the exertion. Thankfully, she still jogged three times a week, and the doctor had assured her that it was all right to continue for months to come. But this wasn't a jog. It was a run for their lives. If she stopped, those rebels would kill them. At least if she ran, they stood a chance. Right now, a chance was all they had.

They hurried through a curtain of thick trees, sending them from the sunlight into near darkness. The air was damp and moldy. It smelled of rotting leaves and other disgusting things. Tree trunks twisted into sinewy coils. There were no animals in sight. No sounds, either, except their gusty breaths and their shoes digging into the spongy ground.

The sweat slipped off Anna's forehead and stung her eyes. Behind her, Rafe maneuvered her in the direction he wanted her to go. She felt limp, but she never stopped moving. To do so would mean surrender, and she had no plans to do that anytime soon. She would survive for her baby's sake.

The cloak of trees didn't last long. As much as Anna had disliked that eerie forest, she'd felt slightly safe there. It didn't last. They soon exited the other side. And were forced to come to a dead stop.

Their chances of survival just went from slim to none.

Chapter 10

Anna looked down and cursed. Rafe echoed much the same on a harsher scale.

Only inches from their shoes was a steep rock cliff that went straight down at least thirty feet. At the bottom was a sliver of a creek that looked about an inch deep. Jumping into it would be suicide.

"What now?" she whispered frantically.

Behind them, she heard the continuous rattle of gunfire, and it seemed to be getting closer. It would only be seconds before those gunmen tracked them down.

Rafe didn't answer. He moved along the ledge, and Anna followed. Keeping their pace at a quick jog, he kept his eyes angled on the cliff wall, studying. He was obviously looking for something, but she didn't have any idea what.

"Hang on," he warned a split second before he pulled her to the ground.

Rafe began to climb down the rocks toward a bush that jutted out from the cliff. For a moment, she thought he'd lost his mind, but then Anna saw what had captured his attention. It was a crevice several feet below, and it just might be deep enough to hide them.

Rafe went first. He eased himself onto a narrow lip beside the crevice and grabbed her wrist to help her. She tried not to waste even a second, even though her hands were trembling. It wasn't a good time to realize that she had a fear of heights, but Anna quickly pushed that fear aside and tried not to look down.

Gripping the scrawny bush, she shimmied down the rocks on her bottom until she reached the spot where Rafe was precariously balanced. He tightened his grip on her wrist, shouldered her into the small space and followed right behind her. After he'd sandwiched her inside, he twisted the bush so that it partially hid them.

The gunfire continued, but she couldn't tell how far away it was. Anna stood there praying. Somehow, they had to get out of this alive.

Inch by inch, Rafe positioned himself in front of her, his weapon ready to fire. And they waited.

The minutes crawled by. Anna pressed her face against his back and closed her eyes, hoping it would shut out the noise.

It didn't.

She wasn't sure how long they stood there braced for the worst and praying for the best. Eventually, the shots tapered off until there was nothing but silence.

"Rafe?" Colonel Shaw shouted.

He was close. Very close. Perhaps just at the top of the ledge. But Rafe didn't move, and he motioned for her to stay quiet.

Anna didn't know how to react to that. So far, Shaw hadn't done a very good job of keeping the rebels away from them. Still, it might be safer with Shaw than forging out on their own.

Might.

But at this point she would trust Rafe before anyone else, including the man she'd known since she was a child.

"Rafe? Anna?" Not Shaw that time but Luke Buchanan. Sheldon joined Buchanan and Shaw, as well, and soon all three men were calling out for them.

Rafe didn't move a muscle. He was as calm as he'd been at the church. Unlike her. She was shaking from head to toe. Anna leaned against him and hoped her legs didn't give way.

The men's voices soon faded until she could no longer hear them. Still, Rafe waited for what seemed a lifetime before he relaxed the grip on his gun and glanced back at her.

"Are you okay?" he mouthed.

Anna nodded. But it was a lie that Rafe must have seen right through. He turned, adjusting his footing until he faced her.

"You did great," he said. He kept his voice soft and low.

"The day's not over yet. I could still go all medieval on you."

Somehow, he managed a smile. He looped his arm around her waist and carefully eased them both to the floor of the crevice. The sharp edges of the rocks jabbed into her back and side, but it was better than facing gunfire.

Because she needed to touch him, to assure herself that they were both alive, she pressed her fingers to his cheek. "Why does this keep happening?" she whispered. "How do the rebels find us?"

"I'd like to know that information myself. But I think it might be a good idea if we put some distance between us and Colonel Shaw."

"You think he had something to do with all of this?" Anna asked.

"Probably not, but somehow the rebels are tapping into our communications equipment. I've got to figure out a way to stop that from happening. But first we have to get out of here. We'll wait a little longer, until they've given up searching this area. Then I'll see what I can do about finding us a safer place."

Anna didn't want to ask if that was even possible. She was beyond the point of just being tired. In the past two days, she'd slept maybe three hours max. The fatigue was catching up with her, and she was too weary to think.

"Get some rest," Rafe encouraged when she put her head against his shoulder. He brushed a kiss on her forehead. "I'll wake you when it's time to go."

With her fear of heights, the idea of resting on the side of a cliff didn't especially appeal to her, but going back into those woods frightened her even more. She ran her hand over her stomach and prayed that they could somehow get out of this alive.

"Rest," he whispered.

Anna didn't fight it. She couldn't. The adrenaline rush had come and gone, leaving her too tired to fight anything. She closed her eyes and gave in to the exhaustion.

Rafe checked his watch, even though the minutes had been ticking off in his head. It'd been a little more than five hours since the last attack, and just slightly less than that since he'd heard anyone from the team call out for him.

He gave his earpiece an adjustment, but there were no sounds coming through it, either. That meant Shaw was out of range.

The area around them was silent. A normal kind of silence. Birds. A gusty breeze. No gut feelings of impending disaster or bad energy in the air.

Hopefully, that meant Shaw and the others were scouring some other area away from the cliff. And that also hopefully meant the latest cadre of rebels were dead. Because soon, Anna and he would have to get the heck out of there. But he didn't want to dodge bullets while he did that. They'd already done enough of that for one day.

Rafe rubbed his thumb over her cheek when she mumbled something in her sleep. She was obviously exhausted. He sure was. But rest for him would have to wait. Things could get much worse before they got better.

What he needed was a damn good plan. And fast. He'd already taken what he hoped was the first step in accomplishing that. Shortly after Anna had fallen asleep, Rafe had phoned Rico's emergency number and left a message about what had happened and asked his friend to call him ASAP.

Of course, if Rico was deep undercover—which he almost certainly was—then "ASAP" might not be for days. Still, it was a chance Rafe had to take. Rico possibly had information that would clear up a few things, and if not, he could at least get them moving in the right direction.

Anna stirred against him, snuggling deeper into the curve of his arm. "Baby," she whispered.

Yes. Funny that she should mention that. Even with everything he had to work out, Rafe couldn't quite get his mind off the baby.

Anna probably hadn't realized that someone had pumped carbon monoxide into the cabin. He'd have to tell her, of course, and he didn't need memories to know that it would frighten her even more than she already was.

Judas.

He had no idea how much of the potentially lethal exhaust they'd inhaled, but as soon as possible Anna would need to see a doctor to learn if it'd had any effect on the baby.

Effect.

The word put a huge knot in his throat.

He eased his hand over Anna's stomach. Over their child. He hadn't wanted to think much about the baby for fear it would break his concentration, but his concentration had seemed practically nil since his return from South America. And now he had to consider that the last attempt on their lives had done something much more than scare them or eat away at their peace of mind. It might have harmed their baby.

As if she'd sensed his thoughts, worry lines bunched up Anna's forehead, and a soft groan left her mouth.

Heaven knew what demons she was wrestling because of this. She'd been through way too much since Monte de Leon. Rico had told him a lot about the day Rafe had rescued her from an abandoned hacienda. If Rafe concentrated very hard, he could almost smell the scent of the cellar where he'd found her. But maybe that was wishful thinking.

God, he wanted to remember.

That was also the day he'd made love to her. Not the best location for such a momentous occasion. A sweltering cellar. The rebels battling it out all around them. Fear. Adrenaline. Relief. Yet, somehow Anna and he had come together and made love. Then he'd asked her to marry him as he put her on the transport that would carry her home.

"Two months ago," he said under his breath. In a cellar with a loaf-size window on the back wall. A two-by-four barricading the door. A rumpled blanket on the floor. And Anna reaching for him. He'd come there to rescue her and send her home.

Saving beautiful photographers is what I do best.

"What?" Anna eased open her eyes and looked up at him. "Did you say something?" she whispered.

Rafe stared at her a moment, trying to figure out if the memory was real or if it was something others had filled in for him. "Just talking to myself."

She glanced down at his hand that was still on her stomach. Her eyebrow lifted a fraction. Rather than say something he didn't want to say, Rafe eased his hand away.

Disappointment went through her eyes. Still, she didn't voice it.

Stretching and making soft sounds of discomfort, Anna sat up but winced when she looked out from the cliff. "How long do we have to stay here?"

Good question. And Rafe hoped he had a good answer. No matter what he did, it was a gamble. A gamble with Anna and his baby's lives. Still, it was just as dangerous to stay as it was to go.

"We'll need to move soon," he told her. "There's a storm coming in."

She looked up at the sky, at the thick curtain of metal-colored clouds. "Wonderful. Just what we don't need." She pursed her lips for a moment. "You'd think eventually something has to go our way, wouldn't you?"

He could only hope.

The phone clipped to his jeans rattled softly, and Rafe answered it, praying it was the one person he wanted to speak with.

It was.

"Rafe," Captain Cal Rico greeted. "I got your message. Let me guess—this call doesn't have anything to do with you needing love advice for your honeymoon?"

"You got that right." Rafe kept his voice to a whisper and continued to keep a vigilant watch around him. "Is this a secure line?"

"Secure enough."

In other words, someone might be listening. That meant Rafe wouldn't give away his position. "Shaw tells me that it's O'Reilly's men after us, but I'm not so sure."

"O'Reilly, huh?" Rico questioned. "Could be. He slipped into the country a couple of days ago."

That didn't surprise Rafe, but he had to wonder why he hadn't already heard this from Shaw. "Did O'Reilly come in by accident or design?"

"Maybe both."

It wasn't the solid assurance Rafe had hoped to hear, but what else was new? "Does that mean we've got a problem with security?"

"If I were a betting man—and I occasionally am—then I'd say, yes. But now you want a name to go with that burger and fries, huh?"

"A name would be nice. Then I'd know what I'm dealing with."

"You're dealing with a weasel, Rafe. A deadly, slimy one. Sorry, though, I can't give you a name, but I've got two theories. Wanna hear them?"

Rafe looked at Anna. Concern, and hope, was all over her face. Maybe by the time he finished with this call, he'd know what they were up against. And knowing that would help him decide what to do next.

"I definitely want to hear what you've got," he told Rico.

"Here's a tasty little tidbit that may mean nothing. Or everything. The Office of Special Investigations just opened a tab on two Alpha Team members, Luke Buchanan and Nicholas Sheldon. Seems Buchanan came into a rather large sum of money that he's buried several layers deep in an overseas account."

Buchanan. Well, Rafe damn sure didn't trust him. But then, Buchanan had been in that cabin with him. He'd sucked in as much carbon monoxide as they had.

Not very smart unless he'd been double-crossed as well. Or maybe Buchanan had taken safety measures that Rafe didn't know about.

"You think Buchanan is on O'Reilly's payroll?" Rafe asked.

"Either that or someone wants us to believe he is. But Buchanan's not the only potentially smelly weasel in the middle of this. I dug up something about Nicholas Sheldon that had bells the size of Texas going off in my head. Remember Eve DeCalley?"

"Is that a trick question? Of course, I do." Security Specialist Eve DeCalley. Just minutes before Rafe had been taken hostage, Eve had been killed during that ambush. Just about everything that could go wrong did that tragic day. Much like now. "What does Sheldon have to do with Eve?"

"They were lovers. Sheldon might be ticked off in a huge sort of way that Eve died while following Shaw's orders."

It was an interesting connection, but in Rafe's mind, a loose one. Most of the civilian security specialists knew one another since they were all from the same private research facility, Sen-tron. And they all knew the dangers they faced with each mission. Still, Rafe didn't plan to discount the connection. He didn't plan to discount anything.

"And what about Shaw?" Rafe asked. "You got anything on him?"

"No. But here's my advice for what it's worth. Don't trust any of them. Too much has gone wrong with this whole damn operation for someone not to have their fingers where they shouldn't be."

"I agree." Rafe did a quick scan of the area. He needed information, but not at the risk of someone sneaking up on them. Too bad there were too many places to hide.

"I wouldn't mind speaking with Quivira to get his take on things," Rafe continued. "Hell, he might even be able to explain why O'Reilly's gotten in on this. Think you could get him a message so I can try to set up a phone call? I'd like to feel him out and see if he'll tell me what information he's looking for from me."

"You think that's wise?" But Rico didn't let him answer. "I guess it's hard to figure out what's wise or foolish at this point. I'll see what I can do about Quivira, but I can't blow my cover."

"Understood. Thanks."

"By the way, how's Anna?"

Rafe glanced at her again. She looked worn out. And incredibly beautiful. How the heck could she manage that? "She's holding up."

"Um, has she said anything about her, well, state of health?"

The vaguely worded question wasn't so vague since Rafe knew how Rico's mind—and investigative process—worked. Rico had no doubt checked into Anna's whereabouts the past two months. And he'd likely learned that she was pregnant.

"We've talked. She's doing as well as can be…expected," Rafe answered.

"Good. I didn't find out until the day of your wedding, but I knew Anna wouldn't keep something like that from you for long." Rico paused. "Are you okay with it?"

"I'm gettin' there." Somehow, his feelings about the baby had gotten mixed up with everything else. Hard to sort through a jumble of feelings when people kept trying to kill them. "I'll be a whole lot better when Anna's safe. Help me out with that any way you can."

"Will do. But the water's a little dangerous this time of year, so be extra careful."

Rafe picked up on that clue, as well. It was a reference to Rico's houseboat at Canyon Lake, a place only about ten miles away. If they pushed themselves, they could be there before nightfall. And hopefully before the storm moved in. The houseboat had a security system, and even better—Rafe had the access codes to get inside. It'd be an ideal hiding place until he could figure out their next step.

"What'd Rico say?" Anna asked after Rafe said goodbye and hung up.

He gave her the condensed version, not mentioning the part about Rico's knowledge of the pregnancy. Rafe checked his watch again. "We need to move. We have to secure another position."

She nodded, not even questioning him. Rafe almost wished she would. That blind trust didn't make him feel any better about what he had to do.

He helped her from the crevice and got them both back on top of the cliff, all the while thinking that they didn't dare stay out in the open long. The gunmen who'd attacked the cabin might be dead, but no doubt there were others ready and willing to try the same thing.

Rafe moved them into the shelter of the woods. It took him a couple of minutes, but he finally found the catbird seat that they needed. A clump of dense cedar shrubs. The ground around them was littered with dead leaves. It gave a perfect view of the cliff while providing them with a hiding place.

"We'll be here for probably a couple of hours," he said.

She went from looking drowsy to wide awake. "Here? But it's still close to those cliffs."

"Yeah." And that's the reason he'd chosen it. "Trust me. It'll be all right."

Anna glanced at the woods around them. "You sure about that?"

"As sure as I can be about anything." Rafe helped her into the shrubs and followed in behind her. He covered them both with the dead leaves before he unclipped his phone from his belt. "I need to call Colonel Shaw. I need to figure out exactly whose side he's on."

Alarm went through her eyes. "And how do you plan to do that?"

"By playing a game that I hope we win." He pressed in the emergency numbers, and Shaw answered on the second ring. "It's me," Rafe said.

"Where are you—"

"Anna and I are safe. For now. But I need to get her out of here immediately."

"Of course. Give me your location."

"We're about a mile and a half east of the bravo site on the west face of a limestone bluff." It was a lie. A necessary one.

"All right. Let's see what I can do."

Rafe listened while the colonel worked out the details with Buchanan. When he finished, Shaw assured him that help was on the way. To the west face of the bluff. Anna and he were on the east side, where they'd hopefully see if *help* would indeed arrive.

"What about the gunmen?" Rafe asked Shaw.

"Eliminated. They were O'Reilly's men."

Judas. So, they were right back in the middle of a civil war. Quivira and O'Reilly had brought their battle to the States. It really didn't matter at this point if Quivira wanted him alive. O'Reilly didn't. Besides, Quivira wouldn't hesitate to kill him as soon as he got the information he wanted.

Rafe issued a hasty goodbye to the colonel, hung up and clipped the phone back onto his belt. "Well, I just set the game in motion," he said to Anna. Maybe it wouldn't blow up in his face. "I gave Colonel Shaw directions to a bogus site, a site we'll be watching carefully to see who shows up."

"How safe is this game?" she asked.

"I don't know. I wish I could promise more, but I can't."

She gave a frustrated sigh. "I'm not blaming you. I'm blaming Quivira and O'Reilly. But no matter who's at fault, I just need this to be over."

"Yeah." Because she looked on the verge of losing it, he touched her cheek and rubbed gently.

The gesture obviously didn't soothe her as he'd planned. "When will you tell me what else is wrong?"

He hadn't realized he'd been that obvious. But then, Anna probably knew him better than he knew himself. He couldn't tell her about the possible harm to the baby. Not now. He couldn't risk how she would react to that.

"I remembered the cellar in Monte de Leon," he

softly explained. "The window. The blanket. You told me that you loved me."

It wasn't a lie—Rafe had remembered fragments of that afternoon—but it wasn't the source of what was bothering him.

He could feel her staring at him, but rather than open himself up to questions he didn't want to answer, Rafe motioned for her to stay quiet.

And he burrowed into their hiding place and braced himself for what he prayed wouldn't happen.

Chapter 11

Anna hid in the camouflage of damp leaves and waited.

For what exactly she didn't know.

Colonel Shaw was on the way, but maybe he wasn't the only one. After all, Rafe had a firm grip on his gun and had obviously braced himself for something unpleasant. She wanted to believe it was that possible unpleasantness that had created the tension she saw in Rafe's face.

But she wasn't so sure.

Anna replayed the conversation she'd just had with Rafe. He had told her of Rico's suspicions about Sheldon and Buchanan. That part sounded believable and would have troubled him. Rafe had then recounted his memory in the cellar and her telling him that she loved him. He also no doubt remembered them making love. Also believable and perhaps troubling. But none of those things should have put him in such a dark mood.

So, what had?

She had to consider the obvious. The fact they were in danger was enough to sour anyone's mood. Or maybe it was the baby who was responsible. After all, on the other occasions when Rafe had faced danger, he turned into the ultimate silent warrior. However, making love had no doubt reminded him of the child she carried. A child he seemed indifferent about.

Or something.

Anna glanced at him, unable to figure out what was going on inside his head. Rafe was on his stomach, buried in the leaves except for parts of his face and hands. He had his attention focused on the cliff wall, which was exactly where it should be focused.

Because she was still watching him, she saw him mouth a curse. Just like that, she felt the blood rush through her head. Her lungs tightened. Her concerns of his dark mood shifted to one even more serious—staying alive.

Rafe's gaze cut to her for a second, and in his eyes she saw the warning to stay quiet.

She did.

A moment later, Anna heard the soft sound. Not from the other side of the cliff, either. Closer. Much closer. A snap of a twig. Maybe. And maybe a lot more than that.

She pulled in her breath. Waited. Listened.

Nothing.

All she could hear was the breeze rattling through the towering live oaks. Without moving, she checked out their surroundings as best she could. Everything looked as it should. But the prickle was still there, along with the gut feeling that something definitely wasn't right.

When her lungs began to ache, Anna quietly blew out the breath that she'd forgotten she was holding. Maybe there was nothing to see or hear other than what she'd manufactured in her own overactive imagination. After all, if there'd been a breach in security, the rebels would be on the other side of the cliff where Rafe had told Shaw that they were.

Anna had almost convinced herself to relax when she heard it again.

Definitely a snap.

Maybe even a footstep.

Her heart began to pound, the sound echoing in her ears. She forced herself to breathe normally so she wouldn't hyperventilate. Beside her, Rafe didn't move a muscle.

The sounds continued. But they were closer now. Definitely footsteps. Despite the roar in her ears, she could measure the pace of whomever it was walking. Slow, methodical steps. Not from the cliff. But from behind them.

God, from behind them.

They were about to be ambushed.

Choking back a gasp, she forced herself not to panic. Instead, she tried to assess the situation in the clinical way that she knew Rafe was doing. Maybe Shaw and the others would have approached them from that direction. Maybe. But at the moment it seemed a lot to hope for.

"Que hay?" someone whispered.

A man's voice. Not Shaw's, Luke Buchanan's or Sheldon's. A stranger's. And even though he'd spoken in Spanish slang, Anna knew the phrase meant that someone was inquiring as to their whereabouts. It evaporated any hope that this was a member of the Alpha Team.

And worse.

That question meant there were at least two of them. Quivira's or O'Reilly's rebels, most likely. Men who would most certainly try to kill them.

Anna prayed. She prayed that the men would just pass them by. But the footsteps grew closer. And closer. It was agony waiting. Pure agony. If the rebels saw them hiding, they could easily shoot them before Rafe could reposition himself to return fire.

Questions and doubts raced through her head. Would the leaves and shrubs give them ample cover? Did the men already know they were there? Would this be one of the last breaths that Rafe and she would ever take? She suddenly wished that Rafe and she had at least talked about the baby. That way, she wouldn't go to the grave doubting how he felt.

From the corner of her left eye, Anna saw the movement. A blur of motion as a man wearing camouflage fatigues darted behind a tree. Thankfully, he didn't seem to be looking in their direction. He fixed his attention on the cliff, and he was armed.

The man had hardly gotten into place when she heard something on the other side of Rafe. She angled her eyes in his direction. He still hadn't moved. But just outside the clump of shrubs was another man. Mere inches away. So close that Anna could smell the sweat on his clothes.

Everything in her stilled, the fear gripping her by the throat. As a photographer, she'd had a couple of tense assignments—the one in Monte de Leon topping the others for situations she most likely wanted to avoid.

But this, this was as close to hell as she ever wanted to get.

The man behind the tree whispered something. One word. In Spanish. Anna didn't quite catch it, but the tone was a warning. An alert. God, had they seen them hiding?

Beside her, she felt Rafe tense. There was no time for her to react or try to figure out what he planned to do. His gun spun to the right.

And he fired.

The sound blasted through the silence. Before the man standing next to them fell, Rafe rolled on top of her, his back against hers. He adjusted his aim and fired again.

At a speed that didn't seem humanly possible, Rafe sprang up from the ground into a crouching position, his feet on each side of her. A split second later, there was another shot.

Anna was no expert in the sounds of gunfire, but the last shot hadn't come from Rafe. Nor had the one that followed. She bit off the scream that nearly made its way past her throat. God. The rebel was shooting at them, and Rafe was literally out in the open.

She looked up at Rafe, frantically checking for any signs of injury, but he moved before she got little more than a glimpse.

"Stay down," he ordered.

With his attention firmly on the man near the tree and with his finger planted on the trigger, Rafe dove out from the shrubs. Rolling over, he came up on one knee and fired. One deadly efficient shot.

Their attacker slumped forward, the gun dropping

from his hand onto the ground. It didn't take long, maybe a second, before the man fell, as well.

Rafe latched on to her hand. "We have to leave. There might be others."

Sweet heaven. She hadn't thought of that. Her mind was a jumble of fear and rage.

Rafe gave her one reassuring glance over his shoulder and led her back into the woods. "I'll get you out of here," he promised.

She believed him. Rafe would indeed get her out of there. But would it matter? Would there simply be more gunmen waiting for them wherever they went?

What had just happened took them well past the theory stage that the rebels had some inside help.

They did.

There was no doubt in Anna's mind. What were the odds that the rebels would be headed in the direction of the bogus rendezvous site unless they'd intercepted— or had been given—the information that Rafe provided Colonel Shaw.

The truth sat cold and hard in her stomach. Someone very close to them had turned traitor. And it'd come very close to getting them killed.

Chapter 12

Rafe didn't like the hesitation he heard on the other end of the line. He'd just asked Shaw what should have been a bombshell of sorts, but instead of the colonel denying it, all Rafe got was silence.

Damn.

"Well?" Rafe questioned. Cradling the phone against his ear, he peeled off the rest of his drenched clothes and stepped into a pair of pants that he'd found on Rico's houseboat. Thankfully, Rico had kept the boat well-stocked and ready for emergencies. Even the phone was a secure line. "After what I learned, should I be suspicious about Buchanan and Sheldon?"

Outside, rain pelted the tiny windows of the houseboat, and a slash of lightning sent a ripple of static through the phone line. The boat was anchored about a hundred yards off the lakeshore, but that didn't stop it from bobbing. Rafe propped his hip against the counter to steady himself.

"I'm not sure what you're asking," Shaw concluded.

"And I'm sure you are, *sir*." In fact, Rafe was more than sure. And God help him, Shaw better have some answers. The *right* answers.

Anna stepped out from the tiny bathroom, a thick white towel draped around her hair. And little else. She wore just an oversize to-the-knees T-shirt, one of the few garments they'd managed to locate among Rico's things. It reminded Rafe of the barely there nightgown she'd donned for their honeymoon night.

With the fresh scent of the shower stirring around her, and her lack of clothes, her mere presence commanded Rafe's attention. Attention he couldn't spare if he hoped to learn anything from Shaw.

She caught his gaze, and her eyebrow lifted a fraction.

"Colonel Shaw," he mouthed.

She nodded, though he saw the questions in her intense brown eyes. Questions as to whether or not it was a good idea to call anyone connected to the Alpha Team. Rafe was asking himself the same darn thing. Too bad this might be the only way to get answers. Maybe now he wouldn't have to pay too high a price for that information.

"Buchanan and Sheldon have been under a microscope lately," Shaw assured him.

But it didn't reassure Rafe of squat—something he'd already anticipated. And that's why Rafe had used Rico's secure line so the colonel couldn't trace the call. Hopefully, that secure line and the security system on the houseboat would buy Anna and him some downtime until he could figure out what to do next.

"Look, I can't make you trust either man," Shaw went on. "Or me, for that matter. But—"

"Do you trust them?" Rafe interrupted. "And save the part about them being valuable members of your team. I've already got enough useless information to sift through, thank you. What I want to know is would you put the lives of people you cared about in their hands?"

There was another of those long silences. "I'm taking precautions. But the point is that you and Anna are in danger. I need to know where you are so I can get you some backup."

It was the second time Shaw evaded answering him and the third time he had demanded that Rafe tell him their location. And for the third time Rafe brushed him off.

"Do you trust them?" Rafe repeated.

Another pause. "No."

Finally! It'd been like pulling teeth, but Shaw had admitted what Rafe had already sensed.

"Tell me about the money in Buchanan's account," Rafe said, trying a different angle.

"He claims his soon-to-be ex-wife put it there. It's possible. You don't remember her, Rafe, but she's vindictive. She'd pull this kind of stunt to get back at Buchanan, but Special Investigations can't figure out where she came up with the money to frame him. She just doesn't have those kinds of funds. In fact, this divorce has left both of them pretty much broke."

Ah. And there was Buchanan's motive in a proverbial nutshell. Rafe knew for a fact that Quivira or O'Reilly would shell out big bucks to get a Justice Department agent on their payroll.

That led him to the next question he wanted to put to Shaw. "So, what does the Justice Department have to say about all of this?"

"That he's a solid agent, but if you don't want him in on this, then he's off the team. The same goes for Sheldon."

The colonel's tone was a little too placating. Rafe didn't think that was a good sign. Still, he wasn't about to turn down that offer. He did want them off the team. Heck, he wanted them as far away from Anna and him as they could get. He could add Shaw to that list, though, as well.

"Suffice it to say that you need two new team members," Rafe continued. "But that doesn't mean I'll stop being suspicious about Sheldon and Buchanan. And speaking of Sheldon—how about his connection to Eve DeCalley?"

"It appears to be a coincidence." No hesitation that time. So, Shaw had at least given it some thought as to how he would respond when Rafe asked. "Sheldon had a few problems after Agent DeCalley's death, but the Sen-tron shrink said he was good to go."

"Pardon me if I reserve judgment awhile longer on that." Rafe's brow furrowed. "I'm not about to trust my life and Anna's on the opinion of a Sen-tron shrink."

Anna gave a crisp, confirming nod and sank down onto the sofa bed. She looked far better than he'd expected her to look. After all, a ten-mile hike through the rain wasn't the best scenario for a pregnant woman.

Maybe that non-exhausted look had something to do with the way that T-shirt skimmed along the curves of her body. Or maybe it was the misty glow she had from the hot shower. And maybe he was unable to get his mind off her simply because this was Anna.

Rafe reached out and skimmed his finger along her cheek. She moved into his touch. Welcoming it. And feeding it at a time when he shouldn't have been touching her.

"Rafe, this renegade attitude of yours won't help Anna," Shaw insisted. "I can get new team members. People that you trust, but you've got to bring her in. Rico should have told you the same."

That comment confirmed what Rafe already suspected—Shaw had somehow learned about their conversation. Hopefully, the man hadn't picked up on Rico's water reference, but just in case, Rafe would check the security system again when he was done with the call. While he was at it, he'd show Anna the escape door that Rico had had installed when he modified the boat.

"You haven't said a thing about the carbon monoxide," Shaw went on.

That immediately put a heavy fist around his heart. Rafe pulled back his hand from her face and stared down at Anna. Her eyes were examining him, and if he wasn't careful, she'd figure out that Shaw was about to discuss something he definitely didn't want Anna to overhear.

He stepped away from her and went to the window to take a cursory glance outside.

"What about it?" he asked Shaw.

"Buchanan tested out all right. No damage. I suspect it's the same for Anna and you."

There was a *but* at the end of that sentence. The baby

wasn't out of the woods yet. There was already so much danger to this child, and now this.

"I have to go," Rafe told him.

"Wait! Tell Anna that Janine's called for her a half-dozen times. She says it's important."

Rafe jotted down the number where Shaw said Janine could be reached. "I don't guess you've had a chance to question her about her old friendship with Victor O'Reilly?"

"I did while I had her on the phone. She said it was water under an old bridge, that she hadn't seen O'Reilly in years. I didn't tell her about the tap, because we're still using it to monitor her line."

"So, how did she explain having coffee with one of his henchmen?"

"Janine said she didn't know the man was connected to O'Reilly."

Yeah, right. He'd heard fish stories like that before. "I'll let Anna know she called." And with that, Rafe ended the call without so much as a goodbye.

"Well?" Anna asked the second he clicked off the phone.

She unwrapped the towel, and her hair tumbled in damp strands against the shoulders of the T-shirt. And the tops of her breasts. Man. He hadn't remembered a T-shirt and wet hair ever looking so damn sexy.

Rafe put the phone on the table and forced his attention away from her and all that…sexiness. "Shaw claimed he doesn't believe Buchanan and Sheldon had anything to do with the rebels getting through to us, but he's bumping them off the team, anyway."

She placed the towel over the back of the chair and rubbed her arms. Probably not because she was cold.

The room was toasty warm. And getting warmer by the minute. "I guess this rules out Janine, huh?"

"Maybe not. She could still be working with someone else. By the way, she called Shaw and says she needs to speak to you. That it's important."

Anna glanced at the phone. "Maybe I should find out what she wants."

Rafe doubted that Janine had anything on her mind, other than maybe finding out where they were. Besides, with that tap on Janine's phone, it was way too big of a risk. Shaw could listen in on every word and might be able to figure out their location.

"It wouldn't be a private conversation," he explained. Rafe grabbed a bottle of water from the fridge and leaned against the counter.

"Something's wrong. I can see it in your face." She stood and walked to the counter. "What aren't you telling me?"

Rafe lifted a shoulder. "Hey, isn't being chased by two groups of rebels enough to warrant a troubled expression?"

"Sure. But there's something else. Something we've been avoiding for a while." Slowly, she eased back around to face him. Whatever she was thinking, it wasn't about rebels and gunmen. "Rafe, I need to know how you feel."

He gulped down some water, hoping it would take care of his suddenly dry mouth. It didn't. "About what?"

She pressed her hand on her stomach. "About this."

Ah, hell. She'd probably overheard Shaw's comment about the carbon monoxide. Rafe hadn't wanted her to learn that way. He'd wanted to prepare her first and give her reassurance that everything would be fine.

But Anna didn't give him a chance to say anything.

She pulled back her shoulders, and her eyes narrowed. "If you don't want the baby then, damn it, just say so."

Anna jumped when thunder pounded through the tiny houseboat, but she wasn't about to let something like a nighttime storm delay this conversation with Rafe. It was long overdue.

"We've been skirting around this since I told you about the baby," she added. Since she needed something to do with her hands, she used her fingers to try to comb out some of the tangles from her shower.

He nodded. Just nodded. He kept his attention focused on the bottle of water in his hand.

Her heart sank. Anna took a deep breath, hoping it would steady her pulse. "I should have said this sooner, but this isn't your responsibility," she offered. "I can raise the baby myself."

It was an out she'd hoped she would never have to give him. But apparently it had come to that after all. During the months Rafe and she had dated, they hadn't discussed having children. Heck, she didn't even know if he liked kids. And this was obviously too much for him to take.

Rafe put the water onto the counter. "Anna, you don't understand."

"I think I do. It shocked me, too, at first. A baby. I hadn't even thought about getting pregnant when we made love—"

He cursed. It was raw and vicious.

The tears instantly came to her eyes. And Anna couldn't blame them just on the hormones. No. This was a horrible ache in her heart. With everything else going on, she wasn't sure she could take Rafe's rejection, as well. He wasn't just her baby's father, he was the only person she could trust.

His head whipped up, snaring her gaze again, and he closed the narrow distance between them with one step. "I swear it's not *that*."

She shook her head, not understanding. "Then what is it, because I need to know—"

"Colonel Shaw told me that O'Reilly's rebels pumped carbon monoxide into the cabin."

Anna had braced herself for almost anything.

Except that.

Rafe pulled her into his arms. A good thing, too, or she might have fallen.

"Oh, my God," she gasped.

"Buchanan tested fine," Rafe explained, his voice a gentle murmur against her ear. "So, you're probably okay, too. And the baby."

"Probably."

It wasn't nearly enough of a reassurance.

He eased away from her and caught her face between his hands. "I didn't want to say anything because I didn't want to worry you. Again, Buchanan's fine, so in all likelihood, you are, too."

She couldn't stop the worst-case-scenario thoughts that went through her head. Anna had no idea of the effects of carbon monoxide on the baby, but it couldn't be good.

God.

It was something else to worry about. Still, she clung to the hope that if Buchanan was all right, then maybe the baby was, too.

"You can be tested," Rafe continued. "I'll try to arrange for you to see a doctor—"

"I thought you didn't want the baby," she blurted out.

He groaned and pressed his forehead to hers. "It was never that. *Never.* And I don't need my memory to know how I feel about this baby."

Relief washed through her, and despite all the other uncertainties, Anna felt the tension drain from her body. She slumped against him, her arms circling his waist. Only after she'd touched his bare skin did she remember that he wasn't wearing a shirt. Hard to forget something like that.

"I tried not to think about the baby," Rafe went on. "I felt I had to concentrate on getting us out of this mess. But it didn't work. There's no way to put something like that out of my mind."

"I know." She almost hated to push this fragile moment, but Anna wanted to know what all of this meant. "If those rebels weren't after us, and if you had your memory back, do you think, well, would you be happy about the baby?"

Rafe didn't answer her right away. At least not with words. He angled his head so that their gazes met and then slid his hand over her stomach. "There're an awful lot of ifs in that question, darling. And you know what? I don't need those ifs because I want this baby, understand?"

She saw it—finally. The look in those clear green eyes that Anna had prayed she would see. Rafe wanted the baby. At the moment, she didn't care if that *want* extended to her. She just needed to hear that he hadn't rejected their child.

He touched his mouth to her forehead. Such a comforting gesture. And so welcome. Maybe it was the relief fueled with the passion that already simmered between them. Or maybe it was the fact they were pressed against each other. It suddenly didn't matter why, but Anna felt the air change around them. An instant awareness that they were man and woman.

Their gazes met. It was little more than a glimpse. And Rafe's mouth came to hers. The heat instantly burned through her. A fire that went from a mere spark to a full blaze with just that one kiss.

"We never get this timing thing right," he grumbled.

Funny. It felt right to her. Under the circumstances, it was about as right as right could get. They were alone. And they were as safe as they could hope for. The storm and security system would hopefully keep everyone else at bay. So for all practical purposes, they were the only two people in their entire world.

She gulped in her breath, taking in the taste of him, as well. From day one, she'd wanted him. Not like this, of course. This was a need that had sprung from the intimacy that only being in love with him could create. Anna wouldn't let herself wonder if Rafe remembered those feelings. For now, this was enough. For now, she only wanted to feel.

As if battling her, and himself, Rafe caught her hands with his and pinned them against the wall. His eyes skimmed over her, and in them, she saw both an apology and a blatant invitation.

"Whatever this is between us, it's not a left-brain thing." He cursed under his breath and shook his head as if disgusted with himself. "Logic tells me to stand guard. To protect you. To move to the other side of the room and leave you alone so I can think straight."

"You're right. This doesn't have anything to do with logic." Anna purposely moved against him. Softly. Slowly. A caress. Her breasts against his chest. The center of her body against his. And because she was so close, she heard him hiss out his breath.

"You might have to set those left-brain thoughts aside," she whispered. "What does your heart tell you to do?"

The corner of his mouth lifted a fraction. It wasn't much of a facial adjustment, but he upped the ante of that blatant invitation. "My heart tells me to do just about everything not dealing with logic. No surprise there, huh?"

Even with that admission, Anna thought he might put duty first and step away from her.

He didn't.

Rafe grasped her wrist and moved her right hand from the wall to his chest. With him guiding her, he slid her palm along the taut muscles that stirred there. And lower. To his stomach.

"You want to play? Okay, let's play," Rafe challenged. "What does *your* heart tell you to do?"

If he thought she would back away, he was wrong.

"My heart tells me to do this." Without moving her hand from his stomach or his grip, she leaned in and kissed him. It wasn't tame. It was long and hungry.

"Not bad." His breath was ragged, and so was the sound that simmered in his throat. "If you want my opinion, darling, your heart's in the right place."

It thrilled her that she was able to do that to him. Of course, Rafe could easily do the same to her.

And probably would.

If she got lucky.

He eased her hand down an inch. "So, what do we do about it?" he asked, obviously continuing the seductive game. "How far does this go?"

"As far as you let it."

That sound in his throat broke free, and he groaned. "Anna, I've given this plenty of thought. *Plenty.* Ninety-nine point nine percent of me wants to strip off any underwear you might have on and take you where you stand." Rafe shook his head. "But I honestly can't give you the words that I know you want to hear."

The words—*"I love you."*

No, he wouldn't be able to say that to her. And Rafe wouldn't lie about something like that. But in her heart, Anna knew those words would come when his memory returned. She knew because Rafe had said them to her in Monte de Leon. Even more, he'd meant them.

She kissed him again, hoping it would save her from giving him an explanation. Because this wasn't something she needed to explain. To make sure she got her point across, she slid her hand lower. Over the front of his loose pants. She moved her fingers over him. Against him.

Around him.

He was already huge and hard, and if there had been any shred of hesitation in her body, that would have eliminated it.

He cursed and jerked away from her, but Anna grabbed his shoulders. "You're not going anywhere," she told him.

He gave her a look that stole her breath. Anna didn't have time to ask his intentions. He fisted his hands in her hair and took her mouth. It was like a flash of fire. All she'd hoped for and more.

Her heartbeat raced. Her body hummed. Every inch of her suddenly seemed desperate. Rafe rocked against her. The hard, rigid part of him against the soft, vulnerable juncture of her thighs. He pressed. Moved. Stroked. Until it wasn't nearly enough.

He slid lower, his body pinning her against the wall. He kissed his way down her throat. Down her breasts. Down her stomach. And dropped to his knees.

The kisses didn't stop.

"You're not going anywhere," he said, repeating her words. "Yet."

Looking up at her, he bunched up the T-shirt and grasped her panties. Since she'd washed them in the bathroom, they were still damp, and Anna felt the cool dampness of the silky fabric as Rafe slid them down her legs. He tossed them aside.

Anna almost asked what he had in mind, but it would have been a stupid question. She knew.

She wanted to resist. Well, part of her did. Not because she didn't want this. It wasn't that. She just wanted him to take this activity in the direction of the sofa bed. The other part wanted to take everything he was offering her right here and now. In the end, it was her need for him that won out. She braced herself for whatever he was about to offer.

Rafe leaned in and kissed the inside of her thigh. She hadn't thought it possible, but that caused the flames to burn hotter. Mercy, she didn't know how much of that she could take without demanding a whole lot more of him.

With slow, deliberate ease, he took her knee and moved it onto his shoulder. "You're not going anywhere," he murmured.

The heat from his moist breath caused Anna to whimper. But it was nothing compared to the heat of his mouth. Rafe took. Sampled. Savored. It was beyond a kiss. It was a primitive claim with his mouth on her flesh, and she hadn't thought anything could feel that good.

Somehow, Anna managed to hold his gaze when that trail of kisses ended at the fiery center of her body. Somehow. But soon her vision blurred. Her need rocketed with every new touch.

He caressed her, gently, with his mouth. With his tongue. Gently and yet exactly the way she needed him to touch her.

"Now you can go," Rafe whispered against that feverish heat.

It didn't take much. A simple brush of his tongue. Anna felt herself soar. Soar. Soar. It was like a spear being hurled through the sky. Until everything within her surrendered. It was far more than she could have even hoped to feel, and yet she was desperate to feel even more.

She came back to earth as quickly as she could, and with the hazy flames still stirring around her, Rafe made his way back up her body. He kissed her. And touched. Until it was Anna who was pushing them toward the sofa bed. Wrapped around each other, they landed on the soft cushions.

It took her a moment to realize that the ringing in her ears wasn't passion-induced. Rafe stopped, cursed and gave her a why-the-heck-now look.

"It might be Rico," he muttered, irritation in his voice.

If so, then his timing was positively lousy. Anna

tried not to groan. Or kick herself. Instead of allowing Rafe to pleasure her, she should have gotten on that sofa with him minutes earlier. Then they would have both been satisfied.

Rafe reached across to the counter and snatched up the phone. He didn't say hello. Or anything else, for that matter. He just waited. But Anna had no trouble seeing the surprise that went through his eyes.

Her first thought—a horrible one—was that this was news about the carbon monoxide they'd inhaled in that cabin. She got to her knees, fixing her T-shirt along the way.

"Who is it?" she mouthed.

"Señor Quivira," Rafe said aloud, addressing the man on the phone. "Mind telling me why the hell you want us dead?"

Chapter 13

Rafe forced himself to remain calm. Hard to do when he was finally speaking with the man who was one of the main reasons Anna's and his lives were in danger. He wanted to reach across the phone lines and send this scum to meet his maker.

"Captain McQuade," Quivira mocked. "You left Monte de Leon without saying goodbye. Poor manners, don't you think? It hurt my feelings."

Quivira's voice went through Rafe like a cold, hard freeze. It was a voice that had tormented him for two months. If there was some emotion beyond pure hate, then that's what he felt for this man.

"I didn't care much for your kind of hospitality," Rafe countered. With the phone cradled against his neck, he started to dress in case they had to get out of there fast. "How did you get this number?"

"From someone who thought it would benefit us both if we spoke." There was no trace of the native accent that Quivira used in the presence of his soldiers. Rafe heard the polish and sophistication of Quivira's Oxford education. Not exactly a common man of the common people that he purported to be. "A friend, you might say."

The friend was no doubt Cal Rico, the man who'd spent weeks infiltrating Quivira's organization. Maybe none of this would jeopardize Rico's undercover mission, but it was a huge risk. Since Rico had set things in motion, Rafe intended to get the most he could for that risk.

"I guess you no longer want anything from me?" Rafe asked, going on the offensive. He glanced at Anna when she rose from the sofa. Without taking her attention from him, she slipped her panties back on and reached for her jeans. "Because that's the only reason I can think of for why you'd want to kill me."

"Rest assured, McQuade, I'm not the one who wants you dead. If so, we wouldn't be having this conversation. Victor O'Reilly's men are after you. And why? Because he thinks you've cut a deal with me for some merchandise that your people promised him. Before he succeeds in eliminating you, we need to take care of a little unfinished business."

Yes. Too bad Rafe didn't remember exactly what that business was. His guess was it had something to do with the virus and antidote, but if so, he'd let Quivira bring up the subject.

"Release the hostages, and that business will no longer be unfinished," Rafe lied.

Quivira laughed. "Such boldness. Under different circumstances, I think we would have become friends, no?"

Not in this freaking lifetime. But Rafe kept that thought to himself. "If you're not in a bargaining mood, then we obviously have nothing to discuss."

"Yes." Quivira paused. "And you'd rather be spending time with your lovely bride, Anna."

Rafe had to clench his teeth to stop himself from saying something he'd regret. Just the sound of Anna's name from this man's lips sent Rafe's blood pressure soaring.

"Let's cut through the bull, shall we?" Quivira suggested. "You tell me what I want to know, and you and your colonel will be rewarded with the release of my... guests."

It was tap-dancing time. Maybe if he asked a few more questions, then Rafe would—

"One day I hope you know what it is to feel a father's grief," Quivira hissed.

Damn him. Damn him. Damn him! It took every ounce of his training, every fiber of his willpower and even a soothing touch from Anna's hand for Rafe to maintain control. How dare this man threaten his child. It cut to the core of what scared him most. And Quivira no doubt knew that.

Before he could unclench his teeth, Quivira continued. "Of course, you need not be a father to know how important it is that you tell me where my son is being held."

Rafe's fit of fury evaporated as quickly as it'd come. "Your son?" he managed to say.

"You make it sound like a question," Quivira commented, his voice turning to a snarl. "A warning, my friend, do not play games with me. Not when it comes to my son. This exchange of information takes place before dawn, or you and your friends will pay."

Hell.

But it was more than just *hell*. Rafe had plenty of blank spots, but Quivira's son wasn't one of them.

The images of battle went through Rafe's head. Specifically, the image of Colonel Shaw shooting the young man. And of him lying dead on the path. Judas Priest! And Quivira obviously thought his son had survived that attack two months earlier.

He felt Anna's touch on his arm, but Rafe turned away from her. He had to think. He had to put the pieces of this together. But he was almost positive it would not be a pretty picture when he was done.

Question one: why didn't Quivira know that his son had died? Answer: Because someone had removed the body from the battle site. If the body had been there, Quivira would have certainly found it, and they wouldn't be having this conversation.

Question two: who had removed the body? Answer: probably the same person who led Quivira to believe that Rafe knew the whereabouts of his son.

No, Rafe didn't like the way this picture was shaping up at all.

"You never did say who told you that I knew about your son." And Rafe braced himself for Quivira's answer.

"Didn't I?" Quivira paused. One second. Then, two. "The leader of your Alpha Team, of course. Colonel Ethan Shaw."

Stunned, Anna listened as Rafe repeated the name of the person who had set this dangerous game in motion.

"I can't believe it," she said. "Why would Colonel Shaw do something like this?"

Rafe shook his head. "I don't know. Maybe it was the only way he thought he could keep the other hostages and me alive."

Maybe. But she didn't think Rafe believed that any more than she did. There were other things mixed with all of this. Things she obviously didn't know about that had placed Rafe, their baby and her in danger.

He led her to the sofa, where they sat side by side. "What I tell you can't go any further than here."

She nodded and tried to brace herself for what she might hear. Hard though to brace herself for what would likely be the details of why someone wanted them dead.

"Luke Buchanan and I were supposed to get together with O'Reilly and Quivira in separate meetings," Rafe started. "It was a setup. They thought we had a new strain of flu virus called Shadow Warrior and its antidote. We told them that we'd sell it to the highest bidder. It was actually a ploy to draw them out of hiding— something we'd been trying to do for months—so we'd stop the rebels from kidnapping any more American businessmen."

"What went wrong?" she asked.

"Everything. First of all, the Shadow Warrior virus really did go missing from the Sen-tron research facility, so Sen-tron alerted their own operative, Eve DeCalley, to track us down. That gave away our position. Then O'Reilly's troops ambushed a convoy of relief workers. Shaw split the team and sent half to try to retrieve those people before O'Reilly could take them deeper into the jungle. Signals got crossed. People weren't in the right position. And Buchanan and

I were caught in the middle between O'Reilly's and Quivira's men."

Anna just sat there and listened. She'd had a taste of being caught in cross fire. It was a helpless, terrifying feeling.

"Shaw had to kill Quivira's son," Rafe continued. "And then we lost Eve DeCalley. Less than a half hour later, I was captured."

"But Shaw didn't have any part of that." The denial didn't ring true when she heard it aloud. "Or did he?"

Rafe shrugged. "Who knows? It was Shaw's plan, and he was the one doling out the orders. He's also lied about Quivira's son right from the start."

She pressed her lips together. "I've known Ethan Shaw most of my life. He was my father's friend. It's difficult for me to accept he'd do something underhanded."

"I know. But someone did. Someone betrayed us. I just don't want to make the mistake of trusting the wrong person."

And there it was. Their dilemma in a nutshell. "But who's the wrong person, Rafe. Buchanan, maybe?"

"Hard to imagine he'd betray us and his country for money, but it's happened before."

Yes. And she could say the same for love. Maybe Janine had turned informant because she was in love with a man who happened to be on the wrong side of the law.

Rafe scratched his head. "The woman who died, Agent Eve DeCalley, was a security specialist at Sentron along with being Sheldon's lover. If he's the one behind this, then I figure it has something to do with her death."

"You mean revenge?" Anna said, thinking out loud. "But if so, then why go after us? You didn't have anything to do with her death, did you?"

"I was there. Right in the middle of it. Maybe he felt I should have done more to stop it." He groaned in frustration. "Someone who's grieving the death of a loved one might go to all lengths to get back at the person they feel is responsible."

Anna agreed. But that didn't just apply to Sheldon; it was the same for Quivira. Once he learned that the CRO team had killed his son in that raid, nothing would stop him from coming after Rafe. Nothing. So, instead of just O'Reilly and this unknown snitch in their midst, they'd have yet another rebel leader out to kill them.

Rafe slid his arm around her. "I'll do whatever it takes to protect you and the baby."

She didn't doubt it, nor did she doubt the tenacity of those men after them. The thought of that caused Anna's stomach to clench. This wasn't over. They were all still in danger.

The phone rang again, the sound echoing through the silence. Rafe swore, apparently anticipating yet more bad news. Anna prayed he was wrong.

Instead of picking up the receiver, he switched on the speaker function.

"Rafe?" Colonel Shaw said.

"What do you want?"

"Well, for starters, I don't want you to shoot me. I'm approaching the boat as we speak."

It didn't take long for Rafe to react to that. He moved

Anna behind him and snatched up his gun. "Repeat—what do you want?"

"We have to talk. Oh, and that's not a suggestion, *Captain McQuade*. That's an order. Now, open up."

Chapter 14

The hellish roller coaster ride apparently wasn't over. Just the sound of Colonel Shaw's order sent Anna's body on high alert.

God, would this never end?

Rafe didn't say anything, but because he had backed her against the wall, she could feel the tense muscles in his body. He was primed and ready to fight. Too bad that it really might come down to that.

There was a knock at the door. Just one. Followed by the terse greeting, "Open up."

It was Colonel Shaw, all right, not that she'd doubted his visit after that order. Anna didn't dare ask what they should do. Either way would be a serious gamble.

Rafe hesitated for several long moments before he reached down and opened a concealed flap door on the floor near the foot of the sofa. "Get in," he insisted.

Anna glanced down the shallow, dark hole. If it had an opening to the outside of the boat, she couldn't see it. Still, it seemed safer than facing down a man who might want to kill them.

"But what about you?" she mouthed.

He didn't answer her. Rafe took her arm and eased her down into the narrow coffin-like space. Anna had to crouch down so that she'd fit inside.

"Just stay put," he instructed in a rough whisper. "Rico equipped this boat with an escape tunnel. It's little more than a crawl space, but if something goes wrong, then use it to get the hell out of here. Then contact Rico at this number." He grabbed a pen from the counter and scribbled some numbers on her palm.

Anna started to argue, to tell him that they should both be trying to escape, but he stopped her. "Think of the baby," Rafe warned. "You have to keep the baby safe."

It was a dirty way to win an argument. But it worked. When Shaw pounded on the exterior door and demanded again that Rafe open up, Anna willingly went into the escape hatch. Rafe pulled out a small gun from a pocket on his pants leg and handed it to her.

"Use it if you have to," he insisted.

She nodded. "Please be careful."

"I will." He touched his mouth to hers before he closed off the opening between them.

Anna held her breath as she heard him walk across the room. Gripping the metal handle of the concealed entry, she peered out through a tiny crack. She caught a glimpse of Rafe opening the door. That glimpse had her heart pounding when Colonel Shaw stepped inside.

Anna had no trouble seeing Rafe's reaction to that. He aimed his gun right at the man.

This was one visit Rafe wished he could avoid, but he'd known all along that it was inevitable. Besides, he needed this visit almost as much as Shaw probably did. There wasn't an eyelash worth of trust between them any longer, and it was time to see the look on Shaw's face when he confronted him with what he'd learned.

Shaw stayed in the doorway, the storm raging behind him. "Where's Anna?" he asked, canvassing the area inside the boat.

"She's safe," Rafe assured him.

For a moment Rafe thought the colonel might demand her whereabouts, but Shaw only motioned toward the gun that Rafe had aimed at him.

"Aim that somewhere else. Whether you believe it or not, we're on the same side."

Rafe made a sound of mild disagreement, but he turned the gun in a slightly different direction. "How did you find me?"

"I had some equipment brought into the area so we could detect any recent movement."

Of course. Rafe knew such equipment existed—and he knew it was a matter of time before Shaw managed to use it against him. Thank God he hadn't brought in the infrared, or Shaw would have known Anna's hiding place. Hell. Maybe he did, anyway. But for some reason, Shaw wasn't playing that hand.

"I don't suppose you've considered that someone is using our own equipment to get to us?" Rafe questioned.

Shaw nodded. "We did have a problem with that, and we fixed it."

"Yeah. Right. Trust me, I'm well aware of that problem. Someone leaked—"

"It was the Justice Department," Shaw offered. "They were monitoring our message traffic but failed to secure it. That's how O'Reilly's been tracking you. But we've stopped the information leak."

Rafe wasn't about to stake his life on that, especially since they had a team member, Luke Buchanan, who worked for the Justice Department. A coincidence that it was that particular agency that was responsible for the leaks? Rafe couldn't buy that, especially since Luke had that unexplained money in his bank account.

"We've fixed the security leaks," Shaw went on. "And we've located the hostages that Quivira's holding. I've already assembled a team to go in after them. Once they're safe, Quivira will have no reason to come after you or Anna."

It sounded good. Maybe too good. There was something a little off with that reassurance. Rafe studied the colonel's expression but couldn't quite put his finger on it. Was Shaw trying to tell him that all was not well with that plan he'd just laid out?

Maybe.

If so, Rafe didn't need anyone to tell him that. For one thing, those hostages weren't free yet. And if securing their freedom was as imminent as Shaw had just made it out to be, then he would have waited until the mission was a done deal before making this little visit. That was standard operating procedure.

So, what did this visit mean, exactly?

Rafe decided to find out. It was time to push a few mental buttons. Little ones, though. He wouldn't bring up what Quivira had told him. Yet. "What about Janine? Is she still a player in this?"

"We don't know. A couple of hours ago she lost the tag we'd put on her."

Great. But it wasn't surprising. If Janine was a bed partner of Victor O'Reilly, then he could have easily gotten her out of the country. Or just out of the way. Rafe didn't intend to let O'Reilly do the same to Anna.

"So, here's the plan," Shaw ordered. "We get out of here right now. And by *we,* I mean all of us, including Anna. I know she's in here with you somewhere. I'm putting the two of you in protective custody until I get news back from the rescue team."

Rafe didn't respond to that. It was an order he didn't intend to obey.

"Quivira called a little while ago" was all Rafe said. "We talked."

It was enough. He could tell by the way Shaw's jaw muscles twitched that he fully understood what Quivira had divulged. The display of emotion didn't last long, though. Shaw quickly regained his military bearing.

"Did you tell him the truth about his son's death?" Shaw asked.

"No."

Shaw's poker face never faltered. No relief. No other emotion. It was the combat-rescue face that Rafe had seen dozens of times. Too bad. It was a hard face to read, and Rafe wanted to know if this man had betrayed him.

"I had my reasons for lying to Quivira," Shaw finally admitted.

Not exactly the huge confession Rafe had wanted. It wasn't nearly enough.

"And what would those reasons be?" Rafe demanded.

"Your life. Anna's. And even the lives of those other men that Quivira's holding. If Quivira knew his son was dead, then I wouldn't have anything to bargain with."

Rafe lifted a shoulder. "You know, you've lied so much that I'm not sure I want to believe that."

"What other reason would I have?"

Rafe could think of one. A bad one. Maybe Shaw had sold out his country and the members of the Alpha Team. And maybe it had something to do with that missing Shadow Warrior virus and antidote. Or all of this could be some elaborate plan to cover up an obviously botched mission. Rafe's silence let the colonel know what he was thinking.

"Quivira is the enemy," Shaw enunciated. "Not me. So, make your choice now, Rafe. Either you're with me, or you're against me. Either you and Anna cooperate with this protective custody, or I'll have you both placed under arrest."

It was the corner Rafe had expected to be boxed into. So, he went into evade-and-escape mode. As far as he was concerned, Shaw was the enemy until he could convince him otherwise, and Rafe had every intention of getting the hell out of there.

"And you think Anna and I will actually be safe in this protective custody?" Rafe questioned.

"I'll do my best. I'll take you to the CRO training facility near San Antonio. We can regroup and wait for information about the rescue of the hostages. If necessary, we can assemble a team to take out O'Reilly and Quivira before they do any more damage. It's time for action, Rafe. I don't want to play by these goons' rules anymore."

Yeah, and all of this *time for action* garbage could include leading the rebels right to them. It didn't matter whose side Shaw was on. Not really. It was obvious that there were holes a mile wide in security.

"Buchanan and Sheldon won't be coming with us to the training facility," Shaw promised. "I'll divert Buchanan to another project. Sheldon's already on his way back to Sen-tron headquarters for reassignment."

Surprised, Rafe just stared at him. It was a start, but it was too little too late. "If you don't trust them, then why did you leave them on the team as long as you did?"

"I thought it'd be safer until I could make other arrangements. The fewer people who knew about this, the better."

It wasn't exactly reassuring, but nothing would have been if it came from Shaw. "So, is all of this really some kind of trap, and Anna and I are the bait?"

"You've been the bait since day one," Shaw said without hesitation. "And you know it. But now it's time to minimize the threat to both of you. Yes, Quivira and O'Reilly might come after you, but they'll do it on our terms. If you're at the training facility, we can better contain them. The first step is for you to get off this boat and come with me."

Rafe would—when they started serving ice water in hell.

Shaw checked his watch. "We'll have to leave now."

"Anna's in the bathroom," Rafe said. "Give us a couple of minutes so she can get dressed, and then we can leave."

The stony look that Shaw sent him was a warning. "Don't try anything stupid. I'll be watching the boat."

Good. Maybe Shaw could keep Quivira's and O'Reilly's men at bay until he got Anna out of there.

"I'll keep this," Shaw said, taking Rafe's gun.

Rafe didn't argue. It was best not to alert Shaw to the fact that he had escape plans on his mind.

"You've got two minutes," Shaw added. And with Rafe's gun gripped in his hand, he stepped outside to wait.

Rafe didn't say a word when he threw open the hatch and climbed into the cramped space with her. Anna had heard the part about "two minutes." Not much time for an escape, but Rafe obviously thought they had a chance. Or else it was a chance he had to take because it was their only option.

He took the gun from her and shoved it into his pants pocket while he maneuvered himself into a narrow tunnel that fed off the hiding space. Rafe threw back the latch.

"We'll have to do this without life jackets," he whispered, apology in his voice. "I don't want anyone to spot us. Think you can swim to shore?"

Anna nodded. She would do whatever it took to get them out of there, but she knew her own limitations. She wasn't that strong a swimmer. "But won't Colonel Shaw be looking for us in the water?"

"Definitely."

That sent her heart pounding. She didn't have time to try to steady it. Rafe opened the small circular door, and without so much as a warning, he slid them both into the dark, cold water. The hatch door snapped shut behind them.

Overhead, the storm pounded the lake, and darkness

was all around them. Rafe pulled her under the water. With his arm around her waist, he began to swim with her in tow.

It seemed several minutes, and Anna's lungs began to ache from the exertion and lack of air. Just when she thought she might panic, he surfaced. For a moment. Only long enough for her to pull in a deep breath. And then he submerged them again.

She didn't even try to look back at the boat to see if Shaw had spotted them. She kept her focus only on Rafe. Somehow, he would get them out of there.

When he neared the shore, he kept them low, in a crouch, and they crawled onto the muddy embankment. Her clothes and shoes were heavy, but Rafe didn't stop. He headed straight for a cluster of cedars and took her with him.

Panting, she heard her own ragged breath above the howl of the storm. "What now?" she asked.

He motioned toward an all-terrain vehicle that was parked near the dock. "We'll borrow that."

It probably belonged to Colonel Shaw, since it hadn't been there when they first arrived at the lake.

"Ready?" Rafe asked.

She took several deep breaths and nodded. Rafe didn't waste even a moment. He latched on to her hand and made a run for it. The night and the storm gave them some cover, but Anna had no idea if it was enough. If Shaw saw them, God knows what he would do to stop them. Maybe he would even shoot at them.

The distance between them and the vehicle seemed to widen with each step, but Rafe didn't let her slow down. Trudging through the mud and slush, he made it to the vehicle, yanked open the door and shoved her inside.

"No keys," she mumbled, looking at the ignition.

That didn't deter Rafe. He reached beneath the dash and hot-wired it.

He had only driven a few yards when she heard the sound behind them. A whirl like a rocket. Or an artillery shell. She glanced back and saw Colonel Shaw dive into the water. A split second later, she understood why. The boat exploded into a thundering ball of flames.

"Did you set explosives?" she asked, already knowing the answer.

"No."

Rafe gunned the engine and got them out of there.

Chapter 15

Rafe was right. The training facility was the last place on earth anyone would have expected them to go. So, why didn't that make her feel better? Maybe it was too much to ask to feel safer simply because they'd moved to a new location.

While Rafe used the computer to check the security system, Anna opened the second-story window and looked out at the nearly deserted facility. It was midnight, and with the storm still raging, it was pitch-black outside. Only the occasional slash of lightning allowed her to see the place where the CROs and security operatives conducted some of their training.

A zigzagging obstacle course. A canine compound complete with at least a half dozen dogs. A winding hedge maze right in the center of the grounds.

In the distance, she could see a portion of a mock vil-

lage and the security police checkpoint at the entrance
of the facility. It was manned with two guards, Rafe
had told her, and that's why he'd carefully avoided it
when he sneaked them inside an hour earlier. Instead,
he had cut his way through a back fence after temporar-
ily disarming a series of perimeter security monitors.

Anna glanced over her shoulder when she heard Rafe
walk toward her. The room was functional and little
else. An office, of sorts, jammed with computers and
other equipment. Earlier, Rafe had changed into his
uniform and put several small pieces of that equipment
into a black duffel bag. Preparing for his mission, no
doubt. A mission that was inevitable. Dangerous. And
necessary.

"Quivira refused to do any negotiations over the
phone," he told her. "That's what I figured he'd say, so
I've set up a meeting with him at his choice of locations.
The cabin we were shot at. I'll give him the information
about his son and tell him, if possible, I'll arrange to
have the body returned to him. Hopefully, that'll start
the ball rolling for a cease-fire."

What Rafe left unsaid was that the meeting was only
a part of what he had to do. He couldn't let Quivira go
free. That was the real reason the meeting had to be
face-to-face. The man was a killer, and as long as he
was out there, their lives and others would always be
in danger. Rafe would have to put an end to that threat
even if it meant eliminating Quivira.

The thought of Rafe facing Quivira made Anna ache.
After all, Quivira was about to learn his son was dead.
God knows how he would react to news like that. A
cease-fire and return of his son's body might be the

last things on his mind. He might come at Rafe with guns blazing.

Of course, Rafe knew that as well as she did.

"What about Victor O'Reilly?" Anna asked. "He wants to kill us, too, and in some ways he's more dangerous than Quivira since he doesn't want to trade any information."

"Rico is going after him. He's already back in the States and on the way to a bravo location where he's arranged to intercept O'Reilly. It's an abandoned house about six miles from the cabin where I'm meeting Quivira. Rico had to blow his undercover identity to find out the man's location, but I couldn't risk having O'Reilly out there any longer."

He was right, of course. "And what about Colonel Shaw? Does he know about this?"

"No. I didn't let Shaw, Buchanan or Sheldon in on our plan. Too risky," Rafe added. "Anyway, Shaw's tied up with the hostage rescue. It should all be over by morning."

He sounded calm. Comforting. Even confident. But it was partly a facade, and they both knew it. Nothing had gone right so far. Well, nothing except for the fact they were still somehow miraculously alive. But that had more to do with Rafe's tenacity than it did anything else.

"I have to stop all of this," Rafe continued as if trying to convince her that there was no other way. Which there probably wasn't. "And I can't take you with me. It's too dangerous. You'll be safe here."

Maybe.

Anna kept that thought to herself. She would certainly be safer at the training compound than she would at that cabin with Quivira and God knows who else. But then, if Rafe had broken through security to get inside the facility, then others could as well.

Anna pushed that thought aside, too.

Rafe stepped closer, until his chest was against her back. He brushed a kiss on her cheek and slid his arms around her. Even after that swim through the lake and the trek through the surrounding woods, he smelled good. Musky and warm.

"You'll be all right," he assured her. "I'll do whatever it takes to protect you."

It wasn't the first time he'd promised that, and there was no sense of *maybe* in it. Anna had doubts about how all of these meetings and the rescue mission would end, but her worries had nothing to do with Rafe's abilities. If it could be done, then he would do it.

She wrapped her arms around his and tightened the grip. "When do you leave?"

"In less than two hours. I have to wait until the task force has gotten the hostages out."

Not much time, considering it could possibly be the last time she would ever see him. But Anna had no intentions of voicing that. She had less than one hundred and twenty minutes to spend with the man she loved, and she didn't intend to waste it with fears and regrets.

"I'm very good at what I do," he whispered. "And I've got a heck of a lot of reasons to finish off this mess and come back to you." He placed his hand on her stomach. "This is just one of them."

Anna smiled in spite of everything. Earlier, she had thought he didn't even want the baby. Thankfully, she'd been wrong.

She could have pushed the moment. And almost did. It would have been wonderful to hear Rafe say that he loved her, but it would have been a lie. Or at least a half truth. He still didn't remember the love he'd once felt for her. And might never remember.

Could she accept that?

It didn't take Anna more than a few seconds to realize the answer. To be with Rafe, she could accept just about anything except losing him.

She turned toward him, sliding her arms around his neck in the same motion. It was the need for reassurance that sent her in search of his mouth. But it was the love she felt for him that made her deepen the kiss.

The taste of him jolted through her. It soothed her. Nourished her. Made her feel as if everything was right with the world. She forgot about the rebels who were after them, the storm, and the mission that still lay ahead. She was safe now and right where she belonged.

His response was instant. A burst of energy. A kiss that matched the need in her. And not exactly meant for reassurance. It was laced with hunger and fire.

For days, they'd been testing and resisting this need they had for each other. Rafe had even managed to show her a thing or two about how he could pleasure her. But they'd yet to make love.

It was time to do something about that.

Anna released her grip on him so she could get closer. Rafe did the same. Until they were pressed against each other. They tried to satisfy the fire with their mouths. With their hurried caresses. With the contact of their bodies. But it wasn't enough.

Not nearly enough.

Anna struggled to hold on to her breath even though she wasn't sure she wanted to breathe just yet. The light-headed giddiness felt like a swirl of magic that had snared her in a sensual web. But she knew the source of the magic was really Rafe.

He backed her against the wall. It was a good thing, or she would have certainly lost her balance. She tugged with the buttons on his battle-dress uniform. And won. She finally managed to get off his shirt so she could put her hands on his naked chest.

Mercy, the man was built.

All those tight rippled muscles. The rough coils of chest hair. The sinewy feel of all that power and strength beneath her hands. His body was a honed lethal weapon, and yet she'd never felt more cherished than she did when those strong arms held her.

"I know this isn't the best time or the best place," she whispered.

"Yeah. We've had a little trouble with that right place, right time thing, haven't we?" He peeled off her oversize T-shirt and tossed it aside. "First that cellar in Monte de Leon. Then the boat. And now this office where there's not a freaking bed in sight."

"We don't need a bed."

He chuckled in that low, sexy way that only Rafe could manage. "My thoughts, exactly. We'll just have to make our own bed...and then lie down in it."

It was exactly what she wanted. *This* was what she wanted. And no, it might not have been the right time or the right place, but this was definitely the right man.

The only man.

Anna went exploring. They didn't have a lot of time, but she didn't intend to skip any of the pleasures along the way. She caressed those taut muscles of his chest and gently circled his nipple with her fingertips. She got her reward when he groaned with pleasure.

Rafe did his own share of exploring. He matched her almost-frantic pace with his hurried kisses and touches. He tugged at her jeans, the snap finally giving way so that he could slide them off her. On his way back up, he planted some kisses on her thighs and stomach.

His movements slowed when he reached her panties. He was gentle. No heated rush even though the clock was ticking. Anna pushed the thought of that clock aside. And everything else. Instead, she concentrated on the kisses. The touches. And Rafe.

"I probably should have said this sooner, but should we be doing this?" he asked. He eased away from her slightly and caught her gaze.

He meant because she was pregnant. "Definitely. The doctor said it was okay."

And Anna pulled him back to her.

Tired of the barriers between them, she rid him of the rest of his uniform, and with the wall still supporting them, they slid down to the floor. Anna took advantage of the new position. Face to face, mouth to mouth, chest to chest, body to body. She eased onto his lap and wrapped her legs around his waist.

"Let's do this now." Anna rubbed herself against his erection, hoping to take him inside her right then and there.

But Rafe obviously had other plans.

He dodged her maneuvers and dropped a line of kisses from her mouth to her breasts. "You're so beautiful."

They were words of seduction, but they weren't necessary. The seduction had not only been mutual but was very near completion. But in her heart, Anna knew she would remember that compliment for the rest of her life.

She said his name. As a plea. And as a promise. His body slid against hers. Damp bare skin against bare skin. His breath brushed over her face.

"Anna," he whispered.

Just the sound of Rafe saying her name was enough to send the fire roaring through her blood. "Make love to me," she insisted.

"Soon."

Rafe fisted his hands in her hair and forced her head back so that he could take her neck. Nothing was slow about this pace. Nothing gentle. He took. And claimed. And savored.

It still wasn't enough.

"More," she insisted.

Rafe flashed her one of those dazzling grins. "More was exactly what I had in mind."

Rafe knew this had already reached the point of no return. *More,* Anna had requested. And that's exactly what he would give her.

"Hang on, darling," he said. "What do you say we go on this ride together?"

She made a soft, shivery sound. Part laughter, part invitation. All need.

Rafe captured her gaze and entered her slowly. Gently. Enjoying every inch of the delicate resistance that he met. Until he was fully inside her.

A few coherent thoughts crossed his mind, but none were exactly the romantic declarations he was looking for. So, Rafe tried a simpler approach.

"This is right," he managed to say.

She nodded, her breath coming out in gentle gusts. "You bet it is."

He stilled another moment. To catch his breath. To absorb the incredible feel of her. Her silky heat pulsed around him. But that heat and warmth that he saw in Anna's eyes put a quick end to that moment of stillness.

Rafe had no choice. He began to move inside her. Need dictated the pace and the intensity. And there was so much need in both of them.

As if his life depended on it, he drove into her. She accepted him, moved with him.

She whispered his name, repeated it, a trembling sound spilling over her lips. He plummeted them both, too quickly, he thought, to that ultimate moment. Any amount of time would have been too little. Too fast. For something he wanted to last forever.

He would tell her that later. Later, when words mattered.

For now, he gathered her beneath him, until all she could do was cling to him to save her.

And he did.

Following her, Rafe did his best to save them both.

With her wrapped in his arms, Rafe let his mind drift. He tried to absorb the enormity of his relationship with Anna, their feelings for each other and everything else.

The night settled in around them. The dark room. Anna's scent on his skin. The gentle rhythm of her heartbeat against his hand. The sound of the storm outside.

And then it happened.

The memories came like video clips. Short bursts of sights, sounds, smells, tastes and touches. Images of Anna. Of the rescue in Monte de Leon. Of that cellar where he'd made love to her.

Everything.

Little by little, it all came back. The small details that were more valuable, more treasured than any tangible possession could ever have been. The first time he'd kissed Anna. The taste of her. The way she'd fit in his arms. And the love. God, the love. It was there. Strong and real. A place in his heart meant only for her.

All of the missing pieces of the past twelve months of his life came back to him.

Rafe caught on to each one. Reliving them. Cherishing them. The pain and the happiness. Most of all the happiness. Before Anna, he hadn't even known what that word truly meant.

Now, he did.

And he would do whatever it took to hold on to that. To hold on to her and their child.

Rafe savored the images and feelings a moment longer before pushing them aside. He couldn't let any of that distract him now.

He kissed her and moved away from her.

"It's time?" she asked.

He nodded, reaching for his clothes. Anna got up also, and they dressed in silence. After he'd donned his battle dress uniform, he put a phone and a handgun on the table near her. He prayed she didn't need either, but they might come in handy if security failed.

Or if *he* failed.

"You'll be careful?" There was a catch in her voice,

but she quickly cleared her throat to try to cover it. She was obviously trying to be strong for him.

"Absolutely." And because he wanted to see that dazzling smile, Rafe looped an arm around her waist and snapped her to him. "Don't worry. All this top-secret kind of stuff is right up my alley, darling. I'll be back before breakfast."

It didn't work. Anna tried to force a smile, but instead her mouth quivered. "Just don't take any unnecessary chances, all right?"

"No plans for that," he assured her. "This will be a quick in and out. Promise. Then Quivira won't be able to get to us anymore."

From his mouth to God's receptive ears. More than anything he wanted to make it back to Anna and their child, and it just might take some help of a divine nature.

"I hate to ask," she started, her voice still low and shaky. "But you do trust Rico, don't you?"

"Of course. I've known him for years."

She lifted a shoulder. "I could say the same about Colonel Shaw. I just don't want you to let friendship blind you to things that might not be right."

It was no easy request. Rico had saved his life not once but twice. That created trust on the deepest level possible. Still, Anna was right. These were not ordinary times. Someone with plenty of insider knowledge had been helping both sides of the rebels. That didn't mean he wouldn't trust Rico to help him with this mission. But he planned to do a lot of looking over his shoulder.

Rafe planted a kiss on her forehead and forced himself away from her so he could finish packing his equipment bag. "Lock the door when I go, and don't leave this room. I'll make sure the security system is set. Plus, there are guards at the gate. Press that red button by the door if you need them."

Anna nodded. And paused. Her eyes slowly lifted to meet his. "What is it?" she asked. "Is something wrong that I don't know about?"

"Everything's fine," he assured her.

It was another of those not-so-little white lies that he'd been doling out lately. He wouldn't tell her that he'd regained his memory. Not now. Not while he was on his way out the door. There wasn't enough time to work through all the implications and conversations of something like that. Later, when he returned, he'd tell her. Later, he would make everything all right.

But first, he had to face down the devil and somehow survive it.

Chapter 16

Rafe had a bad feeling about this. Real bad.

He stayed crouched in the shallow crevice on the limestone bluff and gave his infrared equipment another adjustment. He scanned the cabin. The woods. And even the road. Again. He repeated the procedure to make sure the monitor was working correctly.

It was.

So, why hadn't he gotten a reading to indicate that someone, anyone, was nearby?

Quivira had promised to come alone, but Rafe had automatically dismissed that as a bald-faced lie. He'd come prepared to battle it out with at least a dozen armed men who would try to capture him. Instead, Rafe found himself alone in the woods.

"Status?" he heard Rico ask through the earpiece communicator.

"Too quiet. How about you?"

"The same. The house looks empty. O'Reilly's a no-show."

Definitely not good. So, what the hell was going on?

"Have the SkyWatch pilot do an aerial read," Rafe instructed Rico.

Not that Rafe would trust such an aerial read over the equipment he had in his hands, but it seemed time to get a second opinion.

While he waited for the data, and while the silence lay heavy around him, Rafe couldn't help but think of Anna. Maybe Murphy's Law wouldn't play havoc with them again, and maybe she'd stay safe until he could finish this mission and get back to her.

He was in love with her. No doubt about it. And he hadn't needed the return of his memory to tell him that. Somewhere along the way, in the middle of the chaos, he'd fallen in love with her all over again. There was something comforting about that. No matter what they faced, no matter what the challenges, the love he felt for Anna would always be a constant.

His true north.

And he couldn't get any better anchor than that. Now all he had to do was rid the world of Quivira and make his way back to her.

Rafe heard a slight crackle of static in his ear. "Nothing from the aerial report," Rico relayed to him. "There's been some recent activity, but none in the last hour. This isn't looking good, Rafe."

No, it wasn't.

He considered his options, but there was really only one choice. He had to check out the cabin, to see if Quivira had left a note about a secondary meeting place. Of course, if the man had done that, it would essentially mess up everything. Rafe would lose the advantage of position and territory. And it would mean wasting time here when he should be making his way back to Anna.

But what choice did he have?

"I'm going in," Rafe mumbled.

"You sure about that?" Rico asked.

"No. But I'm doing it anyway."

"Then I guess I will, too. If O'Reilly's in the house, I'll find him. Good luck. Don't break a leg or anything."

"Same to you," Rafe offered.

He took a deep breath, said a quick prayer and climbed out of the crevice. When he got to the top, he stayed in a crouched position and began to make his way down the rough terrain toward the cabin.

The rain had stopped nearly an hour earlier, but the ground was slick with mud. Rafe adjusted the equipment on his back and wormed his way though the mat of shrubs and cedars.

There were no lights on in the cabin, and the dark-colored logs seemed to blend into the moonless night. He glanced at the infrared motion detector to make sure no one had circled around behind him, but he seemed to have the place to himself.

So, why didn't that make him feel better?

He took another reading as he reached the back porch, but when that was negative as well, he put the equipment away and slipped inside.

Rafe paused a moment. Listening. He heard nothing. Not even a whisper of breath. That bad feeling in his gut went up a considerable notch. He went through the kitchen, gingerly stepping over broken glass from Quivira's earlier attack. He moved without a sound, keeping his weapon ready in case he had to fire.

His eyes had already adjusted to the darkness by the time he made it to the living room, so he had no trouble seeing the man in the chair near the fireplace. But not just any man.

Quivira.

"Oh, hell," Rafe muttered.

He went closer, knowing what he would find. Still, he pressed his fingers to the man's neck.

No pulse.

No body heat.

Nothing.

Not only was Quivira dead, he'd been that way for some time. Hours, at least. And that meant the whole meeting had probably been a setup.

"Good news and bad news," he heard Rico say into the earpiece. "The hostages are free. But O'Reilly's already a goner. Not my handiwork, either. He was dead when I arrived."

"Quivira, too."

Both men cursed at the same time.

Rafe hurried out of the cabin, praying he was wrong. He'd never forgive himself if Quivira and O'Reilly's killer had already gone after Anna. But in his heart, he knew that's exactly what had happened.

Anna found herself on her knees in front of the toilet. Talk about a bad time for her first bout with morning sickness. She pressed the wad of wet paper towels to her forehead, hoping it would help. It did, some, but there was still a heavy, queasy feeling in the pit of her stomach.

There was a security light just outside the bathroom window. Just enough so she could catch sight of herself in the full-length mirror mounted on the wall. She had the paper towels in one hand. The gun in the other. Her face was colorless. And she was still rumpled—the remnants of making love with Rafe.

Talk about a visual summary of her predicament.

The only thing missing was a huge sign around her neck saying how worried she was about him. He had to be all right. She wouldn't let herself consider anything else.

The sound of the phone ringing cut through the dull ache in her head, and she got to her feet and raced into the adjoining room to answer it.

"Please let it be Rafe," she mumbled.

But it wasn't Rafe at all.

"Anna?" Janine said.

Stunned, Anna took a moment to gather her breath. "How did you get this number?"

"Colonel Shaw patched me through. We have to talk, Anna. Now."

Mercy. She didn't need this. She already had enough to deal with.

"This isn't a good time, Janine." Anna went to the window and since the glass was coated with condensation, she opened it and checked the grounds. She didn't see anyone, but Janine's call made her very uneasy. If Shaw could patch her through, what else could he do? Could he find her? And if he could, what would he do with that information? "I need to keep this line open in case Rafe calls."

"This is important. Just listen. Someone used me to get to you and Rafe."

Anna's throat constricted. God, it was true. She'd hoped that Shaw and the others had been wrong, that Janine didn't have any part in this. But it appeared that she was the one who was wrong.

"I know about your friendship with Victor O'Reilly," Anna challenged.

"Friendship? Not quite. That would imply a two-way street. He's a user, Anna, and I hadn't heard from him in years until just about a week ago. I had no idea—none—as to what he planned to do, but I think he had someone put something in your wedding ring. A microchip tracking device or something. And I think he's been using it to find you."

Anna's gaze flew to the chunky emerald-cut diamond wedding band. The ring that Janine had no doubt helped Rafe buy from her own jewelry store.

"Get rid of it now," Janine insisted. "Someone had broken into the jewelry store. I think now it was someone who worked for O'Reilly. He didn't take anything so I thought it was kids. I didn't put it together until I talked to Colonel Shaw and he asked if there was any personal item of yours that O'Reilly might have had access to."

"You think he had access to my ring?" Anna asked.

"He had access to the whole damn store. He could have put that tracking chip in the setting before the wedding. I'm so sorry, Anna. I swear I didn't know."

The blood rushed to her head and sent the room spinning. Anna fought it and forced herself to stay focused. She laid the gun aside, cradled the phone against her ear and tugged at the ring.

It wouldn't budge.

God, it wouldn't budge! The only thought going

through her head was that O'Reilly or one of his hench-men was already on his way to kill her.

Frantic, Anna ran to the bathroom and stuck her hand under the running water. The ring finally slipped off. She wasted no time. Anna flushed it down the toilet.

"I got it off," she told Janine.

Anna didn't think the sigh she heard from her friend was fake, and it matched her own.

The relief didn't last long.

"O'Reilly could have already tracked you," Janine pointed out. "Can you go somewhere else—fast?"

"Rafe told me to stay here until he got back."

But the moment she said the words, Anna regretted it. She'd just perhaps told the enemy that she was alone. And vulnerable. Worse, the line went dead.

She pressed the flash button, hoping to reconnect with Janine, but all she got was silence. Silence, until she heard the click. The soft sound came from the lock.

The door opened slowly.

"Good evening, Anna," the person greeted. "I thought I might find you here."

Chapter 17

Anna heard the all-too-familiar voice, and it made her blood run cold. It wasn't Buchanan. Or Shaw. Or even Janine. Nicholas Sheldon was in the doorway of the room.

Every inch of Anna's body went on alert. God, how had he gotten so close without her even hearing him?

"Sheldon. You scared the life out of me." She pressed her hand over her heart. It was too late not to jump to conclusions. She'd already jumped but prayed she was wrong. "What are you doing here?"

Without so much as a word, Sheldon stepped inside and closed the door behind him.

Just that simple gesture made Anna want to take a step back, but she forced herself to hold her ground. She didn't know why, but she didn't intend to let Sheldon know just how much she was afraid of him. "I'll have to ask you to leave. Rafe will be back soon."

"I won't stay long." He leaned against the door, almost casually, and stared at her.

Anna suddenly didn't care if he heard the fear in her voice. "There's nothing we have to say to each other."

"Yes." He paused. "There is."

Somehow, Anna knew what was about to happen. She'd known from the moment she saw him in the doorway. Running from the rebels had honed her survival instincts, and those instincts were screaming for her to get out of there.

She whipped her gaze to the desk. The gun Rafe had left her was still there. Just out of reach. With Sheldon's strength and speed, he could easily overpower her even before she could get to it.

And he would overpower her.

Anna was sure of that.

"You used the tracking device in the ring to find me," she said more to herself than him. She glanced at the emergency button by the door. Sheldon was between it and her.

"No. That was O'Reilly's doing, I guess. I used Sentron's equipment that the Justice Department paid for."

He walked closer, still blocking her path to the emergency button. "This has to be quick." His words were calm. Void of any emotion. He could have been discussing the weather instead of his plans to kill her. "Did I mention these rooms are virtually soundproof? One of Colonel Shaw's idiosyncrasies. He tolerates no information leaks during training. Ironic, isn't it?"

So, no one would hear her if she screamed. Anna fought to keep control of her breath. Her composure. If she panicked, she stood no chance against a man like

Sheldon. She had to keep her wits so she could figure out what to do.

He pulled something from inside his shirt. Something wrapped in a washcloth. With his back still braced against the wall, he carefully unwrapped it, and Anna noticed then that he wore surgical gloves. She didn't have long to dwell on that because cradled in the cloth was a gun fitted with a silencer. She couldn't be sure, but it appeared to be the gun Colonel Shaw had carried that night at the church.

God, was Sheldon trying to set this up to make it seem as if Shaw had killed her?

"Rafe could come walking in here at any moment," she warned.

"No. He won't. He's still very much tied up with his meeting with Quivira. He probably won't figure out that Quivira is dead for…oh, at least another half hour or so."

Dead. Quivira was dead. Not that it would help her now. Had the meeting with Rafe and Quivira been just a ruse? Probably. If so, it was an effective one.

She'd be dead if she didn't do something to save herself. And she would do something. But what? There didn't seem any place to run or hide.

"You're doing this because of that woman who died on a CRO rescue mission?" But it wasn't really a question. Anna just wanted to keep him talking until she could figure out what to do.

"Yes," he readily answered. He winced as if just admitting that was painful. "Eve DeCalley. I was in love with her. An emotion that I'm sure you understand completely. Imagine how heartbroken you'd be if you lost Rafe. Eve's dead because of your husband and Colonel Shaw. Their incompetence killed her. She would have never been caught in that cross fire if it weren't for them."

Anna shook her head and gathered enough breath to speak. "That's not the way I heard it."

"Then you heard it wrong," he calmly assured her. There was a twisted sort of triumph in his voice. "I've already taken care of Quivira and O'Reilly. Dregs of society. You're next, my dear. And then your husband, of course."

"What about Shaw?"

"I'll save the best for last. His won't be nearly as quick and painless. He'll be court-martialed and eventually put to death for killing Rafe and you to cover up his botched mission."

With each word, Anna fought off the despair. She wouldn't let this man win.

Sheldon stuffed the washcloth back in his shirt and raised the gun. Anna did back up then. Just a step. Out of the corner of her eye, she saw the window—the window she'd opened earlier.

He angled his gaze in that direction as well. It was a contingency he probably hadn't counted on. The room might be soundproof, but with an open window, perhaps one of the security policemen would hear her scream.

Now, if she could get close enough for the sound to carry.

"I wouldn't do that if I were you," he warned.

"But you're not me, are you?" she fired back.

A brief smile bent his mouth.

And he took aim.

There was no time to decide what to do—Anna dove onto the side of the table away from him. The shot, hardly more than a swish of air, slammed into the wall above her head and sent a chunk of plaster flying. She didn't stop. She didn't take the time to think about how close Sheldon had just come to killing her.

She yelled, praying the security policemen at the gate would hear her and respond. But she couldn't wait to see if that would happen. She yanked some papers off one of the desks, flung them at Sheldon and, in the same motion, scrambled across the room to try to get to her gun.

Sheldon beat her to it.

He swiped the weapon off the table and threw it well out of her reach. With their bodies only inches apart, their gazes collided. For a moment. And then he sprang toward her. He might have been bigger, but Anna somehow managed to dodge his grip. She hurried around the end of the table and headed straight for the window.

Another shot slammed into the wall next to her shoulder, missing her only because she ducked at the last possible second. It didn't stop her. Nothing would at this point. If she stayed in the room, she'd die.

Anna cried out for help again. She barreled onto the windowsill and climbed out onto the ledge that lipped the building. It wasn't a large space by any means. Mere inches. There was no place for her to hide, so she needed a temporary barricade until she could find a way out.

"It won't do any good to yell," Sheldon told her as he walked closer. "I took care of the sky cops at the gate. You don't think I'd let them interfere with my plans, do you?"

Oh, God. He'd killed them. Not that she had any doubts, but that meant he wouldn't hesitate to kill her.

She slammed the window shut just as the glass shattered from another bullet. Fortunately, the glass was covered with a safety coating so the shards merely cracked and webbed. If it hadn't, she would have almost certainly been cut.

"You're like a cat with nine lives," Sheldon grumbled. "But those lives have already been used up."

Anna screamed again, praying that someone, anyone, would hear her, but she didn't intend to wait around and see. Crouching, she caught sight of the ground below.

"Oh, God," she gasped.

The ledge was probably less than ten feet high, but it suddenly seemed miles away. The jump would perhaps injure her. Or worse, it might hurt the baby, especially if Sheldon could shoot again before she could take cover. But she didn't have a choice. When she heard the sound of him walking toward her, Anna said a prayer.

And jumped.

The scream that tore from her mouth wasn't calculated this time or meant to alert anyone. It was from pain when she hit the ground and twisted her ankle. Anna ignored it. Or tried to and scrambled into a bed of sage bushes. Any moment, Sheldon would come out onto the ledge and shoot at her. If she stayed put, she'd be an easy target.

On all fours, she scurried behind a clumpy hedge and peered up at the window. She cringed when she saw Sheldon already there. His gun, already aimed. Right at her.

Keeping low, she managed to stand, wincing at the almost unbearable pain in her ankle, and darted behind another hedge.

A shot blistered through the air overhead.

She ran and called out for help again. Panic and fear raced through her, nearly choking off her breath. She fought for each bit of air that she managed to pull into her lungs. But she didn't stop. Anna knew she had to put some distance, some space, between Sheldon and her. She had to take cover.

But where?

Still running, she spotted the maze just ahead. Not her first choice of hiding places, but the hedges were thick and high. Maybe Sheldon wouldn't be able to see her from the balcony. That wouldn't stop him from pursuing her, of course, but this way, she at least had a fighting chance.

"Please," she prayed, racing through the entrance of the maze. "Don't let him hurt the baby."

The path between the hedge rows was narrow, probably not even enough room for two people to walk side by side. Obviously not meant for romantic strolls in the moonlight. It reminded her of a spooky carnival ride with its sharp turns and deep shadows. It was so dark, she couldn't even see the ground beneath her feet.

When her lungs ached so much that she thought they might burst, Anna stopped and caught on to one of the hedges. She rifled through the stiff branches, batting them aside. It only took her a moment to realize that she wouldn't be able to escape through the tightly knitted shrubs.

But she saw something that had her heart nearly stopping in mid-beat.

In the distance, she could see the building. And the window. Sheldon was still in it, peering out into the yard at the maze. Even through the murky darkness, she could tell that he didn't have his gun raised. Nor did he appear to be ready to come after her.

He blew into a whistle, the sound high-pitched and shrill. And then he stepped back inside.

Anna had no time to wonder why he'd done that. No time to think. She heard the dogs bark. And knew the sound hadn't come from the pen. They were closer.

Much closer.

Sheldon had sent the attack dogs after her.

The strange sound that Rafe heard had him going still just outside the building where he'd left Anna. He listened. And a moment later, he heard it again. Someone had screamed.

Not someone.

Anna.

Rafe started to bolt inside the building, but he realized the sound hadn't come from there. It was outside. Somewhere on the grounds.

Hell.

Why was she outside?

"Anna?" he called out.

Nothing.

And that caused his heart to drop to his knees.

"Anna?" he shouted even louder. Using the building for cover, he stepped around the side and glanced up at the window of the training room where she was supposed to be.

No one was there.

In the distance he heard the dogs bark. The sound went right through him. He glanced around the area, trying to figure out where the dogs were. And Anna.

"Rafe!" she yelled.

There was no doubt in his mind that she was in the maze, and when he whipped his attention in that direction, he saw the dogs race inside the narrow hedge opening.

Rafe broke into a sprint. God knows why she was there, but he had to get to her before the dogs did. They would tear her to pieces.

He whistled, hoping the dogs would respond to the training prompt. But it was a long shot. One that obviously didn't work. The dogs had been trained to respond to a whistle that the security police used. He didn't know where the cops were, but he couldn't count on them showing up to help Anna.

A shot whipped through the air, smashing into the ground just ahead of him. Rafe cursed and dove for cover. Someone was shooting at him.

But who?

It didn't take him long to come up with that answer. It was probably the person who was responsible for Anna being in that maze.

"Anna, I'm coming!" Rafe shouted.

No gunman or attack dogs would stop him. He used the hedges, running between them, darting in and out of the open yard. He had to keep the movement random. That way, the shooter wouldn't have such an easy target. Easy to say but hard to do when Anna's life was at stake.

Within seconds, he'd reached the back side of the house. Rafe never paused. He raced to a sprawling live oak. Then to another. He heard the dogs again, their incessant barking, and knew they were on Anna's trail.

There was a good twenty feet of open yard between him and the maze. Space he'd have to cover the hard way because there wasn't time to find a circuitous route.

"Rafe?" someone shouted.

Not Anna. Colonel Shaw.

That didn't do a lot to make him feel better about their situation. Rafe knew he only had seconds to react, precious seconds to figure out what to do. If he'd been wrong, if it was Shaw firing those shots, then he'd deal with that—and Shaw—later. Right now, he had to stay alive and get to Anna.

Zigzagging, Rafe darted out into the open space. The entrance to the maze suddenly seemed miles away, and he knew at any moment another bullet could come flying through the darkness. Even if he got hit, he prayed for the strength to save Anna from those dogs and from the shooter.

Rafe whistled again, trying to find the right pitch, but the dogs just kept on barking.

Several shots came at him. One right behind the other. From experience he knew these weren't from a handgun but a high-powered rifle fitted with a silencer. No silencer, however, could muffle that kind of noise, and Rafe was able to pinpoint the direction from where they came.

Inside the house.

The second floor.

And that meant someone had practically an aerial view with which to kill.

Still running, he approached the maze not from the entrance, but from the side. Rafe slid through a narrow crevice between two hedges. He'd known it was there—he'd discovered it and others during the multiple training missions at the facility. He slipped into the narrow corridor, the sharp branches gashing his uniform, and he ran toward the sound of the dogs.

If Anna had known her way around the grounds, she probably could have figured her way out of the maze. It

was basically a mile-long stretch of bends, turns and cir-
cles that had a somewhat predicable pattern. But since
this was probably her first time in it, Rafe had to guess
which direction she might go. The dogs didn't give him
any clues. Their vicious barks filled the air, choking out
any other sounds.

"Anna!" Rafe shouted again.

It would probably give away his position to the
shooter, but it might also get the dogs moving toward
him. At a minimum, the pack might split up, and that
would give Anna a better chance of survival if they attacked.

He prayed they wouldn't attack.

Over the din of the animals, Rafe thought he heard
her answer. He raced through the path, willing himself
to find her, but with each corridor, he came up empty.

And then he heard her scream.

A horrifying sound.

He had no doubts. Anna was battling for her life.

Chapter 18

A dead end.

Damn it! She'd reached a dead end. And she was trapped. The maze pinned her in on both sides, and behind her, she could hear the sounds of the dogs approaching.

God, she didn't want to die.

Shouting out another plea for help, Anna banged her hands against the wall of hedges, knowing the gesture was futile but unable to stop herself.

And then she heard the first growl.

Not some distant sound. No. This was nearby. At least one of the dogs was very close.

Anna turned slowly toward the corridor and prayed she was wrong.

She wasn't.

Even in the darkness, she could see the shimmer of the animal's eyes.

She forced herself not to make any sudden moves. "Stop," she ordered. She even tried whistling, since that's how Sheldon had started the attack in the first place.

Anna couldn't tell if the dog obeyed her order, but she knew this one wouldn't be alone for long. She could already hear the others racing down the passageway straight toward her. When they were together as a pack, then they would no doubt attack as they'd been trained to do.

"Talk to me, Anna," Rafe called out.

His voice gave her hope and made her even more frightened. If he walked into the middle of this, he might be killed as well. She didn't want to risk that, but she didn't want to die, either.

"I need to hear you," Rafe added.

He was trying to find her. But how could he do that in the dark maze?

"The dogs are in here, too," she warned. "And I'm at a dead end."

The dog in front of her snarled even louder, and she sensed that he moved closer. Worse, she heard the others. The pants of their angry breaths. The smell of the run. They were moving in for the kill.

Anna fought the black wave of panic that washed through her. She couldn't give in to it. She rammed her hand into the hedges and cursed when she felt the metal rods that braced the trunks. The rods were only inches apart. Like the bars in a jail cell that had imprisoned her. Still, she tried to pry them from the ground.

"Rafe? Where are you?" she called again.

"Inside the maze."

Not necessarily close to her, though. Anna just couldn't tell. But even if he did manage to get to the correct corridor, there was a possibility he wouldn't be able to stop all the dogs before they attacked.

"Damn you, Sheldon," Anna mumbled. Keeping her gaze locked on the dog, she whistled and heard Rafe do the same.

She reached behind her again and tried to latch on to the hedges so she could hoist herself up. They were thick, matted together in a thorny tangle with the metal rods, but the fronds simply snapped in her hands. She kept hold of one of the larger branches, hoping to use it to protect herself. It wasn't much, but it was better than nothing.

Another dog raced around the corner and into the corridor. He wasn't alone. Since her eyes had adjusted to the darkness, Anna had no trouble seeing a third. And then a fourth. They fanned out as much as they could and stalked toward her.

She backed against the hedges and kept the branch raised in front of her like a shield.

"Anna?" Rafe called out.

He was close, but she didn't dare answer him now. The dogs would almost certainly attack her if she made any sudden noise or if she tried to climb over the hedges. Of course, they'd likely do the same if she stayed perfectly quiet. Still, she wanted to buy herself as many seconds as she could.

The dog in the front of the pack growled. He moved. Not inches. He sprang forward. At the same time, the others moved as well. All lunging at her.

On a ragged scream, Anna grabbed on to the hedges to try to hoist herself up.

Rafe felt his way along the hedges and cursed the darkness. With just a few threads of light, he would have already found what he was looking for. Thank God he had at least an audible way to locate her.

Too bad the audible included her frantic, terrified screams and the sounds of the dogs as they made their way toward her. From the way the hedges rattled, she was obviously trying to climb over them.

An impossible task.

Rafe knew because he'd tried that himself. The hedges simply weren't designed to support weight. Not the weight of a person, anyway. And the bramble beneath would cut flesh to shreds.

He didn't waste time reassuring her but prayed she would hold on long enough for him to reach her. While he was at it, he added a prayer that the maze was the same as it had been since he'd first done training there. If not, then he could be in a hell of a lot of trouble.

And Anna and his baby could be dead.

But Rafe didn't intend for that to happen.

He shoved his hands through the hedges, working at a frenzied pace until he came to the spot—the slit that he'd wormed his way through to beat the designated enemy at the maze game. One of dozens of slits that the designer had included in the dead ends in case a trainee was smart enough to try some creative evade-and-escape maneuvers.

Like now.

"It's me," he shouted. "Take my hand."

"Where?"

Rafe didn't wait for her to locate it. He felt around until he latched on to her arm, and with a fierce jerk, he pulled her through.

His gun was already in position to fire, but first he shoved her behind him. He aimed the shots high, hopefully over the dogs' heads, but if he had to, he would shoot to kill. Without a silencer, the two rounds he fired exploded with a deafening blast.

He paused. Waited. And listened.

When he heard the animals running away, he knew the shots had done the trick. Now he waited to see if the gunfire had also alerted the person who wanted them dead.

He hooked his arm around Anna's waist and roughly pulled her to him. "Sheldon," she said, her breath coming out in rough, loud gasps.

"Sheldon?"

"He's the one behind this. He tried to kill me because of the woman who died on one of your missions."

Yes. And Sheldon was no doubt the one who'd killed O'Reilly and Quivira—in retaliation for Eve's death. He'd also likely fired those shots at him. And from the sound the shots made, he'd used a rifle. Which might be equipped with a night scope. If so, he wouldn't have any trouble tracking them when they left the maze.

"Judas," Rafe muttered, still holding Anna. "I should have known."

"You couldn't have." She pulled him closer still, clinging to him.

She was wrong. The signs were all there, but he hadn't been able to stop Sheldon from coming after them to get his revenge.

"So what do we do?" she asked.

He stared down at Anna, meeting her eyes in the darkness. There wasn't enough time to let her know all the things he felt in his heart.

Anna spoke before he could say anything. "Just tell me what you need me to do, and I'll do it."

It was a generous offer, one that terrified him more than anything else about this situation. He couldn't leave her in the maze in case the dogs returned. Or Sheldon. Yet, taking her with him was a huge risk as well.

Too bad he didn't have a choice.

"Come on," Rafe said before he could change his mind. He took her by the arm and started running toward the mouth of the maze. "I don't want you to take any chances," he instructed. "If you hear shots, get down and stay down, understand?"

"And what about you?"

"I have to get inside the building. Since we've messed up his plans, Sheldon will probably go after Colonel Shaw and then try to double back to come after us."

They'd covered several yards before Rafe noticed Anna was limping. She had been injured, but there was no time to question her about it or curse the fact that Sheldon had hurt her. Rafe scooped her up in his arms, swung her over his shoulder and kept running.

It was like a nightmare. Running through the dark maze, wondering what would be at the end waiting for them. But Rafe had something on his side that Sheldon didn't. Sheldon's quest for revenge had driven him to this point. Rafe knew his motivation was much stronger. Anna and his baby's lives were at stake.

He stopped about twenty feet from the maze entrance and deposited her on the ground. With each step that he'd run, Rafe had tried to come up with a plan, and he thought he finally had one. Not necessarily a good one, but it might work if they got lucky.

Very lucky.

He pressed the gun into her hand and pulled back the hedges to reveal another of the man-made slits. "Wait in here until I get back. Kill the dogs if they return."

She shook her head. "But what will you do? God, you can't go unarmed after Sheldon."

Yes, he would. He didn't have a choice. "I'll find a weapon as soon as I'm inside." Maybe. And if not, he'd go after Sheldon with his bare hands.

Rafe couldn't waste any more time so he maneuvered her into the slit, pushing back as many of the branches as he could to minimize the scratches and scrapes. He pressed a quick kiss on her mouth.

Anna caught his arm when he started to move away. "If something goes wrong—"

"It won't," Rafe interrupted.

And, damn it, it was more than an empty parting promise to help calm her. He wouldn't lose her. One way or another, he would stop Sheldon and come back for her.

"If something goes wrong," Anna repeated. "I just want you to know I love you."

I love you. Hard to hear words like that from Anna and not let them affect him.

Pushing aside her hand, he caught her by the back of the neck and kissed her. Not a brief touch of reassurance. A real kiss. One he hoped she'd remember in case it ended up being their last.

Rafe had already broken the embrace and was ready to run across the open lawn when he heard the nearly muffled shot. It was another round from that rifle, and Sheldon had fired it into the maze.

Damn it—in the maze.

Maybe he'd already finished off Shaw and had returned for Anna. After all, Sheldon certainly would have had enough time to double back, shoot Shaw, and then return to the second floor to make sure the dogs had taken care of Anna.

Rafe didn't waste any time cursing Murphy's Law. "There's been a slight change in plans. You have to come with me."

He grabbed her and ran. When they reached the entrance, he stopped to check out their surroundings and motioned for Anna to stay behind him.

There were just enough interior lights for Rafe to spot the shooter's location. A rifle was sticking out the window of the room where he'd originally left Anna.

And yes, the rifle was aimed right at the maze.

Either Sheldon had already located them with some infrared equipment, or else he would continue to fire random shots in the hopes of getting lucky. Rafe didn't care much for either scenario.

That meant he had to act fast.

The easiest way to do that was for Rafe to shoot him. It would be a tough shot, though, since he couldn't actually see Sheldon's position. And if he missed, Sheldon would know their location and would almost certainly get off some rounds. Perhaps at Anna.

However, if he kept Sheldon occupied while he got closer to the building, then Anna and he would both be safe. Well, as safe as he could make them considering there was a gunman apparently hell-bent on killing them.

From somewhere in the maze, he heard one of the dogs. A gruff snarl. Not nearby, though, so Rafe dismissed it.

Until he heard the next shot.

It went straight in the direction of that gruff snarl, and Rafe heard the dog yelp in pain. That told him exactly what he needed to know. Sheldon did indeed have some kind of night scope on the rifle, but it wasn't accurate enough to distinguish between the dogs and them.

Rafe looked at her over his shoulder. "I have to go—"

She grabbed on to him. "No!"

"Yes. Sheldon will shoot at anything that moves. Especially you. I need to do something to lead him away from the maze."

"But what about you, Rafe? You can't just make yourself a target."

He could. And would. But there was no reason to let her know that. "When you hear shots, slide through the opening and head toward the storage depot. It's nearby, not far to your left. Shut yourself in and wait."

"No. There has to be another way. You can take me with you. Both of us can divert Sheldon."

Rafe had already opened his mouth to tell her that wasn't going to happen, but he heard a shot. A partially silenced blast of deadly power. This one slammed into the maze. Close. Too close. Seconds later, Sheldon fired again.

And again.

Rafe scrubbed his hand over his face. Since the moment when Sheldon fired that first shot, Rafe had known all along what the most logical thing to do was. Too bad it didn't feel logical. And time was running out. Fast.

"Can you run with your foot hurt?" he asked, taking the gun from her.

She nodded.

He hadn't thought she would say differently. Now he only prayed it was true.

"Stay behind me," he instructed. There was no way he could leave her in that maze with Sheldon firing a deadly barrage of bullets that might never end until he hit his ultimate target—Anna.

I love you.

Her words burned through his head as his pulse pounded in his throat. He forced himself to push her confession aside. Forced himself not to think about exactly what was at stake here.

Rafe took her through the crevice. It was their best chance at creating a blind spot for Sheldon. Still, Rafe didn't count on that. He pulled her through to the lawn and pushed her to the ground.

He waited—long agonizing seconds—to see if those bullets would come their way. Sheldon continued to fire, but it seemed random. Or else he wanted Rafe to believe it was, anyway. It was possible that the moment they moved farther into the yard, Sheldon would already have them targeted.

Keeping his gun aimed and ready, Rafe maneuvered Anna behind him and started across the yard. The nearest tree, the one he'd used earlier for cover, was mere feet from them. It seemed miles away. Each inch they had to cover would mean Anna was in danger.

"Let's move," he ordered.

She stayed behind him, and they moved in unison. One step at a time.

The shots stopped.

They were still a few feet from the tree when Rafe latched on to her arm and dove for cover. Just in time. The next shot slammed into the tree only inches from them.

So, he had his answer.

Sheldon knew exactly where they were.

But then, Rafe knew where Sheldon was as well. Now that he was no longer in that maze, he had a much better angle to put a stop to all of this. Nicholas Sheldon was going down.

Rafe crouched behind the tree and took aim. Even though he couldn't see Sheldon, he could see the position of the rifle, and he estimated Sheldon's location. Rafe aimed and double tapped the trigger, pumping two shots into the narrow opening of the window.

Silence followed.

The rifle didn't move.

From the corner of his eye, he saw a slash of motion that came from near the front of the house. A man. Rafe braced himself to fire, but it wasn't Sheldon making his way across the lawn.

It was Colonel Shaw.

"What's he doing out here?" Anna asked.

Rafe didn't have an answer for that, but it was the worst possible time for Shaw to put in an appearance. "Get down, Shaw!" he yelled.

But he didn't. Shaw lifted his hand, an act of surrender, and continued to walk across the lawn right toward them.

"Shaw!" Rafe yelled again. His instinct was to go after him, to get him away from Sheldon's aim.

But it wasn't his first instinct.

Rafe's first instinct was to protect Anna and their

child. At all costs. Even if it meant violating a cardinal rule of not losing a fellow combat rescue officer.

"Sheldon?" Shaw called out. He stopped and faced the balcony. He lowered his hands and propped them on his hips, an almost cocky stance. Rafe could just make out the pistol that Shaw had tucked in the back waist of his battle-dress uniform. Not that it would do him much good. Before he could even draw his weapon, Sheldon would kill him.

"It's me that you want," Shaw continued. "You want me to pay for Eve DeCalley's death. All right, here's your chance. Just leave Rafe and Anna out of this."

Rafe didn't wait for Sheldon to respond because he figured that response would be a shower of bullets. He shoved all thoughts from his head and relied on his training. Rote skills that had been honed for situations just like this. It was combat and rescue in its purest form.

He rolled out from behind the tree, moving away from cover, and came up on one knee. His aim was automatic since he never took his eyes off the target. Rafe emptied the rest of his rounds into the space around the rifle.

Sheldon staggered forward. There was blood. But not enough. None at all in the chest area, which meant he was probably wearing a bulletproof vest. Even though Rafe had managed to wing him a couple of times in the arm, Sheldon still had the rifle clutched in his hand.

And Sheldon aimed the rifle at Shaw.

"Stay put," Rafe ordered Anna, and using the trees for cover, he started across the yard toward Shaw. He would have given just about anything for one more bullet to finish Sheldon off.

"You shouldn't have had Eve as the lead on that mission," Sheldon ground out. "She wasn't ready." He stumbled, but the windowsill stopped his fall.

Shaw was still in danger.

Sheldon took aim again. "You shouldn't have allowed her to die."

"Eve was just doing her job."

Damn it! Why was Shaw antagonizing him? He should have been trying to talk Sheldon into putting down that gun. Rafe didn't dare shout yet, but he would if he had to divert Sheldon's attention from Shaw.

"So, kill me," Shaw invited. "Go ahead."

Sheldon fired. One shot. Just as Shaw dove to the side. The bullet slammed into Shaw's right hand. His shooting hand. Rafe heard the colonel groan in pain.

As Rafe got closer, he could see both sleeves of Sheldon's shirt covered with blood. The man wouldn't last long, but he didn't need to last long to fire one final shot.

"Sheldon!" Rafe yelled.

He stepped out into what he knew was a direct line of fire. Sheldon swung the rifle toward him, just as Rafe had hoped he would.

What he hadn't counted on was hearing Anna's voice. "Sheldon!"

Rafe whipped his gaze in her direction, fearing the worst, and soon having that fear confirmed. She wasn't behind the tree but out in the open, and she was running across the side of the yard. Not toward him. But away. In an attempt to divert Sheldon's attention.

"Get back, Anna!" It took Rafe a moment to realize he hadn't shouted that, but Shaw had stolen the words from his mouth.

Rafe lurched forward into a crisscross run, praying Sheldon would focus on him.

He didn't.

As Rafe feared he would do, he turned the rifle on Anna. She was the common denominator between Shaw and Rafe. Sheldon could hurt them both by killing her.

"Rafe," Shaw called out.

It happened fast. Shaw pulled the gun from the back waist of his uniform and tossed it to Rafe. Rafe had his stance braced even before he snatched the pistol from the air.

He fired.

And fired.

Sheldon never even dropped the rifle. Still clinging to it, he toppled out of the window and fell to the ground below.

With his gun still poised to shoot, Rafe ran to Sheldon and checked to make sure he was dead.

He was.

When he turned around to tell the others, Anna was already on her way to him. They covered the distance in just a few short steps.

Rafe pulled her into his arms and held on.

"It's over?" she asked. The words were all breath, no sound. And there were already tears in her eyes.

"It's over."

Epilogue

"You're trembling," Anna whispered.

"Am I?" Rafe stroked his mouth over hers. "It's the effect you have on me. Don't mention it to Rico, though. He'll make wussy jokes about it."

From over his shoulder, Anna caught a glimpse of Cal Rico, Rafe's best man. The wink he gave her let her know that he would indeed make wussy jokes about it. It was one of the testosterone-mandated requirements of Alpha Team members. And close friends.

Rafe would no doubt enjoy every minute of the banter.

"How about you?" Rafe asked her. "Are you doing any trembling?"

"From head to toe." Anna smiled. "But it's a good kind of trembling."

"Then we must be doing the right thing." Rafe gently

took her hand and slipped the wedding ring on her finger. "No turning back now, darling. You just promised to love, honor and cherish me in front of all these people."

Anna made a passing glance of those people. All four of them. Janine, Luke Buchanan, Rico and Colonel Shaw. Even though it'd only been three days since the ordeal with O'Reilly, Quivira and Sheldon, none of them looked the worse for wear. Well, with the exception of Shaw, who had a bandage around his wounded hand.

Still, it was something of a small miracle that they'd all managed to survive and were here to share this special day with them. Everyone was safe, including their baby. They'd had test after test, and all of them confirmed that the carbon monoxide hadn't caused any damage. Those results were the answers to many prayers.

"Okay, here's the deal, darling." Rafe kept his voice low and intimate. The words were meant only for her. "This might be just a simple ring, but all that forever-together symbolic stuff goes right along with it. I'm talking a permanent hip-joining of me, you and our little officer trainee that you're commissioning inside you. So, if you have any doubts—"

"I don't."

Anna looked down at the delicately etched white-gold band. It was perfect. Like her husband. Like her healthy unborn child. Like everything else in her life. "I guess this proves you love me. You married me twice."

"Darling, you didn't need this ceremony to prove that. I do love you."

The words sent a warmth through her whole body. She'd never tire of hearing Rafe say that to her. "I love you, too."

The minister cleared his throat, apparently a gesture to get them to hurry things along.

They ignored him.

"I'd marry you a thousand times, Anna McQuade," Rafe added. "Make that a million. And that includes any honeymoon duties expected of me." Rafe grinned and looked at the minister. "Can I kiss her now?"

"Absolutely."

Rafe slipped his arm around her waist and eased her to him. "Brace yourself. I want you to remember this for the rest of your incredibly long life."

Despite the warning, Anna didn't even try to brace herself. She wanted to surrender to whatever Rafe had in mind.

He kissed both of her cheeks first. Not basic husbandly pecks, either. Lingering caresses with that incredibly sexy, damp mouth of his.

It was just the beginning.

Rafe dipped her back. Just slightly. Just enough to throw her a little off-kilter and make the candlelight shimmer in his eyes. The jungle-hot look he gave her had Anna zinging even before his mouth came to hers.

His lips were soft and warm. Amazing. About a million steps past clever. He gave with those lips. Took in return. Satisfied. Aroused. Promised. It was pure, uncut intimacy, and like everything that Rafe McQuade did in life, it left her in awe.

He pulled back and gave her a satisfied smile.

There were no jolts. No funny feelings. And definitely no doubts. Everything was as clear as fine glass.

Anna looked into Rafe's eyes and knew she was and always would be well loved.

* * * * *

We hope you enjoyed reading

Out of the Darkness

by *New York Times* bestselling author

HEATHER GRAHAM

and

Marching Orders

by *USA TODAY* bestselling author

DELORES FOSSEN.

Both were originally Harlequin® series stories!

From passionate, suspenseful and dramatic
love stories to inspirational or historical,
Harlequin offers different lines to
satisfy every romance reader.

New books in each line are available every month.

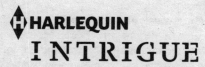

⬥HARLEQUIN
INTRIGUE

SEEK THRILLS. SOLVE CRIMES.
JUSTICE SERVED.

Harlequin.com

Lena Love kicked a rock out from underneath her foot, then bent down and tightened the twill shoelaces on her brown leather hiking boots.

The crime scene investigator, who doubled as a forensic science technician, stood back up and eyed Los Angeles's Cucamonga Wilderness trail. Sharp-edged stones and ragged shards of bark covered the rugged, winding terrain.

"Watch your step," she uttered to herself before continuing along the path of her latest crime scene.

Lena squinted as she focused on the trail. Heavy foliage loomed overhead, blocking out the sun's brilliant rays. She pulled out her flashlight, hoping its bright beam would help uncover potential evidence.

An ominous wave of vulnerability swept through her chest at the sight of the vast San Gabriel Mountains. She spun around slowly, feeling small while eyeing the infinite views of the forest, desert and snowy mountainous peaks.

The wild surroundings left her with a lingering sense of defenselessness. Lena tightened the belt on her tan suede blazer. She hoped it would give her some semblance of security.

It didn't.

Lena wondered if the latest victim had felt that same vulnerability on the night she'd been brutally murdered.

"Come on, Grace Mitchell," Lena said aloud, as if the dead woman could hear her. "Talk to me. Tell me what happened to you. *Show* me what happened to you."

A gust of wind whipped Lena's bone-straight bob across her slender face. She tucked her hair behind her ears and stooped down, aiming the flashlight toward the majestic oak tree where Grace's body had been found.

Lena envisioned spotting droplets of blood, a cigarette butt, the tip of a latex glove...*anything* that would help identify the killer.

This was her second visit to the crime scene. The thought of showing up to the station without any viable evidence yet again caused an agonizing pang of dread to shoot up her spine.

Grace was the fifth victim of a criminal whom Lena had labeled an organized serial killer. He appeared to have a type. Young, slender brunette women. Their bodies had all been found in heavily wooded areas. Each victim's hands were meticulously tied behind their backs with a three-strand twisted rope. They'd been strangled to death. And the amount of evidence left at each scene was practically nonexistent.

But the killer's signature mark was always there. And it was a sinister one.

Look for
The Heart-Shaped Murders *by Denise N. Wheatley,*
available June 2022 wherever
Harlequin Intrigue books and ebooks are sold.

Harlequin.com

Love Harlequin romance?

DISCOVER.

Be the first to find out about promotions, news and exclusive content!

f Facebook.com/HarlequinBooks

Twitter.com/HarlequinBooks

Instagram.com/HarlequinBooks

Pinterest.com/HarlequinBooks

You Tube YouTube.com/HarlequinBooks

ReaderService.com

EXPLORE.

Sign up for the Harlequin e-newsletter and download a free book from any series at
TryHarlequin.com

CONNECT.

Join our Harlequin community to share your thoughts and connect with other romance readers!
Facebook.com/groups/HarlequinConnection

HARLEQUIN

Heartfelt or thrilling, passionate or uplifting—Harlequin is more than just happily-ever-after.

With twelve different series to choose from and new books available every month, you are sure to find stories that will move you, uplift you, inspire and delight you.